THE SOUL DESTROYER

The Soul Summoner Series Book 7

ELICIA HYDER

Inkwell & Quill, LLC

GET A FREE BOOK
at www.eliciahyder.com

Robbery · Arson · Murder
And the one-night stand that just won't end.

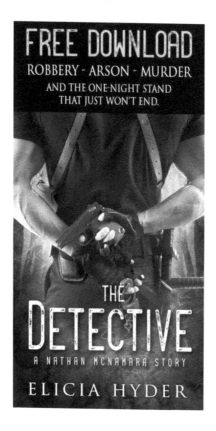

CHARACTER LIST

Warren Parish
the Archangel of Death. Father of Iliana. Son of Azrael and Nadine.

Nathan McNamara
Warren's best friend. Married to Sloan Jordan. Commander of SF-12.

Sloan Jordan
Mother of Iliana. Married to Nathan McNamara. Daughter of fallen Angel of Life Kasyade.

Azrael
Former Archangel of Death. Father of Warren and father of Adrianne's unborn child. Owner of Claymore Worldwide Security.

Reuel
Angel of Protection. Now in charge of the Angels of Protection (aka Guardians).

Adrianne Marx
Sloan's best friend. Girlfriend of Azrael.

Fury (Allison)
Member of SF - 12. Human daughter of Abaddon, the Destroyer. Twin sister of Anya. Former girlfriend of Warren.

Anya
(presumed deceased)
Seramorta Angel of Protection. Twin sister of Fury. Daughter of Abaddon, the Destroyer.

The Morning Star
Fallen Angel of Life and Angel of Knowledge.

Johnny McNamara
Uncle of Nathan McNamara. Father of Fury's unborn child.

Abaddon "The Destroyer"
(Deceased)
Father of Fury and Anya. Former guardian of Nulterra, and former Archangel of Protection.

Phenex
(Deceased)
Mother of Alice. Fallen Angel of Life.

Alice
(Deceased)
Childhood best friend of Warren.

Ysha
(Deceased)
Father of Taiya. Fallen Angel of Life.

Taiya
Seramorta Angel of Life. Daughter of Ysha and Melinda Harmon.

Shannon Green
Nathan's former girlfriend. Now possibly pregnant with an angel.

Kasyade
(Deceased)
Biological mother of Sloan. Fallen Angel of Life.

Nadine
(Deceased)
Mother of Warren.

Audrey Jordan
(Deceased)
Adoptive mother of Sloan.

Robert Jordan
Adoptive father of Sloan.

Enzo
Special Operations Director of SF-12

Samael
Angel of Death who guards the spirit line.

Ionis
Messenger Angel.

Sandalphon
Angel of Prophecy and Knowledge (Born on Earth)

Metatron
Angel of Life and Ministry (Born on Earth)

Members of Sf-12 (*denotes ability to see angels):
1. Enzo*
2. Kane*
3. Cooper
4. NAG* (Mandi) - pilot
5. Lex
6. Doc*
7. Wings - pilot
8. Cruz
9. Pirez
10. Justice
11. Dalton
12. *Fury* (Retired)

THE SOUL SUMMONER SERIES ORDER

Book 1 - **The Soul Summoner**
Book 2 - **The Siren**
Book 3 - **The Angel of Death**
Book 4 - **The Taken**
Book 5 - **The Sacrifice**
Book 6 - **The Regular Guy**
Book 7 - The Soul Destroyer

COMPANION NOVELLAS
The Detective
The Mercenary

For Chris.
My everything, and then some.

VENICE, ITALY

"*I* won't hurt you."

My hands were raised like I was creeping toward a madman with a gun. Only it wasn't a gunman. It was a very young woman, terrified and weeping in the corner. In her mismatched brown and green eyes, *I* was the madman.

"I want to help you." I took another slow, careful step forward. "What's your name?"

Her trembling hands shielded her face, and she pulled her knees closer to her chest. "S...Sofia."

I knelt in front of her. "Hi, Sofia. My name's Warren. These are my friends, Samael and Jaleal."

She peeked through her fingers at the two Angels of Death standing in the doorway behind me.

I offered her my hand. "We're here to take you home."

"Home?"

"Yes. Are you ready?"

She flinched away.

"It's OK. You have my word."

Cautiously, she inched her hand toward mine. The instant our fingertips touched, her shaking calmed. Her eyes cleared.

I smiled gently. "There. Better?"

She nodded.

As I stood, I pulled her to her feet.

Radiating off her soul was a sparkling deep-amethyst haze. It moved like smoke, twisting and curling around her. Samael had been right; I'd seen nothing like it either.

Sofia's spirit was shielded from anything unsettling, so she didn't even glance over as we passed her mutilated body on the bed.

"Jaleal?" I said quietly.

Selecting Jaleal for this job hadn't been random. She was the most innocuous of us all at five feet tall and barely a hundred pounds.

Jaleal took her arm. "Hi, Sofia. Let's go for a walk." Her voice was melodic and soothing as she led Sofia from the room.

Samael stepped over beside me. "This is victim number four. The second one here in Venice."

I walked over to the body and examined Sofia's severed head perched on the bedpost. "Her eyes were gouged out while she was still alive." Blood had streamed like tears down Sofia's cheeks.

"The mark on her chest too. The wounds are much deeper this time." He was leaning over her torso.

"Maybe. But why is the mark here at all? No one this side of the spirit line knows what it means."

"That, I do not know." Samael sighed. "But it worries me. Azrael will be interested to see this."

"I'm sure I'll see him soon." My phone buzzed in my pocket. I pulled it out and looked at the screen. It was a text message from Fury.

On our way to the hospital. My water just broke.

I showed it to Samael.

He put a hand on my shoulder. "Go. I'll call if there's news."

"Thank you." Before leaving, I walked to the head of the

bed again and looked down at Sofia's bare chest. In its bloody center was a carving of what looked like a Roman cross with two *S*'s mirroring each other.

It was *my* mark. My calling card.

The mark of the Archangel of Death.

CHAPTER TWO

*M*y right knee wouldn't stop bouncing.

I wasn't even sure why the hell I was so nervous. It's not like *my* kid was being born today.

Maybe it was because I was in a hospital. God knows, my presence in such a place wasn't good for anyone.

Maybe it was because the most dangerous angel in all of history might be coming into the world via emergency C-section in the very next room.

Or maybe all my anxiety was because of *her*.

She was certainly the reason my eyes kept flicking toward the entrance. Never mind that I'd spent over four decades in Eden away from her; my heart quickened like it still beat on Earth's time. For here, on this planet, it had only been a year since Sloan Jordan—err, Sloan *McNamara*—had almost become my wife.

And now she was married to my best friend.

And they were raising my daughter together.

And a slight possibility existed that she might walk through the door at any second...

The waiting-room door opened.

It was Reuel returning from another trip to the vending machine. My partner, a hulking guardian angel, was stress eating a fourth bag of potato chips since he'd arrived. *Crunch, crunch, crunch.* And two candy bars were tucked into the front pocket of his shirt.

He caught my eye, looked mildly guilty, then smiled. At least his crumb-covered mouth smiled. His worried eyes were fixed with fright. It was almost funny seeing such a huge and lethal angel reduced to a bundle of nerves.

But he loved the mother-to-be down the hall in surgery—platonically, of course, the way all the guardians surely grow to love their charges. He'd been with Fury almost exclusively since he and my father found her twenty-something years ago.

"You all right?" I asked, looking up—way up—at him.

He grunted and sat down beside me.

I patted his bulky shoulder. "She'll be fine. Fury's strong. There's nothing to worry about."

"Akal ai vevru ta," he said in our language, *Katavukai,* without meeting my eyes. Translated, he said, "She's different now."

My eyes fell to the speckled tile floor. He was right. Fury *was* different. I saw it in her soul—whatever *it* was—the first time I laid eyes on her after she became pregnant. She knew it too, though I doubt she'd ever admitted it to anyone but me.

Fury was good at keeping secrets.

Reuel looked at my bouncing knee. *"Mas alis kavalai par kalai?"*

I snapped my fingers and pointed at him. "Yes! That's exactly it. I'm stressed about the murders." I sank back in my seat. "Thanks, Reuel. I'm not stressed about—"

The door opened again. I jolted upright, then immediately slumped upon seeing my father, Azrael. He was alone.

He frowned. "Don't look so happy to see me, Warren."

Beside me, Reuel was chuckling.

"Sorry." I stood and greeted him with a hug.

Mortality suited Azrael, except it was a shock to see age on his face and his once-eternal frame. He'd only been mortal for a few months, but it was already showing in the tiny crinkles at the corners of his eyes and mouth. And, for the first time, Azrael was shorter than me. Only millimeters perhaps. Something hopefully only my keen eye would detect.

"Have I missed anything?" he asked when he stepped back to greet Reuel.

"Not yet." I looked at the thick black tactical watch encircling my wrist. "She went into labor seventeen hours ago and toughed it out at home until her water broke. John came in a little while ago and said they're doing a C-section because her cervix isn't dilating."

"But she's OK?"

"Yeah, she's all right." I looked over his shoulder. "You're alone?"

"Yes."

"Oh."

He must have noticed my face fall. "Are you disappointed?"

"I was hoping to see Adrianne."

He laughed.

So did Reuel.

"Bullshit," Azrael said.

Heat rushed to my cheeks, but I hoped no one would notice as we sat down.

"I'm not completely alone. Nathan dropped me off at the entrance. He's parking the car."

"Where's Iliana?"

"Your daughter is safe at Echo-5." After a beat, he added, "Sloan is with her if you're wondering."

"I'm not."

"Sure." He lowered his voice even though we were the only people in the room. "We're taking extra precautions with Iliana now that it's been over a year."

That made me feel both better and worse.

My daughter—the *Vitamorte*, the most powerful angel in existence—had recently been moved into Echo-5, a supernaturally-secure building hidden in the mountains of western North Carolina. It was outside Asheville on the Wolf Gap compound, a division of my father's private military company, Claymore Worldwide Security.

Iliana couldn't be any safer than at Wolf Gap with her own personal security team, SF-12. They were each hand-selected by Azrael. Twelve (or currently, eleven) men and women with special-ops military backgrounds, combat experience, and most importantly—hands-on training to deal with threats from *my* world. To say they were elite and unique human warriors wouldn't come close to being an adequate description.

But the cause for high alert had me worried.

Angels came to Earth in many forms. Most stayed as spirits, completely unseen and almost undetectable to mortals. They could influence humans to some degree but not cause bodily harm.

Other angels possessed human bodies—bodies that could be alive or dead. Those angels were a threat, but their powers were limited and they were fairly easy to dispatch.

The most dangerous angels to the human race were those reborn on Earth into bodies infused with immortality. They were almost limitless in their abilities, easily camouflaged among the living, and they could reproduce. Demon spawn were a very real thing. I would know because, technically, I was one.

I was born a *Seramorta*: part angel, part human. And though he was on the right side of heaven now, Azrael was once a coerced member of the fallen. My mother had been completely human, and for a time, she was held hostage through demonic possession by the Morning Star himself.

She'd died a little over a year ago, the exact moment the

Morning Star had been dispatched into the stratosphere. That was when the waiting game began. It would be a year before the Morning Star would be strong enough to possess another human—or be reborn into a new form.

Enter our current predicament.

I looked at my father. "If the Morning Star does return as Fury's kid, that will almost be easier for all of us."

Azrael smirked. "You want to go through Fury to take her child away?"

"She's not exactly the maternal type."

"Parenthood changes people, son. Never discount that."

Reuel crumpled his chip bag. "*Akal kaval*"—he held up his finger and thumb in the shape of a pistol—"*pew, pew.*"

We had no word in our language for "gun."

"Fury gave up shooting completely?" I asked, surprised. Fury was an expert marksman, or marks*woman,* I guess. She made me, a former sniper for the Marine Corps and a Claymore firearms instructor, look like I'd done a little target practice with a BB gun.

Azrael nodded. "I heard that too. The doctor warned her about the decibel level of gunfire during her pregnancy, and that was it."

"Wow. Good for her though. That's as it should be." Still, Fury being mom-like was weird. Crazy weird.

"Has the Council decided on a game plan if the Morning Star happens to be born among us?" Azrael asked.

"Not yet. It's on the floor for discussion now. They've been debating it for weeks and are supposed to send for me when there's a decision."

"You know what you're most likely going to have to do, right?"

Nausea churned in my stomach, which reminded me of the situation in Italy. "I need to talk to you about something else pretty serious. Not here though." A maternity ward was no place for talk of beheaded women.

"Sounds ominous."

"I'm afraid it is."

He opened his mouth to say something else, but the waiting-room door opened. I looked up as Nathan McNamara walked inside. My nemesis. And my very best friend.

He wore his signature olive-drab ball cap with the "Regular Guy" patch I'd given him fixed to the front. Appropriate, since he was the only human in our group.

His goofy, lopsided grin broke on his face when he saw me. I stood as he put a couple of bags down on a nearby chair.

"There's my favorite Area 51 Reject," he said, opening his arms.

With a laugh, I stepped forward to embrace him. I clapped him on the back. "Good to see you, Nate."

"You too, man."

When I pulled back, Reuel was standing beside me.

Nathan laughed and hugged him. "Reuel, my old friend, it's been too long."

With a grunt, Reuel lifted Nathan's feet off the ground.

"You haven't seen each other in what, almost a year?" I asked when Reuel put him down.

"Ten months, I guess. Not at all since Iliana was born. Been staying busy?" Nathan asked him.

Reuel nodded and pointed at me.

"I know. I'm a dictator," I said.

Reuel smiled. *"Kitak es ket alis appa."*

He and I both looked back at Azrael.

"Almost as bad as me?" Azrael pointed at him. "Nobody said you had to work for either of us. You volunteered, so just eat your snacks and keep your mouth shut."

Reuel's shoulders shook with silent laughter.

"Speaking of snacks..." Nathan reached for the bags he'd put down and handed one of them to Reuel. "I made a pit stop on the way here and brought you a treat."

Reuel pulled out a box from Southside Sweets, an Asheville bakery I was sure could have been kept in business by Nathan and Reuel alone.

With a gleeful grin, Reuel hugged Nathan again. *"Gratalis."*

"You're welcome." Nathan handed me the other bag, a black gift bag with a teal-ribbon handle. "Sloan sent you this."

"How is she?" I asked as I accepted it.

His smile widened. "She's amazing. Such a great mother. You'd be really proud."

"I knew she would be." I looked into the bag. "What's this?"

"Open it," Nathan said, sitting in a chair across from us.

I sat down and pulled out the tissue-paper wrapped object inside. It was a book. A photo album. And my baby girl's face was on the cover. A lump the size of a watermelon rose in my throat. I tried to swallow it back down with a painful gulp.

"Sloan thought you might like to have pictures that were bigger than the size of your phone's screen."

I was half tempted to put the book back into the bag without looking at it, because I knew if I did, there was a high probability of tears in front of my friends. But Reuel was already leaning over my shoulder to look, dropping sprinkles from his donut on my sleeve.

When I opened the cover, a slip of paper floated to the floor. I picked it up and saw Sloan's familiar sloppy cursive.

Dear Warren,

I hope this letter finds you well. Not a day passes that we don't think of you. Iliana is happy and healthy, completely caught up (and then some) with the other babies her age. Can you believe she'll be a year old soon?

She's crawling all over the place now. Nathan has it on video, so be sure to remind him to show you.

We don't leave the penthouse much these days, for obvious reasons. I'll be so thankful when the Morning Star resurfaces, and we know exactly what we're dealing with. I swear, the nervous wondering and waiting is almost worse than facing him in the flesh. Rest assured, everyone on this side of the spirit line is on high alert, as I'm sure you are as well.

Enjoy the book. Wish you were here.

Love always,
Sloan

I blinked a few times to stop the tingling at the corners of my eyes. Then I flipped to the first page of the book. Someone, probably Nathan, had drawn a handlebar mustache on Iliana's face. Reuel and I both laughed.

"It was chocolate sauce," Nathan said, leaning over to look at it upside down.

"Of course it was." Nathan ate more junk food than any other human I'd ever known. I looked more closely at the picture. "Is that a bow?"

"Yeah, Adrianne tapes one to her head every time we see her now. Poor kid. I don't think she'll ever have any real hair."

The next page was a photo of Iliana holding Sloan's face. They were nose-to-nose and both laughing. My heart twisted, and a bubble of unstoppable emotion creaked out of my constricted airway. I tried—and failed—to mask it as a cough.

Nathan caught my eye and put his hand on my shoulder. "I want to show you something." He pulled his phone from his pocket and swiped the screen with his thumb. After a few taps, he turned it toward me.

It was a video. I expected it to be of Iliana crawling. Instead, it was a clip taken over Nathan's shoulder from behind. He was holding Iliana in the crook of his arm while he held a picture album in his hand. The book was open to a photo of Sloan. "Illy, who's this?" he asked her.

"Mama!" she chirped happily, clapping her tiny hands.

He turned the page. "And who's this?" It was a photo of Sloan's dad.

"Papa!" She looked off-camera and pointed, probably because Dr. Jordan was somewhere in the room.

"Good girl." Nathan turned another page. "And who is this?"

It was a picture of me, wearing a black T-shirt and jeans, stretched across the white bed I'd shared with Sloan. It was taken a few days before Iliana was born.

Iliana lunged forward and grabbed the book. "*Appa!*"

Appa. The word for *Father* in Katavukai.

I covered my mouth with my hand as a few rogue tears escaped down my cheeks.

Nate squeezed my arm. "She knows you, brother."

Sniffing, I pinched the bridge of my nose, then swiped away the tears. I cleared my throat and finally looked up. "Thanks for that. Will you send it to me?"

"You bet."

I tucked the photo album back into the bag. "I'll finish looking at this later."

Nathan nodded. "So I'm guessing Satan hasn't been born yet?" He was looking around like *Satan* might be standing behind him.

Azrael groaned. "That's not even funny."

Nathan held up his thumb and index finger an inch apart. "It's a little funny. I got a group text from Johnny saying they were doing a C-section."

"Supposed to be doing it now," I said.

Azrael sat back and folded his arms over his chest. "You

know, it's probably a good sign that they had to rush her into surgery."

We all looked at him in confusion.

"The Morning Star is an Angel of Life and of Knowledge. There shouldn't be complications with childbirth if his spirit is present."

I hadn't considered that.

Reuel relaxed a little.

Nathan nodded toward the door. "But we're sure it's an angel popping out of that uterus?"

"It's something," Azrael said, staring at the ceiling.

The look on his face was puzzling. "What's the matter?" I asked.

He let out a deep sigh. "I wasn't going to say anything until I knew for certain, but I'm concerned about Adrianne as well."

I turned toward him in my seat. "You're joking?"

"Afraid not."

Azrael's girlfriend, Adrianne Marx, was also pregnant. Angels could only produce one angelic offspring with a human, and Azrael had met his quota when I was born.

"Are you telling me there's a possibility that my wife's very best friend on the planet might be carrying the Morning Star?" Nathan's face was as white as the wall behind him.

Azrael didn't answer.

I held out my hand. "Photograph, please." I could tell a lot from a picture.

He angled to the side and pulled out his phone. "I think it's still too early to tell. We don't even find out until Friday if it's a boy or a girl."

"When's she due?" I asked as he passed me his cell phone.

"Late August."

Reuel looked at the phone over my shoulder.

On the screen was a mirror selfie of Adrianne in a sports bra. She was turned to the side to show off her baby bump. The picture was captioned, "Nineteen Weeks. Baby is the size of a mango!"

Had the baby been completely human, I would sense nothing more than a general feeling of virtue—as my gift could judge the righteous souls from the wicked. Instead, a rippled haze—like heat waves off asphalt in summer—radiated around Adrianne's bare midsection.

I swallowed hard and handed the phone back to him. "Your suspicion is valid."

"*Verdad,*" Reuel agreed.

Azrael froze, then his knuckles turned white around the phone before he hurled it across the room at the wall.

My hand flew forward and stopped the phone midair before it collided with the drywall.

Nathan gasped. Then, because he was closest, he got up and grabbed the phone where it was suspended. He shook his head as his hand closed around it. "You think I'd be used to this shit by now," he said, bewildered. He carried the phone back to Azrael and set it down cautiously, two chairs away from him.

"Az, when did you notice a difference?" I asked.

His eyes were closed, and for a long time, he didn't answer me. "Adrianne's had severe morning sickness, all-day sickness really, since the beginning. But that passed a few weeks ago. Then I started noticing her sickness seemed to follow her visits with Sloan."

"You mean, her visits with Iliana," I said.

He nodded.

There were physical side effects when angels in human form were together. It was the primary reason I had to leave Sloan and my daughter when she was born. My presence could warp Iliana's developing brain.

We'd also recently found out what Iliana could do to an angel in the womb. Whenever Fury was around her, Fury's unborn son would kick and tumble so much, she'd experience motion sickness. And the effects became worse as the fetus and Iliana grew older. It became so bad that Fury had refused to visit Echo-5 at all in the past few months.

"Well, shit." Nathan stood with so much force that his chair slid backward a few inches across the tiles. "What will I tell Sloan?"

"Nothing until we know more," I said.

He shook his head. "I don't keep stuff from her, Warren. Not ever."

Had to respect that. Even though I rationalized it as protecting Sloan, I couldn't say as much when she and I were together. Maybe he had learned from my mistakes.

Just then, the sound of a slot-machine jackpot filled the room. Nathan reached for his phone. "I'd say speak of the devil, but that's a little too heavy-handed for this group. It's Sloan. Excuse me."

He walked out into the hallway, and my eyes followed him.

"Her ringtone on his phone is a jackpot," I said aloud to no one in particular as I stared at the door closing behind him.

My father put his hand on my arm. "You made a good choice, Warren. The *right* choice."

I took a deep breath and blew it out slowly. "I know."

And I did.

Still, some days were harder than others. Because while time really does heal all wounds, love never fades. It never dies. Not even with a lifetime apart. And I'd spent enough time on Earth this day for the wound of losing her to feel as fresh as the day I left.

But I couldn't let myself dwell on it. Fortunately, the intercom above our heads chimed. Then it played the first few bars of Twinkle, Twinkle, Little Star.

"He's here," I said, looking up.

Azrael's head snapped back. "Who's here?"

"The baby."

"How the hell do you know that?"

I tapped my temple. "Omniscience. It's a new perk of the job since you left."

He scowled.

I laughed and pointed to the sign by the door. "When you hear the nursery bells, a new little angel has been born."

Azrael shoved my shoulder, and I laughed harder as Nathan walked back into the room. "What's so funny?" Nathan asked.

"Azrael can't take a joke. Did you hear the bells?" I pointed to the sign again for Nathan.

He turned and read it. "Shit. I'll bet that sign has never been so literal."

"I guarantee it hasn't," Azrael said.

Nathan reclaimed his seat and looked at me. "Sloan sends her love to everyone."

My heart torqued. Thankfully, no one seemed to notice.

The minutes ticked by slowly on the clock above the waiting-room coffee pot.

Reuel tore open a candy bar.

Azrael's knee was bouncing in time with mine.

And Nathan was chewing on his thumbnail. Finally, he broke the silence. "So when you guys see Fury's kid, you'll know if it's the Morning Star?" Nathan wagged his finger between me and Reuel.

I shifted on my chair. "No. I'll only know if it's an angel or human or Seramorta."

"Seriously?"

"Seriously. It's not like we're born wearing name tags, Nate."

"The last time I saw you, you told me we should know soon enough which baby was the Morning Star."

"And compared with time in my world, that's true. A few years on Earth is nothing."

Nate pointed at Azrael. "Warren, you're becoming as bad as him with all the ambiguity and shit."

I smiled. "I'm sorry. I'll try to use simpler speech you can understand."

"Thank you—" His mouth quickly snapped shut as he recognized the thinly veiled insult. "Glad to see immortality hasn't cured you of being a dick."

We all laughed.

The door swung open, and Nathan's uncle and Fury's boyfriend, Johnny McNamara, burst through the door in a set of pale-blue scrubs and a paper cap. He was red faced and sweaty with wide eyes and an even wider smile. "It's a boy! He's beautiful."

We all stood.

Azrael stepped toward him. "How's Fury?"

"She's great! They didn't have to do the C-section. Once they doped her up, her body relaxed, allowing her cervix to dilate. He was born naturally. She's still groggy, but they're both perfectly fine."

Reuel breathed a sigh so deep with relief that it shifted our row of connected chairs.

I got up to shake Johnny's hand. "That's good news. Congratulations."

"Yes. Congratulations," Azrael echoed.

Nathan hugged his uncle.

"When can we meet him?" I asked.

Johnny jerked his thumb over his shoulder. "The nurses took him to clean him up. They're moving Fury to a regular room, and once she's feeling more alert, we'll have y'all back to see her."

"Excellent," I said.

"Don't go anywhere. I'll be back soon!" With a little skip, Johnny spun on his heel and left.

I couldn't help but smile.

Nathan pointed at me and Reuel. "How long will you guys stick around near the baby?"

I knew what he was getting at. If Fury's child was an angel, our presence wasn't healthy.

"They don't have to stay, but they do need to see the child." Azrael's gaze fell enough for me to notice. "I can no longer see angels."

"Oh yeah. Sorry Az."

Azrael waved his hand to dismiss it.

I sat back down. "We won't be here long."

"So will this baby be Seramorta like Sloan and Warren were? Half-angel?" Nathan asked.

"Not unless Fury has been sleeping with an angel while she's been with Johnny," Azrael said.

All eyes in the room turned toward me.

I put my hands up in defense. "What the hell? I haven't slept with Fury!"

Nathan cocked an eyebrow.

"OK, I haven't slept with Fury *recently*." Fury and I had history, but it was ancient. Even more ancient for me than for her. That pinged another idea. I leaned back and folded my arms. "Did John have a paternity test done when they found out she was pregnant? He'd had a vasectomy right?"

"Not that I know of. They assumed Sloan healed *that part* of him when she healed his severed jugular last year," Nathan said.

Sloan was formerly a half Angel of Life with the gift of healing. She'd saved Johnny's life after almost accidentally killing him in a training exercise.

"How does that work? Angel DNA?" Nathan asked.

"The child's DNA won't match the parents' at all. And the child will have Rh-null blood," Azrael said.

Nathan's head tilted. "Could you do a blood test on Adrianne's baby?"

Azrael's eyes widened. "Good thinking, Nate."

"Excellent idea," I agreed.

Smiling, Nathan leaned back and linked his hands behind

his head. "Good to know my investigative skills aren't getting too rusty."

"Speaking of, how are you liking the new job, *Commander?*" I asked with a grin.

"Training days are fun. Shooting shit never gets old. The day-to-do is slow here lately, but I'm not complaining. I hope it stays that way."

Nathan was Special Operations Commander of SF-12. If his job ever got exciting, it was bad news for everyone.

"What about you? Are you still planning to take Fury to Nulterra to find her sister?" Nathan asked me.

"As soon as she's ready." I looked at Azrael. "I need to deal with Nulterra soon. The situation there is increasingly unstable."

"What situation?" Nathan asked.

"Basically, Abaddon's demise and the Morning Star's departure left the throne of Hell without a successor," Azrael said.

"And now, the different players are vying for power," I added.

Nathan laughed. "Hold up. Like *Game of Thrones?*"

My head bobbed from side to side. "Sort of. Azrael, I'm afraid it will come to war if the angels don't intervene."

"War in Hell sounds like it should be on HBO," Nathan said, still smiling.

"Problem is, the war won't stay in Hell." I pointed at the floor. "It's only a matter of time before they bring the fight here."

"Why here?" Nathan asked.

I shrugged. "What greater claim would someone have than if they possessed what the Morning Star wants the most?"

Nathan sat up straight, the amusement suddenly gone from his face. "You think they'll come after Iliana?"

No one answered.

Nathan looked desperately at Azrael.

"It's what I would do." Azrael appeared almost forlorn. It must not have been easy for him to have once been so powerful and suddenly be so helpless.

"There have already been threats," I said.

"Well, what are you waiting for?" Nathan's panicky voice was almost at shouting volume. "Go! Go now!"

I held up a hand to silence him. "I will, but not yet."

"Why? Because of Fury? To hell with her sister. We're talking about my daughter!" Nathan's mouth snapped shut as soon as the words left it. "I'm sorry, Warren. I didn't mean to—"

"I know." I took a slow breath. "Trust me, no one is more concerned about Iliana's safety than me. But first, we might have the biggest bargaining chip of all on our hands."

"The Morning Star himself," Nathan said.

I nodded. "And he might be right next door."

"Then why are we still in here?" Nathan stood and walked to the exit. He pulled it open and looked at me expectantly. "Aren't you still able to open locked doors?"

CHAPTER THREE

The four of us huddled in front of the nursery-room window. Clear plastic bassinets were parked in a row on the other side of the glass. A plump female nurse swaddled a squirming baby with a pale-blue blanket.

Nathan searched the name placards on each bed. "Which one is he? None of these baby boxes says McNamara."

"How do you know she'll give him your family name?" Azrael asked.

"Because it's cool." Nathan said his last name again, letting the syllables pop off his lips. "Mc-Na-ma-ra."

I shook my head. "Fury's baby isn't here. All these are human."

The nurse, whose back was to me, lifted her head and turned her ear toward us.

I leaned toward Reuel. "Did I say that too loud?"

He shook his head, and the nurse returned to swaddling. Maybe the vibrations of my voice had carried into the room, but after checking the seal of the window against all edges of the wall, I seriously doubted she'd heard me. It had to be a coincidence.

"What are you guys doing in here?" Johnny McNamara's voice made us all turn. Down the hall, he was closing a door behind him.

"A nurse let us in," Nathan lied.

"Sure they did." Johnny rolled his eyes as he neared us. "Y'all are going to get us kicked out of the hospital."

Azrael stepped to the front of our group. "Can we see them now?"

Johnny hesitated, then finally nodded. "Come on." We followed him to the room he'd just exited. He held up a hand to stop us. "Just a second. Let me tell Allison."

Nathan looked up at me. "It's weird when he calls her *Allison*, right?"

"It's weird she lets him." I grinned. "I asked if I could call her Allison once when we were"—*dating* sure as hell wasn't the right word—"whatever we were doing. She threatened to cut my tongue out and staple it to my forehead."

Nathan laughed. "Sounds about right."

We waited in the hall for what seemed like an eternity.

Nathan rocked on his heels in front of me. "So...feel anything weird?" He wiggled his fingers in the air. "Crazy juju or anything?"

"Nathan, shut up."

"I'm serious."

"No, I don't feel anything weird."

"That's a good thing, right?" he asked Azrael.

Azrael rolled his eyes. "It means absolutely nothing."

It would be easier if I *could* feel something. Evil humans gave off warning vibes like they were radioactive. Angels were trickier, even those literally *born* evil like the Morning Star. We'd have to wait and see.

Johnny came back out into the hallway. He looked at me. "She wants to see you first. Alone."

Azrael huffed and crossed his arms.

I nodded and took a deep breath before walking through the heavy wooden door. Once inside, I closed it gently behind me.

Fury's eyes were closed. She wore a white-and-blue diamond-print hospital gown that was gaping open at the top until it disappeared under the white sheet that covered her. A baby in a blue cap was asleep against her chest.

"Warren," Fury whispered, her sleepy eyes fluttering open. Her mismatched blue and green eyes reminded me of the brutal scene in Italy.

I walked toward the bed, bent, and kissed her damp forehead. "Hey. How are you feeling?"

"Tired."

"I bet." I sat down on the edge of the bed beside her. The whole thing creaked under my weight. "I think you just had the workout of your life."

She laughed softly. "You can say that again." Reaching up, she tugged the blanket away from the sleeping baby's face. My heart twisted in my chest, making it nearly impossible to breathe. "Warren, I'd like to introduce you to John Jett McNamara."

"McNamara, huh?" I asked, leaning forward for a better look. "Interesting choice."

"Why?" When she met my eyes, hers were filled with tears. She must have been exhausted. I'd never seen Fury cry.

I put my hand on hers. "You know why."

Her eyes fell to the baby. "Because he's not John's."

"Fury, he's not yours either."

And he wasn't. There was nothing about this baby that was human other than the skin that contained him. Baby Jett was an angel incarnate. But *which* angel was the question.

Fury broke then, tears spilling down her cheeks like someone had turned on a faucet. I bent and rested my forehead against hers. "That doesn't mean he's the Morning Star."

My words didn't help. She buried her face in my shoulder and sobbed, her whole body shaking as she tried to muffle the sound with my shirt. "You can't ever tell John," she begged. "You can't ever tell anyone."

I pulled back enough to look her in the eye. "I have to tell Azrael and the Council."

"No, Warren." Her chin trembled. "They'll take him away from me."

I tucked her hair behind her ears. "Nobody will take him."

What the hell are you saying, Warren? I nearly shouted at myself, knowing what I'd just said couldn't be further from the truth.

She looked at the baby boy again. "He can't be the Morning Star. It has to be one of the others. That Shannon-girl's baby. Or even Adrianne's."

I blinked.

"Don't think for one second I haven't noticed the way Azrael watches her now."

"I wouldn't bring it up if I were you."

"I'm not stupid. Has he told Adrianne?"

"No. And I doubt he will."

"Is she here?"

I shook my head.

"Is Sloan?"

My jaw twitched. "No, but Nathan is. So are Az and Reuel. I think Reuel's cleaned out the vending machine because he's been so nervous."

She smiled and wiped her eyes. "I can't wait to see him."

I glanced toward the door. "Want me to send him in?"

"In a second. I need to talk to you about something else."

My brow lifted.

"My sister was seen *alive* boarding a chartered yacht in Thailand four days after Abaddon attacked us in Mogadishu."

Fury's sister, Anya, had been missing for over three years,

since the sisters were attacked by their father, Abaddon, the Destroyer, in Somalia. Until now, there had been zero proof that Anya had survived aside from Fury's adamant insistence. Still, I was planning to take her to Nulterra to investigate.

"How the hell did you find that out?"

"I told you, my team has been following leads all over for the past few years. Something was bound to turn up eventually. I got so excited, I think it put me into labor."

I ran my hand over my face. "And you still want to do this? Even now?" I gestured to the baby.

"Especially now. I know you haven't met my sister, but Anya makes me look like a fruitcake. If the Morning Star is reborn in human form and is preparing for a war with Iliana, don't you want her to have all the help she can get?"

I scowled. "Are you manipulating my heartstrings right now?"

"Bet your ass I am."

"You know that's unnecessary. I'll help you either way."

Her face softened. "I know. In all seriousness though, Anya is one of the fiercest women alive. And just like Iliana, she's more angel than human."

A chill rippled through me; perhaps that was the feeling of heartstrings for an Angel of Death. "It's still a long way off, but I won't stop until we find her."

With a rare and grateful smile on her plump lips, she put her hand on mine and squeezed.

As she pulled her hand away and adjusted the baby's blanket, I caught a flash of charred skin tissue on her palm. I caught her wrist and turned her hand over. "What did you do?"

As she yanked it away, I caught a flash of a circle with a line through it. "Burned it a while ago."

"Burned it on what? The sun?"

She shot me the bird.

The baby stirred.

I graced my knuckle against Jett's tiny cheek. "I hope you're ready to have a ball-buster for a mother, little guy."

At my touch, his eyes fluttered open. One of them was dark blue, like most babies; the other was a shocking emerald—just like his mother's.

Mismatched eyes in humans was often a sign of the gift of discernment, the ability to see angels. Fury had the gift, and it was hereditary.

"Warren, look at those eyes and tell me again that he's not mine," she said.

I kept my mouth shut and wished she was right. Genetics were irrelevant; baby Jett wasn't human. That much was a fact.

An even more disturbing thought churned in my mind. If this was the Morning Star, our problems had just multiplied. Fury's gift was unlike others similar to it. She could see more than just angels—she could see the angels' powers, which are mostly invisible even to someone like me. Their energy—their *intentions*—were as clear to her as if they'd brandished a shining sword.

The only thing I could compare it to was how we used infrared in battle when I was in the military. Our night-vision goggles had a setting to view infrared, and our weapons had special infrared lasers we called "night lights." When we switched our goggles to infrared, a previously dark battlefield would suddenly look like a maze of green glowing beams.

Fury didn't need goggles to see how angels were using their powers. It was apparently something her father, Abaddon the Destroyer, could do as the Archangel of Protection. A gift he didn't lose when he fell. A gift he passed on to his daughters when they were conceived.

Even as powerful as the Morning Star had always been as an Angel of Life and Angel of Knowledge, he'd never had that kind of advantage before. And it was an advantage my daughter would never know.

I jerked my thumb over my shoulder. "We'd probably better let Reuel in before he takes the door off its hinges."

She smiled and nodded, still looking down at the baby.

I got up and pulled open the door. "You guys can come in now."

Reuel pushed his way in first and went straight to her bedside. He bent, kissed her head, and spoke softly to her in Katavukai, which Fury spoke fluently.

Azrael caught my arm as everyone else filed past me. His brow lifted in question.

I just shook my head slightly.

His expression was unreadable.

Nathan and Johnny walked to the other side of Fury's bed. Nathan patted his uncle on the back. "Congratulations, John." He bent over Fury for a closer look. "He's a cute kid. Please tell me his name is Chaos or Hercules."

Johnny laughed. "Jett. John Jett McNamara."

Nathan looked at Azrael. "Told ya."

I leaned toward my father and lowered my voice. "John Jett kinda sounds like a cartoon character, doesn't it?"

"Or a seventies rock star," he replied.

I chuckled softly.

"Can I hold him?" Nathan asked Fury cautiously.

She nodded and weakly offered him the baby. Nathan scooped him up and held him to his chest. "He's tiny," Nathan said, his voice full of wonder.

"Just under six pounds." John looked at Fury. "They'll keep a close eye on him. Make sure everything's working properly."

"That's a good sign, right?" I asked Azrael, hoping for some encouragement.

He nodded, sort of. Then he crossed the room to stand by Nathan. Fury shifted in her bed like she might be going for a weapon she probably had concealed somewhere.

But Azrael didn't make a move for the baby. He looked over

Nathan's shoulder. "He's a fine boy, Allison." Azrael only called Fury by her real name when he was feeling sentimental—or manipulative.

"Thanks, Az. We thought about naming him Azrael."

His head snapped up. "Really?"

She smirked. "No."

We all laughed.

"Are you OK?" he asked her.

She flopped back against her pillow. "I'm beat."

Azrael put his hand on Nathan's shoulder. "We'll get out of your hair and let you rest."

Reuel made an indignant squeaking sound and held his hands toward the baby. Azrael laughed and backed out of the way. "After Reuel's held the baby, of course."

Nathan carefully handed the bundle over to the massive angel. Reuel curled his arms around the baby and held Jett carefully against his chest. Reuel laughed. *"Cak."*

We all looked closer. Jett's eyes were open, and he looked to be smiling at Reuel. A tiny hand lifted from the mound of blankets, and Reuel lowered his face so Jett could touch his cheek.

Azrael and I exchanged a loaded glance. Fury caught my eye. She gestured toward them as if to say, "There's no way this kid is the Morning Star."

I hoped to the Father she was right.

"Warren, may I have a second?" Azrael asked when we were all outside the hospital room again.

Nathan slapped Reuel on the arm. "I'm starving. Want to walk with me to the cafeteria?"

With a grunt of confirmation, Reuel nodded.

"We'll catch up with you," I said.

Azrael and I turned to follow them, but we both walked

very slowly. When they were out of earshot, Azrael spoke quietly. "What is that thing in there?"

"It's a baby, you insensitive prick."

"I'm an insensitive prick? Earlier you said it would be easier if Fury gave birth to the Morning Star so we can take it away. Who's insensitive?"

I sighed. "I don't know if it's the Morning Star, but it's not human at all. Fury knows it too. She didn't want me to tell you."

"I feel bad she has the sight. It would be better if she had no idea," he said, looking down the hallway.

"Like Adrianne?"

He didn't answer.

"Did you see that baby's eyes?" I asked him.

"I did. I'm afraid of what that could mean."

"Me too."

"Warren, hold up!" Johnny called behind us.

Azrael and I both stopped and turned around. Johnny was jogging to catch up. "Allison asked for me to tell you that she wants you to come by the house when they let her go home from the hospital."

"Does she know when that will be?"

He shrugged. "Not sure, but I imagine they'll keep her for a day or two, at least."

"OK. Tell her to call me. I'll be"—I looked left and right —"around." I meant I'd be on Earth and reachable by cell phone.

"Will do."

I extended my hand toward him. He accepted it. "Congratulations, John. I'm happy for you." Although, I wasn't exactly sure if that was true.

"Thanks, Warren. That means a lot coming from you."

I wondered if it meant a lot because I was the Archangel of Death. Or if it meant a lot because once upon a time, I was the one sleeping with his girlfriend and this was my way of conceding the victory to him. I suspected it was the latter. And judging from Azrael's grin, he suspected the same.

"I'll tell Allison to call you," Johnny said, backing away from us.

"You do that." I waved as he retreated.

When he'd turned fully away from us, Azrael nudged me with his elbow. "Humans, huh?"

I laughed. "Yeah."

We continued toward the exit. "You know, I thought once the baby came, Fury might stay home and let you go to Nulterra without her," Azrael said.

I held open the exit door for him. "Motherhood might change people, but nothing will change Fury *that* much."

"You might be right, son." He stopped walking and turned toward me. Folding his arms across his chest, he looked at the floor. Finally, he met my eyes again. They were serious. Worried. "If Fury's child is the Morning Star, you know what the Council might require you to do."

A lump rose in my throat. "That hasn't been decided yet."

"You need to prepare yourself, Warren."

"There's no way I can—"

"If they mandate it, you won't have a choice. Trust me as one who knows, the last thing you want is to be thrown out of Eden."

I suddenly felt sick. "But it's a child."

He pointed at my face. "It's not a child. You *know* that."

"What do you think they'll expect me to do? Find and kill him every time he's reborn?"

"Yes. At least until your daughter is old enough to destroy him permanently."

"So maybe we don't separate him. Maybe we imprison him. Keep your enemies close, right?"

He shrugged. "It's what I would do, but the Council has a

history of choosing the immediate path of least resistance. They tried to have me do this once before."

I ran my hands down my face. "Let's say I could get over the whole idea of infanticide...I still couldn't do that to Fury."

"As much as I disagree with it, you would be doing her a favor."

Shaking my head, I looked up at the ceiling. "I can't believe we're even having this conversation."

"How do you think it will affect her when this comes to war and SF-12 goes to battle with the Morning Star?"

"She's not part of SF-12 anymore," I reminded him.

"Then what if she fights on the side of her son?" His words landed like a boulder in between us. "Are you ready to kill Allison?"

I sighed. "You're crazy."

"You know I'm right."

"And what if it's Adrianne? Are you ready to let me kill her child?"

He visibly swallowed.

"Not so easy when the tables are turned, is it?"

A muscle worked in his jaw. "I'll let you do what's necessary. There's no other option if it's the Morning Star."

He was serious.

I felt like my head might explode.

"Did Nathan tell you a few of them went to see his ex-girlfriend, Shannon?"

"No, but Enzo left me a voicemail about it. He and Kane both agreed her child, too, might not be human. I'll pay her a visit the next time I'm in Asheville. When is her baby due?"

"It's a couple of months away still." Azrael sighed. "Never have I seen anything like this. One angel birth is rare. Two is unheard of."

"Iliana's unheard of. I feel like her birth is upsetting all the norms."

"It certainly is," he agreed.

"Come on. We can't do anything about it today," I said, continuing down the hallway. "What are you doing after this? I really need to talk to you about a situation developing in Italy."

"How about you join us for dinner? I'd like you to see Adrianne anyway."

I stopped walking again. "In Asheville?"

He pulled on my sleeve to tug me forward. "No, not in Asheville. Adrianne came with us and is at Nathan's parents' house not too far away in Durham. She had absolutely no desire to see Fury."

I chuckled. "A loyalist even now that Sloan married Nate?"

"Even now."

No one had been angrier than me when Fury showed back up in my life, but for Sloan, that hadn't eased the blow of having my ex suddenly thrust in her face. So Adrianne hated Fury as any best friend should, even beyond the expiration date of Sloan's relationship with me.

"I'd be happy to see her, but don't the McNamaras believe I'm dead?"

The official story was that I'd been killed in action on assignment with Claymore in the Middle East.

"Nathan will send them here to see the baby as soon as we get back to the house. You can wait in the car until they leave."

"Yeah. I'd love to see her then."

He squeezed my arm as we walked. "Excellent. I already told her you might. She was thrilled."

"Did you tell Sloan you'd be seeing me?"

Azrael looked at me. "It's hard for you this time, isn't it?"

"You're the only one I'd confess this to, but it's hard every time." I sighed as we neared the elevator. "This trip back to Earth has been worse than I expected."

"Because you thought you'd see Sloan?"

I didn't answer. I didn't have to.

He pressed the down button on the wall. "Because you truly loved her, it won't ever leave you completely, son." He leaned toward me and lowered his voice. "It won't ever leave her completely either, if that's any consolation."

It wasn't.

"The less time you spend on Earth, the better."

"That, I know."

"Just keep reminding yourself that you did the right thing for Sloan and Iliana."

"I wish that made it feel like less of a kick to the balls every day that I'm here."

He patted my shoulder as we stepped onto the elevator. "I know how you feel. How's your mother?"

The elevator doors slid closed, and I pressed the button for the third floor. "She's well. Still asks about you."

"Does she know about Adrianne and the baby?"

I nodded. "She's happy for you."

"I knew she would be. I still miss her though."

We were silent the rest of the ride down, and when the elevator doors opened, Reuel and Nathan were waiting for us. "Cafeteria's closed," Nathan said with a shrug.

Reuel's sad eyes fell to the floor.

"It's OK though," Nathan said, gripping the angel's shoulder as they got on the elevator. "Mom said she's keeping dinner warm for when we get back. And *nobody* cooks like my mother. Warren, are you coming with us?"

"My first home-cooked meal on Earth in almost a century?" I said with a smile. "I wouldn't miss it."

CHAPTER FOUR

"*D*o you know how long it's been since I've ridden in a car?" I asked from the back seat of Azrael's black SUV.

Azrael looked at me in the rearview mirror. "How long have you been here this time?"

I looked at my watch, which was always set on Asheville's time zone. "About six hours."

"You've been at the hospital all that time?" Nathan asked.

"No. I was in Italy when I got the text about Fury's water breaking. I met Reuel at the hospital after that."

"Italy? I thought you'd be in Eden," Azrael said.

"I was, and I'll have to go back very soon."

"What's it like there?" Nathan asked.

"In Eden?"

"Yeah."

My lips instinctively tipped up in a smile. "It's beautiful. It looks similar to here, but everything's brighter and greener—"

"And cleaner," Azrael said, checking his blind spot before merging onto the interstate.

Reuel grunted and nodded in agreement. "*Nira icai.*"

I smiled. "Yes, there's also a *lot* of music. And it's just peaceful. There's still work to do and decisions to make, but it's free from the day-to-day drama and stress you experience here on Earth." I took a deep breath. "Kinda like being on the ultimate vacation all the time."

Azrael glanced back at us. "There's a reason they call it paradise."

"I bet you miss it," Nathan said to him.

He sighed. "Every single day."

I understood. In Eden, we could remember our lives on Earth, but they were so far removed from us that it was like we'd read a biography about someone else. Thinking of Iliana and Sloan in Eden was so much easier, joyful even sometimes.

But this side of the spirit line was just *heavy*. Even for a temporary visitor like myself. My dead heart hadn't hurt like this since the last time I'd been here.

"So you just sit around on a cloud eating bonbons and drinking cherry lemonade every day?" Nathan asked.

I chuckled. "Some people do, but I have a job, remember?"

His eyes narrowed. "What's that resume look like these days?"

"My job is much easier now that I've gotten caught up on *someone's* backlogged workload." I could see Azrael grinning in the mirror.

"Sorry. Not sorry," he said.

I rolled my eyes.

"What workload?" Nathan asked.

"The Archangel of Death is the only being with the power to inflict the second death on a human. Lots of souls got backed up over the thirty-one years Azrael was stuck here," I said.

"You just blink them out of existence?"

"I don't *blink*, per se, but yeah. I obliterate them."

He blew out a sigh. "I'm glad you're on my side now."

Azrael smiled in the mirror again. "Kinda gives a whole new

meaning to that 'till death do you part' bit in your marriage vows, huh?"

Nathan's face whipped toward me. "You wouldn't."

I shrugged. "I have thought about it."

His jaw dropped.

I laughed. "You're safe, for now."

"You're an asshole."

"I know."

Nathan crossed his arms. "How many people do you obliterate in a day?"

"A day on Earth? Not too many. Most are permitted into Eden. The final death is reserved for those who have allowed remorseless transgressions against others to mutate their souls—"

"Mutate?" Nathan asked.

"Remember how Sloan and I could tell the good souls from the bad ones?"

He nodded.

"There's no coming back from that, even in Eden, so the Father mercifully allows them eternal rest."

Azrael glanced back. "Except for a special few. The most heinous offenders go to Nulterra."

"Anyone I know?" Nathan asked.

An evil grin overtook my face. "Remember Larry Mendez? The guy who was trafficking little girls for Sloan's demon mother?"

"How could I forget?"

"Let's say, he's getting what he deserves."

Nathan gave a thumbs-up. "That's a relief. Will he stay there forever?"

"Until the pit devours his soul," I said.

"A pit sounds amazing. Can we get a few for the Justice Department here in the US?" Nathan asked.

"They have them in Thailand," Azrael said, flashing a grin

over his shoulder. Following the GPS's directions, he changed lanes toward the next exit.

Reuel chuckled and started a story in Katavukai that began with, "Remember that one time in Thailand—"

Azrael slammed on the brakes, pitching all four of us forward as the wheels screamed against the asphalt. I "mom-armed" Nathan across the car to keep him from slamming face-first into the back of Reuel's seat. Then I looked back just in time to throw my power toward the car barreling toward us. It veered right and missed our bumper by a couple of inches.

The driver swore out his window as he passed on the passenger's side.

"What the hell, Azrael?" Nathan shouted.

We both looked ahead to see an angel standing in the dead-center of the road.

Azrael was out of the car and charging forward before I could even remove my seatbelt. Immortal or not, safety first.

"Who's that?" Nathan asked.

"Ionis," Reuel answered.

Nathan looked at me. "Who?"

"A messenger." I grabbed the door handle and pushed it open. "Come on, Nate. Az is about to show you how to kill an angel."

Azrael grabbed the small messenger by the collar of his flashy jacket and lifted his feet inches from the ground. He screamed in his face. "Are you trying to get someone killed?"

Ionis smiled, kicking his legs. "Testy now that we're mortal, are we?"

Azrael hurled him against the concrete wall dividing the offramp from the interstate below. His hair was a shocking white, cut short and pushed back in a wave. He wore a bright-blue striped shirt under the jacket, skinny jeans, and sneakers with no socks.

I walked over and grabbed his jacket to haul him up. "What are you doing here, Ionis?"

"I have news," he said.

Nathan held up his hands. "Whoa, whoa, whoa. He's speaking English. Is he a demon?"

Angels weren't permitted to speak anything but Katavukai. It was a mark of their loyalty, and a tell-tale sign for the fallen. Because I was born human, the rule didn't apply to me.

"I'm a messenger, not a demon," Ionis snapped, dusting off the seat of his pants. "Geez. Stupid humans."

"He is speaking Katavukai. You just understand him in English because he's a Messenger," I said. "And he's OK. A friend from Eden."

"A friend," Azrael huffed, folding his arms.

Nathan leaned close and lowered his voice to just above a whisper. "Is your friend...male? Female?"

"Technically, neither. You can refer to Ionis as a him though." I turned back to Ionis. "Do we need to do this in the middle of the road, or can we get back in the car?"

"I'd love a ride. Where are we going?" he asked, his voice chipper as always as he started toward the car.

Azrael pointed at him and then around to the rest of us. "*We're* not going anywhere. We'll drop you off on the side of the road somewhere."

"Your manners never cease to impress me, Azrael," Ionis said with a smirk.

Azrael held up his middle finger.

Ionis puckered his lips. "You're such a blessing." I suspected that if he hadn't been afraid of Azrael, he would have pinched his cheeks.

Az just glared.

A horn blasted behind us. Cars were stacking up down the exit ramp. Nathan waved them around as we got back in the

SUV. Ionis slid into the middle of the back seat between me and Nathan.

"Hello, Reuel," Ionis said.

Reuel waved over his shoulder.

"Why the bad blood between you two?" Nathan asked, gesturing between Ionis and Azrael.

Azrael put the transmission in drive.

Reuel chuckled and answered in Katavukai.

I translated. "Ionis likes to report all the dumb stuff Azrael does on Earth back to Eden."

Ionis sighed dramatically. "It's a full-time job, but somebody's got to do it."

Nathan bit down on the insides of his lips to keep from laughing.

Azrael put on a blinker to turn right at the intersection onto the main road. "What's so important that you almost killed us?"

"Did the Council reconvene with a verdict?" I asked.

Ionis shrugged. "Hell if I know. That's not why I'm here. I was sent to find Azrael."

Azrael groaned. "Lucky me."

"Hey, Az, have you heard about the new *magic* in Eden?" Ionis wiggled his fingers like magic might shoot from them. His middle fingernails were painted a glittery blue.

"Magic, really?" Azrael probably would have laughed had he not sounded so annoyed. "That's the dumbest thing I've ever heard."

"Tell him, Warren." Ionis split a glance between Azrael and myself.

"That's what I wanted to talk to you about," I said.

"Magic in Eden?"

My head bobbed from side to side. "Not necessarily *in* Eden."

Ionis leaned closer to Azrael's seat. "Samael says he's never seen anything like it."

Nathan nodded, impressed. "That's a big statement coming from a guy who's been around since the beginning of time."

Azrael looked at me in the rearview mirror. "He's serious?"

"Afraid so. And it gets worse."

"We have another *serial killer.*" Ionis's voice jumped up an octave with excitement.

Nathan grinned. Reuel chuckled.

"What's he talking about?" Azrael asked me.

"There have been four people with the gift of discernment murdered in the past few months," I said.

"Unusual."

"The first one was a woman from Thailand. The second was a man in Turkey. But the last two were murdered on the Calle dei Morti."

Azrael swerved the SUV over the rumble strips on the side of the road. Ionis slammed into me, and Nathan grabbed onto the back of Reuel's seat.

Azrael's eyes were wide in the mirror. "The Street of the Dead?"

Nathan chuckled. "The Street of the Dead. What an appropriate place to commit a murder."

"More appropriate than you think." I looked at my father. "This isn't the first time."

"The Calle dei Morti has a rich history of violence and death. I'm very familiar with it," Azrael said.

"I know. I think we're dealing with a copycat killer."

"What makes you think so?"

"There have been four victims so far: three women and one man. All of them were beheaded with their eyes removed."

"Were the eyes found in the throat or back of the mouth?" Azrael asked.

I nodded.

"Were the heads mounted on something near the body?"

"On a bedpost twice. On a lamp once."

Ionis shuddered. "Ew."

Reuel was shaking his head.

"*Il mostro di Venezia.*" Azrael's voice was full of wonder.

"What?" Nathan asked.

"Not what. *Who*," Ionis said.

"The monster of Venice," I translated. "He was one of the most brutal killers in European history. Azrael killed him in 1797. Vito Saez is the reason the street's called the Calle dei Morti."

"I've studied a lot of serial killers over the years. That name nor the MO ring any bells for me," Nathan said.

I looked across Ionis at him. "I almost forgot we met because of a serial killer. God, that seems like a lifetime ago."

Ionis's head tilted. "For you, it was."

"Good point," I said. "I've done some research. There are a few mentions of Saez buried online. They weren't easy to find, but they *were* out there."

"What does that have to do with *magic*?" You could tell it was almost painful for Azrael to use that word.

"What drew Samael's attention to the deaths in the first place was this strange purple..."

"Say it," Ionis whispered, wiggling his fingers again.

I rolled my eyes. "It was a weird purple energy on the first girl's spirit. Very faint, but still conspicuous. When he discovered she had the gift as well, he started to investigate."

"And?"

"All the victims have had my mark carved into their chests."

Azrael's face crumpled with confusion. "What?"

"You heard me correctly. My mark, carved right into the skin."

"What mark?" Nathan asked.

I leaned forward to look at him. "Angels of Death only escort souls across the spirit line. We rarely kill them. When we do, the spirit is branded with a mark, a signature of which angel did the deed. My mark looks like an old Roman cross with two S's facing each other."

"They're snakes," Azrael corrected me.

"Really? They don't look like snakes."

Reuel chuckled. *"Mat ene Azrael yat vorai."*

I laughed, and Azrael held up his middle finger.

"What'd he say?" Nathan asked.

"He said, 'Only because Azrael can't draw.'" I laughed again.

"The point is"—Azrael overemphasized his words—"the mark is only visible to other Angels of Death. It's not even commonly known in Eden—much less on Earth. It certainly isn't found in a Google search."

"The last one, the girl we found this morning, was young. Still a teenager, maybe."

Reuel's hands clenched into fists. He hated violence against women and children most of all.

Nathan leaned forward to look around Ionis at me. "That's a punishable-by-Nulterra offense, right?"

"You'd better believe it is. Our deal with Nulterra was actually created with those who hurt children in mind."

"What deal?" he asked.

Ionis's head tilted. "You're cute, but not too bright."

"He's very bright. He's just been on a need-to-know basis," Azrael said.

Nathan whimpered and dramatically put his hand over his heart. "Az, that may be the nicest thing you've ever said to me."

"You'd better write that shit down somewhere, Mr. McNamara," Ionis said.

"How do you know my name?" Nathan asked.

Ionis just sighed and rolled his eyes. He looked at me. "Is this guy for real?"

I ignored him and looked over at Nate. "When the Morning Star and his followers were kicked out of Eden, the Morning Star created Nulterra. From what we know, its main energy source comes from the destruction of human souls, much like the way nuclear energy is created by splitting atoms."

Nathan cringed. "Geez."

"In the beginning, they were taking souls straight from Earth to the pit," I said.

"How? Aren't there rules against them messing with humans?" Nathan asked.

Ionis cocked an eyebrow. "Ever heard of selling your soul to the devil?"

"No shit?"

"No shit," Ionis said.

"But we put a stop to it quickly," Azrael said.

I nodded. "Azrael's idea was to furnish the Morning Star with the souls of the ultra wicked in exchange for the gate from Earth being sealed and completely hidden."

At the top of the ultra-wicked list were pedophiles, and it brought me comfort knowing the first ever human I'd killed was rotting away in Hell.

If anyone deserved damnation, it was Charlie Lockett.

"Why would they agree to that?" Nathan asked.

"Because except for the Morning Star, the fallen were once again allowed to travel via the spirit line. Never back through the Eden Gate, but they could travel to and from Nulterra and throughout the Earth," Azrael said.

Nathan frowned. "Didn't you think about the consequences of that? Now I have to worry about baby snatchers across different dimensions."

Azrael didn't bother to respond. We all knew it was a problem.

The GPS was telling Azrael to turn left. Looking out the windshield, I saw the name on the mailbox we were passing: McNamara.

"Is this your parents' place?" I asked Nathan.

"Yep. This is home sweet home."

The two-story farmhouse came into view at the end of the long gravel driveway. The white house had a covered wraparound porch and a tall stone chimney that was billowing gray smoke.

My heart ached at the sight. I was supposed to have visited here with Sloan. She'd always talked about how much she loved it. About how at home she'd felt under the McNamara's roof. Now, the same place that had quickly become a second home to her was a glaring reminder of how great an alien I was.

The wheels rolled to a stop on the loose gravel. Azrael put the SUV in park. "Warren, you and Ionis stay here until the McNamaras are gone."

Nathan pointed around the left side of the house. "You'll see them leave in a silver Jeep. I'll hurry them along. Reuel, you can come inside with us. We told them you might be at the hospital."

Reuel looked back at me for my blessing.

"We'll see in you inside." I pointed at him. "Save me a plate."

He smiled.

When they left, Ionis slid into Nathan's vacated seat. "Long time no see, Warren."

I scowled. "I saw you this morning."

"Yes, but that was like a month ago for me."

"It's not like you felt it," I reminded him.

He laid his white head back against the headrest. "But I felt it when I got here. Ugh."

I pulled the photo book Nathan had given me from the bag at my feet. I knew *exactly* what he meant.

CHAPTER FIVE

Nathan's mom had cooked a turkey. A full Thanksgiving spread, really, with dressing, green bean casserole, mashed potatoes, and fresh-baked biscuits. Apparently, it was Nathan's favorite meal.

The house was exactly like I imagined it. Warm, cozy, inviting. It smelled like the holidays and happiness. Family pictures covered the walls, and children's artwork covered the fridge. Etched into the wooden doorframe between the kitchen and dining room were lines marking different heights. Each line had its own name and date. *Chuck, 2-8-1983. Lara, 11-17-1987. Nathan, 1-06-1988. Ashley, 9-16-1989.*

Ionis was looking into the curio cabinet against the wall. "Nathan, is this you?"

Nathan carried his plate over to see where Ionis was pointing. "Yep. Halloween, 1989. Even back then I wanted to be a cop. Mom made the costume."

I looked over Ionis's shoulder. In the photo, Nathan was dressed in a black police officer's uniform and proudly holding a plastic jack-o'-lantern. He was missing his two front teeth. "Do you miss it?"

"Halloween? The biggest candy holiday of the year? Always."

I rolled my eyes. "Police work."

He sighed and walked back to the stove. "Yeah. Don't get me wrong. I love my life now and wouldn't change it for anything, but I miss it." He handed me an empty plate. "Eat up, brother."

Reuel pulled both legs off the bird and laid them across the piles of food heaped onto his plate. When he saw me eyeing him, he picked one of them back up and offered it to me.

"No thanks, buddy," I said with a smile. "Where's Az?"

"Upstairs with Adrianne," Nathan answered, plucking two rolls from the bread basket.

"This is a great house, Nate." I scooped up a spoonful of potatoes.

Ionis was in line behind me. "It's so *Leave it to Beaver*."

I chuckled. It really was.

We carried our plates into the dining room, and Nathan passed around a glass pitcher full of sweet iced tea. Azrael walked in just as we started to eat. "Adrianne will be down in a little while. She's resting. Nate, when should we expect your parents to return?"

"I asked Dad to send me a text message when they are leaving the hospital."

"Thank you," Azrael said.

Nathan pointed a dinner roll toward the kitchen. "Az, go make yourself a plate. There's plenty of food."

"I'll eat with Adrianne." Azrael pulled out the chair at the head of the table and sat down. "We need to figure out how to determine the identity of the Morning Star, otherwise it will be a long wait until the child comes of age and names itself."

"How long does it usually take?" Nathan asked.

"The Morning Star isn't *usual*, but if we're talking averages... thirteen years, give or take. It's different for all of us."

"You were thirteen or fourteen, weren't you?" I asked.

He straightened, surprise widening his eyes. "How did you know that?"

I reached across the table and hooked my finger around the chain encircling his neck. I pulled the blood stone from under his collar.

He clenched it in his hand. "Of course." Then his eyes narrowed. "Someday, you and I need to have a long father-to-son talk about all you learned from my memories in the blood stone."

I smiled. "You've had some fun times, haven't you?"

If my father had been a blusher, he'd have turned beet red. Instead, a thin but loaded smile was fixed on his normally-stern face. "Son, you have no idea." He tucked the necklace back into his shirt.

"Better not let Adrianne hear you say that," I said.

On the other side of me, Reuel chuckled.

Azrael's blood stone had been given to me when I became the Archangel of Death, the day my daughter was born. It contained most of his memories from the spiritual world and his few thousand years on Earth. They were colorful, to say the least. The memories had faded some for me now that I'd returned the necklace to him, but a few would be forever scarred in my mind.

"Why can't 'the Father'"—Nathan actually used air quotes —"identify the child?"

"He could, if he was in Eden," I said, skewering a forkful of green beans. "The Father has been on Earth since he brought Sloan back from the dead."

"Really?" Nathan asked.

"That's what I hear. I may have to hunt him down though and get him to go back home. He's all but powerless here."

Nathan looked worried. "God is powerless?"

"By his own design. He never wanted to be tempted to rule the Earth," Azrael explained.

"That's why we were sent here to help humanity," Ionis added.

Azrael smiled. "Some of us are more helpful than others."

Ionis leaned on the table. "I'd like to remind you that you're no longer helpful to anyone."

"Ooo," Reuel said with a grin.

Azrael moved to get up, but I used my power to hold him in his chair. "Can we please stay on topic here? You two can kill each other later when such important matters aren't pressing."

Azrael glared at him.

"Are Metatron or Sandalphon powerful enough to identify the child?" Ionis asked.

I put my fork down and looked at Azrael. "That's a very good question. Are they?"

"I remember Sandalphon, the creepy old guy who could see the future, but who's Metatron again?" Nathan asked, squinting like he was getting a headache from so much information.

"He's another angel similar to Iliana and Sandalphon, except he's both Angel of Life and Angel of Ministry. If you think of spirit beings in a hierarchy, the Father is at the very top, then Iliana, then Metatron and Sandalphon, and then all the rest of us." I turned back to Az. "Do you think it's possible?"

Azrael was considering it. Possibly trying to come up with a way to admit Ionis might be right, without admitting Ionis might be right. "We've never had to do this before, so I really don't know. It would be worth asking either of them to try. Think you can find them?"

"I can try. Sandalphon should be present at the reading of the Council's verdict. But Metatron...I don't even know where to start looking."

In the century I'd spent in Eden, I still hadn't met the guy. But Eden was an infinite place, so that wasn't saying a whole lot.

There were plenty of people I hadn't met yet that I wanted to, like General Douglas MacArthur and Elvis.

"Getting him to help might be a tougher matter than finding him. And finding him will be hard." Azrael pointed at Ionis. "You could aid him with the search."

It was true. The messengers were like the gossip hub of the heavenlies.

"Maybe, but you must ask me nicely," Ionis said, smiling over the rim of his glass.

Azrael ignored him. "So, Warren, what's your plan for taking Fury to Nulterra?"

I sighed and shook my head. "I would appreciate your help, Ionis. *Please.*"

Ionis put his hand on my arm. "For *you*, I'd do anything."

"See, I didn't have to be nice," Azrael said, grinning. He reached over to Reuel's plate and stole one of his extra rolls. Reuel's mouth dropped open, but Azrael smiled and bit into it.

"Why can't the other Angels of Death help you find him?" Nathan asked. "Aren't you their boss?"

"Yeah, but they're busy here. You don't want a bunch of ghosts wandering the Earth, do you?"

"Sure don't," Nathan said.

"And they're already working with reduced numbers as it is," Ionis added.

Azrael's head pulled back. "Why?"

Ionis pointed at me. "Because *someone* put them on a rotation to give them time off."

Azrael crossed his arms. "Really? How's that working out?"

"It's been a few years in Eden now, and the world hasn't fallen apart. Reuel even instituted the practice with the guardians."

Reuel nodded.

"How did *that* go over with the Council?" Azrael asked.

"They weren't happy about it."

"I'll bet they weren't." He chuckled. "You're running the choir like a human."

"And it's working just fine. It's boosted morale for all of them."

Nathan grinned at Az. "Good god, he's running Heaven like a Marine."

I lifted a shoulder.

"Whatever he's doing, it's working. The death choir has never been more tolerable." Ionis pointed his fork at Azrael. "Maybe if the practice had been instituted sooner, you wouldn't be such an insolent colon ulcer."

Azrael started to get up, and again, I held him still.

"I'm going to send you guys to the backyard. Have you two always been like this?" Nathan asked.

"Since he was, unfortunately, created," Azrael said with a grumble.

Ionis winked at him. "You love me."

"Ionis, why are you even here? I doubt it was to tell me about the magic"—Azrael wiggled his fingers—"in Eden."

Ionis's eyes popped open. "Right! I almost forgot. I have a gift for you." He leaned to the side and pulled a small black box from his pocket.

I recognized it. It was a trinket carrier designed to help small items survive across the spirit line. They were very rare. "Where'd you get that?"

He handed the box to Azrael. "I have no idea. It was left for me at the *Avronesh* with explicit instructions to give it to Azrael." Ionis looked at him across the table. "You're supposed to open it when you're alone."

"That's strange," I said. "Who would send you something from Eden?"

"Your mother?" Az suggested.

I shrugged and reached for the box. He put it in my hand,

and I turned it over, looking at it. "Mom doesn't have access to these. And she would have sent it by me if she did."

"Open it," Nathan said, leaning toward me.

"He can't. Only Azrael can." Ionis looked at him again. "And the instructions were clear. When you're alone."

"So mysterious," I said with a chuckle, handing it back to Az.

Nathan nudged my arm. "Let me hold it. I've never seen anything from Heaven before."

Reuel reached over and shoved him, then gestured around to all of us angels sitting around the table.

Nathan laughed as I gave him the box. "Besides you guys, of course." He gazed into its shiny cover, then tapped its corner against the table. "What is it made of? Some kind of metal?"

"They say the boxes are made of pure solidified darkness," Ionis said.

Nathan's eyes widened. "Really?"

Ionis's face pinched with a smirk. "No."

Rolling his eyes, Nathan gave the box back to Azrael. "Are all angels assholes?"

Reuel shook his head and raised his hand.

Nathan pointed at him. "You, Reuel. You're the only one."

Reuel winked at him.

Azrael put the box in his pocket. "Warren, what's your plan with Fury?" he asked, revisiting his earlier question.

"We still don't have a plan. No angel I've talked to can sense Anya's spirit. Not in Eden. Not on Earth. They all think she was destroyed—"

"Myself included," Azrael said.

I held up a finger. "But if Abaddon is dead and Anya is dead, why didn't the mantle of the Archangel pass to Reuel?"

"It didn't?" Nathan asked.

Reuel shook his head.

"No, but it should have if Abaddon was destroyed without an heir." I looked at my father. "Correct?"

Azrael didn't answer.

"And Fury told me today that Anya was seen boarding a chartered yacht in Thailand four days after Abaddon attacked them," I said.

"Didn't Fury tell us she saw Anya get dragged into Nulterra alive?" Nathan asked around the bite in his mouth.

Azrael shook his head. "She didn't see it herself. She's believing the vision of a prophet."

He looked annoyed, probably because Azrael had never held much respect for the Angels of Prophecy. Or, come to think of it, most angels whose gifts were less concrete than the power to inflict death, give life, or strong-arm their adversaries (like Reuel).

"Theta, the Archangel of Prophecy, showed Fury the vision of Anya being taken into Nulterra alive." I looked at my father. "I believe her."

"I've known more than one prophet to twist the facts to suit their agendas," he said.

"Says the master of fact-twisting himself," Nathan said with a smirk.

"Preach," Ionis said, holding his tea glass in the air.

Azrael ignored them. "Who saw Anya boarding a yacht?"

I skewered a bite of turkey with my fork. "Fury has had a team working for her since Anya disappeared three years ago. Two private investigators and one of the best hackers I've ever heard of."

"Who is it?" Nathan asked.

"Somebody named Chimera," I said.

Azrael scoffed. "Nobody's better than my staff."

Ionis laughed. "Oh, that's hilarious."

"You don't think so?" Azrael asked. He looked at me. "My

team killed you off easily in every database on the planet, didn't they?"

"They did, but the word is, it was Chimera who hacked the National Data Bank in 2013."

"Bullshit," Azrael said.

"I got it on good authority."

"Whoa, I heard about that," Nathan said with wide eyes.

I smiled. "What you probably didn't hear was that the Department of Defense had just contracted a white-hat hacker team from Claymore to try to break into it. Off the record, our guys said the system was secure. And right before they were about to send their all-clear report to the Pentagon..."

Nathan looked from me to a brooding Azrael. "Somebody broke in?"

"No one knows who it was," Azrael snapped.

I mouthed "It was Chimera" to Nathan.

He chuckled.

"If this guy's so good, how can Fury afford him?" Azrael asked.

"She can't afford him. She blew through her savings trying to find Anya." I pointed at Azrael. "Which is the only reason she agreed to come back to work for you last year."

Azrael leaned back in his seat. "Not the only reason."

"You think Fury came back for me?"

"I know she did."

Nathan raised his hand. "I know she did too. And I hate to say it, but she used the shit out of my uncle to take a jab at you."

Having suddenly found an ally, Azrael leaned toward Nathan. "And when this guy found out"—he pointed at me—"he was *pissed.*"

Nathan laughed. "Yeah, he was."

"Then you should've told her I was with Sloan," I said to Az, dodging their taunts.

Nathan stopped laughing. "Fury didn't know the two of you were together?"

"She would have if her hacker was any good," Azrael said with a laugh.

Nathan snickered again along with Reuel.

"What's so funny in here?" Adrianne asked, walking into the dining room.

I stood as a wide smile broke on my face. "Adrianne." I crossed the room and engulfed her in my arms.

She hugged me. "Warren. God, it's been too long. You look great. Really great."

"Hey, hey," Azrael said, snapping his fingers toward us. "You can cool it with the 'you look great' nonsense."

Laughing, she pulled back but still held onto my shoulders. "What do you expect me to say? He looks just like you."

Azrael smiled. "That's better."

Reuel walked over and hugged her.

"My favorite guardian angel," she said as he lifted her feet off the floor. "How are you, Reuel?"

He grunted.

"Still a man of many words, I see."

He laughed and settled her back down.

She stepped over to me again and put her hands on the sides of my face. "You, dear sir, have been terribly missed."

"You have no idea." I took her hands and a step back. "Let me have a look at you."

Azrael got up and stood beside us.

Adrianne hadn't changed much. Her hair was a darker shade of auburn than I remembered, and it had grown out past her shoulders. She wore a fitted white top to display the bump around her middle.

I reached toward her stomach. "May I?"

"Of course," she said.

I placed my hands on either side of her belly, and a faint

wave of energy pulsed through my fingers. The sensation was wildly different from what I'd felt around Fury, something unexplainable. Something powerful.

"What do you think?" Azrael asked.

"What does he think about what?" Adrianne asked.

"He wants to know if the baby is human." I looked over at him. "I really don't know. It's too early to tell, but if it is human, it's certainly not an average one."

"What the hell, Warren? Of course it's human. What else would it..." Her mouth widened as she turned toward Azrael. "Oh my god. You think I'm giving birth to a demon."

He took a step back. "Not necessarily. I'm not convinced it's a demon."

"What kind of father thinks their kid is a demon?" she asked.

Ionis jabbed his finger toward Azrael. It was hard for me to stifle a laugh.

"And who is this guy?" Adrianne asked, waving a manicured hand at the messenger.

Ionis got up and pushed his way between us. He went to hug her, but she palmed his forehead to stop him. "Um, no. Who are you?"

He smiled. "My name is Ionis. It's nice to meet you, Adrianne Marx. I'm sure your son will be as beautiful as his mother."

All our faces whipped toward him.

Adrianne's lips parted. "My—my son?"

"You didn't know?" Ionis covered his mouth. "I ruined the surprise."

"A son?" Azrael said, grabbing Ionis's sleeve. "Is it human?"

Ionis shrugged. "That's the rumor in Eden. Congratulations, Azrael."

"Rumor from who? I haven't heard anything," I said.

"I told you, you've been gone a *long* time," Ionis answered.

Azrael stepped over to Adrianne. She laughed through the tears streaming down her cheeks as he embraced her. "It's a boy," he said, tangling one hand in her hair and resting his forehead against hers.

"It's a boy," she repeated and kissed him.

Ionis leaned toward me. "Aww...you'll have a baby brother."

Reuel laughed.

"Oh." I frowned. "I hadn't thought about it that way."

Nathan's face soured. "That's weird."

I shook my head to clear it as I sat back down. The thought of having a sibling was too weird to process over a turkey dinner. For that, I'd need whiskey. Or something otherworldly stronger. I pushed my plate away from me. "If the baby's human, how do you explain the weird vibes from that womb?"

"*Nanum,*" Reuel agreed, meaning he felt them too.

Ionis drummed his nails on the tabletop. "As much as I hate to say it out loud, Azrael was one of the most powerful angels that's ever lived. And he's the *only* angel to ever become mortal. There's no telling what kind of abilities that kid might have."

Nathan raised an eyebrow. "Like Adrianne might give birth to the next Harry Potter?"

Ionis smirked. "Or the next Lord Voldemort."

As if on cue, a thunderous boom shook the entire house. The windows clanged against their frames. The dishes rattled on the table.

Ionis flinched.

Reuel jumped up from his chair.

Adrianne screamed.

Nathan looked up like something might crash through the roof. "What the...?"

I slowly closed my eyes. "That was an Angel of Death."

CHAPTER SIX

*S*amael was coming up the steps two at a time when Azrael opened the front door. "Azrael. Good, you're both here," Samael said before I even appeared in the doorway.

Unlike the rest of us, Samael typically dressed the part of the Angel of Death. This visit, his flowing black robe shimmered with the pink-and-orange rays of the setting sun, and the magic of the spirit line still glistened on his mocha skin. Even I was impressed. It almost made me wonder who should actually be in charge: me or him?

"Samael, what's going on?" I asked, stepping in front of Azrael. "Has the Council sent for me?"

"Yes. They have reached a verdict, but I'd like to talk to Azrael before we go."

Nathan pulled me backward. "Let the man in. Let the man in."

As I moved out of the way, Ionis leaned toward me and lowered his voice to a loud whisper. "He knows Samael's *not* a man, right?"

"He knows." I pushed him backward as Samael walked inside.

Samael reached for Nathan's hand. "Mr. McNamara, a pleasure to see you again. I hope you don't mind my unannounced intrusion."

"You wouldn't come if it wasn't important." Nathan closed the door behind him. "Come on in. You know everyone, right?"

Samael's bright golden eyes swept the group. "Yes. Hello, Adrianne. How are you feeling?"

She greeted him with a hug. "Good, as long as you're not here for one of us."

He laughed. "Not here for a house call."

"Then it's wonderful to see you. Sloan will be so jealous."

"Please give her my regards."

"I will."

"Samael, come on back," Nathan said, leading us all down the hallway.

On the other end of the house was a dimly lit family room with a couple of couches and overstuffed armchairs. I sat next to Samael near the fireplace.

"If you boys will excuse me, while you talk angel business, I'm going to stuff my face with all that delicious food in the kitchen," Adrianne said.

"Do you need my help?" Azrael asked her.

She kissed him quickly. "I'm perfectly capable of feeding myself. Thank you. Stay here. I know you eat this shit up."

I grinned.

When she was gone, Azrael came and sat on the arm of the sofa beside me. "I heard you've got some dead bodies bearing my mark."

"My mark," I corrected him.

Azrael laughed. "The mark of the Archangel. Better?"

I nodded.

"Did he tell you about the purple haze?"

"Ionis used the word *magic*," Azrael added, his skepticism clear.

Samael nodded. "Magic is a good way to describe it. It's a power unlike anything I've ever seen."

"So we've heard. Got any theories?" Azrael asked.

"I hoped you might," Samael said.

Azrael crossed his arms. "It's hard for me to speculate on something I haven't seen for myself."

"Which is why I'm here. I think I know how to show you," Samael said. "Do you have the blood stone?"

"Yes." Azrael sounded surprised. He reached both hands behind his neck and released the clasp of the chain holding the blood stone. He handed it to me. "Put this on."

"Good idea," I said, ashamed I hadn't thought of it myself. Samael could show me the scene again, and the blood stone could record it. I put the necklace on and turned toward Samael. "Go ahead."

Samael gripped my forehead with his large hand, pressing his fingertips into the sides of my skull. My eyes rolled back as I dipped into his memory.

The spirit of the girl from Thailand was staggering slowly toward me. She was hunched over and crying like she was in pain. Surrounding her spirit was a faint glistening purple haze. It moved like smoke, twisting and curling around her.

The second victim, a man from Turkey, had the same swirling haze.

So did the first victim from Venice. Finally, I was looking at Sofia from Samael's point of view in the room.

I pulled away from Samael's hand and opened my eyes. Then I took off the necklace and returned it to Azrael. "Here, see what you think."

Nathan leaned toward Ionis. "This shit is still so weird."

Ionis wiggled his fingers again and whispered, "Magic."

Nathan laughed.

Azrael's eyelids fluttered as he watched the vision through the blood stone. Finally, he looked at us again. "I have no idea what that is, but I don't think it's possible for a copycat to know our mark. I know Jaleal is working the area now, but who sent the first spirit over?"

"Jeshua. He was the first to notify me of the mark on the body."

"We'll keep searching. We'll find out who did this," Samael said.

Azrael nodded. "I have no doubt."

I turned toward Samael. "Shall we get back to Eden then?"

"They are waiting for you."

Dread pooled in my stomach like acid. I stood, prompting everyone else to rise around me. Azrael reached for my hand. "Let me know what they say."

"Of course."

He walked to the dining-room door and pushed it open. "Adrianne, Warren's leaving."

I looked at Reuel. "You ready?"

He nodded.

Nathan came over and pulled me into a one-armed hug. "Take care of yourself, brother."

"Always, man. Give my love to my family," I said.

"You know I will."

I held up the bag containing the photo album. "And thanks again for this."

"You gonna be able to take it with you?" he asked, curiously cutting his eyes at me.

"Unfortunately, they don't make trinket boxes big enough. But I can stash it outside the Eden Gate."

He sighed and shook his head. "So freaking weird." Then he stepped back to hug Reuel.

Adrianne came over with her arms outstretched. "Don't leave. I thought we might video chat with Iliana."

My heart wrenched as I hugged her. "As much as I would love that, I'm not sure I could keep my shit together for her."

"Next time?" she asked.

"Hopefully. Kiss my baby girl for me?"

"I will."

I touched her belly again. "And take care of this one. He's going to be pretty special."

She covered my hand with hers. "I'm already planning his marriage to Iliana."

"I think that's incest," Nathan said, his face souring.

Her eyes doubled. "Oh, I didn't think about that."

Laughing, Azrael put his arm around her.

"Ionis, are you coming with us?" Samael asked.

"Unless Azrael wants me to stay with him." Ionis flashed a smile across the room at Az.

Azrael pointed toward the door. "Get out."

Ionis laughed.

Azrael, Adrianne, and Nathan followed us to the front door and lingered in the doorway as we descended the stairs and walked down the gravel driveway.

Samael and Ionis disappeared with a loud *crack* first. Then Reuel. Then I turned around backward and waved with a sad smile.

All three of them waved back. Adrianne blew a kiss.

I checked my tactical watch and started a new timer. It was 6:48 p.m. on March 24.

Then I breached across the spirit line with a thunderous *boom*.

The inside of the spirit line always reminded me of the colorful corridors that connected the terminals of Chicago O'Hare. Light from Earth and Eden filtered through its walls, splintering from the pressure of both space and time into a metallic rainbow mist all around us.

In a sense, it even had a moving sidewalk, as walking or flying wasn't necessary. Our intention was enough to guide us to the Eden Gate through this living, breathing bridge between realms.

This time, we were moving quickly through it, a little like Willy Wonka's psychedelic boat ride. But it was possible to linger in the gap between worlds. To gaze through the membrane at life on the other side.

It was torture for the demons who longed for home in Eden.

And it was torture for me, gazing back on the life I gave up.

Through this veil, when Iliana wasn't hidden safely inside the Echo-5 fortress, the entire spirit world kept watch over my daughter. Those who would do her harm; and those who would destroy themselves to save her.

There would be no stopping now to check in on her. The walls around us were becoming thicker, the path was solidifying, and a sublime melody was growing louder in the distance.

Home was near.

At the end of the eternal corridor, both sides of the passageway widened farther than my eyes could see and stretched higher and higher until they disappeared into the kaleidoscopic lights above. Before us were the moonstone steps, hundreds of them, framed by alabaster columns.

The steps led to the colossal entrance, a gate made of moonstone and pearl. It had three arched doorways. The largest in the center led to Eden. The door to the left led to Nulterra. And the door on the right led to Reclusion—my chamber, where souls would await their final death.

Four large columns framed the doors. The two in the middle, on either side of Eden's entrance, were etched with two verses in Katavukai. In English, they read:

"The world is but a bridge. Pass over it, but build no houses upon it."

And,

"He who hopes for a day, may hope for eternity; but the world endures but an hour."

The great gate that once stood outside Constantinople was carved with the same words. The design had been inspired by a *very* near-death experience of the architect. Apparently, the makers of a gate still standing in India had copied that one.

"Time to drop our stuff," I said, walking toward the wall on our left at the base of the stairs.

There was a split where the wall overlapped itself, forming a narrow hallway. Inside it were rows of safes, small lockers we could use to store our items from the physical world. Each box had face recognition. Mine opened when I stepped in front of it.

Inside, I carefully placed my cell phone, my watch, and my wallet inside. Then I stole one last glance through the book Nate had given me.

Beside me, Reuel sighed heavily. When I looked, he was frowning at the last candy bar he still hadn't eaten.

With a laugh, I put my hand on his shoulder. "Don't be sad, my friend. Manna awaits."

He nodded and stuck the candy bar in the locker.

Down the row, Ionis was stripping down to his briefs.

"What *are* you doing?" Samael asked. He was waiting for us at the entrance as he had nothing to leave behind.

"I'm not letting this outfit get burned up through the gate. That's a seven-hundred-dollar jacket," Ionis said, stuffing it into his locker.

I rolled my eyes, put the book in the back of my safe, and closed the door.

As the four of us ascended the steps, human souls materialized around us.

Samael was the Angel of Death who guarded the spirit line. He decided which spirits and human souls could cross into

Eden, which humans should come to me to suffer the second death, and who must be turned over to Nulterra.

He hadn't been gone very long, hours only. Still, thousands of newcomers had gathered, and thousands more of their loved ones had come outside the gate to greet them.

Thankfully, no one seemed to care or notice that Ionis was nearly naked.

For now, the newcomers looked similar to the way they had before they crossed over. But once they crossed all the way into Eden, everything would be made new.

Music flowed over the walls and through the entrance, and joyful chatter echoed all around us. The gate was always a happy place, usually even for those who'd never make it inside.

Halfway up the steps, Samael grabbed my arm to stop me. He pointed, and I followed the direction of his finger. On the left side, near the base of a column, Sofia sat alone. She was still surrounded by the shimmering purple haze.

I turned toward Reuel and Ionis and pointed to Sofia. "There's the *magic* if you want to see it for yourself."

Ionis stretched on his toes to look over the heads around us. Reuel looked too.

"Got any ideas what it could be?"

"The purple sparkles?" Ionis asked.

"Yeah."

"Looks like something from an acid trip," he said.

I rolled my eyes. "You really are no help. Reuel?"

He just shrugged and shook his head.

I started in her direction. "Come with me."

We crossed the staircase through a maze of souls. Sofia's knees were pulled up to her chest when we reached her.

I knelt down at her feet. "Hello, Sofia. Remember me?" I asked gently in Katavukai. Much like when Ionis spoke on Earth, all spirits, no matter their native language, understood Katavukai once they were released from their earthly bodies.

She was no longer shaking, but her face still glistened with tears, something unusual for such a jubilant site.

Pain, sickness, the sting of death...all those things were left behind as souls crossed over. But the more violent the death, the harder it was for the effects to be burned away by the spirit line.

For her to still be upset, the death must have been horrific —so horrific it had aftershocks in the afterlife.

"Warren. You helped me." She answered in Italian, and even though I didn't speak the language, because she was a spirit, I understood her too.

"Sofia, do you know where you are?"

She looked around. "Heaven?"

"That's right. You have nothing to be afraid of here." I dried the tears on her cheeks and she didn't flinch.

One of the nicest things about the afterlife was no one feared me. On Earth, I'd gotten used to people going out of their way to avoid me; it was like I was born with a force field. I would later learn they weren't actually afraid of me, only afraid of what they could sense inside me.

Here, death was a thing of the past. And like most fears, once they're faced, they lose their sting.

She sniffed and wiped her nose on the back of her hand. "I'm not afraid. I'm not sad either." She covered her face. "I'm not sure what's wrong with me. Maybe I miss my mother and my sister, Gianna."

Samael crouched beside me. "Nothing's wrong with you. Do you see what's happening around us?" He gestured toward the masses hugging and laughing on the steps. "These are families just like yours. You'll see your mother and Gianna again."

I put my hand on hers. "Sofia, what's the last thing you remember before you met me?"

This was Eden, so she wouldn't remember anything upsetting.

"The Club Venezia. I was at work. I loved my job. Is that wrong?"

"That you worked in a nightclub?" I asked, smiling. "No, that's not wrong."

"Sofia? Sofia, is that you?"

Sofia looked over my shoulder. *"Nonna!"* The girl scrambled to her feet and ran past me to the woman who had called to her.

I looked at Samael as we stood. "You need to get back to Venice."

"May I come with?" Ionis rubbed his palms together. "I love Venice. The Carnival is my favorite."

Samael frowned. "No." He looked around at the people surrounding us. "Once we've heard from the Council, and once I've taken care of all this, I'll go back."

"We'd better get going." I started toward the gate and stopped beside Sofia and her grandmother. "Sofia, would you like to see inside?"

"More than anything," she said, beaming.

I offered her my hand, and she gladly took it. "Right this way."

Together, we passed through the gate into euphoria. Perfect peace and love washed over us, melting away all our cares. All the stress of the world was gone in a blink. Some humans around us couldn't handle the quick release, and they fell to their buckling knees on the soft ground. Sofia remained steady, her eyes closed, her mouth smiling.

Closing my eyes, I breathed in deep the scent of honeysuckle and sea salt as the Eden light from its two distant suns warmed my face. Every nerve ending tingled with all the best emotions: joy, hope, gratitude, and complete acceptance.

Every time was like the first time.

Home.

The jeans and T-shirt I'd worn in North Carolina were gone,

replaced with a similar outfit from my closet in Eden. The threads were finer, stronger, and softer...literally formed from photons of light.

When I finally looked at Sofia again, the purple haze and my mark had evaporated. Both were gone, along with everything else she'd experienced in the world we'd left behind. Her ghostly form had materialized, and she now wore a pure white dress, a blank slate for the new life she'd build here.

Her wide eyes looked around the garden entrance, a maze of every vibrant flower one could imagine. Colors I'd never even known existed sprouted up from the emerald grass, stretching toward the topaz sky.

Sofia squeezed my hand. "Thank you."

"Welcome home, Sofia."

"May I go with my nonna?" she asked.

I smiled. "You may go anywhere you like."

The two of them join hands and ran down the path together.

Reuel stepped beside me and put a hand on my shoulder. He still spoke in Katavukai, but I understood him in perfect English. "It's good to be back," he said with a smile.

"Yes, it is." I looked down the path toward the busy Eden streets—yes, they were gold. "And now it's time to go to work."

CHAPTER SEVEN

$\mathcal{T}$he Principality Council was the governing angel body in Eden. It was comprised of nine Angels of Knowledge, all of whom were widely accepted as the wisest in the celestial hierarchy. The Father had veto power over any decision that was made, but it was rare he got involved.

The few times he had gotten involved, the Council was *pissed*. Most recently, when he appointed Sandalphon to the Council. Not to say the Council members are elitists (even though, they totally are), they weren't happy to have an angel born on Earth added to their numbers.

Sandalphon was the angelic child of two Seramorta, and was born an Angel of Prophecy and Knowledge. In Eden, he was known as the *Oragnosi*, which loosely translated to "old wise dude." He was, indeed, both.

I expected him to be at the Council hearing. Alas, his seat was empty when I entered the Onyx Tower.

Instead, the angel Cassiel seemed to be presiding. She was seated in the center of the long marble table with a silver book in front of her.

Only three angels of the nine had been born into physical

bodies on Earth. None of them had Seramorta children, so they were free to pass through the spirit line at will. Cassiel was one of them, and she could have been the angel who'd been the muse for so many paintings. Long golden-brown hair. Icy-blue eyes. Smoking body. Because we were in Eden, I could see her wings, made of light, resting behind her.

To her right was Zaphkael. He had olive skin and jet-black hair and a snarl that reminded me of a Disney villain. The guy clearly hated me, but no real surprise there—a lot of angels did.

To Cassiel's left was Dumah, a strikingly beautiful woman who could've passed for Samael's sister. They both had the same sparkling golden eyes. It was said that Dumah had taken an eternal vow of silence.

The other six angels had no definite form. They were simply bodies of light and energy; even their wings were indistinguishable. They could, however, take on the form of anything they wished, often resembling humans when they interacted with the souls around them.

My mother sat in a pew to my right. The only human I could see and the most beautiful being—human or otherwise—in the room. I gave a slight wave, and she smiled. Reuel and Samael went to join her. Ionis had vanished.

"Warren, you're late," Cassiel said, tapping the end of a silver pen against the marble tabletop.

I approached the podium before them. "Forgive me for keeping you waiting. I've been with Fury. Her child was born today."

Cassiel's brow rose. "And?"

"The child is an angel, but it was unclear who or what kind." I looked around the room. "Where's Sandalphon?" At least he had proven in the past to have the best interest of my family at heart.

"Not here."

I waited for her to explain. She didn't. "Has the Council reached a decision regarding the Morning Star?" I finally asked.

"We have. Cassiel will deliver our decision," Zaphkael said.

Cassiel opened the book and read, "By the order of the Principality Council, any physical vessel harboring an angel who has not received written permission granted by this Council—"

"Excuse me?" I turned my ear toward the table, certain I'd misheard. "Did you say *any* angel who has been born into human form without permission?"

"Yes."

I laughed, though it wasn't remotely funny. "Is that even a thing? Angels have to ask the Council's permission now?"

"We feel it is best given our present circumstance with the Morning Star. Henceforth, all angels who desire to be born into human form must first acquire permission of this Council."

"Good luck with the riot you're about to have on your hands."

She leaned over her book. "May I continue?"

"You're the boss," I said with a smirk.

"Any physical vessel harboring an angel who has not received written permission granted by this Council and is aged less than two years shall be destroyed immediately upon discovery—"

"Destroyed?" I shouted.

With her expression pinched, she folded her hands on top of the book. "I know you're new around here, Warren, but no one interrupts this Council."

I gripped the sides of the podium to force myself to stay behind it. "You want me to destroy any angel less than two years old?"

"You don't have the power to destroy an angel," Eaza, one of the spirits, said.

"We only require that the Angels of Death destroy the vessel," Cassiel clarified.

I took an angry step back. "Does that mean my daughter? She's an angel less than two years old."

"No, we'll discuss the Vitamorte in a moment." Cassiel lifted the top of the book, her eyes asking again, "May I?"

I gestured for her to go ahead.

"This shall include but is not limited to an infantile commencement or a mature or juvenile mortal acquisition."

I looked up. "Hold on. Juvenile mortal acquisition? Are you saying that if the Morning Star possesses a child, you want us to take the child's life?"

"That's exactly what we're saying," Cassiel said with a completely straight face. "All unidentifiable beings shall be destroyed. The Morning Star has masqueraded as a child before to conceal his identity. Destroying all unknowns is the only way we can be sure he isn't as powerful as he could be."

Leaning my elbows on the podium, I cradled my heavy head in my hands.

"Should any angel encounter an unidentified spirit in any form and willingly fail to destroy the vessel or report it to an Angel of Death with the power to do so, that angel will be considered hostile to the throne of Eden and will be banished to the Earth."

"You have got to be kidding me," I mumbled, slumping over the stone lectern.

"As for your daughter..."

I straightened to attention.

"In order to protect the integrity of the spirit line and maintain our connection with the mortal world, it is the decision of this Council that the Vitamorte shall be brought to Eden before her first birthday to become a seraph."

A chill ran down my spine. "A seraph? What does that mean? She'll grow up here?"

"It means she won't grow up at all," Zaphkael said.

It felt like the world disappeared beneath my feet. My knees gave way, and I caught myself on the podium before I fell. "What?"

"The demons' plan all along has been to use Iliana's power to destroy the spirit line, forever separating Earth from Eden. The risk is too great with the unrest in Nulterra and the whereabouts of the Morning Star unknown. Bringing Iliana safely here will protect us from—"

"You're talking about robbing her of everything! A family. A home. A life. I gave up my life to make sure she had those things."

Cassiel's face softened. "We are all aware that you still have a sentimental attachment to this child—"

"You think?"

Zaphkael pointed at me and raised his voice. "If you interrupt this council one more time, I will personally have you thrown into *Cira*."

"Really? You're talking about destroying my daughter's life and angel jail is supposed to worry me?" I was shouting again.

"Warren," Cassiel said gently, "think of the positives. You and Iliana can be together. She'll be safe. What kind of life could she have that's better than here? Especially considering she'll have to grow up inside that fortress created by your father."

"Growing up at Claymore is better than not growing up at all."

The gentleness faded from her voice. "There are certain things we cannot allow to happen. The Morning Star using your daughter to destroy the spirit line is chief among them. A close second is the risk of the demons convincing her to join them."

"That is complete madness."

"Is it? They didn't have such a hard time convincing your father," Zaphkael said.

I couldn't argue with that.

Cassiel closed her book. "We will appoint a guardian to bring Iliana to Eden."

"No." I shook my head. "No one goes near my daughter but me."

"Then you have until her first birthday to bring her here," Cassiel said.

My face fell.

Zaphkael leaned toward me. "And should you fail, you will be stripped of your title and banished from Eden. Are we clear?"

I felt like I might vomit. "I beg you to reconsider."

"Our decision is final!" he shouted.

"Then I'd like to see the Father." I looked around the room. "Does anyone know where I might find him?"

A thin smile spread across Zaphkael's face. "Hoping for a reversal of our decision?"

"It's worth a discussion on both matters. You're talking about killing innocents and stripping Iliana of her potential. She's destined to claim the empty seat of the Morning Star as the most powerful angel in all of Eden—" I heard the words as they left my mouth, and I drew back with alarm. "My god. That's what this is about, isn't it?"

Cassiel rolled her eyes.

I pointed at her. "It is. The Council was only formed after the uprising of the Morning Star and the first angel war. If Iliana takes her rightful place here in the kingdom, she'll outrank all of you."

"That is insanity," Cassiel said.

Zaphkael shook his head. "Worse. It's blasphemy."

"Blasphemy can only be committed against the Father. And I really want to know what he thinks about all this. It flies in the face of his intentions for Iliana."

"How do you know the Father's intentions with Iliana?" Eaza asked.

"He personally sent Sloan back to Earth to raise her. You think he would have done that if he thought it was better for Iliana to be locked up here?"

The spirits exchanged glances, and there were murmurs between a few of them I couldn't make out. Finally, the third angel from Cassiel's left spoke. His name was Mueren, and his light pulsed with his words as he spoke. "The Father is currently aiding with the hunger crisis in the Horn of Africa."

"Where exactly?"

"The nation of Malab, near the coast."

"Thank you, Mueren."

Cassiel looked around the mostly-empty room. "Are there any further questions?"

I just shook my head.

"We need to make clear our instructions concerning the Morning Star." Cassiel held up a white scroll bound with a red seal. "This commandment shall be sent to the messengers at the close of this meeting."

Even though angels could communicate within their choirs, the messengers always passed official announcements from the Council or the Father.

With a heavy sigh, I walked toward the table. "I'll take it to the *Avronesh*. I'll speak with Gabriel when I leave here." Perhaps I could convince the Archangel Gabriel to buy us some time by delaying the message. I reached for the scroll.

"Absolutely not. We can't trust him," Zaphkael said.

For a second, Cassiel held it out of my reach, searching my eyes for any sign of deceit. I wondered what she saw. Finally, she gave it to me and stood. "Very well." Beside her, Zaphkael huffed. She ignored him. "The Council is adjourned."

When I turned, my mother caught my eye. She was sadly shaking her head. She knew firsthand what it meant for an innocent to be killed for the sake of hindering the Morning Star.

I crossed the room, and she stood and greeted me with a hug. "Hi, Mom."

She rested her head against my shoulder and rubbed my back. "Hello, son. I've missed you."

I gestured toward the remaining members of the Council. "I'm so glad I hurried back for this."

"You'll figure something out. You always do." She pushed my black hair behind my ears. "How's Fury?"

"She's well. The baby is..." I raked my fingers through my black hair. "The baby is going to be a problem."

She sighed. "I gathered that. I'm so sorry you're burdened with this. Can I help?"

"I must find Gabriel right now, but dinner tonight at home would be great. I need a quiet place to think and plan. Maybe we could invite Alice too."

"That sounds lovely." She looked over her shoulder at Reuel. "I assume you'll be joining us?"

With a wide smile, he nodded. *"Gratalis."*

"Warren, a word?" It was Cassiel, standing behind me.

"One second," I said to her.

My mother looked past me, her dark eyes sparkling with Cassiel's light. "You can invite her too if you'd like."

I chuckled. "Even now, Mom? She wants to freeze Iliana as a baby and have all humans like you killed."

"Maybe you can make her see the error of her ways," she said with a smile.

"I'll see you at home. It could take a while because Samael and I also have work to do." I pointed to where Samael was waiting for me.

"We've got all the time in the world," she said.

I sighed. "I wish that were true. Iliana turns one in just a few weeks."

"I love you, son."

"Love you too, Mom."

I turned back to Cassiel. "If you want to talk, keep up."

The Angel of Knowledge fell into step beside me as we walked down the center aisle toward the exit of the tower. I motioned for Samael and Reuel to follow us. They did.

"I'm sorry. I know the mandate will be hard for you," she said.

"You don't know shit, Cassiel. Not only is what you're asking me to do not going to be effective, it's *wrong*."

I held the door for her as we walked outside.

"Then what would you suggest instead? Putting the Morning Star in a cell he can walk right out of?" she asked.

I shook my head. "He can't walk out of all cells."

"You are referring to the facilities built by your father?"

"The Echo buildings on the Claymore properties are secure. I've tested a few of them myself. By the same design, Azrael could create a prison cell that would hold him."

She laughed. "You think we trust Azrael?"

"The Father forgave Azrael. Why can't you?"

"Because Azrael broke our code."

I smirked. "Now you sound like a Marine."

"Angels never side with humans over other angels. He put us all at risk by trying to save your mother. Or to go a step further, he put us all at risk by having you."

I turned to face her and crossed my arms.

"It's true, Warren. Had you not been born, the fallen Angels of Life would have never conspired to create Sloan. And if the two of you had never met, there would be no threat to the spirit line."

"So you're saying it would be better if I'd never been born."

Her perfect mouth closed.

I turned and walked away from her. "And I thought you liked me."

"I do like you, Warren." She double-stepped to catch up with me, and when she did, she grabbed my arms to stop me.

"But this is bigger than us. This could destroy everything as we know it."

Trying to dismiss her, I tore myself from her grip and walked on.

"Are you ready to be separated from your daughter for all time?" she called behind me. "Because that's exactly what will happen if the spirit line comes crashing down and Iliana is on the other side."

That got my attention. I turned to face her.

"She's immortal; so are you. You'd be on the opposite sides of forever if the Morning Star succeeds." She came toward me again, this time snaking her fingers around mine. "This is really the only way. You'll still have Iliana."

I stared down at our joined hands. One of her powers as an Angel of Knowledge was the ability to force people to tell the truth. She could even read someone's mind, if she had ahold of them long enough. My jaw tightened. If she wanted honesty, that's exactly what she'd get.

"What do you not understand about the fact that I gave up my whole family so that Iliana might have a full and happy life on Earth? Don't talk like you understand what it is to love anyone other than yourself."

Her lips pressed together.

"I will find another way." I jerked my hand free. "Excuse me. Unless you know where I might find Sandalphon or Metatron, I really have no use for you."

"Metatron, no. But Sandalphon willfully entered Cira today for a time of reflection."

My heart nearly imploded. If Sandalphon was in Cira, there would be no way to reach him. "Why?"

"We've had issues with him lately. He said he needed time away to think."

I gripped my forehead. "That makes two of us."

"What do you want with Sandalphon and Metatron?"

"Goodbye, Cassiel." Without answering, I turned and walked away.

"Warren!"

I glanced back.

"Don't do anything stupid."

I was wrong.

It was possible to feel sadness in Eden over things on Earth.

"What will you do?" Reuel asked as we walked with Samael toward the Avronesh, the sanctuary of the messengers. We could see its tall golden domes rising up into the blue sky in the distance.

"I have to find the Morning Star. It's the only bargaining chip I might have to convince them to let Iliana stay on Earth until she's grown. If either of you have any ideas on how I can convince Gabriel to delay the message, I'm all ears."

Silence hung between the three of us as we crossed the Idalia Marketplace.

"It wouldn't delay the message, but you could add that any Angel of Death must notify you before executing any judgment on Earth," Samael said.

"I can do that?" I asked. "I can make them notify me before they use their killing power?"

"You can, and the Council can't argue. It's in the Canon *they* wrote."

"You're a genius, Samael." I looked over at him. "Any idea why Sandalphon would have checked into Cira?"

"It's not that unusual. He disappears frequently," Reuel said.

"To Cira? Where *nobody* can reach him?"

He grimaced. "Well...no."

"That is unusual," Samael agreed.

After the spectacular fall of the Morning Star and his

followers, Cira was created to be a cooling-off zone for spirits teetering on rebellion. Most of the time, we were forced there —hence, the reason we called it "angel jail." But I'd been told, it was originally meant to be a voluntary place of respite. A great cosmic time-out for anyone tempted to do something everyone might regret.

I'd just never known anyone to actually *choose* to be there. Once an angel was locked inside, all the excess of Eden was stripped away. There was no peace. No hope. No joy. And worst of all in my current circumstance, there was zero communication.

"Can we even get him a message?" I asked.

Reuel shook his head.

"Not until he chooses to leave," Samael said.

I swore. "He was my best chance at an ally on the Council."

"And between him and Metatron, he was your most likely aid in identifying the Morning Star," Reuel added.

"Thanks, buddy," I said, shaking my head. "What can you guys tell me about this seraph thing? Are there others here?"

"Yes, but not many," Samael said. "The first was the Angel of Knowledge Mariel. She was brought here around the age of six. She'd been stolen and raised by the demon, Amaiah. By the time we found her, her mind was so warped by her extended proximity to Amaiah that she was exhibiting psychotic behavior—"

"Like what?" I asked.

"Mutilating animals, harming other children...Had we left her alone, there's no telling what she might have become," Samael said.

"Why not just separate her from the body?"

"It was discussed, but we weren't sure if the damage done had affected her spirit. We were unsure what we might have released into the world. Bringing her to Eden seemed like a safer option."

"And she's OK now?" I asked.

"Yes, but she'll never come into her full power again."

I swallowed. "And the others?"

"There were only two others, both Angels of Protection. Gaelish and Ofaniel were beheaded by Herod the Great when they were one and two, respectively. Beheading an angel complicates the process of healing or destroying the body, so they were brought here."

"Herod the Great?" I asked.

"The king of Judea a couple thousand years ago," Reuel said. "Late in his life, a traveling prophet told Herod a new king would be born to replace him. In a fit of paranoia, he ordered all boys under the age of two to be slaughtered. Gaelish and Ofaniel happened to be among them."

I scowled. "Under the age of two? Sounds familiar, doesn't it?"

Reuel sadly nodded his head.

"Where are they now?"

"Have you been to Lunaris?" Samael asked.

"No."

"It's about a day's journey past your mother's place at the Eternal Sea. Beautiful orchards out that way."

We started up the stone steps, but I stopped and turned around. "Wait. Samael, I need you to go to Venice. We still need to find out what happened to those humans. Just hurry because I'm going to need you here."

He took a step back down. "You can count on me."

"I know I can." I turned back to climb the stairs again.

"Warren," Samael said.

I stopped.

"Good luck."

"Thank you."

He spread his radiant wings. With one powerful thrust, he soared from the ground.

"Why don't you ever fly?" Reuel asked as we watched Samael disappear into the clouds.

I started back up the steps. "I fly."

"Not often."

"It feels weird. I'm supposed to be here as a human."

"But you're not a human."

My head bobbed from side to side. "I still feel human. Some of the time, anyway."

When I permanently chose Eden as my home—the day Iliana was born—the Father gave me wings. I could fly on either side of the spirit line, though as Reuel had said, I usually didn't. Human souls in Eden, like my mother and Alice, couldn't fly, and I certainly felt more like them than I ever felt like the other angels.

Two massive bronze doors led into the Avronesh. Ionis was inside, drinking a glass of wine with two other messengers. He stood when he saw us.

"You disappeared on us," I said, though I wasn't really sorry. Ionis couldn't keep his mouth shut, and the longer the news of the Council stayed quiet, the better.

"I didn't think you'd miss me. Politics aren't really my thing." He held up his glass. "Would you like a drink?"

Would I ever.

I shook my head. "Wish I could. I need to see Gabriel."

"You know where to find him. I'll see you two later," he said, going out the door through which we'd come in.

Reuel and I walked down the long haul to Gabriel's office. "Knock, knock," I said at the open door.

The Archangel Gabriel was seated behind a large desk. He was tall, larger than the rest of the messengers, and had long black hair and dark-tan skin. He looked like he'd been born into a Native American tribe. Hell, maybe he had been.

He looked up. "Warren, come in. Hello, Reuel."

"I'll let the two of you talk." Reuel pointed over his shoulder. "I'm going to check in at the Keep. See you at dinner?"

"Yeah, I'll see you later." When he was gone, I closed the door behind him. Then I walked over and sat down across from Gabriel in a chair that molded to me like a cloud. I relaxed back against it.

"How can I help you, Warren?"

"The Council has a couple of announcements for you to make."

He leaned back in his chair and folded his hands across his stomach. "I'm listening."

"The first is that the Council is now requiring all angels who wish to be born on Earth to register, to request permission from them before they act."

Gabriel's eyes widened. "You're serious?"

"Afraid so."

"That's not written in the Canon."

I shrugged. "Maybe they'll add it."

He stood so forcefully that his chair slid back and slammed against the wall. "They are taking away one of the very few freedoms we have?"

It was hard not to smile. His reaction would do nothing but help me. "I know. Bummer, right?"

"The news won't go over well."

I put my hands up in defense. "Don't shoot the messenger," I said with a joking smile.

He laughed, sort of. "What's the other message?"

"They've also decided that if any angel encounters an unidentified spirit in any human form, they are supposed to destroy its body or report it to an Angel of Death to be destroyed. This includes infants and children, specifically infants under two."

Gabriel settled slowly in his chair. "What if a demon has taken a child and the child is still alive?"

I dragged the tips of my fingers across the center of my throat.

He balanced his elbows on the table. "What?"

"Read it for yourself." I handed him the scroll. "Any angel who fails to do so will be declared hostile and excommunicated."

He broke the seal and opened it.

When he finished reading, Gabriel cradled his skull in his large hands. Worry radiated off him.

I knew the feeling.

"They can't do this."

"And yet they are."

"They're willing to kill innocents just to take the Morning Star out of commission for a year? Does the Father know about this?"

"He will soon enough." I scooted closer to the desk and lowered my voice. "Which is why I need you to add an addendum to the message for the Angels of Death. Before any of them execute a judgment on a human or an angel-child under the age of two, I must be notified."

"That's in the Canon. I can do that without either of us getting into trouble. We'll start delivering the message tomorrow to give you peace for the night. I think that will be reasonable enough for the Council."

"Thank you, Gabriel. You can mark Samael and Reuel off your list. They were in the courtroom with me and heard the message themselves."

Nodding, he made a note. Then he pointed at a line on the paper. "Is this other part in here about your daughter true? Are they bringing her to Eden now?"

I stood. "Not if I can help it."

CHAPTER EIGHT

When she was human, my mother had always wanted a house by the ocean. Now, she had one, on the cliffs overlooking the Eternal Sea. It was a bay off the even larger Eden Ocean.

A cobblestone path led around the front of the house, and the double doors were open, looking out over the water. I stopped out in the yard to admire the view. The waves splashed and retreated as if they were dancing with the rocks below.

I closed my eyes, soaking in the quiet serenity. It would be so easy to let the whole business of the Morning Star simply wash out to sea.

The quiet moment shattered with a happy bark coming from the house. Before I could turn, my dog was bouncing around my boots. She had been a gift from Reuel to welcome me to Eden, a brown-and-white English bulldog .

Reuel had named her Skittles.

"Hey, girl," I said, getting down to my knees on the soft grass. With her feet happily prancing on my thighs, she licked my face and nuzzled her smushed snout against my hands as I tried to pet her. "Did you miss me?"

She barked.

I hugged her and scratched her wrinkled sides until she flipped over onto her back. Begging for a belly rub, she wiggled in the grass. I gladly obliged.

Two cool hands covered my face from behind. "Three guesses, but you only need one."

I'd recognize my best friend's voice anywhere in eternity.

Laughing, I turned around in Alice's arms and stood, pulling her against me. "God, I've missed you." I lifted her feet off the ground in a tight hug, then put her back down.

"Me too." She rested her head against my chest and sighed. "I'm so glad you're back."

Alice was the first person I'd ever loved, though it had only ever been in the filial sense, never romantic. When I was alive, she was the closest thing I'd ever known to family, and she'd always felt like what I imagined a sister would be. And the feeling was mutual. Even in Eden, Alice would introduce me as her brother. We were family and the very best of friends.

Skittles barked and pushed her way in between our feet.

"Somebody missed you even more than me," she said, still clinging to my middle.

"Was she good for you?"

"Always is, but we're both glad you're home." After a moment, she looked up and smiled. "How was the melancholy land of depression and gloom?"

"Excruciating, as usual." I released her, and started toward the house with Skittles and her stumpy legs at a full gallop to keep up. "What have you been up to without me here to keep you out of trouble?"

"I've been keeping myself entertained. Did you know that if you bribe Forfax with enough strawberry manna, she will fly you to the *auranos* and let you create a star?"

"I had no idea." I laughed. "That's what you've been up to? Making stars with Forfax?"

She grabbed my hand to stop me, then spun me back toward the cliffs. She pointed up toward the sky. "See the pink one? She named it the *Alys,* after me."

"Why did you make it pink?"

"Why wouldn't I make it pink?"

Fair enough. I wasn't even sure why I asked. Everything Alice had in Eden was pink, including her entire wardrobe. Her sweater that night was soft, fuzzy, and the color of Pepto-Bismol. She'd also gotten Skittles a pink moonstone collar.

I smiled. "You and Forfax, huh?"

She skipped along the path beside me, her blonde hair bouncing around her face. "I dunno. We'll see. She's beautiful, and she knows all the best places to watch the sunrise over Earth."

"And she lets you make stars."

"And she lets me make stars." She hooked her arm through mine. "What's with you and Brainiac Barbie? Should I expect her at dinner tonight?"

"Absolutely not. And after today, you might never see her again."

"What happened today?"

"The Council wants me to do something I completely disagree with."

"So don't do it."

I cocked an eyebrow. "If I don't, I could get kicked out of Eden."

She stopped walking. "Warren, that's serious."

I pointed to my face. "Hence, all the stress."

"Your mom told me you had a tough time at the Onyx Tower. She didn't let on that it was that bad."

"My mother is an incurable optimist." All human souls were in Eden, really.

"I'm sure you'll make the right decision. Is it about Fury?"

"Partly. Her child isn't human, and they want me to kill all newborn nonhumans."

Alarm washed over her face. "Even Iliana?"

"No, but they want me to bring her here."

She clapped her hands together. "That sounds wonderful. Doesn't it, Skittles?"

Skittles barked again.

I shook my head as we walked into the house. "No, it really isn't. She'll be frozen as a baby. Never able to grow up."

Alice shrugged. "Maybe that's not such a bad thing."

"You only say that because your childhood was shit."

And it was. Alice and I had gone through the foster system together. She was the reason I killed Charlie Lockett, one of our caregivers, when I was just eight years old. What he did to her...even in Eden, I still couldn't stomach the thought. Unfortunately, his extermination hadn't saved her from the damage done to her mortal heart, and the life of addiction and depression that had followed ultimately killed her.

On Earth, Alice had died in my arms.

Alice leaned against my shoulder. "Not all of it was shit. The parts with you were wonderful."

I smiled and kissed the top of her head.

There was a basket of fresh, warm manna on the counter. It was a delicacy in Eden, and to put it in earthly terms, it was like a yeast roll and a pound cake got together and had a delicious baby. A baby that induced a feeling of ecstasy, like catnip for humans—or heroin that can't kill you (Alice's comparison, not mine). It came in all sorts of flavors. This one looked like butter cheesecake, my very favorite. I plucked out a slice and lifted it to my lips.

"Warren," my mother said, her tone scolding.

I bit into it anyway. "This is Eden," I said around the bite as I fed a piece to the dog. "No rules."

Mom laughed and swatted me with a dishtowel.

Yes, my mother still liked to do dishes...and cook and keep a tidy house. I think it was part of realizing the dream she'd wanted on Earth—a quiet domestic life with my father. He'd been here with her for a long time before they decided together it'd be best for him to return to help raise Iliana. I knew my mother missed him, but Eden gives us all a different perspective on time; a life on Earth is but a blink in respect to eternity.

I sat down at the elegantly set table, and Alice put arms around my neck from behind. She bent to rest her head on my shoulder. "How long can you stay?"

I put my hand over hers. "Not long enough, I'm afraid. I must go back tonight and find the Father."

"Where is he?"

"Africa."

"Bring me back a giraffe?" she asked, turning her face toward mine.

I laughed. "I'll see what I can do. Where would we put it?" Alice and I shared a house on the beach nearby.

"You could build a fence in the side yard."

"It would have to be a tall fence."

Alice kissed my cheek, then moved to the chair beside me. "Can you take care of Skittles for a little longer?"

At the sound of her name, Skittles headbutted my calf under the table.

"Of course. Is Reuel going with you?" She reached for the carafe of red wine in the center of the table.

"I hope so."

"Where is he? Nadine said he was coming," she said, filling her glass and mine.

"He said he'd be here, but knowing him, he was probably sidetracked by the manna carts on the way through the village."

Alice handed me my glass and held up hers. "Cheers."

"Cheers. Thank you." We clinked our glasses and drank. The silky wine flowed over my tongue, rapturing my taste buds.

The doorbell rang, sending Skittles barking toward the door. "That must be him now," I said, getting up.

"I'll get it." Mom wiped her hand on the towel. "It might be your grandparents."

"You invited Yaya and George?"

"Yes. I hope that's OK," she said, walking to the door.

"Of course it's OK."

Alice stood beside me. "Yay, I love Yaya."

Growing up, Alice was the closest thing to family I had. Here, in Eden, I had more relatives than I could count. The closest of which, besides my mother, were my maternal grandparents who had passed away in the '80s and '90s.

My mother had been an only child, so my grandmother had never had grandchildren when she was alive. Now, she insisted I call her Yaya, being that she was Greek. My grandfather, on the other hand, was happy to be called George.

The door opened, and my grandmother raised her hands (one of which was holding a wine bottle) over her head. "Warren, you're home!"

Though she had died from pancreatic cancer in her late sixties, Yaya's age had been reset to her mid twenties. Physically, she looked even younger than me, as my aging process had stopped at thirty-one. I wouldn't age any more as long as I stayed in Eden.

"Yaya brought wine!" I teased as I walked over to hug her.

During her lifetime, Yaya had been part of a very strict church that condemned all consumption of alcohol. Obviously, booze wasn't an issue in Eden, so Yaya seemed to be making up for lost time. It was rare to see her without a drink in her hand. It was a good thing alcoholism wasn't a problem in the spirit world.

She handed me the bottle. "It's from the *Pallata* region. Have you been? George and I just got back. Beautiful countryside. Puts Sonoma and Napa Valley to shame. I daresay it's even prettier than here."

"Not possible," Mom said, greeting her with a kiss on the cheek. "But I'm glad you had a nice time. Dad, how are you?"

"If I was doing any better, I'd be scared to death," he replied, kneeling down to greet Skittles.

"Is that Alice I see hiding back there?" Yaya peeked around me. "Warren, be a dear and open this wine."

"Sure thing, Yaya."

Alice waved and walked over. The two women hugged. "It's good to see you, Yaya."

"Mom, are you ready to eat?" Mom asked going back to the kitchen to stir a large pot on the stove.

"Yes, you know I'm always hungry. It smells wonderful in here, Nadine."

"Thank you. Warren, should we wait on Reuel?" Mom asked.

"Nah. We'll save him a plate."

"Oh, I love that Reuel," Yaya said as we all gathered around the table. "So funny."

My mother carried a large bowl of creamy white pasta over to the table and placed it in the center. We all sat in our usual places. For an orphan like me, having a "usual" seat at any family table in itself was a miracle. A miracle for which I'd be eternally grateful. I picked up my wine and smiled.

George leaned over the dish and inhaled slowly. "That smells like—"

"Heaven?" Alice asked with a giggle.

"Exactly. It looks delicious," he said.

"It's a recipe I learned from Giorgia Larson, our neighbor when I first moved to Chicago with Azrael. It tastes much better here, of course, but it was always one of his favorites."

Alice folded one leg underneath her. "Maybe you could teach me to make it, Nadine." She leaned toward me. "I'll bet

Forfax would love it. No telling what she might let me do with the sky."

I chuckled and rested my arm across the back of her chair.

"Forfax...is that the dark-skinned young girl who plays in the sky?" Yaya wiggled her fingers in the air.

My mother passed me a basket of bread. "If you mean the guardian angel who controls the heavens, then yes," I said with a smile.

"That's the one. Lovely girl," Yaya said, taking a long drink of her wine before accepting the breadbasket from George.

"Yes, she is," Alice agreed, blushing enough for me to notice.

"Warren, how is your father?" Yaya asked.

"Az is doing well. He's having another son in a few months."

My mother put a hand over her heart. "It's a boy?"

I nodded.

"I know he's happy about that." Mom had a genuine smile as she filled George's plate with pasta. Jealousy and sadness didn't exist in Eden.

"I think he's just happy it isn't the Morning Star."

Yaya paused as she reached for the bowl of shredded white cheese. "The Morning Star is real? I thought that whole story was made up."

"The angel war was very real. It happened a very long time ago," I said.

"And your great-granddaughter will be even more powerful than he was," my mother said as she filled Yaya's plate.

Alice leaned toward me and lowered her voice. "If we were back on Earth, this conversation would be about soccer stats and the honor roll."

I chuckled quietly.

"How is sweet Iliana?" George asked.

"Growing fast. She will be a year old soon." As soon as the words left my mouth, the urgency of the situation returned.

"Only a year?" Yaya asked.

"As hard as it is to believe," I said, feeding Skittles some shredded cheese under the table. I decided *not* to tell them about the Council's ruling. I wasn't sure how they'd take the news, and hopefully, I'd prevent it from happening.

Movement near the open back door caught my eye. Reuel walked in carrying an armload of manna. He took a deep breath and smiled. "It's so good to be home."

Alice laughed and picked up her wine. "Reuel, you'd better be glad calories don't affect your waistline."

"Or the arteries around his heart," George added. He'd died of a heart attack.

"You are just in time for dinner. Come on in," Mom said, gesturing toward the empty seat at the end of the table.

Reuel walked in, deposited his load onto the counter, and came back to the table. "Sorry I'm late." He pulled out the chair and sat down. "The Heavenly Delights sisters made Death by Chocolate manna."

I grinned at Alice. "I told you."

The dog trotted over to him and put her paws on the side of his leg. "Hi, Skittles," he said, rubbing her head.

"Skittles, go get in your bed," Alice said.

The dog huffed and crossed the kitchen to her pink pillow by the door to the den.

Mom held out her hand. "Warren, pass me Reuel's plate."

I handed his plate to her, and she piled it higher than the rest of ours with pasta.

"So, boys, what's new on Earth?" George asked.

I thought about what news might interest him. "The Patriots beat the Seahawks in the Super Bowl a couple of months ago."

He laughed. "I haven't thought about football in...I don't even know how long. How are the Houston Oilers doing?"

I looked at Reuel for help; I'd never cared much for football.

"The Houston Oilers are the Tennessee Titans now," Reuel answered.

"No kidding?" George asked.

"That's right. They're in Nashville." I looked at Reuel for confirmation. He nodded, and I smiled proudly for knowing the answer. "Yes, Nashville."

"Well, isn't that something?" George said, shaking his head.

Dinner was filled with more laughter and stories. Yaya drank and told us all about their trip to Pallata. George talked about the boat he was building. Alice talked about Forfax, Reuel ate, and Mom listed all the new flowers she'd planted in the front garden.

Except for the Council's ruling, I told them all about Iliana. How she was talking now, and how she'd started crawling. I wished I could've brought along the photo book Nate had given me, but items from Earth wouldn't survive crossing into Eden. Perhaps I could get a new memory stone for Mom and fill it with Iliana saying, "Appa."

When we finished the meal and had helped Mom clean up, Alice and I walked out to the backyard. She laid down in the hammock I'd made for my mother while I stretched out in the grass with Skittles.

Alice used her fingertips to push against the ground to rock the hammock. She looked over at me. "When do you have to leave?"

I rubbed the dog's belly. "Honestly? Now. The longer I stay here, the less I want to leave."

Such was Eden's only curse when, like me, one also had responsibilities elsewhere.

"Five more minutes," Alice said, holding up five fingers.

Because of the time difference, I wasn't in a terrible rush to get back, but it was dangerously easy in Eden to let minutes turn into hours, hours into weeks, weeks into eons. For here, the old adage was definitely true: time *does* fly when you're having fun.

I smiled and rolled onto my back. Skittles plopped her round head on my chest. Inside the house, Reuel was telling a wild story, I think about the time Abaddon the Destroyer had impaled him on a tree. Whatever he was saying, Yaya must have thought it was hysterical. She was screaming with laughter. Then again, maybe it was all the wine.

God, I didn't want to leave again. I closed my eyes and curled my arm around my dog.

Definitely more than five minutes later, Reuel finally walked outside. "Your grandmother is drunk."

"I am well aware." I opened my eyes and looked up at him. "Are you ready to go?"

"Whenever you are, but if we leave now, isn't it the middle of the night in Africa?"

"True, but if I spend tonight here in my bed, I might never leave."

Reuel nodded, understanding what I meant. "Should we wait for Samael?"

"Not unless he shows up in the next minute or two. He knows how to find me."

"I didn't want to bring it up over dinner, but I have more confirmation that the Father is in North Africa. Barachiel recently saw him in a village near the Adwa River in Malab."

"Excellent. Thank you, Reuel."

"I also ran into Ionis on my way here. He said he heard Metatron is in Lunaris."

I sat up. "Lunaris?"

He nodded.

Since Samael had told me about the place, I had really wanted to visit the home of the seraphs.

"Why are you looking for Metatron?" Alice asked.

"I'm hoping he can identify the Morning Star."

With a laugh, Alice pointed at the sky. "Speaking of stars, Reuel, have you seen mine? Guess which one it is."

I smiled, only a little envious of how carefree she was.

"I don't need to guess. It's the pink one," he said.

She let out a gleeful gasp. "That's amazing!"

I looked at her. "He's a guardian. He's actually in charge of Forfax."

We all laughed, and it felt good. Too bad it wouldn't last.

Finally, I gave Skittles one last rubdown and pushed myself up. "I hope whatever is keeping Samael, he's able to resolve it quickly. We've got a lot to do and not enough time to do it."

Reuel looked out over the cliff. "Maybe that's Samael now."

I stood beside him. Like a meteor, a ball of light was coming in fast over the horizon. It grew larger and larger as it approached, and it slowed just before reaching the precipice.

"That's not Samael," Reuel said, shaking his head.

"No." I frowned. "It's Cassiel."

Skittles started barking.

Cassiel's wings spread wide as she gracefully lowered her feet to the ground in front of us. "Good evening, Warren, Reuel. Hello, Alice."

Alice gave a small wave from the hammock, then clicked her tongue. "Come here, Skittles."

"Hello, Cassiel." I put my hands on my hips. "Come bearing good news?"

"I'm not sure how you'll take it."

My brow creased.

She had changed from her formal robes as a Council member to tight, midnight-blue pants, a white corset top, and a long dark hooded cloak that was tied at her neck. A brown bag was strapped diagonally across her chest, and her golden hair was pulled into a high ponytail. She looked like a mystic sage about to time travel...

Holy shit. Because she *was*.

"Oh no," I said, shaking my head as I walked toward her. "You are absolutely not coming with me."

"Did you visit the messengers today?" she asked.

"I went to see Gabriel right after I left you."

"Why was there an addendum to the message we gave you?"

I shrugged. "I don't know, you'll have to ask Gabriel."

She crossed her arms. "You're aware I can see when you're lying, correct?"

Shit.

"I told him to add that any Angel of Death must clear it with me before they use their power on the living. And that's in the Canon, so you can't argue."

"Perhaps not, but we can change the Canon, and we already did."

Anger bubbled up inside me. "You changed the Canon?"

"Zaphkael changed it before the decision was even made." She pointed at my face. "And I'm coming with you to Earth."

"No, you're not. I outrank you, remember?"

"You don't outrank the Council, and this was a Council decision. Besides, you shouldn't have anything to worry about unless you're planning on doing something dishonorable."

Behind me, Alice laughed. "Warren Parish do something dishonorable? Not a chance."

Cassiel took a step and twisted the button on the front of my shirt. She cut her eyes up at me. "Even where his daughter is concerned?"

My jaw clenched.

She smiled and flattened her palm against my chest. "Where shall we go first? Asheville? Africa?"

I took a deep breath. "Chicago."

CHAPTER NINE

My eyes burned when we landed in Chicago outside my makeshift earthly residence. I checked my watch and stopped the time clock.

It was still March 24. Only now, in the Central Standard Time Zone, it was *earlier* than when I'd left Earth. 5:59 p.m. The time clock had been running for eleven minutes, and I'd just spent the better part of a day in Eden.

I would never get used to that.

"What is this place?" Cassiel asked.

Claymore's Chicago safe house didn't look like much from the street. And it was clear not much had changed in the time I'd been away. The front-porch roof was still falling down. The front steps were still caved in. And boards were tacked up over the windows thanks to the squatters I'd run off the last time I'd come.

If only they'd known what lay beneath that old shack.

The three of us carefully navigated the front porch to the door. I waved my hand over the deadbolt, and the lock tumbled back in place. "Welcome to my humble earthly abode," I said, pushing the door open and stepping out of their way.

Reuel walked right in.

Cassiel hesitated.

"Is there a problem?" I asked.

She nervously shook her head. "Just making sure the floor doesn't fall through before I walk across it."

"I can assure you it's safe."

"Under the circumstances, forgive me for not being confident in your assurances." Through the buildings across the street, the setting sun almost formed a perfect halo behind her head. I would have laughed had I not been so pissed she was there.

I walked inside ahead of her, turned around, and jumped up and down on the dusty but solid floor. "There are eighteen inches of concrete and steel underneath the subflooring. It's not going anywhere."

She clenched her fists at her sides and carefully walked to me.

"See?"

She didn't respond.

I pulled the string of the single light bulb dangling from the ceiling in what used to be the living room. It illuminated the fact that the interior of the house wasn't any nicer than the exterior—at least not the part we were standing in.

The drywall had been stripped to the support beams, where the squatters had cut the copper wiring. They'd set up camp on the floor with dirty sheets and half-melted candles, and the whole room reeked of urine. In the kitchen, the refrigerator door gaped open, dangling only from its bottom hinge.

"Nice place," Cassiel said, pinching her nose closed.

"This way." I waved for them to follow me down the dark hallway to the coat-closet door. Inside was the broken mop and old work towels right where I'd left them. I felt blindly along the inside of the doorframe until my fingers found the switch they were searching for.

The hydraulics hissed in the walls as the shelves slid back and then rose out of our view. A steep staircase was hidden behind it. The lights below flickered on.

Reuel was grinning like it was the first time he'd ever seen it. He turned sideways to wedge himself into the narrow closet.

Cassiel looked impressed, probably against her will.

"Ladies first," I said, leaning against the doorframe.

She cautiously inched forward, and I followed her down the stairs. At the bottom was an open living room with a flat-screen TV. One whole wall was a steel cage that housed enough fire-power to level the block. Beyond it, the state-of-the-art kitchen had stainless-steel *everything* and a table that could accommodate twelve.

One side of the bunker had a dorm-style bathroom and a massive room full of bunk beds. On the other was my small bedroom with a king-sized bed, another TV, and its own bath.

"I must say, I'm pleasantly surprised," Cassiel said, taking it all in.

"It's not Eden, but it'll do."

She spun on her heel toward me. "You should know, one advantage for you in having me along is the Council has agreed that either of you might speak any language deemed necessary during our travels."

I crossed my arms. "Why should I care? I'm not bound by that law anyway."

"No." She pointed at Reuel. "But he is."

Reuel perked up.

"Wouldn't it be easier if your muscle could communicate along the journey?" she asked.

I scowled, but unfortunately, she had a point and she knew it. "Excellent news. Any other upsides to this arrangement you'd like to inform me of?"

She didn't answer, so I walked past her to my bedroom. Reuel went to the dormitory.

Cassiel followed me. "What are we doing here?"

Reuel and I had collected our things from our lockers before we left the spirit world, so I tossed my phone and wallet on the bed. Turning toward her, I unbuttoned my shirt, hoping for a reaction out of the nosy angel. I didn't get one.

"We're changing. We'll stick out bad enough in Africa without wearing clothes made from the fabric of the universe."

"We're really going to Africa?"

"Yes."

She put her hands on her hips. "You know the Father can't just leave and come back to Eden, right?"

"Why not?"

"When he comes to Earth, he has to stay for a solar year. It's part of the limitations he put on himself. For him to return to Eden early, you'd have to dispatch him from his body."

"I knew that." I *totally* didn't know that. In my head, I was swearing. "He can get on a plane though."

"But he won't. He probably can't even recognize the Morning Star in his human form."

The Father had intervened for my family before. Perhaps he would do it again. "Feel free to go back to Eden, but if you're coming with me, go change."

She looked down at the outfit she was wearing. "This really won't work?"

"It might if we were attending a Renaissance festival."

She scowled.

I pointed out the door. "Grab something from the locker marked 'Fury' in the dormitory." I looked Cassiel up and down as I unzipped my pants. "You're about the same size."

"Anything else?" she asked, annoyed.

"Yeah, dress in layers and start with something lighter than that crap you've got on. We're going to one of the hottest and driest climates in this world."

"Are you planning to be rude the entire time we're on Earth?"

"Probably. Why? You wanna go home?"

"I'm not the enemy here. I'm just trying to do my job."

"Spare me your attempts to ease your conscience, Cassiel."

She stepped dangerously close. "You're stuck with me either way, so if you want to make this trip even more miserable for yourself, keep up your execrable attitude."

Before I could argue—or clarify that execrable meant *bad* —she turned and left the room.

I swore and threw my shirt on the bed.

I quickly changed into olive-drab tactical pants and a black T-shirt. Then I picked up my phone and tapped Azrael's name in my recent-call list.

He answered on the first ring. "That was fast."

I kept my voice low. "We need to talk, but not right now. The Council sent a chaperone back with me. I'll need you to stay available if I check in."

"You got it. Was their decision what you feared?"

"Worse. I'm heading to Malab now to talk to the Father. I would say pray that he helps fix this mess, but I know who's listening."

Azrael groaned on the other end of the line. "OK. Touch base when you can. We're heading back to Asheville tonight."

"You might see me there soon, but I sincerely hope not. Keep Iliana in the penthouse."

"We will."

"Tell Azrael I said hello." Cassiel's voice behind me was startling.

I ended the call and turned around.

Holy hell. Cassiel was wearing Fury's desert-camo fatigue pants, a suction-tight black tank top, and desert-tan boots. She smiled...because I'm pretty sure I gave her the reaction I'd been looking for earlier.

If she'd been trying to disarm me, it worked.

I cleared my throat. "That'll do."

It was clear she was tempted to laugh. Instead, she held up the bag she'd brought along. "Can I bring this, or is it too conspicuous as well?" Her tone was full of snark.

I had to turn away from her. "It's fine." The bag could have been a cherub with a zipper on its forehead and I wouldn't have noticed.

Was it hot in here? Just me?

One thing was certain: Fury would be pissed to know another woman was wearing her clothes, and wearing them *that* well. Good god.

Thankfully, Reuel walked into the room, once again wearing his street clothes. Then he took one look at Cassiel and started laughing.

He knew me too well.

I gritted my teeth and mouthed the words "shut up" while Cassiel was looking back at him. That didn't help. He doubled over, bracing his arms against his knees.

"What's so funny?" Cassiel asked.

"Nothing."

She pointed at my face. "You're lying again."

I grabbed her finger and pushed it down. "You've got to stop doing that. This is Earth. My planet. My rules."

"That's really not the way this works, Warren."

I wanted to say to her, "It's a good thing you're hot," but I knew she might throw me into Cira for a century of solitude and hard labor.

Instead, I looked at my watch. "We've got time to kill before it makes any sense to go to Malab."

Reuel patted his stomach. *"Akai uno."*

Cassiel rolled her eyes. "Of course you could eat."

I smiled. "Cassiel, are you hungry?"

Her nose wrinkled. "For food here? Is that a joke?"

"Then you can stay here and wait. We're going out for a few hours."

With a smirk, she draped her bag over her shoulder. "And let the two of you abandon me in this den of roaches? I don't think so."

I sighed heavily. "Then are you ready to go?"

"As always, Warren, I'm waiting on you."

The Horn of Africa was the peninsula that jutted out from the northeast corner of the continent. It was the jagged section on the map that looked like it had broken off from Saudi Arabia. Maybe it had? I made a mental note to ask someone when we got back to Eden.

I could have asked Cassiel, but I decided against it because she tended to be smug when answering questions. I also wanted to avoid telling her about the suspicious killings Samael had discovered in Italy, lest the Council be given anything else to potentially blame on me.

Beside me, she was kicking her boots against the cracked earth behind a crooked hut made of mud and grass where we'd appeared. "I've never been anywhere on Earth like this before."

My head pulled back. "Really?"

"No. I've spent most of my limited days on Earth in Europe."

"I guess that explains the *Braveheart* getup from earlier."

Reuel chuckled.

"You're from America. What were you doing in a place like this? Were you here with the military?"

"Don't you know? I kind of assumed you knew everything about me."

"I know a lot. But not this."

Perhaps she had mentally heard me accusing her of being

smug. "I haven't exactly been *here*, but I spent a lot of time in the region during my days working for Claymore. My first assignment with them was farther south in Somalia, but I'd say it's similar."

"You worked for Azrael then," she said as we walked around the front of the hut toward a building made of stone and clay with a tin roof.

My head tilted from side to side. "Yeah, I just didn't know it then. I thought I worked for some faceless ex-special-ops guy named Damon Claymore. I didn't find out Claymore was Azrael and that Azrael was my father until much later."

"How did that make you feel?"

I lifted an eyebrow. "Are you trying to get inside my head?"

She smiled, barely. "Why? Are you trying to keep me out?"

"Definitely."

"Do you know where you're going?" she asked.

I shrugged. "Sort of. The Father's close. I felt him as soon as we crossed the spirit line."

It was the middle of winter in Malab and not too long after sunrise when we arrived. Still, it was warm enough for the local children to be in shorts. Most of them were shoeless, but I doubted that was by choice given the state of the ragged clothes hanging off their skinny frames.

A few boys were kicking a bright red ball around a small patch of grass beside a pasture with three bony cows behind a knotty fence. They stopped playing immediately when they saw us, and their faces broke into wide smiles.

Funny thing about kids, they were never afraid of me. Adults usually were, some more terrified than others because nearly all adults feared death. Never kids.

These boys immediately ran to us and began going through our pockets. They were all laughing and begging for something. I kept recognizing the word *karamela* as they pulled on us.

I held my hands over my head in surrender. "What's happening?"

"They want candy," Cassiel translated.

Reuel chuckled and reached into his shirt pocket for the candy bar he'd grabbed from his safe. He tore open the wrapper and broke the chocolate into chunks. When he passed out the pieces, the boys squealed with delight.

"The Father always has candy in his pockets for the children. He must be close." Cassiel looked around the quiet village square, then back at the boys. She spoke to them in a language I didn't recognize.

The boys excitedly pointed down a road to our right. They kept saying "Abo John" so I assumed they were telling Cassiel where to find him. Father John was the name he often went by on Earth. It was the name he'd used when Sloan and I met him the very first time in San Antonio, Texas.

"They say the Father is at the river…" Her head fell to the side. "He's hosting a fishing tournament." She sounded as confused as I felt. Funny, for an Angel of Knowledge. She looked up at me. "A fishing tournament?"

"Are you sure you translated correctly?" I asked with a grin.

Her brow pinched. "Really?"

"I heard He was at the river too. Let's check it out," Reuel said.

The tallest boy near Reuel motioned us forward. He wanted us to follow. All the other boys joined him—the youngest took Cassiel by the hand—and the group led us down the street.

"What are their names?" I asked as Reuel and I followed behind.

Cassiel spoke to the boys in their language, then translated their answers. "The oldest here is Ezana. And this is Jima and Dawit." She looked down at the boy holding her hand. "And this is—"

"Kelyle," he answered for her with a wave.

I waved back. "Hello, Kelyle."

We walked about a half mile outside the small village before the boys turned right onto a small dirt path. From what I gathered through Cassiel's translations, the Father had been in this particular village for a little over a month. He had been helping them build boats and learn how to fish.

The boys were very interested to know if we had ever eaten fish. Reuel and I both told them yes to their great delight. Cassiel said no.

"You've never eaten fish?" I asked as we crested a berm through a broken wooden fence.

"Once, maybe, when I was in Ireland near the coast. But I assure you it wasn't on purpose."

"You don't eat fish, and you won't eat in Chicago. What do you eat?"

"When I'm here, I try to stick to fruits and vegetables if I can find them without all the pesticides and growth hormones your kind uses."

I laughed and shook my head. "I had no idea you were such a snob, Cassiel."

"And I had no idea you were so ignorant."

With a smile, Reuel nodded toward her, up ahead of us, as he walked beside me. He spoke quietly in Katavukai. Translated, he said, "Never trust a woman who can't appreciate the four basic food groups." Then he counted on his fingers. "Steak, bread, potato chips, and chocolate."

I chuckled.

I could hear water up ahead. "We must be close."

The vegetation of the land thickened as we neared the water, but the boys led us through a break in the shrubs and spindly trees. Male voices carried over the sound of the water. Finally, we saw them. Twenty or so men fishing from the riverbanks or out in small boats.

Father John was by the river's edge, working with an older

man to wind a long fishing line around a scrap of wood. He looked up before he could have heard us, sensing our presence as we could sense his.

"Ah, my friends. How lovely to see you!" He cheered, waving to us. The first time I met the Father he was dressed as an actual priest in a long black robe. Today, he wore a short-sleeved, button-up tan shirt tucked into dark trousers with rainbow suspenders.

Reuel leaned toward me. *"Akai unmai minpi."*

"I know." I scratched my head and shrugged. "He's *actually* fishing."

Father John pulled on the old man's arm. "Come, meet my friends."

The boy who led us to the river ran to the water and waved to two men in a boat. The three younger boys followed him.

We met Father John halfway. He greeted Cassiel with a hug first. "Isn't this a pleasant surprise," he said in Katavukai as he embraced her. "I'd like you to meet my new friend, Absame. Absame is an elder of the Barid tribe." Then he spoke to the man in his native language. All I understood was our names.

Absame and the Father exchanged a few more words before Absame returned to the river.

I crossed my arms and looked out over the water. "It's good to see you, Father. What *are* you doing here?"

The Father laughed, sounding a lot like Santa Claus. He was plump and nearly bald, with a birthmark that looked like South America bleeding over onto his forehead. "We are having a fishing tournament, Warren. What does it look like?"

"Yes, but why are you having a fishing tournament?" Reuel asked.

Cassiel looked at the Father. "Is this to do with the famine crisis?"

The Father nodded. "And even more to do with the government crisis. There hasn't been a hunger crisis like this since the 1980s. That famine killed about four hundred thousand people. This one will rival it if something doesn't change soon."

"Has there been a drought?" I asked, knowing it would be easy for him to bring rain.

"There was, yes, and it killed the harvests, but that's not why these people are starving now. The corrupt prime minister of Malab is withholding stores of food for his people, aid sent here from around the world to feed them. So I have come to teach these good people how to pull fish from the two vibrant river systems they have access to. Can you believe fishing is such a novelty here?"

I answered no, and Cassiel answered yes at the same time. We exchanged a private smile.

"But why not go straight to the government and force them to release the food?" I asked, confused.

The Father put his hand on my shoulder. "I'd like to tell you the old 'teach a man to fish' proverb, but it seems a little satiric."

"I'll go deal with the prime minister," Reuel said, watching the boys throw sticks out into the water.

"And I'll let you." The Father looked at the men on the riverbanks. "But my place is here, for now."

"What do they get if they win the tournament?" I asked.

The Father smiled. "Pure gold."

My brow lifted. "Really?"

The Father reached into his jacket and pulled out a bright yellow tub of *Old Bay Seasoning.* "Best thing in this realm to put on fish, you know."

Reuel and I both laughed. Cassiel took the container to study the label.

"The idea is to teach them to bring in enough food to feed their families and to sell at the market," the Father said.

"That's brilliant." I shook my head. "It's still *really* random."

The Father chuckled again. "Tell me, what brings the three of you so far from Eden?"

Cassiel turned toward me and folded her arms across her chest.

I took a deep breath. "Father, are you aware that the Council has sanctioned the killing of innocents to prevent the Morning Star from taking human form?" I kept my eyes away from Cassiel.

He looked at her. Then he looked back at me. He put his arm around my shoulders. "Take a walk with me, Warren." We walked away from the group, back toward the tree line we'd come through. "Did you really come all the way to Africa to tattle on Cassiel?"

"Yes."

He smiled. "I appreciate your honesty."

"They're talking about killing innocents, even children."

He turned to face me. "You understand that it's nearly impossible for an angel to take a human child? That the child would have to be next to death anyway and completely unable to survive on their own."

"Yes, sir, I do."

"And that in all cases of demon possession of an adult, it's a willing partnership between the spirit and the human soul making them not-so-innocent after all."

"Yes, but—"

He held up a hand to silence me. "Why don't you tell me what you're really upset about."

"Father, Fury just gave birth to a son, an angelic son. Under the new laws, I'm obligated to destroy the child."

He put his hands on both my shoulders. "But it's *not* a child. And you're not destroying anyone. The body is but a shell, remember?"

"I know, but Fury won't see it that way. Even she knows the truth, and still—"

"And still she's grown an emotional attachment to the child. Have you considered that might be by design?" he asked, leveling his gaze with mine. "Do you think it was a random choice of a woman you once loved to bear an angel?"

My face fell.

"Duty is never easy, my son."

"There's more." I swallowed down all the emotion that threatened to boil over inside me. "They've decided I must bring Iliana to Eden as a baby."

"When?"

"By her first birthday. She's not even walking yet."

He looked at the ground for a long moment. "Warren, do you know why I appointed the Council?"

I shook my head.

"To make these kinds of decisions. The hard calls no one should have to make." He sighed. "I trust it was not an easy or thoughtless ruling, and as much as I hate it for you, I must stand behind them in this."

My heart tumbled.

He lowered his voice. "However, if you find the Morning Star before she turns a year old, I'll see what I can do. I'll talk to the Council."

"Thank you, Father." Hope swelled in my heart again. "Will you come with me to see Fury?"

He shook his head. "My place is here, for now." He took both of my hands. "I have faith in you, Warren. If I didn't believe you could handle this job, I wouldn't have entrusted you with the mantle of the Archangel. Never forget that."

I bowed my head, honored but still discouraged. "Thank you."

Behind us was a loud *splash!* followed by screaming. I looked over the Father's head to see the youngest boy, Kelyle, thrashing around in the river.

The current was swift, dragging him under as he fought

unsuccessfully to keep his face above water. Reuel, Cassiel, and I took off running along with the local men toward him. I was the closest to where Kelyle was swept downriver.

Without thinking, I threw my hands forward and unleashed my power, parting the Red Sea like Moses. A wall of water peeled back away from Kelyle, damming the river and dumping him in a sputtering heap onto the muck of the riverbed.

One man rushed through the opening and lifted the child in his arms. Then he paused with a look of horror on his face as he looked at the growing wall of water in front of him.

The other men began screaming and motioning him forward. His boots were sinking in the mud, making each step a challenge, and the wall climbed higher and higher as I held the water back.

Finally, the man reached the riverbank and pushed the child into the arms of his friends. Then he clawed at the ground trying to get out. A friend grasped the back of his shirt, hauling him up on the back. One of his shoes was sucked off his foot by the mud.

I unleashed the wall like a tidal wave. Fifty feet or more of water crashed back down onto the riverbed, and I held it within its banks to keep anyone else from being sucked downstream.

On the ground, Kelyle was coughing and spewing water from his lungs. But he was alive.

When the river calmed, I collapsed to my knees, breathless and sweating under the African sun.

Cassiel came over and touched my shoulder. "Well done, Warren. You saved his life."

I used the tail of my shirt to wipe my face, then I rocked back onto my feet to stand.

The locals gawked at me in fear.

"I think that's my cue to leave," I said, taking a step back.

The Father patted me on the arm. "I'll see you back in Eden before long. Are you going there now?"

"Soon, but first, we'll pay a visit to the capital of Malab."

"Excellent."

"Father, do you know if Metatron or Sandalphon have the power to identify the Morning Star in infancy?"

He laughed with surprise. "You know, I really don't." He lowered his voice. "Not in this form anyway."

"Of course." I offered Him a sad smile. "Goodbye, Father."

He gave me a rare, very human, handshake. "Goodbye, Warren."

CHAPTER TEN

The capital city of Tigahb was physically only eighty miles away from the Barid village, but it was light-years away in terms of modernization. Tigahb didn't just have cars and electricity; it had interstates and skyscrapers.

"Are we sure this is the place?" Cassiel asked when we walked out of the alleyway we had appeared in.

I double-checked the map on my phone. "This is it. We're only a few blocks from the Capitol building."

"What will we do when we get there?" Cassiel asked.

Reuel smiled. *"Ala cey en me vi."*

Cassiel's eyes narrowed looking up at him. "You know you can speak English, right?"

"Oh, right." As soon as the words left his mouth, he clapped his hand over it. Then he lowered his voice to a whisper. "I've never spoken English out loud before."

I laughed and patted him on the back. "Congratulations, my friend."

"But remember, they don't speak English here," Cassiel said as we walked along the alleyway.

"What is it they speak?" I asked.

"Tigrinya. I can translate for you both."

"Is there any language you can't speak?"

She just laughed and rolled her eyes.

So smug.

"All the angels except you can understand anything. Did you know that?" she asked.

"Did you know that," I mimicked in a high-pitch voice. "Yes, I'm aware. Thanks for rubbing it in."

"You're welcome."

It was said all languages descended from Katavukai, and those who were created speaking it—all the angels but me—could interpret other languages *through* it, like it served as a universal cipher key to unravel the spoken word.

Because my job spanned the globe, language barriers were a very real thing for me. Fortunately, the bulk of my work happened across the spirit line, where all souls and spirits could inherently speak and understand Katavukai.

We crossed the busy street and turned right, following the turn-by-turn directions of my phone's app. People were everywhere, walking along the sidewalks and weaving in and out of traffic. Shops and restaurants lined the road to the Capitol building, and the food smelled amazing. Sweet and spicy, unlike anything I'd ever smelled before.

As we neared an intersection, commotion behind us caught my attention. A male voice was shouting over the noise of the block. Cassiel turned her ear toward the noise. "Someone is shouting *wait*."

The three of us turned. A man with a hefty bodyguard was pushing his way through the crowd to reach us. A quick scan of his soul revealed nothing sinister, so I allowed him to approach. He wore a sharp navy suit and shiny shoes, and his guard was nearly the size of Reuel. When the man was close enough, I saw his eyes. One was black; the other was gold.

Cassiel put her hand on mine. "He knows us."

"Well, see what he has to say."

The man was chattering a thousand words per minute. Cassiel put her hands up to stop him and spoke to him in Tigrinya. He panted for a moment, trying to catch his breath. Finally, he had collected himself enough to speak to her clearly.

"He wants to know if we've come to deal with the prime minister's secretary," she translated.

"Who is the prime minister's secretary?" I asked with a shrug. "And who is this guy?"

She spoke to him again and then listened intently. "This man's name is Umar Tadese. He's the chairman of the People's Liberation League, the largest political party here in Malab." Cassiel looked impressed. I, on the other hand, knew *nothing* about politics. "He says he's been waiting for someone to come and deal with Idris Baria."

Reuel looked confused. "Who?"

She asked him then turned slowly toward me. "Idris Baria is a spirit."

"A good or bad one?" I asked.

Her head tilted. "If he's starving a nation, I don't think I'd put my money on him being a good guy."

Damn it. I looked away and stuffed my fists into my pockets. Sometimes my stupidity begged for her smugness.

"He's a bad one," Umar said.

We all turned toward him. "You speak English?" I asked.

"I speak eleven languages."

My head pulled back. "Wow. That's impressive. Can you get us into the prime minister's office?"

"First, tell me why you are here," he said.

I looked at the bodyguard and lifted an eyebrow.

Deciphering my meaning, Umar waved his hand. "My guard, Romodan, is loyal to me. You may speak freely."

"It is our understanding that your government is withholding aid from the starving people of Malab," I said.

Umar nodded emphatically. "Yes, we are, but it's only at the insistence of the prime minister and his aide, Idris Baria. Baria is not human. He is like you."

I shook my head. "He is *nothing* like us."

Umar smiled. "Of course not. Are you here to remove him from power?"

"If that's what it takes," Reuel said.

"Is Baria the one calling the shots for the prime minister?" I asked.

"I believe so."

"Where can we find him?"

He looked at his watch. "They are at the Capitol right now. There is a foreign-affairs meeting in progress."

"Can you get us in?" I asked.

"Of course I can."

Cassiel took a step toward me and lowered her voice. "Given his title, he's one of the most powerful men in the government of Malab."

I looked at Reuel. "Good enough for me," he said.

I gave a slight bow to Umar. "Lead the way."

Worry suddenly washed over Umar's face. He turned to the left and to the right before gripping his skull with both hands— a universal sign of freaking out.

"What's the matter?" I asked.

"My wife is in the café back there. She'll be furious with me for breaking our date."

I chuckled. "I can understand that."

"Come, come. I will only be a moment," Umar said, walking backward toward the café.

We walked with him and waited near the door. Another guard was inside near the table he approached. Umar was having a lively conversation with the woman at the table. There were lots of arm gestures and head shaking, but she must have consented to let him leave. He picked up a brown leather brief-case and carried it over to us.

His wife was glaring at me. I waved.

"I apologize. It isn't often she and I can have breakfast in the city," he said when he reached us.

From there, we followed him and his guards to a black full-sized SUV waiting at the curb. It was clearly armored, much like the ones at Claymore. The driver opened the back door and Umar and his guards climbed inside. The guards went to the very back, Cassiel and I sat in the middle seat with Umar, and Reuel got in the front.

I suspected we could have walked to the Capitol in the time it took us all to squeeze into the car, but whatever.

"What's the story with this guy, Idris Baria?" I asked as we pulled away from the curb.

"Seven months ago, my predecessor, Saare Kelifah, was elected to the minister's office. But about a month after he took control of the country, there was an assassination attempt on his life. He very nearly died. When he came back to office, Baria was brought in to be his first advisor." He reached into the seat-back pocket of the driver's seat and produced a magazine. He handed it to me. "Our prime minister hasn't been the same since."

I froze. The man on the cover had a black goatee and deep-set eyes. He wore an expensive suit with the flag of Malab tacked to the lapel.

Something was off. Way off.

Cassiel gripped my thigh.

I looked at Umar again. "*This* is your prime minister?"

"Yes."

Cassiel took the magazine. "This isn't possible."

"You notice something strange about him, yes?" Umar asked.

I only nodded.

The only other time in my life I'd ever seen anything like it was the first time I looked at a photo of Sloan's biological mother. We'd mistaken her for a murder victim because neither Sloan nor myself could see a human soul. Back then, I could only see humans. Now I could see angels too, and this guy...was neither.

———

The Malab Capitol building looked a lot like Fort Knox without all the fences and security cameras. It was a gray, two-story slab-like structure with small windows uniformly lined across the front of each floor. A small, flat pyramid rested on top with a tall antenna of some ancient communications system jutting from the peak. In the center of the bottom floor, concrete steps lead up to a covered entrance.

We took the steps two at a time with Umar and his guards leading the way. "Please don't speak to anyone unless spoken to until we get past security. It's the only way in."

Reuel chuckled. "It's not the *only* way."

I smiled.

Umar stopped and turned toward us. "Are any of you carrying weapons?"

My smile widened. "Not the kind that will set off a metal detector."

Obviously satisfied, he motioned us forward. The front doors opened into a wide lobby. Two security guards were waving metal-detection wands over people waiting in line. Umar took us to a separate area where security recognized him immediately. He said something to a guard in a green uniform who was sitting behind a large desk.

Cassiel leaned toward me. "He's telling the guards we're here for a meeting with the prime minister."

The guard checked the computer in front of him, then

shook his head. Umar waved his hand, clearly arguing with the man. After a moment, the guard carefully looked us over. Then he pointed to the security line.

"It sounds like they'll let us in, but we have to allow the guards to check us out," Cassiel said. "Apparently, they're having trouble with their computer system."

I looked at Reuel. "Did you have something to do with that?"

He smiled and pointed at a security camera above our heads on the ceiling.

"Good job, Reuel. You're gonna have to teach me how to do that."

Umar waited for us behind the ropes. Reuel was carefully studying everyone in the room. "What are you thinking?" I asked him.

He crossed his huge arms. "I'm hoping this isn't a setup. You?"

I turned my palms up. "Well, now I'm hoping this isn't a set-up too. Thanks a lot."

He grinned.

The guards made us empty our pockets, which contained nothing interesting, and once we passed the guys with the metal wands, we were free to rejoin Umar. "Security is extra-tight lately. There have been death threats against the prime minister."

Death threats against a dead guy. Interesting.

We took an elevator up to the second floor and walked down a long tiled hallway. When we passed two glass double doors, Reuel grabbed my arm to stop me. Inside was a group of people gathered for a meeting.

My attention pulled like a magnet to the *death* at the head of the table. It was the prime minister. And his being dead wasn't the most interesting thing about him—a glowing purple haze swirled around him.

Before anyone saw us, we moved out of the way of the door. I looked at Cassiel since as a general rule, she always knew more than the rest of us. "What was that?"

"That was a dead guy in a purple cloud and an angel," she said.

"An angel? I was too distracted by the dead guy to even notice."

"I didn't get a good enough look to see who it was. What is that purple fog?" she asked.

"I was hoping you could tell me." No more keeping the secret now. "Samael is in northern Italy investigating a few human souls who carried that same purple fog across the spirit line, except not so bright. Have you ever seen anything like it?"

"Never."

I looked over at Umar, who was watching us carefully. "Is there anything weird about the prime minister other than the angel he's working with?"

"Yes..." He visibly swallowed. "I think the prime minister is dead."

A chill made me shudder. "Why? You can't see human souls, right? Only spirits."

"Because I've known Saare Kelifah for many years. Whoever is here now, is not him."

Just then, the conference doors opened, and the men who were inside filed out. I looked at Reuel. "Do you have a plan?"

He held up both his fists.

"At least one of us is prepared." I let my power build and sizzle at my fingertips as the men dispersed in the hallway. The prime minister and the angel I hadn't noticed were not among them.

Umar nudged me forward. "You might not get another chance to catch the Prime Minister alone. You should go in now."

"If we take him out, can you make sure the food and supplies get to the people?"

"Yes. Without Kelifah in power, I will take his place until another election can be planned."

I offered my hand. "I'm trusting you, Umar."

He shook it. "I'm happy to do what is right for my country."

"Stay out of sight. No one needs to see you involved in this," I said.

He nodded, then took off down the hallway.

Reuel went first. Cassiel and I were right behind him. A third man had stayed behind with the prime minister and his aide. When they saw us, the aide—the *angel*—said something to the man, and he left quickly.

The angel's back was to us, but he stood and slowly turned around. I didn't recognize him, but Cassiel grabbed the back of my shirt. "Moloch," she whispered.

The fallen Archangel of Knowledge.

The prime minister stayed in his chair, but from this distance, I could get a better look at him. His dark skin was ashy, more gray than it was black, and it had a waxy quality, almost like it was made of plastic. When he looked at me, I saw sparks somewhere in his eyes. The body was dead, for sure, but there was some form of a human soul present.

"Cassiel," Moloch said, his voice deep and even. He tucked a cell phone into the inside pocket of his gray suit jacket, then buttoned the front. He was about my height, broad-shouldered, and appeared to be in his late forties. The body he occupied wasn't his own. A fact that thankfully weakened him. He wouldn't likely pick a fight with us.

He could, however, outsmart us all—probably even Cassiel.

"Hello, Reuel," Moloch said.

Reuel didn't answer, but his fists were still clenched, ready for a fight.

Moloch offered me his hand. "And we haven't had the pleasure of being introduced. However, one look at you tells me you're Azrael's son. Hello, Warren."

I knew better than to touch him. Instead, I let my power dance in my palm as a warning. He smiled, and it was so bright and perfect it creeped me out.

Cassiel stepped closer to the prime minister for a better look at him. "Moloch, what have you done?"

"Whatever do you mean?" Moloch asked, his voice mockingly melodic.

She leaned closer to the prime minister. "Who are you?"

The man (I think?) looked up at her. "My name is Saare Kelifah, prime minister of the great country of Malab." His voice was flat, almost robotic, like he'd been programmed to respond.

Cassiel grabbed the man's hand. "Who are you *really*?"

His eyes pressed closed, and he twisted like his entire upper body was being wrung by an invisible hand. "Haile Menelek," he choked out.

She released him and took a step back. "Haile Menelek," she echoed.

"Who is that?" I asked.

"He was the leader of Malab during the famine in the early 1980s. Azrael killed him and banished him to Nulterra. History is repeating itself," Cassiel said, her voice full of something alarmingly akin to wonder.

I looked at Moloch. "How did you do this? Human spirits can't cross back into this world."

"Oh really?" His wicked grin deepened.

Cassiel stepped toward the prime minister again, and he flinched away from her hand. "Where is Saare Kelifah?"

The man's eyes rolled in different directions as he focused on her face. "Saare Kelifah is dead."

I pushed up my sleeves. "Then he won't miss his body." My power surged as I took a step toward the prime minister.

I paused.

"What's the matter?" Cassiel asked, her voice laced with panic.

"I want to see his spirit. If it's really him, his spirit will have Azrael's mark. But if I use my power and it's *not* him..."

"The spirit will still have the same mark," Cassiel said.

I patted my hip where I'd always kept a weapon when I was human. Now, there was nothing there. I also didn't want to use my bare hands to kill him. Maybe I could—

"I'll do it." Before I could react, Moloch produced a semiautomatic handgun from inside his suit jacket and fired a round through the prime minister's temple. The man slumped sideways over the arm of his chair.

I flinched with shock.

"You're welcome," Moloch said.

A siren blared through the halls.

I turned to Moloch just as Reuel's fist connected with his stunned face. He flew backward into a bookcase, rocking it sideways and collapsing two of its shelves. Books spilled out onto his head as he fell to its base.

Before he could pull himself up, Reuel grabbed him by the lapel of his suit jacket and hauled him to his feet. Moloch swiped away a trickle of blood from the corner of his mouth onto his sleeve.

"Warren, look," Cassiel said.

I turned back toward the prime minister. The spirit of a man who looked nothing like Saare Kelifah, the *real* prime minister, stood slowly. Then he looked at me, smiling. His whole form swirled with the purple mist, and in the center of his chest was the mark of the Archangel, just as I'd suspected.

I held up my palms facing each other and conjured the power of the final death. Unlike any of my other powers, it looked like a smoking black hole suspended between my hands.

Cassiel took a step back. "You can do that here?"

"Of course I can."

"Is it a good idea?"

"Don't want to risk him getting out again, do we?"

She opened her mouth to say something else, but it was too late.

My hands shot forward, releasing my power. It exploded inside the spirit with so much force it shook the building and blew out the windows. The purple seemed to catch fire and burn away in a flurry of tiny ruby sparks.

A wave of insane nausea hit me, and I staggered sideways. Cassiel grabbed my arm to steady me, curling one arm around my lower back. My head was spinning.

"You know, you really shouldn't inflict the final death here on Earth," Moloch said from where Reuel had him pinned against the wall.

I covered one eye with the ball of my hand to stop the spinning. "You'd like that, wouldn't you?"

"He has a point," Cassiel said quietly. "Inflicting the final death this side of the spirit line could have consequences. There's a reason it's forbidden."

"It's obviously not forbidden now that the power is mine." The queasiness was easing, but my head was pounding. "Besides, it's got to be better than the alternative." I turned toward Moloch.

He was smiling over Reuel's shoulder as I closed the space between us. "Will you destroy me now too, Warren?"

I opened my right hand and conjured my killing power into it. While I couldn't destroy him permanently, I could separate him from his body.

Reuel slammed him against the wall one more time and moved out of my way. Moloch tore open his white shirt, exposing his smooth black chest, then spread his arms wide and laughed.

My power landed hard in the center of his chest just as Cassiel screamed, "No!"

Light fragmented Moloch's body with fissures, like cracks through an eggshell. Suddenly, they detonated, sending blinding light through the room with another thunderous boom.

The lifeless body crumpled at my feet, its eerie smile still cemented in place.

I spun toward Cassiel. "Why did you scream?"

"That was exactly what he wanted." She clutched my arm. "He didn't even put up a fight."

Before I could process what she was saying, a small army ran into the room, weapons drawn. They looked at us, then at the bodies of the prime minister and his aide. Moloch's body was in bloody pieces. The prime minister's eyes were open and lifeless.

I sidestepped in front of Cassiel as the men opened fire.

It wasn't the first time I'd been shot. That checkbox had been ticked off back in Iraq when I was still with the Marines. And under a hail of gunfire was how I'd died the first time. This wasn't exactly new.

But getting hammered from two assault rifles and two handguns all at once was something else. The pain actually drove me to knees. And the Malab soldiers were no respecters of persons. I was sure Cassiel took almost as many rounds as me, especially after I fell in front of her.

Reuel was taking most of the heavy brass as the logic of the guards was simple: aim the big guns at the big guy. Still, he was unfazed enough to use his force to disarm one of the shooters and sling the assault rifle through a glass case along the wall.

Finally, the gunfire ceased. My arms were braced against the carpet, barely holding my body upright. I looked around for Cassiel. She was on the floor behind me.

"Are you all right?" I reached for her, then swore in pain, crumpling forward again.

"God, that hurts." I wondered if He could hear me nearby. I

glanced down at my shredded shirt, and my head swooned, not in a good way.

"Warren." Cassiel's tone reflected the concern on her face. Her eyes were fixed on my head. If the pain radiating from my skull was any sign of what she saw, my head was splitting, maybe literally.

Gently touching my forehead, I felt a hole. When I pulled my fingers away, they were bloody. "Well, shit."

The soldiers looked on, petrified with fear, as I sat back on my heels. I pushed my hair back. Then I pinched my nose closed, took a deep breath, and tried to blow the air out of my closed nostrils.

My left ear popped.

Then my right.

Then a 9 mm bullet squeezed out the inside corner of my left eye. It plopped out onto the floor and rolled across the hardwood.

One man cried out in horror.

Reuel was grinning a few feet away.

I squinted and shook my throbbing head. "That'll hurt for a while."

I'd felt the larger bullets from the assault rifles tear straight through my torso. They ripped through flesh, muscle, bone, and what would have been vital organs had I still been human.

And I hadn't gone to the floor simply because of the pain— though that was definitely part of it. A bullet had destroyed my left knee. Thankfully, the round was something smaller than a 5.56. Otherwise, the healing situation would've been a hell of a lot more complicated.

I forced myself to stand, and it wobbled underneath me. Something ached in my lower back; I suspected a round was lodged in my spine.

"This," Cassiel said, pulling herself off the floor. "This is why I hate coming to Earth."

"You get shot a lot over in Europe?" I asked, pulling up the front of my shirt to inspect the damage.

"Shut up, Warren."

Two more bullets slid out of oozing holes in my chest and stomach. One from between my sixth and seventh rib on my left side. The other from just beneath my right collarbone. They toppled to the floor in a splash of blood and lung tissue.

Then all the holes, all six of them that I could see, closed slowly. I swore.

"What's the matter?" Cassiel asked, holding her hand over a bloodstain on her side.

"Everything's closing." I twisted my spine. "And I still feel brass in my lower back."

The guards were finally starting to regain their mobility, but panic was setting in. They were yelling at each other in their language and waving their guns around in the air.

Cassiel was checking the holes in her outfit. "They want to know what kind of body armor we're wearing. And that guy is calling me a witch."

When she pointed, two of the men cowered back in fear, dropping their weapons in surrender. The other two lit us up again.

With a painful yowl, I limped my way forward through the wall of bullets. I grabbed the end of the rifle first and yanked it out of the man's hands. Flipping it around, I used the butt to break the nose of the guy still firing his 9 mm at me. Then I swung the rifle like a baseball bat to knock the final guy off his feet.

The two who hadn't shot at us a second time ran and crawled screaming from the room. The man on the floor scrambled back toward the door. And the guy with blood pouring out his nose had passed out cold.

I walked over and stuck my finger through one of the holes in Reuel's chest. "That hurt?"

He shoved me sideways, then held up his middle finger. "What's with you falling to the floor like a crying tiny canine?"

My head swirled around. "Like a what? I'm trying to be offended, but I have no idea what you said."

He spoke in Katavukai.

I laughed. Then I doubled over, laughing harder until the bullet pinched a nerve in my back. I straightened and patted Reuel's shoulder. "You need to work on your English, my friend. The phrase is whiny little bitch."

"That's you." He pointed at my face. "Whiny little bitch."

"Crying tiny canine is a hell of a lot funnier." As my laughter faded, I looked over at Cassiel. "You OK?"

"All the bullets are out, but I need more clothes again," she said, pulling Fury's bloody tank top away from her stomach.

"I think we all do," I agreed.

Reuel grabbed my arm so hard I winced. Then I spun toward him and saw his worried eyes. "Something's wrong." His hand covered his face. "The guardians at Echo-5..." He tapped his forehead and stumbled over his words. "They sent me a message."

The phone in my pocket rang out with alarm bells. Miraculously, it hadn't been hit by the spray of bullets. I pulled it out and looked at the screen. It was an auto-generated warning from the security system called Ahab in Iliana's building. The message made my throat tighten.

Atmospheric Breach.

Iliana was under attack.

CHAPTER ELEVEN

*T*he journey back to Asheville took less than a second, but it felt like an eternity. Inside the breach, I searched for my daughter's spirit and couldn't find it—a good sign. If she was hidden from me, she was still hidden from those who might hurt her.

We came in too fast through the spirit line and landed *hard* in the front yard of Echo-5. Normally, it would have been no big deal, but that was before all the cartilage and bone in my knee had been shredded. And before a bullet was lodged between my L3 and L4. Stars twinkled in my eyes at the impact, and I went down on my injured knee.

Reuel hauled me to my feet. Searching the darkness, I took a step forward, and blinding pain seared through my spine and leg again. Bones were harder to heal than flesh, and sooner or later, that bullet would have to come out. I didn't have to be a prophet to know pain would be in my future for a while.

But no time to worry about that now. My eyes, darting from side to side, spotted nothing out of place. Still, the property was buzzing with supernatural activity. It was so strong, gooseflesh rippled my skin. But I didn't see anything anywhere. "Reuel, think you can brighten this place up?"

With a grunt, he stepped in front of us and held both hands toward the sky. He whispered something even my keen ears couldn't hear to whoever was watching in the auranos. Then a streak of stars brightened, illuminating the grounds.

"Where are your guardians?" I asked him, looking around us. A unique power to the guardians who were in spirit form was the ability to camouflage themselves from other angels.

"*Kavalar, nikal tiyar,*" he said.

Four hulking angels revealed themselves, standing guard at all four points of the building.

From the front, Echo-5 didn't look like much, just a concrete block with rows of dark shuttered windows. In reality, even without its supernatural protection detail, it was probably the most secure building on the planet. It was made of steel, concrete, lead, and a composite metal foam known as high-Z.

A team of scientists had developed high-Z to be bulletproof and radiation proof. As an added bonus, it was also angel proof —making it more valuable than all the gems in Eden.

Beyond the building was a crater about the size of a football field where Azrael and Nathan were overseeing the construction of an underground bunker. When completed, it would be able to withstand almost any natural disaster, a nuclear war, or a full-on demon attack. Too bad it wasn't ready tonight.

Next to the crater, a communications tower, poorly designed to look like a pine tree, loomed over the property. It was about ten stories tall, twice the height of the building, and it only had pine branches covering the top half. Someday it might blend in with the normal-sized trees that were planted around it, but it wouldn't be in anyone's lifetime that I knew.

Tonight, the compound was dark and silent. Another good sign. Because with Ahab's alarms going off on my phone, I was sure the sirens were even louder inside the building. Still, there was only silence from out here.

I hoped the windows had been completely sealed off prior to the breach between worlds. Surely it had been sealed before everyone went to bed. It was after two in the morning, after all.

The only thing worrisome was the complete lack of light *outside*. Our arrival in the yard should have triggered the motion-sensor perimeter lights. And at the very least, the parking lot lights should be on. Instead, it was a total blackout.

I swiped open my screen and checked Ahab's status again. *Ahab secure.*

I texted Nathan. *I'm here, hoping you're all locked up inside. Don't come out until I tell you it's clear.*

He didn't answer.

"Reuel, could the guardians have breached here and set off Ahab?" I asked as I limped toward the building.

Reuel commanded the team of guardians that guarded Echo-5 from the auranos, a ripple of the spirit line through space. They literally kept watch over my daughter from the stars.

He answered me in Katavukai, saying no, the alarm went off before the guardians arrived. Maybe I'd made him self-conscious of his English skills.

"It was Moloch. I know it," Cassiel said, following behind me.

"Maybe so, but where is he now? There are more angels here than the four of them and the three of us. Don't you agree?"

"I do, but I don't know where he could be."

"Reuel, talk to the guardians. See if they know what happened," I said.

He nodded and started toward the building.

Cassiel followed him. "I'll come with you."

My eyes carefully scanned the area. "We're missing something."

The sound of an engine and gravel shifting under tires was coming from behind us. I turned as two SUVs screamed to a stop. The doors opened and several bodies climbed out with guns raised in our direction.

"I swear I'll kill you, Warren, if I get shot one more time," Cassiel called out.

"Nobody told you to come," I reminded her over my shoulder.

"Warren?" a man called out.

I waved. "Point those barrels away from us, Enzo."

"Yes, sir. Good to see you here, sir."

"Quit calling me *sir*, Enzo."

"Yes, sir."

I rolled my eyes. Enzo was the Special Operations Director of SF-12. Three men and one woman were with him. All of them were armed with military-grade firepower. I knew none of them.

Considering I'd gotten there within seconds of the alarm, their response time was impressive—for humans.

"What happened here?" I asked.

"Not sure. Got a notification that Ahab detected a breach nearby. I was hoping it was you again."

"Not this time." I'd shown up unannounced a few months before and scared the bejeezus out of everyone. "I came here when I got the alarm. Have you heard from Nathan?"

"Had him on the radio just now. Everyone's safe inside, but he said something hit the building."

"Or someone."

Enzo looked at the crew with him. "Search the perimeter."

"Can we trust your people?" I asked.

He looked at me like I had two heads. "Can we trust SF-12?"

I blinked. "Those were SF-12 members?" A sharp pain seared in my skull. I winced and pressed my eyes closed.

"Do you need me to call Doc?" Enzo asked.

As the pain subsided, I opened my eyes. "Probably not a bad idea." I arched my shoulders forward to relieve the pressure in my aching spine. Perhaps damage to my spinal cord was causing the headache.

I pointed my finger at all the dead light posts. "Who killed the lights?"

"They're down all the way to the guardhouse. Looks like a transformer was blown," he said.

"Is it this dark inside?"

"No. Echo-5 is on a separate transformer. And if that was taken out, it has a backup generator that can power the emergency lights, the cameras, and the air-filtration system. As long as nothing got in, they're fine in there."

"Do you think anything got in?"

He smiled. "No, sir. They've been on Security Level Bravo since the solar year passed. All the shutters stay closed and the doors locked." He pointed to Reuel and Cassiel near the building. "Is that our boy?"

"Yeah. The female is with us too."

Like they'd heard us talking about them—maybe they had—Reuel and Cassiel turned and came back toward us. Hopefully, with news.

Enzo shined his flashlight on my shirt. "What the hell happened to you, Warren?"

"Long story."

Before Reuel and Cassiel reached us, the beam of the headlights behind me snagged on something in the woods. All my senses focused on the flicker beyond the parking lot, and I dialed my vision in on the spot.

Two glowing green eyes stared back at me.

Then four.

Then six.

Then eight.

"Bingo," I whispered.

Reuel stepped close beside me and looked in the direction I was staring. "What is it?" he asked, this time in English.

In my peripheral vision, I saw Enzo's face whip toward him. He'd only ever heard Reuel speak in Katavukai before.

"It's weird, right?" Reuel asked him.

I held up a finger to silence them. "Shh."

Cupping my hands together, I let my power pool in my palms. Then I curled my hands around it and held a tiny break between my thumbs to my lips. I blew into my hands—as one might do in the cold—and the heat of my breath mixed with my power, creating a bright orb of light. I hurled it toward the tree line, and it landed in front of the group of demons like a bonfire.

Their faces lit up.

Saleos, the Sorceress.

Uko, the Torturer.

Nybria, the Goddess of Confusion—her self-given title.

And Elek, the fallen Angel of Life who once commanded the weather for all the universe.

"Reuel, I think it's time for the wings," I said, spreading mine behind me. Their energy lit up the whole property almost as bright as daylight.

"Yes," he whispered, clenching a victorious fist.

With a powerful thrust that tweaked my back, I sailed into the air. Reuel and Cassiel followed me across the property. All the demons withdrew into the woods.

As we neared, Elek's arm extended toward the sky, then sliced sideways through the air. A powerful wind from the east howled, pitching us across the sky.

I tightened my wingspan behind me, went headfirst into the wind, and turned back toward them. When I was near enough, I dropped my wings and came down so hard that the ground shook and my boots left deep impressions in the soil.

Inside, I was screaming in pain, but I refused to let my bad knee buckle again.

Using all my force, I blasted Elek backward. He landed hard on his ass, and the wind ceased as quickly has it had come. I was panting hard, and I was pissed. "Shall it be war tonight then?" I growled.

Their whispers sounded like a pit of snakes from where I stood. Appropriate.

"Your time will come soon enough, Archangel," Nybria hissed.

Reuel and Cassiel joined me.

I looked at my watch. "Well, if that's not happening in the next few minutes, can you please move along? I have a very busy night ahead of me."

"You have no idea," Uko said, brandishing a silver sword from a sheath on his back.

As I was trying to figure out what he might have meant by that, a ball of light like a meteor slammed into the building. The ground vibrated so hard with the impact that I had to lift off the ground to stay upright. The building shook but didn't falter as the light fizzled to a faint ripple.

Moloch.

The giant spotlights on top of the building switched on. A deafening siren wailed through the mountains. And all our phones chimed.

Moloch's light burned bright again, then shot straight up through the sky. Taking that as some kind of cue, the demons all disappeared at once with loud cracks of thunder through the atmosphere.

Reuel looked up at me from where he stood on the ground below, ready to pounce. "They're running?"

"I guess so." I settled beside him and lowered my wings. They darkened and disappeared as I searched the atmosphere for activity. All was still and quiet again. This time, lacking the buzz of nearby spirits.

"Was Uko carrying a sword?" Cassiel asked.

"Yeah." I looked between her and Reuel. "That's weird, right?"

Reuel nodded and scratched his head.

"Come on. Let's get back to Enzo and the others."

The members of SF-12 had shouldered their weapons and had come back together between the two Claymore SUVs.

"They've gone," I shouted over the siren as we neared them.

"What was that?" the only female in their group asked.

Enzo held up his hand, then pulled out his phone. He swiped the screen, tapped it several times, and the siren stopped.

"I said the demons left," I repeated as I settled on the ground. I looked around at all their faces. God, who were they? I knew that I knew them, but for the life of me, I couldn't remember their names.

"Who was it?" the largest male asked.

Cassiel landed next to me. "Saleos, Uko, Nybria, and Elek. They were here with the Archangel—"

All their weapons immediately locked on Cassiel's face. She ducked behind Reuel.

The woman's mismatched eyes narrowed. "Who are you? And why the hell are you speaking English?"

I held up my hands. "Weapons down! Don't make me lower them for you."

The operatives were reluctant, but they slowly lowered their barrels toward the ground. "Who is she, Warren?" the woman asked again.

"Her name is Cassiel. She came with me from Eden," I said.

One of the other guys looked ready to lean on the trigger of his gun again. "And why is she not speaking Katavukai? You know what that means."

Cassiel stepped around me. "I'm the head of the Council that made that law. Therefore, I have the authority to disregard it."

"How convenient for you," the youngest guy said with a smirk.

"It is *quite* convenient. I know." Her angry blue eyes dared him to say something else.

He didn't.

"Moloch was here?" Enzo asked, pointing at the ground.

"Yeah, and unfortunately, I think that's my fault. I blew up his body about ten minutes ago on the other side of the planet." I sighed and rested my hands on my hips.

The big guy nodded toward my chest. "Is that what happened to your shirt?"

I tugged at the hem. "Those were caused by a one-sided shootout with the prime minister of Malab's security detail. You'll probably hear about it on the news."

"Why?" Enzo asked.

"Because Warren killed the prime minister," Cassiel said.

They all reacted. Dropped jaws, flinching heads, wide eyes.

The young man gave an impressed nod. "Damn."

I touched my throbbing head. "Guys, I'm going to level with you. I took some spinal damage during the shootout, and I'm having an impossible time remembering your names."

They all exchanged a confused glance.

"Just tell me your names again."

The big guy spoke first. "Kane."

"Lex."

"Cruz."

"NAG," the woman said.

"NAG?" Cassiel asked.

"It stands for Not A Guy," Enzo explained. "Her real name's Mandi."

My memory flared to life along with another surge of pain. I immediately remembered all of them. "Of course. I remember now. God, I don't know what's wrong with me." I felt stupid.

Cassiel touched my arm. She looked genuinely concerned.

"We've got bigger worries than a headache." I massaged my temples. "Have any of you ever seen a swirling purple fog around any humans?"

Enzo exchanged confused glances with the rest of the team. Most of them could *see* the supernatural the way Umar in Africa could see us. "Like a smoke bomb?" Lex asked.

That wasn't a terrible description. "Sort of. A spiritual one, but yeah."

"I haven't," Enzo said.

The others shook their heads.

My phone rang. I pulled it out and looked at the screen. "Nathan." I tapped the answer button and put it to my ear. "Everybody whole?"

"Everybody's fine. What's going on out there? Looks like you guys are about to have a picnic on my front lawn."

I turned toward the building and waved to the security cameras.

"I see you. What happened?"

"You were just dive-bombed by an Archangel demon."

Nathan swore. "Well, we're still here. Ahab did what it was supposed to do." There was commotion on his end of the line. "Hey, Warren, looks like we're about to have more company. Az just pulled through the gate."

"OK. Where's Iliana?"

"She's with Sloan in the safe room."

Headlights appeared down the road. "Az is here. Let me call you back."

"Warren, is it safe to come out?" he asked.

"Give me a minute. I'll have Reuel send a guardian to cover your exit."

"I'll watch for the all clear on the camera."

"OK. See you in a minute." I ended the call as my father pulled up in front of us. I gripped Reuel's shoulder. "Can you have someone cover the Echo-5 door? Nathan wants to come out, but we need to know it's secure."

"Akai viru cerah," he said with a nod.

"Thanks, man." I squeezed his arm.

Azrael opened the driver's side door and got out. "What happened?" His black hair was standing on end, and his sweatshirt was inside out.

"There was an atmospheric breach at two oh nine a.m." Enzo gestured toward me. "These guys were here when we arrived."

"We came as soon as I received the alarm on my phone. I just talked to Nate. He said Iliana is fine. Nothing happened inside the building."

Azrael sighed with relief. "Thank the Father for that."

"We believe it was Moloch. There were others here as well," I said.

"What others?" Azreal asked.

I thought for a second. "Saleos, Elek, Nybria..."

"And Uko," Cassiel added.

Azrael's eyes narrowed. "Hello, Cassiel."

She waved but otherwise didn't greet him.

"No Morning Star?" he asked.

I shook my head.

He looked up at the moonless sky. "Why now? Why tonight?" he asked no one in particular.

Cassiel raised her arm toward Echo-5. "Because you're harboring a devastating weapon here."

I lowered my voice. "You're not helping."

"I believe this was planned," she said.

My brow crumpled. "You believe Moloch knew I would be in Malab to kill him today, when I just decided to come last night?" I shook my head. "He's smart, but he's not a mind reader."

"No, but he clearly knew what he was doing tonight." She stepped closer. "He wanted you to separate him from his body so he could move as a spirit again. Maybe we surprised him, and because it happened unexpectedly, his plan fell apart once he got here."

I shrugged. "It's possible I guess, but has he been waiting in the Capitol building all these months for an Angel of Death to happen by? That's a little ridiculous."

"He had to have known the Father was in the area. And he was keeping the Angels of Death busy there with the famine."

"That's true."

Everyone looked past me. When I turned, Nathan was crossing the yard with Reuel and another SF-12 member, Justice. Nathan wore blue plaid pajama pants and his black SWAT hoodie, which brought back memories like a tidal wave.

My eyes drifted over their heads to the building, and for the first time since we'd arrived, I had a chance to consider that my daughter and Sloan were *right there*.

"This many angels in my front yard is never a good sign," he said as they approached. Lines from his pillow creased the right side of his face. "What happened?"

"It looks like this was the first major attempt to take Iliana," Azrael said.

Nathan shook his head. "Definitely not the first."

Az rolled his eyes. "OK. The first since she's been here, where she's supposed to be safe."

I put my hand on his shoulder. "She was safe. Nothing happened. This is why you built this place, remember. Everything functioned the way you designed it to."

"But it was a close call, and certainly not the last attempt," Cassiel said.

Nathan turned toward her, his eyes wide with worry. "And who are you?"

"Sorry," I said. "Nathan this Cassiel. She's from Eden and she can speak English, so don't freak out. Also, Reuel can too now."

Reuel waved. "Hello."

Nathan took a step back. "Whoa."

"It's crazy, I know." I crossed my arms. "Now I need to know what happened inside."

"The internal alarm sounded, just like the time you showed up unannounced around Christmas. I checked the video feed on my phone's app and didn't see anything, so I put Sloan and Iliana in the safe room with Pirez and went to the control room downstairs.

"That must have been when you got here because you were on the screen when I walked in. Justice was already going over all the cameras. Neither of us saw anything out of place except you jokers stalking the yard.

"Then, *boom!*" Nathan was using wild hand gestures. "Shit got real and the big sirens went off."

"That was exactly what was supposed to happen," Enzo said.

Smiling, Nathan clapped his hands. "Bravo, Az. Your system works."

"This time." Cassiel was not impressed. "Moloch doesn't fail. He tests and recalibrates. This was a training exercise."

"You're just a ball of sunshine, aren't you?" Nathan asked, his smile now bent with sarcasm.

"My job is to think of the scenarios everyone else can't. Moloch will be back."

"And we'll be ready," Enzo said.

Cassiel nodded, but it was clear she didn't agree. "Until Moloch figures out a workaround and defeats the system."

He smirked. "There's a complicated series of steps to bypass Ahab. It doesn't just have an on-and-off switch."

Cassiel stared at him a moment. I knew the look. She was sizing Enzo up. "Moloch has the most advanced consciousness in existence next to the Morning Star. Your fancy computer system isn't smarter than he is. "

"What do you suggest we do?" Azrael asked, surprising no one more than me...except maybe Cassiel.

But she was smart enough not to answer around a crew carrying loaded guns. She looked at me.

"We'll talk later," I told him.

"Just to be safe, tomorrow I'll call in the Nerd Platoon from New Hope to come double-check the system," Nathan said.

"Commander"—Enzo's tone was scolding—"human resources says you're not allowed to call them that."

"Yeah, yeah." Nathan rolled his eyes. He looked at me. "Where are you staying tonight?"

"Somewhere close. I want to keep an eye on the activity around here," I said.

"There's plenty of room at the command center," Enzo said.

The command center was the house I'd bought for Sloan.

I gulped. "Thanks, but no thanks. I'll stay with Az." I looked at him. "Is that OK?"

He looked surprised. "Uh...yeah. Of course."

I lifted an eyebrow.

"*We* will stay with Az, you mean?" Cassiel looked at Azrael. "Because wherever he goes, I go."

Azrael scowled and looked a little...worried? Angry?

"Great," he grumbled.

Yep. Angry.

"And I need to talk to you," she said, taking a step closer to him.

His brow lifted, and he took a small step back. No, he was *definitely* worried.

"We've just come from Malab. Another human spirit was controlling the body of the country's prime minister."

Azrael's shoulders relaxed. But then his head tilted. "Wait. What?"

"The Prime Minister's body was possessed by a *human* spirit." She lowered her voice. "The soul identified himself as Haile Menelek."

If Azrael could have looked shocked, he would have. "I killed Haile Menelek myself and sentenced him to Nulterra. He must have been lying."

"People don't lie to me, Azrael. They can't," she said.

"And his spirit had your mark," I added.

"But that's impossible."

Cassiel shrugged. "All the more reason to be worried."

Azrael ran a hand through his wild hair. "We'll not figure it out standing here in the middle of the night. My brain needs sleep these days to function properly."

I pushed my shoulders forward again to try to ease the throbbing in my back. "Az, I need to see Doc soon."

"Why? What's wrong?"

I tugged at the front of my shredded shirt. "Between the three of us, we took about thirty rounds back in Malab a little while ago. I've got some brass lodged in my spine that's killing me."

He smiled. "No, it isn't."

"You know what I mean."

He walked toward his car. "I can't wait to hear about that."

"We're also traveling light. We all need some new clothes," I said.

"You can have something of mine." Azrael looked over to where the rest of SF-12 was standing a few feet away from us. "NAG, go back to the command center and bring clothes for Cassiel to my house. You're about the same size."

Reuel raised his hand.

Azrael shook his head. "I don't know what we'll do for you, Reuel."

"I've got a couple of tents back in storage," Nathan said, jerking his thumb toward the building.

Reuel shoved him back. "Donkey hole."

Nathan blinked. "What?"

I laughed. "It's *asshole,* Reuel."

"Asshole," Reuel repeated.

"What the hell?" Nathan asked, laughing.

"The language is new for him," Cassiel said. "He understands English perfectly well, but it's interpreted for him in literal meanings. Your moronic insults and idioms make no real sense to us in Katavukai."

"I like it." Nathan gave Reuel a thumbs-up. "I'm going to start calling people donkey holes."

Reuel winked at him.

Nathan yawned. "I'm calling it a night, my friends. Think it's safe for me to let Sloan and Illy out of the panic room?"

I searched the sky with my gift again. "It should be fine. Everything's calm now."

Nathan shook his head. "You're so weird, man."

"And you're a donkey hole. I'll let you know tomorrow how long I'll be in town."

Nathan laughed and waved to the group. "Goodnight, everyone."

"Make sure they get inside OK?" I asked Reuel.

He nodded and jogged to catch up with Nathan and Justice. I watched them, and then stared at the building for a long moment, silently wishing I could go inside.

"Warren?" Cassiel gently took my hand.

A supernatural calm washed over me. I took a deep breath and released it slowly. "Sorry. Let's go."

CHAPTER TWELVE

*D*oc, the medic for SF-12, stood over me with a scalpel. "I'm afraid this will sting...a lot."

I was shirtless, in the prone position across Azrael and Adrianne's dining room table. Az, Reuel, Enzo, NAG, and Cassiel all looked on.

"Can't you give him morphine?" NAG asked.

Azrael shook his head. "His body would metabolize it so quickly it'd be a waste."

I clenched my teeth and closed my eyes. "Just do it, Doc."

The blade sliced deep into my lower back, through the skin and muscle tissue. I gripped the edge of the table above my head until I nearly cracked the wood.

Metal hit the table; he'd put the knife down, probably to pick up the six-inch tweezers he'd pulled from his bag earlier.

"Shit," he said.

My eyes popped open. "What's the matter?"

"The incision closed."

I groaned and thumped my forehead on the table.

"I need to do it again." Doc paused. "I don't have retractors to hold it open while I remove the bullet. Reuel, come here."

Reuel came closer to the table, and I looked back over my bare shoulder. His face twisted like he'd smelled a bunch of rotten eggs.

"When I make the incision, use both hands to hold the skin back out of my way."

Reuel made a vomiting noise.

"Give me a break, you big baby. Do you remember losing your arm to that train in Chicago? That was way worse than this," I said.

He sucked in a sharp breath and held it.

I felt Doc's hands on my back. "You ready?" he asked me.

I nodded and braced against the table.

The knife sliced through me again. I groaned loudly through gritted teeth. This time, Reuel's cold hands grabbed the center of my back and pulled it apart.

Enzo swore.

NAG looked away.

Cassiel covered her mouth.

Scalpel down. Tweezers up.

With my eyes pressed closed, I was silently praying he would get it out quickly.

"What the hell is going on in here?" Adrianne asked.

Reuel let go.

"Shit!" Doc shouted.

"Not again," I whimpered.

I opened my eyes as Adrianne walked into the dining room. Azrael put his arm around her shoulders. "Sweetheart, you should go back to bed."

"Why is Doc performing surgery on my grandmother's table? Good lord, is that Warren?"

I wiggled a few fingers to wave. "Hi, Adrianne."

"Warren was shot. Doc needs to remove a bullet from his spine," Azrael said. "You might not want to watch this."

"The hell I don't. Let me go." She pushed him away and walked right over beside my head. She patted my shoulder. "You're groggy I hope?"

"Not even a little bit."

"Ooo, sucks for you."

Doc sighed. "Ready to go again?"

"Last time, man. I can't take much more."

"Last time. Reuel, ready?"

I turned and pointed at Reuel. "Don't. Let. Go."

He nodded and rubbed his hands together. All his fingers were bloody. I wished I hadn't looked.

Doc cut into my back a third time, making this incision even longer than the others. I said a few bad words, and Adrianne put her hand on top of mine. Oddly, it helped.

Reuel gripped both sides of the incision and pulled. It felt like he was ripping me apart. I would have screamed had I not had an audience. The toes of my boots bent back into the table.

For what felt like eternity, Doc pushed and pulled around my spine. "I can see it, but the bullet won't budge. I might have to go in from the front so I can pull it out the way it went in."

"Hell no," I said. "Azrael, rip that shit out."

"You got it."

As good as Doc was, he couldn't help but treat me like a human patient. Azrael wouldn't be so careful. He also wouldn't be gentle, but the job would get done without anymore cutting.

Doc moved out of the way, and Azrael bent over my back. There was more pushing and pulling and jabbing with the tweezers. "Screw this shit," he finally said. "Adrianne, get the pliers from my toolbox in the garage."

"Hurry," I said, tears of pain leaking from my eyes.

She ran from the room, and Cassiel knelt by my head. "Hold on, Warren."

I stared into her blue eyes, wishing I could get lost in them.

For the first time, she looked helpless and afraid. "You sure this can't kill me?"

"I promise." She smiled and held my hand. "Not much longer."

"I think this is worse than getting shot." I forced a smile.

She pushed a loose strand of hair back behind my ear. "The audience probably doesn't help."

Adrianne finally returned a million years later with a pair of pliers. "Here."

"Thank you." He bent over me again and jammed the cold metal into my back so hard I didn't know how my spine stayed intact.

He braced one hand against my rib cage and pushed as he yanked the pliers.

I screamed the F-word.

Finally, the tension broke, and I inhaled for the first time in minutes.

"Got it!" he shouted.

Everyone clapped, and Reuel released the incision.

Adrianne bent to look at me. "Are you OK?"

"I am now." I patted her hand. "Sorry we woke you up."

"I'm sorry you got shot."

Azrael held the bullet in front of my face. "Ta-da! Want a souvenir?"

"No thanks. You can keep it."

"Yeah, put it on a necklace," Enzo said, laughing.

I pushed myself up carefully in case the pain returned—or, God forbid, the headache and the memory loss. "Thanks, everybody." Reuel looked a little pale. I squeezed his arm. "You did well."

"Come on, Reuel." Adrianne tugged on his shirt. "Let's get you a snack as a reward."

He smiled and followed her to the kitchen.

"Sorry I couldn't get it," Doc said, offering me his hand. "The ligaments and cartilage healed around it, fusing it in there."

I squeezed his hand and released it. "You're not telling me anything I don't know. I've felt it for the past couple of hours." I picked up the clean black T-shirt Azrael had given me. "Thanks for trying. Can't feel a thing now."

"Good."

"Hey, Doc, could that bullet have caused a bad headache? My head hurt so bad earlier I was forgetting things."

"Like most of us lowly humans," NAG said with a laugh.

Doc sighed and ran his fingers through his hair. "Headaches, sure. But shit, Warren, that bullet would have paralyzed most people. Who the hell knows how it might affect you."

I chuckled. "Yeah. Good point. Thanks again."

"Don't mention it."

Cassiel was standing in front of me, watching me put on the shirt. "That was brutal. Are you sure you're all right?"

"I'm fine now. Thank you." I pulled the T-shirt over my head and stood up, arching my spine backward. "Oh, that feels glorious."

Enzo and NAG walked over. Both of their eyes were mismatched. Enzo's were blue and green. NAG's were brown and green. "Now that the show's over, I guess we'll go home," he said with a smile.

"Thanks for everything you guys do. And NAG, thanks for getting the clothes." She'd brought clothes for Cassiel and had visited the Big and Tall section of a 24-hour Walmart for Reuel.

"Don't mention it," she replied.

"Will you be around for a while?" Enzo asked.

I shrugged. "I really have no idea. Iliana's safety is my first priority, but I need to get back to Eden to find Metatron."

"I still haven't met him," he said.

"That makes two of us."

"Take care of yourself, Warren. Hope the back is OK," he said.

I twisted at the waist. "Just like new."

As Enzo and NAG walked to the door. Cassiel followed them. I heard her thanking NAG again for her clothes.

When they were across the room, Azrael looked at me with a clenched jaw. "Why did you bring her here?" he whispered angrily.

"I told you, the Council is watching me."

"Why?"

I took a step closer to him and lowered my voice as much as I could. "They've ruled that I must bring Iliana to Eden by her first birthday."

His head drew back in alarm. "They plan to make her a seraph?"

"They plan to try."

"You know what that means, right?" he asked.

I nodded. "They also want me and the other Angels of Death to destroy any human body harboring an angel under the age of two."

"Fury's baby." His mouth widened with shock, and he turned away from me. "I wouldn't have been surprised if they had ordered the destruction of the Morning Star, but *all* babies?"

"All of them."

He stared through me for a moment, gripping his forehead. He looked at Adrianne and Reuel in the kitchen, then at Cassiel, Enzo, and NAG at the front door. "What's your plan?" he finally asked.

"I need to find Metatron. If he can identify the Morning Star, I might have a chance to save Iliana and spare Fury's kid."

"What about Sandalphon? He's generally easier to—"

"Sandalphon's locked himself in Cira."

"Why?"

I shrugged my shoulders. "Nobody knows."

Azrael steepled his fingers and pressed them down the center of his face. His eyes bounced nervously back and forth. Finally, he shook his head. "We must get Fury somewhere safe."

"Where? She's still in the hospital right now."

"You don't think an angel can walk out of a hospital with a baby?"

True.

"Don't worry about Fury. I'll take care of her."

"Where will you take her?"

He shook his head. "The less you know, the better."

I looked across the room. Cassiel was talking quietly with Enzo at the door. My eyes narrowed as I watched her touch his arm.

Azrael jabbed his finger into my chest. "You need to work on a backup plan. I'm not sure Metatron can recognize the Morning Star. And even if it's possible, he's not the easiest angel to work with. He's powerful, and he knows it."

I grinned. "Sounds like somebody else I know."

"I don't know what you're talking about."

"Of course you don't."

"Did you speak with the Father?"

"The Father won't leave Malab, but He says he'll help persuade the Council against making Iliana a seraph if I can find the Morning Star."

"Which brings you back to the problem."

"Yep."

"What are you two talking about over there?" Cassiel's voice made both of us turn. She was closing the front door behind Enzo and NAG.

"I could ask the same question about you and Enzo," I said

"Enzo was assuring me he had the security situation under control here." She broke eye contact with me.

I crossed my arms. *Now who's lying?*

"What are you talking about?" she asked again.

"Sleeping arrangements," Azrael lied.

She lifted a skeptical eyebrow.

I huffed. "I was filling Azrael in on the Council's ruling."

"See? Was it so hard to be honest with me?"

Azrael looked around the room. "But we do need to talk about sleeping arrangements."

"Right," Adrianne said, walking in from the kitchen. "Where is everyone sleeping?"

"I meant to tell you guys, congratulations on the house. This place looks great," I said.

Since I'd been gone, Azrael and Adrianne had bought a house together closer to Wolf Gap. It was an older home, a '70s-style ranch, but the inside had recently been renovated.

Adrianne put her arms around Azrael's waist. "Thank you. We like it." She kissed his cheek.

"And speaking of congratulations..." Cassiel walked over and extended her hand to Adrianne. "We haven't officially met. I'm Cassiel. Congratulations on the baby."

Before Adrianne could shake Cassiel's hand, Azrael tightened his arm around her and moved Adrianne back a few steps. "Thank you, Cassiel," he answered for her.

Adrianne elbowed him. "I'm still a grown woman, Az. It's nice to meet you, Cassiel. Any friend of Warren's is a friend of ours."

"She's not a friend," Azrael said quickly.

Adrianne put a hand on her hip. "Are you ever going to learn the manners of humans? You're in the south for crying out loud."

"Sleeping arrangements," he blurted out. "We have two

spare bedrooms. One has a full-sized bed, and the other has a queen."

It was obvious Azrael wanted to move the conversation along, so I helped. "Reuel needs a bed. He won't fit on the couch."

At the kitchen island, Reuel had a mouthful of reheated meatloaf. He smiled, showing ketchup in his teeth.

"And Cassiel can have the other bed. I'll take the couch."

Cassiel laughed and crossed her arms. "So you can sneak off in the middle of the night while I'm asleep? I don't think so. We can share the bed."

All eyes turned slowly toward me.

"Share the bed?" I asked.

Azrael had a taunting smile. "We have a queen. It would be big enough for both of you."

I wanted to give him the finger. "No thanks. If we have to sleep in the same room, I'll sleep on the floor."

Cassiel sighed and shook her head. "Suit yourself." She looked at Adrianne. "May I use your shower? I'd really like to wash off all this blood and get out of these ruined clothes."

"What happened to you guys?" Adrianne asked.

"An army," Cassiel said.

Adrianne's face soured. "You know, Warren, things have been so peaceful since you've been gone."

"And I'm working hard to keep it that way," I said.

"I'm sure, but it's like you show up and suddenly armies are shooting people up and demons are storming the compound."

Cassiel smiled at me. "He *is* the Angel of Death, you know."

"I guess." Adrianne pointed to the door behind Cassiel. "The bathroom is down the hall, the second door on the left. There are towels and washcloths under the sink."

"Thank you, Adrianne."

"Do you need something to wear? I could try to find something with legs short enough to fit you."

"That's OK. NAG brought me a couple of things to choose from." Cassiel turned toward me. "Can I trust you for five minutes?"

"Are you sure you don't want me to sit on the bathroom floor while you take a shower?"

I swear she blushed a little.

"Five minutes," she said, dodging the question.

As she walked away, I watched. "We're plotting against you while you're gone."

"I expect no less," she said with a laugh.

When the bathroom door closed behind her, Adrianne turned to Azrael. "I'm going back to bed."

He kissed her. "I'll be in there soon."

"Will I see you in the morning?" she asked me.

"Most likely."

"Give me a hug just in case."

I hugged her. Then she went to the other side of the house.

When we were alone, and the shower turned on in the bathroom, Azrael grabbed my arm. "You have to get her out of here."

"Why are you so worried?" I asked.

"She's too inquisitive. I don't want her around Adrianne."

"But your baby's human."

"That was a rumor from Ionis. I'm not trusting Adrianne's life to the Council until we have solid proof."

"You think they'd hurt her?"

"I'm not taking any chances."

Azrael had already lost one pregnant wife to dangerous angels. Couldn't blame him for being cautious with Adrianne.

"We'll leave tomorrow, I'm sure. Unless you want her out of here tonight."

He put both hands on his hips. "No, tomorrow is fine. I still need information from her about what happened in Malab."

"We'll talk over breakfast, and then she and I will go."

He nodded.

"Speaking of Malab, what do you know about inflicting the final death this side of the spirit line?" I asked.

"It's forbidden. I've never been able to do it, even though I wanted to a few times."

"I can do it."

His head snapped back.

I held up my hands and conjured the final death.

His eyes doubled. "Whoa."

I let the power fizzle out.

"It must be because you were born with free will. Did you destroy Menelek?" he asked.

"Yeah. Felt super sick afterward. Cassiel and Moloch both said it was a bad idea to do it on Earth."

"Moloch *would* say that, wouldn't he? He was working with Menelek."

"You're right. He was. That doesn't explain why Cassiel would say the same."

He looked at me seriously. "Don't mistake her voice for one of reason. She's not here to help you."

"You're right."

"Of course I'm right. Now tell me, what happens if you don't take Iliana to Eden?"

"Then I assume I'll be moving into your guest room."

"I figured as much."

"They said they'll send the guardians for her."

His tired eyes fell to the floor. "I can't believe they're doing this again."

"What do you mean *again?*"

"It's not important." He put his arm on my shoulder. "They can be stopped. It just might take everything you've got to do it."

"There's nothing I wouldn't do for my family."

He smiled and squeezed my shoulder. "I know."

The water in the bathroom shut off.

"That was fast. She doesn't mess around," I said, looking down the hallway.

Azrael pushed my cheek to turn my face back to him. "No, she doesn't. Don't let your guard down around Cassiel for a second."

"Don't worry. I won't."

CHAPTER THIRTEEN

*R*euel took the full-sized bed, and Cassiel and I went to the queen bedroom. As promised, I arranged blankets and pillows on the hardwood floor. She laid down on the bed facing me. "You're being ridiculous. There isn't even carpet in here."

I stacked two pillows behind my head. "It's your fault for not letting me sleep on the couch."

"Warren, I don't bite."

"How can I be sure? Most snakes do."

"Very clever." She stared at me for a second. "Are we going to talk about Adrianne's baby?"

"There's nothing to talk about. We already know Adrianne's baby is human."

Her eyes narrowed. "There's power there. Can't you sense it?"

"Yes, but it's Azrael's biological child. Who knows what kind of power it might have. Just look at Fury."

"I think it's more than that," she said.

"Ionis came with a message confirming the baby wasn't an angel. The word was straight from Eden."

"Given by whom?"

"Does it matter right now? Should I plan on killing pregnant women too?" I asked, raising my voice.

"Of course not. Calm down. I'll check into it when we get back."

"For tonight, is it too much to ask that we drop it and go to sleep?"

"Fine."

Using my power, I turned off the light switch and the room went dark. My brain began turning on Azrael's advice: get a backup plan. But, hell, what could that be? I hardly had a preliminary plan, one with *lots* of giant holes in it.

"Was it hard for you being at the Claymore property tonight?" Cassiel's voice ripped me from my thoughts.

I stared up at the darkness above me. "You want to talk about my feelings now?"

"I'm trying to understand you, Warren. There's never been another like you before."

"I am pretty special," I said with a cocky smile she couldn't see in the dark.

"There's never been another human turned Archangel...or any angel, for that matter."

"I know what you meant."

"So was it hard for you being so near your old life?" she asked—or pried, really.

"It's hard every time I come to Earth."

There was a beat of silence. I hoped her inquisition into my thoughts and emotions was finished. It wasn't.

"Do you miss Sloan?"

I sighed. "Only when I'm here."

"Do you ever—"

"*Goodnight*, Cassiel."

I heard her roll over in the bed. "Goodnight."

Nothing in me wanted to talk about Sloan. Or about my old

life. But that apparently wouldn't stop my brain from thinking about it. Turning their faces over and over in my mind. Replaying Sloan's very last words to me...

"With everything I am, I love you."

Pressing my eyes shut, I tried willing myself to sleep, or at least willing my brain to shut off. Too bad that wasn't happening.

Sleep wasn't going to come easy. My body might have been immortal, but after being shot up and cut open, it was sore. And the floor sure as hell wasn't helping. I turned onto my left side, then my right. Then onto my stomach, and then onto my back.

Finally, with a huff, Cassiel turned on the bedside lamp. "I swear to the Father, Warren Parish, if you don't get into this bed, I'll get on the floor myself."

I ignored her.

She threw the covers back and swung her legs off the bed. Then she stood and grabbed her pillow. "Don't believe me? Scoot over."

I sat up, and she towered over me. She wore tiny gray shorts under a thin white T-shirt. She also wore no bra. Why? Because they weren't necessary in Eden. They certainly weren't necessary for Cassiel—not that I noticed. My pulse suddenly thumping, I darted my eyes away. "Fine. I'll get in the bed."

The shirt had nothing to do with it. I swear.

I pushed myself up, then took my pillows around to the other side of the bed. We both laid down the exact same time.

She rolled toward me, then using her finger, she drew a line down the center of the bed. "This is my side. And that is your side. I'll stay on my side. You'll stay on your side. This isn't that complicated."

"Shut up, Cassiel."

With a victorious smirk, she turned off the light.

In the morning, I awoke to angel chatter in my ear. The mandates from the Council had been announced, and the Angels of Death were *pissed*.

I groaned and opened my eyes. I was hugging my second pillow to my chest in a weird and loving way that made me wonder what I'd been dreaming about. My bare feet were tangled up with Cassiel's.

Her back was to me, and had we been any closer, I'd have been spooning her and not my pillow. It was a good thing she was almost a foot away. Morning wood was still a thing in the afterlife. Who knew?

Slowly, I tried to withdraw my feet before she noticed them.

"Warren?" she asked softly.

"Yeah?"

"You're on my side."

I snatched my feet away, and she turned over to face me.

"How did you sleep?" I wasn't sure why I'd asked. It's not like I cared. Maybe it was my brain working overtime to think about anything other than what was *literally* between us under the covers. The scent of her so dangerously close wasn't helping.

"Very well, actually. I think getting shot a half dozen times really wore me out."

I laughed, and it felt good. Too good.

"You're up early," she said.

"It's your fault."

"My fault?"

I tapped my ear. "My angels are livid about your decree." I pulled the pillow over my head. "They won't shut up."

"Here, let me." Between the pillows, her hands slid up my jaw.

Oh god. I closed my eyes and gulped. Touching me—even my face—was dangerous at the moment. My heart raced.

She pressed her fingertips beneath my earlobes until there was a soft click. All the voices went silent.

My eyes popped open. "What did you do?"

"You've been an Archangel for how long and didn't know you had a silence button?"

"Holy shit. That's amazing. How do I turn it back on?"

"If you hold those two spots again, or if you broadcast a message to all your angels, it will turn back on for all of them. Otherwise, it will turn on one by one as you contact them."

"So I should probably contact Samael since he's supposed to be getting back to me with information."

"If you want to hear it."

"Thank you, Cassiel." The words felt strange in my mouth.

"You're welcome." She rolled onto her back. Then she lifted her head and pulled her long golden hair from beneath her, letting it spill across the bedsheets beside me. It smelled like honeysuckle.

My whole body was throbbing. Thank the Father I was in the fetal position on my side.

"How's your back this morning?"

"Still sore if I lay on it." I closed my eyes, hoping she wouldn't notice I was fibbing.

Silence.

I peeked out one eye and saw her staring at me. "Why are you lying about that?"

I sighed. "This honesty shit is getting old really quick."

"Why would you lie about something so stupid as laying on your back?" She threw her hands into the air. "And you wonder why I don't trust you."

I'd finally had enough. Pushing the covers down to my thighs, I rolled onto my back. "Because I'm trying to be a gentleman!"

"What?" She looked down. Then her eyes doubled. They shot back up toward the ceiling. "Oh my." Pink bloomed in her cheeks.

I pulled the blankets back up around me, my erection slowly starting to wilt. "It's been almost a hundred years, and my body still won't believe it's not human anymore."

She covered her face with her hands. "Oh my stars."

Laughing, I pulled her hands away from her face. "Are you embarrassed, Councilor?"

"Humiliated." Her cheeks were cherry red. "I'm sorry, Warren."

"Forget it." I needed to forget it. Her giggles were resolidifying the situation.

She sat up, fanning her face. "I need to get out of this bed."

I wondered what she meant by that.

Sitting up, I took care to keep the covers pulled over my lap. I pressed a finger against my ear and called out to Samael. "Can you hear me?" I asked inaudibly.

"Loud and clear. Still gathering info, so stay tuned. Lots of activity here," he replied.

"What's the plan for today?" Cassiel stood and turned to face me, then gathered her hair into a knot on top of her head. The T-shirt lifted in the front, exposing the smooth patch of skin between her belly button and the sagging waistband of her cotton shorts. "Earth to Warren."

I pulled my eyes back up to hers. "Sorry."

"What's our plan?" she asked again.

"I want to call and check on Fury." Which was true, but I really wanted call and *warn* Fury. I just couldn't tell Cassiel.

"Does she really believe her sister is alive in Nulterra?"

"She does. In fact, she received intel that might prove Anya is alive."

"What kind of intel?"

"Details about her sister's movement after Abaddon took

her. She's hoping the information might lead us to the Nulterra Gate."

Cassiel spread the clothes NAG had given her on the bed. "How much do you know about the Nulterra Gate?"

"Only what Azrael has told me. And what I saw through his blood stone."

"Shall I tell you what I know about it?" she asked, picking up the pair of cargo pants.

Truth be told, the reason I had sought out Cassiel in the first place (many months earlier) was to hear what she was hopefully about to tell me. When the deal was struck between Eden and the demons, the Council had been responsible for laying out the parameters of the agreement.

I only knew what Azrael knew: the demons were allowed to access the spirit line so that souls could be delivered to Nulterra; and the gate on Earth was to be permanently sealed. Azrael wasn't much for details.

"I'd love to hear it." I propped my pillows against the headboard and reclined, lacing my fingers together over my stomach.

She unzipped the cargo pants and held them out in front of her.

My hand shot forward. "If you're getting undressed, save the story for later. There's no way I'll remember if you tell me while you're getting naked."

She smiled, and for the first time, I realized she had a slight dimple in her left cheek. "I'll change in the bathroom. Don't worry."

I wasn't *worried* exactly.

She sat down on her side of the bed. "We tried to find out the location of the gate from the demons during the negotiations, but they refused to tell us. They did, however, agree to have two keys created for the gate. One was for Abaddon. The other for us."

"I haven't heard anything about a key."

Her head tilted. "Did you assume there would be no lock on the door to the most volatile place in existence?"

Good point. "Honestly, I never even thought about it."

She smiled again. "Honestly? Have we finally gotten to that mountaintop in our relationship?"

I touched the center of my chest. "You help me, and I'll help you."

"Fair enough." She turned to face me. "Because the key was Nulterra-borne, it could not cross the spirit line. It certainly couldn't be brought into Eden. So it was entrusted to an angel here on Earth"

I straightened. "Who?"

"A guardian named Mihan."

Mihan. That name sounded very familiar. So familiar it stirred a sick feeling in my gut.

She must have noticed how it affected me. "You fought against her with Azrael and Sloan at a place called Calfkiller River. She'd possessed the body of a human woman. A brunette, if I remember correctly."

The battle of Calfkiller River was where I'd died the first time—or at least that's where my human spirit died. Azrael brought me back as a full angel. It was the first time we fought Abaddon, the Destroyer. Mihan, a woman, had battled alongside him against us. Sloan had killed her.

"Why would you entrust Nulterra's key to a demon?" I asked.

Cassiel shook her head. "Mihan didn't fall with the Morning Star. She was converted later and joined Abaddon's ranks after she'd been given the key."

I raked my fingers back through my hair. "You've got to be kidding me."

"Afraid not. And unfortunately, the key was lost."

"So if we find the Nulterra Gate, how the hell will we get inside? I assume my power won't work to open it."

"No. Your gift won't open it anymore than it could open the gate to Eden."

I swore under my breath. "Have any suggestions?"

"The keys would not have been destroyed along with their masters. Abaddon's key must still be in existence, probably passed to his daughter, Anya."

"And Anya, if she's still alive, is in Nulterra. That does us no good."

"Mihan's should still be somewhere here on Earth."

"Did she have any children?"

"No. Her key would have passed to another guardian."

"What do the keys look like?"

She shrugged "I never saw them."

"Who did?"

She stared at me, pressing her lips closed.

"Let me guess, Mihan and the Destroyer?"

"Yes."

"I thought you were supposed to know everything, Cassiel."

Her lips spread into a thin smile. "Only most things."

I sighed. "Fury won't be happy about this." I sat back, letting the back of my skull thump against the headboard. "Can you hand me my phone? It's on your nightstand."

She picked it up, unplugged it, and handed it to me.

"Can I have some privacy?" I asked.

"Nope."

Shaking my head, I swiped open the screen and searched for Fury's name in my recent-call list. When I found it, I paused.

"What's the matter?" Cassiel asked

"I can't remember which day Fury had her baby."

"It's been two days here."

I pinched the bridge of my nose. "You know what I'm thankful for?"

Her brow lifted.

I held up my phone. "Cell phone towers and satellites that keep track of which time zone I'm in. This shit hurts my brain."

She laughed. "I wish I could say it gets easier."

I tapped Fury's name in the call list, and the phone dialed her number. It was just after six in the morning. Any other time, Fury would have been awake. Certainly having a newborn would only increase those odds, right?

The phone rang. And rang. And rang.

She finally picked up. "Hello?" Her voice was gravelly and quiet.

"Did I wake you?"

"Yes."

"Really?"

"I just had a baby, Warren, and I'm on narcotics. What do you want?"

I decided to save the bad news about the key for when she was feeling a little less lethal. "I just wanted to make sure you and the baby were all right."

"At six a.m.?"

"Sorry. There was an attack on Wolf Gap last night. Moloch, the Archangel of—"

"I know who Moloch is."

"I don't think I like you on drugs," I said.

"Oh my god, Warren."

"We think Moloch tried to attack Echo-5 last night. There were several demons with him."

"So why are you worried about me? They're after *your* kid, not mine."

Her bitchiness might prove useful. "Are you sure about that?" I asked slowly.

There was silence on her end for a second. "What do you mean?"

Cassiel was watching me.

"How long are they planning to keep you at the hospital?"

"You're being weird. Is someone listening to you?" Her voice was quiet.

"I just wanted to know when you're going home. Azrael said he can help out if you need him."

God, I hoped she understood my cryptic meaning. I couldn't say much more without evoking the wrath of Cassiel.

"I'll call him now," she said.

"You should do that. How are you feeling?"

"Goodbye, Warren." Her *tone* had returned.

"Bye, Fury. I'll be in—" The line went dead. I pulled it back and looked at it. *Call disconnected.* "She hung up on me."

Cassiel stood back up. "What's with the two of you? Your whole demeanor shifted when she answered the phone."

"There's nothing with the two of us."

She pointed at me. "Lying. Again."

"You really have to stop doing that."

"How about a compromise? If you can't tell me something, just don't say anything. I'd rather have silence than deceit."

"And you won't force me to tell you something I don't want to?"

Her head tilted. "Depends on how badly I want to know."

"Figures."

She picked up my clothes off the floor and tossed them to me. "Get dressed. You need to find me something decent to eat around here. Or is that even possible out here in the boonies?"

"Oh yeah. It's possible." I smiled. "How about Tupelo Honey?"

CHAPTER FOURTEEN

*M*aybe breakfast at Sloan's favorite restaurant wasn't my smartest idea. Even Adrianne looked at me funny when I suggested it that morning. Still, she and Azrael and Reuel went with us.

"Has anyone talked to Nathan?" I asked.

"Briefly this morning. I told him we were going to breakfast," Azrael said.

I dialed Nathan's number. It went to voicemail, so I left a message. "Hey, it's Warren. We're on our way to Tupelo Honey in South Asheville if you'd like to join. Call me back."

He responded via text a second later. *Way ahead of you, man. Be on my way soon. Picking something up at the command center.*

I wanted to ask Nathan how many I should add to our party, but I didn't.

"Have you seen the news this morning?" Azrael asked, looking in the rearview mirror.

"No. Why?"

"Malab is all over it."

"What's Malab?" Adrianne asked.

"A small country in northern Africa. Warren killed their prime minister yesterday," Azrael said.

Adrianne whipped around in her seat.

I rolled my eyes. "Their prime minister was already dead. I killed a dangerous imposter."

"Can you look it up on your phone?" Cassiel asked. She was sandwiched in the middle seat between me and Reuel.

"Good idea."

She nudged my shoulder with hers. "I'm pretty smart."

I chuckled and swiped the phone's screen open. I googled Malab, and the entire first screen was filled with news articles announcing the death of its leader. I clicked on the first story, then played the video that popped up.

An anchorwoman was speaking over a recorded video of the windows being blown out of Malab's Capitol building. "A nation is grieving today after the mysterious death of Saare Kelifah, the prime minister of Malab."

"I think *grieving* is a stretch," I said.

"Witnesses say an explosion occurred only minutes after the close of a Cabinet meeting. The prime minister and his aide were found dead at the scene. Guards have reported two white males and one white female were present after the explosion, but their whereabouts and their involvement is currently unknown. Security footage seems to have gone offline shortly before the incident occurred."

I looked over at Reuel. "Nice job taking out the cameras."

He gave me a thumbs-up.

"Umar Tadese, chairman of the People's Liberation League, will serve as the interim prime minister until the party chooses a new leader. Tadese was unavailable for comment."

I ended the video. "Hopefully because he's busy distributing food to his people."

"Nice work, son," Azrael said.

"I couldn't have done it without these guys," I admitted.

Cassiel smiled. Reuel reached around her to offer me a fist bump. I obliged.

Azrael changed lanes. "Anyone else find it funny that Moloch was nothing more than a footnote to that video?"

"So funny," Cassiel agreed.

Reuel nodded. "I'll bet he's going to be urinated."

The entire car burst out laughing.

The restaurant was just as I remembered it. Trendy. Eclectic. Super Americana. And it smelled the closest to Eden as any place I'd been on Earth.

"How many?" the hostess asked just inside the front door.

"Six, maybe seven," I answered with a gulp.

Azrael glanced over. "Think she'll come?"

"No, but just in case."

He looked at Adrianne. "Do you think Sloan will come?"

I was so desperate to know, I wondered if anyone might sense the anxiety radiating off me.

Adrianne shrugged. "I texted her, but she didn't answer."

Cassiel was watching me carefully. Then she put her hand on the small of my back. My heart rate slowed and the tense muscles at the base of my neck relaxed.

As much as I hated the Council's ruling, and as much as I hated Cassiel being my unshakable shadow, it wasn't *all bad* having her around. Reuel was great company, but Cassiel seemed to understand me.

She was also easy on the eyes, which was never a bad thing. NAG had given her a pair of black tactical cargoes and a loose gray T-shirt. It didn't have quite the same effect as Fury's suction-tight tank top (few outfits did), but now she looked like she belonged in civilized society and less like she was heading to the set of the next *Lara Croft* film.

I smiled, gratefully, at her. And she hooked her arm around mine.

The hostess led us to a round table tucked into a nook in the back corner of the room. I pulled out a chair.

Adrianne pointed to a seat across the table. "Save that corner seat facing out for Nathan. Otherwise, he'll be looking over his shoulder the whole time at what's happening behind him."

"Why?" Cassiel asked, sitting next to me.

"It's a cop thing," Azrael answered.

"He's a police officer too?" she asked.

I shook my head. "Not anymore."

The waitress, a young redhead, stopped at our table. "Good mornin', folks. What can I getcha to drink?" She looked at Adrianne first.

"Orange juice."

"Same," Cassiel said.

Azrael ordered coffee.

"Coffee for me too, please," I said.

She looked at Reuel.

I started to answer for him. "He'll have a—"

"I can order for myself," he said with a wild grin.

I chuckled and balanced my elbows on the table. "That's right you can."

The waitress was looking at us weird.

"I'll have milk, chocolate." He hovered his hand about a foot off the tabletop. "Big one."

She smiled and scribbled on her notepad. "You got it."

When she left, Adrianne shook her head. "It's so strange hearing you talk, Reuel."

"It's really funny when he gets stuff wrong," Azrael said, looking over his menu.

"What do you recommend ordering?" Cassiel asked me.

"Everything's good."

"My favorite is the Pecan Pie French Toast," Adrianne told her. "Or the Carolina Steak and Eggs or any of the omelets. The biscuits are amazing too, with gobs of blackberry jam."

I grinned. "Hungry, Adrianne?"

She stuck out her tongue at me. "Shut up, Warren. I'm eating for two."

"When are you due?" Cassiel asked.

"August twenty-fourth." She beamed at Azrael, who was scowling at Cassiel. "We just found out it's a boy."

"Congratulations," Cassiel said. "Have you thought about names?"

Adrianne looked at Azrael. He gave a slight nod.

"We've talked about naming him Michael." Adrianne smiled at me. "After his big brother."

"Really?" I asked, sitting back in my chair.

Azrael put his arm around Adrianne. "If that's OK with you."

"Of course it is. I'm honored."

"I never knew Michael was your middle name until Azrael recently told me," Adrianne said.

"It's more than a middle name." Cassiel turned toward me. "That's the name registered in Eden."

"Like Sloan's demon mom used to call her *Praea*?" Adrianne asked.

Azrael nodded. "Exactly. When an angel or Seramorta is created, they're often give two names. One for Earth, and one for *elsewhere*."

"Michael doesn't sound like an angel name. Sounds like a human name," Adrianne said.

"Very much so." Cassiel leveled her gaze with Azrael across the table. "It's been discussed if that was by design."

"What do you mean?" I asked her.

Azrael spoke before she could. "She means she's over-thinking this as she does everything else. But I guess it is part of her job description."

The waitress interrupted the conversation with our drinks. "Any questions about the menu?"

I was still staring at my father, and he was doing his best to avoid making eye contact. "I think we're all ready to order," he said, signaling the end of our conversation.

As I ordered the Shoo Mercy Omelette, a familiar sound turned my head toward the window. A moment later, a black Dodge Challenger SRT Hellcat pulled into the parking lot.

My car.

I got up from my seat. "Excuse me."

"Men and their toys," Adrianne said as I walked to the restaurant's front door.

Nathan was angling out of the driver's seat when I walked outside. It appeared he was alone. I stood on the curb and crossed my arms. "I knew that sound a mile away. You here to rub it in?" I asked as he crossed the parking lot.

He tossed me the keys, and I caught them midair. "You said it had been a while since you'd ridden in a car. Thought you might like to drive one."

I hooked the keyring over my middle finger and jingled them. "I wonder if I remember how."

"Like riding a bike, my friend."

"Nice hat," I said, reading the "Zombie Response Team" patch on the front. "Speaking of zombies, you're gonna love our story from Africa."

"Ooo, can't wait to hear it." He took a step backward off the curb. "Come on, tell me about it while we cruise up the mountain and back."

"Later. Maybe we can take the car over to see Shannon after breakfast. I need to check on that situation."

"I'm sure Shannon would *love* to see us," he said with a sarcastic laugh as we neared our group.

I thought of Cassiel. Nothing in me wanted to tell Cassiel about Shannon Green, Nathan's ex. Much less did I want Cassiel to meet her. But given the circumstances, if there was a chance Shannon's child was the Morning Star, I needed that information sooner rather than later.

Cassiel was watching through the window. "Not sure what to do about my warden though," I said with a frustrated sigh.

"That woman you're with?"

"Yeah."

"She looks like an elf from *Lord of the Rings*," he said quietly.

Couldn't argue with that.

"Are you and her...?" He made a fist with one hand, then inserted his other index finger into it.

"Ha. She wishes."

He laughed.

"Where's the woman with you?"

"Sloan and I talked about her coming. Even called her dad to see if he could come hang out with Iliana." He looked down at his boots. "But she decided at the last minute it probably wouldn't be a good idea for anyone." He grinned. "Least of all, me."

I laughed to cover the sadness surely etched in my eyes and turned toward the restaurant door. "No more issues at Echo-5?"

He opened the door and held it for me. "The rest of the night was quiet."

"Thank the Father for that."

"What's your plan? You sticking around for a while?"

"Iliana's safety is my priority, but as soon as we're sure the compound is secure, I must go. I have some pressing matters to deal with."

"The stuff with Samael?" he asked as we walked by the bar.

"Yes." At least Nathan couldn't tell when I wasn't being completely honest.

He deserved to know the truth about the Council's ruling

against Iliana, but that didn't mean I would actually tell him. Hopefully, I could find the Morning Star before Iliana's birthday and change the Council's mind, and no one would have to be the wiser.

Reuel, who was sitting at the end of the table, got up to let Nathan squeeze past him to the chair in the corner. I sat back down next to Cassiel.

In my absence, the waitress had delivered two baskets of biscuits: one for Reuel, and one for the rest of us.

Cassiel peeled one open, and steam rose off the fluffy, flaky insides. "This looks promising," she said, reaching for the blackberry jam.

"Have you guys ordered?" Nathan asked, picking up the menu at his place.

"Yeah, we didn't know when you'd be here," Azrael said.

Adrianne looked over at Nathan. "How's my goddaughter this morning?"

"She was still sleeping when I left. She is not a morning person, just like her mama."

My heart twisted.

Cassiel picked up her biscuit and bit into it. Her eyes melted with delight. Then she slowly wiped buttery crumbs off the corners of her mouth. "OK. I'm a believer, not all food on Earth is pure *kupai*."

I laughed and handed her a napkin.

Adrianne looked confused. "Kupai?"

"It means *shit*," Azrael translated.

"Can I ask you a question?" Adrianne asked Cassiel.

Cassiel wiped her mouth and nodded her head. "Sure."

"Azrael told me last night you are part of the group that made up the rule that angels can't speak English. Why is that?"

"That's a good question." Cassiel put her napkin down beside her biscuit and folded her hands in her lap. "When angels were first sent to this planet, it was a safeguard to keep us from being too powerful here on Earth. It's difficult to recruit followers if you're unable to talk to them."

"That's not the only reason," Azrael said.

Cassiel sighed. "We also hoped it would discourage intraspecies relations."

"You didn't want the angels mating with humans?" Nathan laughed. "How did that work out for you?"

"Obviously, not as well as we had hoped. And that really isn't the reason any longer. After the first angel war, the fallen disregarded the rule, and began tempting man with their powers and abilities." Cassiel looked at me. "That was how they were luring souls to Nulterra before the gate was sealed."

"That was when the language became a sign of allegiance. Only the fallen spoke the earthly languages," Azrael added.

"What about you, Az? You didn't talk to Warren's mother?" Nathan asked.

He shook his head. "Not in English."

"He taught her Katavukai," I said. "She speaks it better than I do."

"Don't you think the law is a little outdated?" Adrianne clearly wasn't convinced. "I mean, Warren and Azrael haven't tried to take over the world, right?" She pointed at Cassiel. "And do *you* plan to take over while you're here speaking English?"

A satisfied smile spread across Azrael's face. He crossed his arms and looked at Cassiel. We all did. And for a moment, she was speechless.

"I've learned from my years in law enforcement that bad people intent on doing bad things will find a way regardless of the rules. I'm sure it's the same for your people," Nathan said.

Reuel cupped his hand around his mouth and lowered his voice to a loud whisper. "We are not people."

Nathan elbowed him. "You know what I mean."

"Maybe your rules are doing more harm than good." Adrianne laid her head against Azrael's shoulder. "Nothing bad has come from this union."

Cassiel stared at them for a moment. Then she slightly bowed her head. "Perhaps you are right, Adrianne. The Council is not above changing its mind."

God, I hoped so.

The waitress returned to our table with a pot of coffee and poured Nathan's mug full without having to ask him. "Good morning, Mr. McNamara. What can I get you for breakfast?"

"Hi, Ruthie," he said, smiling up at her.

Azrael scowled. "First-name basis? Really?"

Nathan shrugged. "It's my wife's favorite place." He handed Ruthie the menu he hadn't even opened. "I'll have the sweet-potato pancakes and a side of bacon. Remind me before I leave, I need to place a to-go order."

"Of cheese grits?" the girl asked.

Sloan's favorite.

"Yes, ma'am," Nathan said, handing her his menu.

"I'll have it ready."

Thankfully, Azrael diverted the conversation. "Have you heard anymore about the situation in Italy?"

I sipped my coffee. "Yes and no. You know how Cassiel told you about the prime minister of Malab saying he was that guy...?" I couldn't remember his name. Snapping my fingers, I pointed at Cassiel.

"Haile Menelek," she said.

Azrael nodded. "Yes, I remember."

"His soul was purple as well."

Azrael crossed his arms on the tabletop. "And you really think Haile Menelek came back from the dead?" Azrael asked, looking at both me and Cassiel.

Nathan sat up straight in his chair. "Zombies?"

"He wasn't eating brains or anything, but yeah. Sort of," I said.

Nathan pointed to his hat. "Sign me the hell up."

I grinned.

Azrael shook his head. "Zombies aren't possible. I don't understand. I killed Haile Menelek and sentenced him to Nulterra myself."

"If you killed him, that would explain why he had the Archangel's mark," I said.

Adrianne's held up her hands. "Human inbound. Please stop talking about killing people," she said in a loud whisper.

The waitress returned and gathered the empty bread baskets. "Can I get anyone else anything right now? More biscuits, maybe?"

Reuel nodded with a wide smile.

"Coming right up," she said, walking back to the kitchen.

When the waitress was safely out of earshot, I turned back to Azrael. "If you killed him, that would explain the mark, but it wouldn't explain the purple magic."

He sighed. "It's not magic."

"Then the power, or whatever it is," I said.

"Fury can see power. Have you asked her?"

"I didn't think about it, actually."

"Because you're too busy thinking it's magic." With a huff, he pulled out his cell phone, tapping the screen a few times before putting it to his ear.

I pointed at the phone. "Be warned. She's bitchy."

Nathan chuckled. "What else is new?"

"I need your help," Azrael said a moment later without a greeting. "Hold on. I'm putting you on speakerphone."

Azrael tapped the screen again, then laid the phone in the center of the table. "Fury, it's a little loud in here, can you hear me?"

"Yeah. Az, I'm not on your payroll anymore. What do you want?"

Nathan and I exchanged a smile.

"I'm here with Warren. What do you know about the color purple?"

"It's what you get when you mix red and blue."

A few of us (not Azrael) chuckled.

Az frowned. "I'm talking about spirits, Fury. Do you ever see colors when you look at angels or their powers? Like a purple mist or smoke?"

There was a pause. "Nulterra has a purple mist. I saw it in Theta's vision, and I've seen it on angels who have recently come from there."

Everyone at the table sat up straight, including me.

Azrael picked up the phone again. "Thanks, Fury. That was very helpful. We'll call you later." He ended the call and put the phone down by his cutlery.

"You didn't tell her *why* you wanted to know?" I asked

"Fury has enough to worry about."

Cassiel touched my arm. Then she covered her mouth with both hands.

"What is it?" I asked.

"The keys."

"Right. They're missing. You already told me that."

"What if they aren't missing? There's only one way a human spirit could have come back to Earth." Her words had all the gravity of a planet.

"Shit. The Nulterra Gate," I said.

"What if the gate was opened, and it really was Haile Menelek we encountered in Malab?" she asked.

"I'm a little afraid to ask what the hell y'all are talking about," Adrianne said.

Nathan balanced his elbows on the table. "I think they're saying someone opened the gate to Hell and let out a bunch of criminals. Am I right?"

I just nodded.

Adrianne's face wilted into a frown. "Yep. Sorry I asked."

The blood drained from Azrael's face. He put his hands on his head and scooted his chair back from the table. He looked at me and visibly swallowed. "And Vito Saez is in Italy."

"Excuse me?" Cassiel asked.

"The murders Samael is investigating in Italy. Same MO as Vito Saez."

Worry filled her eyes. "The monster of Venice?"

"Yes. If it's true...I hate to think what else might be possible," he said.

Cassiel touched her temples. "I'm afraid to think about it."

"But, Warren, didn't you tell me the victims' souls have been purple?" Azrael asked.

"Yeah."

"That makes little sense. They haven't been to Nulterra."

I shrugged. "If Saez has spent the last two hundred and seventy years soaking up the energy of Nulterra, maybe it transferred onto them."

"I think Iliana rubs off on people," Nathan said. "When Azrael's memory was jacked up without the blood stone, we noticed he improved around me and Sloan even when Illy wasn't around."

Cassiel nodded. "It might be possible. The Father has always said humans can comfort others with the comfort they have received from the Angels of Ministry."

"So this Vito guy would be even more deadly?" Adrianne asked, looking a little bewildered.

No one answered. Probably because no one wanted to.

I turned toward Cassiel. "Do you think the gate could still be open?"

"I don't know, but I think you'll have a lot more help looking for it now."

I looked at Azrael. "I need to get back to Italy."

"Yes, you do. Don't worry about things here. Echo-5 is secure," he said.

I stood from the table. Cassiel followed. Reuel looked sad that we were leaving before our food came.

"You know what?" I put my hand on his huge shoulder. "I want you to stay here. Protect Iliana for me?"

He stood and offered me his hand. "Of course I will."

I pumped his massive fist. "I'll see you in a couple of days. Maybe sooner."

"Be careful, Warren," Adrianne said.

"Always."

Azrael got up. "Go by the command center. In the armory, you have a go-bag already packed in the closet. In it, you'll find a passport and a credit card with your new identity. I packed the rest of the supplies myself."

"I have a new identity?" I asked.

Nathan grinned. "Yeah, you do."

"Did you have something to do with it?"

He just kept smiling.

I groaned. "I can only imagine."

"We won't need passports," Cassiel said.

"No, but we might need cash." I pulled my keys—err, Nathan's keys—from my pocket. "Mind if we take the car?"

"It's yours, isn't it?" He jerked his head toward Azrael. "I'll catch a ride home with these guys."

"Thanks."

"Enjoy it."

I gripped the keys. "Oh, I will. When I get back, we do need to visit Shannon."

"I can't wait," he said, laughing.

Cassiel and I started away from the table.

"Wait." Azrael grabbed my arm.

When I turned, he was taking off the blood stone necklace. "Wear this. I want to see what happens when you get back."

I gripped the chain, letting the stone dangle from my hand. "Won't your memory be affected?"

"My memory will be fine for a while. I've taken it off periodically to be sure. If it is Saez, my memories will be more important to you than to me. And if I can see what you see, maybe I can help."

"OK." I put on the necklace and tucked it beneath my shirt. "I'll see you when I get back."

He went to shake my hand, but I pulled him into a hug. I lowered my voice as much as I could. "I didn't tell Nathan about the ruling against Iliana, but if anything happens and I don't make it back..."

"I'll do what's necessary. Don't worry. She's not going anywhere."

"And Fury?"

"I've already talked to her. I'll make sure she takes the child somewhere safe."

I pulled back and nodded.

When I turned to Cassiel, she was glaring.

"You ready?" I offered her my hand.

She looked at my hand but didn't accept it. "Yes. Let's go."

The V8 rumbled to life underneath me as Cassiel got into the passenger's seat. I laid my head back against the headrest, closing my eyes to enjoy the gentle vibration. I smiled. "Oh yeah."

"Do you two need some privacy?" Cassiel asked, slamming her door.

My eyes popped open. "Whoa. Why are you so pissed?"

"What did you say to Azrael?"

I kept my mouth shut.

She crossed her arms, looking at me expectantly.

"You told me this morning you'd rather have my silence than my deceit. So I'm not lying to you."

She reached for my hand, and I jerked it away from her. I wagged my finger in front of her face. "Oh no. That's cheating."

"Did you tell him to hide Iliana?"

I bit down on the insides of my lips.

She sat back hard in her seat and stared out the windshield. "We will find her, you know."

"You may not have to if I can find the Morning Star first."

"The Council won't change their minds."

"I'm not trying to change the Council's minds. Just yours." I put the car in reverse and looked over my shoulder to back out of the space.

"My mind is made up. You'd better get used to that idea."

"We'll see," I said, turning the car. I glanced back at the restaurant. Our group inside was watching from the window. I waved and revved the powerful engine. "You might want to buckle up."

"Are you serious—"

I dropped the clutch and peeled through the parking lot.

Cassiel swore and grabbed the handle by her head.

I laughed and slowed the car before pulling onto the freeway. "I told you to buckle up."

She snapped her seatbelt, then held onto the door handle.

"You can relax," I said, glancing at her white knuckles. "Enjoy the view. Asheville's beautiful."

It certainly was this time of year. The purples and yellows of early spring were just popping against the rich green canvas of the roadside. I turned onto my favorite winding road and let the wheels hug the turns as we wound up the mountainside.

Cassiel was still gripping the door handle like she wasn't immortal. "Where are we going?"

"Home," I said with a sigh.

"Home?"

"You'll see."

We rode the rest of the way in silence drowned out by the

engine. God, I loved this car. I finally turned into my old driveway and put the car in park in front of the three-car garage.

Cassiel looked up at the house. "What is this place?"

I leaned against the steering wheel and stared up. "It used to be my house."

She turned and looked at me.

I sighed and pushed the door open. "Come on. Let's get this over with."

We climbed the front steps to the path that led to the front door. The locks had been replaced. I used my power on the deadbolt, but nothing happened. It actually made me smile. I tried my fingerprint on the reader instead. There was a small chime and a *click*. I opened the door. "Welcome to my former abode."

Cassiel walked inside first. My heart sank as I followed. The place looked almost exactly the same as I'd left it. Memories flooded back like a tsunami.

Watching college basketball with Nate in the living room.

Our friend Taiya dancing drunk on the dining table.

Kissing my almost-wife in the very spot we were standing.

I cleared my throat and walked past Cassiel. "I wonder where they've set up the armory."

I walked down the hall first. Big mistake. At the mouth of the hallway, the large wooden door on the left led to the master bedroom. The bedroom I'd shared with Sloan.

Cassiel stopped in front of its heavy wooden door. "What's in here?"

"I don't want to go in there." Then I noticed the lock panel that had been installed. "But that's new."

"It's sophisticated too. Retina scan," she said.

"I guess it wouldn't hurt to have a look." I leaned toward the scanner. The panel lit up green and the lock tumbled. She pushed the door open. I fell back a step.

"Looks like we found the armory," she said.

The walls were covered in pegboard with hooks holding what looked like every kind of firearm known to man. Long-range rifles to our left. Assault rifles to the right. A smaller collection of handguns lined the wall surrounding the door; handguns were almost useless against the supernatural.

Against the far wall, a large safe covered the only window. I suspected explosives were inside. And where my king bed had once been, a large padded table was set with cleaning supplies.

"They know they can't kill us, right?" Cassiel asked, wandering the room in a daze.

I smiled. "Yep. They also know how to slow us down."

"Where's the bag you're looking for?"

"In the closet."

I walked into the bathroom and stopped. It was completely unchanged. My eyes fixed on the tub Sloan had loved so much. It had been one of the selling points of the house.

"Warren?" Standing behind me, Cassiel's hands came to rest on my sides. Peace flooded from her fingertips, and I relaxed.

After a second, I turned around. "What are you doing to me?"

"Helping," she said.

"How?"

"Just imparting a bit of home."

"It feel like..." My brain was struggling to find the words.

"I imagine it feels a lot like when you first met Sloan," she said.

I fell back a step. "How did you know that?"

"It's who we are. The spirit in us is part of Eden. It's probably what drew you to her in the first place."

Nothing in me wanted to discuss my feelings for Sloan. "The closet is in here."

On the other side of the bathroom, the master closet had been stripped of most of its shelves. The wall where Sloan had once hung her clothes was now covered with hooks holding tactical backpacks. They were all labeled. The thinnest of them had my name.

I picked it up and looked inside the main zipper. From what I could see, there were a couple of changes of clothes inside. The front pocket had the passport. I flipped it open.

"Oh my god."

"What's the matter?" Cassiel asked.

I turned it around to show her my photo and new name.

She covered her mouth to stifle a laugh. "Angelo Suave?"

I stuffed it back into the bag. "Nathan thinks he's funny."

"He is. That's hilarious."

I smiled, caught off guard that she had a sense of humor. Then I turned back to the wall. Fury's pack was on the bottom left. I grabbed it and handed it her. "Get the clothes out of here. We'll put them in my bag."

There was a crackle like static in my ears. Then I heard Samael's voice far away. "Warren, we have victim number five. Can you come to Venice?"

"On my way."

"What?" Cassiel asked, handing me Fury's clothes.

I stuffed them into my backpack. "It was Samael. He's found another body. We need to go."

CHAPTER FIFTEEN

*I*t was chilly and raining when we crossed through the spirit line onto the mainland near the airport outside Venice. Cassiel decided our arrival on any of the small, crowded islands that made up the city might be too conspicuous. "Water taxis are this way," she said, looking at a map. Then she walked off without waiting for me.

"Cassiel?"

She stopped and turned.

"Water taxis aren't free."

She looked surprised. Not because we needed money, but probably because I'd thought of it before she did. I grinned as she walked past me in the direction the sign was pointing toward the airport entrance.

"We'll need euros," I said, jogging to catch up with her.

"I know that, Warren."

I winked as I held the door. She cracked a small grin and walked inside.

My eyes searched the lobby until they landed on a sign with major credit logos on it. "Foreign exchange this way."

The woman behind the desk smiled as we approached, but

the smile faded as I neared the counter. So typical. She greeted us in Italian.

I took out my wallet. "Do you speak—"

"*Buona sera,*" Cassiel said with a smile. Then she handed the woman my credit card, and (I assume) asked for euros.

The woman looked at the card, then at me, then back at the card. Her smile magically returned. "Damn it, Nathan," I whispered, shaking my head.

When the woman finished, she handed Cassiel the cash and handed me the card. "Signore Suave," she said, unable to tame her teasing lips.

Cassiel snickered behind her hand.

"Thanks," I said, shaking my head at both of them. I looked at Cassiel. "You ready?"

"Oh yeah. This might even be fun." She held onto my arm, and I let her, trusting that she wouldn't use her powers for evil. As we neared the door we'd come in, she stopped and looked up at a television mounted overhead.

It was a news report, but I couldn't understand what the reporter was saying. One word in the caption was clear: *omicidio.*

"Are they talking about our victim?" I asked her.

She nodded. "I think so. They say another gruesome discovery was made this afternoon at an apartment building near Piazza San Marco, St. Mark's Square. They are calling it too graphic for public television."

I shuddered. "I'll bet that's where we find Samael."

"Let's go."

Our water taxi across the lagoon was a large orange boat with a tight inside cabin. We moved all the way to the back of the U-shaped bench, and there was a very obvious gap between me and the skittish woman to my right. Cassiel moved closer to me. "Take my hand," she whispered.

I narrowed my eyes.

"It will make you less conspicuous to the people here. They're already terrified. Let's not make it worse."

"No funny business?" I asked.

"I promise."

When our hands touched, and our fingers meshed, her warm energy flowed through me. *Home.*

Instantly, the other passengers relaxed. When Sloan and I were together, she had a theory that our powers somehow balanced each other out. I wondered if Cassiel had a similar effect.

Looking down at our hands, I felt the stress of Earth ease in my chest.

"Better?" she asked as if she could sense it.

"Yes."

She squeezed my fingers.

"Mind if I check out for a minute and take a quick trip down Azrael's memory lane?" I asked.

She looked at the lump under my shirt where the blood stone rested. "Do you know how rare that thing is?"

"Yes, I do. Do you mind?"

"No."

I closed my eyes, and the world around me faded to black. I thought back to the first time Azrael ever encountered the work of il mostro di Venezia. His memory took over as *my* memory.

It was dark, and I was walking along a cobblestone street... or maybe a wide alleyway between buildings lit only by moonlight. A woman's wails drifted along the quiet breeze, the only sound louder than the staccato *clip clop* of my heels against the stones.

I stopped at the open front door from which the cries were emanating. Fresh death seemed to make the building breathe. Its walls seemed to expand and contract as I stepped into the narrow entryway.

The sound was coming from the top of the stairs.

I took them two at a time until I reached the landing. Looked right. Looked left. Golden light flickered against the wood grain of an open door.

I stepped inside. A man was holding a woman in a night-dress as she screamed over the body of a young woman on the bed. The man drew back with alarm when I entered, pulling the crying woman away from me. I held up both my hands and took each step slowly toward the dead girl.

Picking up the candlestick holder that teetered dangerously on the edge of the bedside table, I moved it over the corpse on the bed. Her body was naked, ribs protruding like a washboard. Bruises covered her pale arms and legs, signs of beatings with a rod or a cane.

Her head was mounted on the headboard post, missing its eyes I knew to be brown and green. This girl, an orphan raised by the church, had approached me only days before near the fish market in the *piazzetta*. Her curiosity had given away her gift long before I'd been close enough to see her eyes.

Now, her mouth was gaping enough for me to see something white inside. I pried it open, and a bloody green eyeball rolled out. I barely caught it in my gloved hand.

"*Smettila! Smettila!*" the man screamed, still holding the woman.

I looked around the room. The girl's spirit had to be close, as I was the only Angel of Death in Venice. That was when I saw her crouched in the small space between the bed and the wall. Placing the eyeball carefully on her body's chest, I walked toward her, cautiously kneeling near her feet.

She was crying.

I offered her my hand. "*Ceyet ai kayam,*" I said gently, telling her not to be afraid.

Shaking, she put her hand in mine. Then together we walked out of the house.

"Only one more stop." The voice of the boat's captain jarred me from the vision. Quickly glancing around the boat, I saw we were the last passengers on board.

"Are you Americans?" he asked, his accent as thick as his black hair.

"Yes," I answered before Cassiel could deny it.

"Lots of excitement at the square today. Be careful," he said.

I straightened in my seat. I didn't realize I'd slumped against Cassiel. "Are you talking about the murder? We saw it on the news at the airport."

"Yes. They say we have a serial killer. Three murders now in the past two weeks."

"Do you know where?" Cassiel asked.

He pointed off the side of the boat. "The one they found today is just over there. See the yellow building with the flag?"

I looked out the window. "The red flag?"

"Yes. That's it. I heard the body was, how do you say..."

"Decapitated?" I asked.

"Yes. Decapitated."

Cassiel looked at me. "How did you know that?"

I still hadn't told her I'd known about these suspicious murders for a while. In lieu of an answer, I pulled the blood stone out from under my shirt.

She nodded.

"They say all the victims eyes were found in their throats," the boat driver added.

Cassiel made a sour face.

I leaned against her shoulder and spoke quietly. "Same MO."

"Were the other murders close by?" she asked him.

"All of them. The bodies have been found on the Calle dei Morti, which makes it, how you say...creepy? In English it means the Street of the Dead."

I sighed. "So I've heard. Do the police have any leads?"

He shrugged as he steered the boat toward the dock. "If

they do, they are not telling the public. And I think they would. The city is afraid. My boat is always full. The past few days, less than half."

Once the boat was secured to the wooden dock, Cassiel and I got up. I shook the captain's hand on our way out. "Thanks for the information."

"You are welcome. Be safe," he said with a smile.

Even in the drizzling rain, Venice looked like a postcard. Exactly how I'd imagined it would be. A clock tower and domed cathedrals in the distance. Ornate buildings lining the water. Arched bridges marking the inlets. The air smelled of fish and seawater.

A street vendor was selling umbrellas by the docks. Other things too: Carnival masks, shot glasses, magnets of the statue of *David's* penis. I selected a black umbrella and handed the vendor the cash.

"Thank you," I said, taking a step back and opening it over my head and Cassiel's. "You ready to go check out the mob?"

"Where's Samael?" she asked, searching the sky like he might fly by.

"Close." I pressed a finger to my ear and called out to him. "I'm near St. Mark's Square. Where are you?"

"Follow the police," he replied in my mind.

I looked around us. A block up ahead along the lagoon, two police officers in black uniforms with safety-yellow vests were guarding a temporary metal fence blocking the side street. "This way." I nudged the small of Cassiel's back.

As we approached, a cop stepped forward with his hand raised to stop us. He said something in Italian that I assumed meant the area was closed. Cassiel argued with him. He argued back.

It was kind of entertaining.

Beyond them, a crowd of reporters and police were gathered at the entrance to the yellow building we'd seen from the boat.

Samael wasn't among them, but he was somewhere, maybe inside.

With an exasperated huff, the officer finally motioned us forward.

"Come on," Cassiel said, leading me through the gap in the fence.

"What did you say to him?" I asked.

"I told him we had a vacation rental from an owner of one of the apartments and that we were late for check-in. He said the building was closed, but I insisted that we be able to look for our host. When he refused, I threatened to call the American embassy. I guess he decided I wasn't worth the hassle."

"Sometimes I feel the same way," I said with a grin.

She elbowed me in the ribs.

"American, huh?" I asked, surprised.

"You're the one with a passport."

The street was paved with large concrete bricks, and it was a block and a half to the three-story building. Samael was walking out the front door when we reached it. It was weird seeing him in modern clothes: khaki pants and a navy polo under a tan raincoat. On his shoulder was a leather bag. When he spotted us, he gestured us forward.

I collapsed the umbrella to make it easier to press through the crowd, but the onlookers were reluctant to let us pass. I looked back at Cassiel, then dropped her hand. Immediately, the crowd moved away from me—like a clove of garlic dropped into a sea of vampires.

Another set of officers tried to block our way as Cassiel followed me up the steps to the entrance. Samael stepped between them and spoke in Italian. Then he looked at me. "Come. I told them you are with me."

My head pulled back. "Who do they think you are?"

He reached into his inside-jacket pocket and produced an ID badge.

I smiled. "Interpol, David Miller." He'd been wearing a David Miller name tag the first time we'd met on Earth. "Very impressive. Nice man purse."

He held up the leather bag. "It's a satchel."

"OK," I said with a laugh. "What's going on here?"

The entrance hall was crowded with uniformed and plain-clothed police. We followed Samael up the stairs. "The body was found here this afternoon when she failed to report in at work. She's a shopkeeper for her family's jewelry store near the Rialto Bridge."

"Is the body still here?" Cassiel asked when we reached the second floor.

"Yes, but they are getting ready to move it. You're here just in time." He turned right and flashed his badge to another officer standing watch at one of the doorways. The man moved out of our way.

The apartment was small and dimly lit by a single bulb in the overhead lamp and the storm-filtered sunlight barely making it through the window. A photographer was snapping pictures. A forensics team was looking for fingerprints.

Samael led us to the bedroom where the naked body of a woman was stretched across the bed. Like the others, the center of her chest had been mutilated, and her arms and legs were each tied to the bed's four posts. Staring at us from the footboard post was her head, the eyes missing and the cheeks streaked with dried blood.

"My god," Cassiel whispered, covering her mouth.

A tall woman—as tall as me—walked over from where she'd been giving directions to a second photographer. She had silky black hair and wore an expensive-looking navy pants suit. Her hand was outstretched as we approached. "You must be the other agents from Interpol," she said in perfect English with a beautiful Italian accent.

I shook the woman's hand but didn't give our names.

"I am Inspector Santoro. I'm afraid we have little need for your services, as this is a local matter."

Cassiel shook the inspector's hand, then held onto it. "It's lovely to meet you. Please give us your *full* report."

The woman stared blankly for a moment. Then she nodded. "The victim's name is Amalia Cosentino, age nineteen. The body was discovered at approximately twelve o'clock today by Dario Cosentino, the victim's father. Like the others, she was strangled first and then decapitated.

"The eyes were removed and the chest carving was done while the victim was still alive. You can see that by the amount of blood present on the skin."

"The eyes are in the mouth?" I asked, taking a closer look at the head.

"The examination has not yet been preformed, but it's a reasonable assumption."

Cassiel walked to the bedside. "Warren."

I joined her.

"It's your mark," she whispered.

Once again, my mark had been carved into the victim's chest with something sharp. Probably the same *something* used to gouge out her eyes. I wasn't surprised, but I tried to fake it. "Oh wow."

Cassiel's eyes narrowed with suspicion. "Did you know about this?"

I tried to contain a guilty grimace and failed.

Looking back at the inspector, Cassiel pointed to the girl's chest. "Did the other bodies have this same symbol?"

"Yes. The very same."

"No one heard screaming? A commotion?" Cassiel asked.

The inspector shook her head. "We found residue from tape on the other victims' mouths. We assume this will be the same."

"What leads do you have?" I asked.

"None that are substantial. The apartment was rented to the victim's father. No one saw her leaving or coming back."

I looked at Samael. "Have you met her father?"

He nodded. "He checks out."

"We questioned him extensively," Inspector Santoro said.

I didn't care about her opinion. Only Samael's judgment really mattered. A murderer couldn't be more plain to him if they were wearing a flashing neon sign.

I looked around the room, specifically between the bed and the wall. There was nothing. Aside from us, there were no spirits, human or otherwise. And no purple smoke.

I reached for the inspector's hand again. "We'll let you take it from here. Thank you for letting us invade your crime scene."

Confused, she shook my hand. "You're welcome?" She didn't sound so sure.

When we were back outside, I picked up the umbrella I'd left near the door. The three of us used it as an excuse to huddle together and talk quietly on the street.

"Did Jaleal take the girl's soul across the spirit line?" I asked Samael.

"Yes. I considered waiting for you to get here, but..."

I shook my head. "No, you did the right thing. It's unfair to keep them here suffering for any longer than they have to be."

He looked relieved.

Cassiel grabbed me by the jacket and spun me around. "You've known about this."

"Yes."

"And you didn't think you should tell me?"

I shrugged. "I didn't know it was related until we got to Malab." *That* was the truth.

Frustrated, her head tilted toward the sky, and she pressed her eyes closed.

"So you were here soon after?" I asked Samael.

"I only missed the killer by minutes, I'd say." He looked at me. "I also just sent Jeshua to cover for me at the gate while we sort this out. Did you pass him in the breach?"

I shook my head. "We came here from Asheville. Moloch attacked Echo-5 last night."

"What do we know about these victims?" Cassiel asked.

Samael pulled a thick black file folder from his man purse and gave it to her. "I've been collecting information since I was in Thailand. The only similarity between our victims is that they all have mismatched eyes, and they were all found in the same state as what you saw upstairs."

Cassiel flipped through the file.

Samael leaned toward her and lowered his voice. "All of Vito Saez's victims died the same way a few centuries ago, so we think it might be a copycat killer."

I sighed and shook my head. "We don't think that anymore."

His brow lifted.

"We need to talk," I said.

Cassiel looked around. "Preferably somewhere dry with food. I'm famished."

I looked up and down the Street of the Dead. "Looks like there's a restaurant on the next block. How does Italian food sound?"

"Right now? Almost as good as manna. Lead the way," she said.

Osteria da Emiliano was slow (it was too late for lunch and way too early for dinner in Venice), so we were able to secure a private table in the back. The waiter brought us water, and Cassiel ordered a carafe of the house red wine. He lingered for our food order.

The entire menu was in Italian. "Cassiel, will you order for me?" I pointed at her. "And *not* fruits and vegetables. I've never been to Italy before, and dammit, I want pasta or pizza or something delicious."

Still smiling, she looked down at the menu. "It appears pizza is their specialty here."

"I mean it, Cassiel. Don't screw this up."

She laughed softly, then spoke to the waiter in Italian. She thanked him and handed over her menu. "I ordered the house-specialty pizza for all of us to share."

"*Gracias*," I said.

She rolled her eyes. "It's *grazie*, Warren."

"Same thing."

When the waiter left, Samael leaned his elbows on the table. "What's your news?"

Cassiel took a deep breath. "We believe the Nulterra Gate may have been opened."

Samael sat up straight. "Really?"

"There was an incident in Malab," she said.

"I heard the prime minister was killed."

I held up a hand. "Guilty. But he wasn't their prime minister."

"He identified himself to me as Haile Menelek," she said.

"Was it the truth?"

She nodded. "We saw him."

"His soul bore my mark," I said, tracing the symbol with my finger on my own chest.

Samael rubbed his hand down his face. "And if this is Saez, that means two souls sentenced to Nulterra have come back to Earth. Does the Father know?"

I shook my head. "We haven't had the chance to tell him because we've been jumping crisis to crisis since we left Africa. Besides, he's very busy teaching the people of Malab how to fish."

Samael's eyes narrowed with confusion. "He's what?"

"Not important. Bottom line is, he's busy and he's not coming," Cassiel said.

Samael sighed. "So now we hunt a serial killer."

I crossed my arms. "Well, if it is this Saez guy, he'll be easy to spot if he walks around in public."

"Why?" Samael asked.

"The guy from Malab had the same swirling purple *magic* as the girls, only much brighter. I could see it as plain as I could see his suit."

"What do you think it is?"

"Azrael asked Fury about it, and she said it's what Nulterra looks like. She can see it on demons who have recently come from there," I said.

Cassiel turned toward me. "So what do you want to do? Wander around Venice for however long it takes to be in the same place as the killer?"

I thought about Iliana's first birthday. "I don't have that kind of time. Too bad Sloan doesn't still have her powers. She could summon Vito Saez to us."

Cassiel straightened. "Sloan might not be able to do that, but another Angel of Life can."

"Right! Metatron can, and I need to find him anyway." I started to get up, but she grabbed my arm to hold me still.

"I swear if you drag me out of another restaurant before I get some food, I'll use your powers against you."

I cocked an eyebrow. "You can't do that," I said, though honestly, I wasn't so sure she couldn't.

Samael slid the file folder over to me. "We might have some luck on the ground ourselves. The new victims are very similar to Saez's old victims, and if he continues to follow the same pattern, we might find him."

With a heavy sigh, I opened the file. Inside were homicide reports with photos of victims stapled to them. My stomach knotted. "I'd really hoped to never see one of these again."

"You know you're the Angel of Death, right?" Cassiel asked.

"Yes, but this"—I tapped my finger on the first photo

—"isn't my job. I haven't seen reports like these since I was hunting down missing people with Nathan."

I looked closely at the first photo. The girl's eyes were mismatched.

An image flashed through my mind of the young woman Azrael had met near the market. The woman whose eyeball he'd held.

"Do all these victims have the ability to see us?" I asked.

"No. Two of them simply had an ocular defect or injury," Samael said.

"Tell me about what happened two hundred years ago." I pulled the blood stone out from under my shirt again. "I know some of the story, but I just got this thing back and everything's hazy. Fill me in on the important stuff."

"Azrael came to Venice to investigate the deaths of three girls." Samael held up three fingers. "Benedetta Giuliani, Maria Testa, and Rosannah Guerra. All of them had the ability to see angels. It was curious they'd be murdered so close together. It seemed as though someone was targeting humans with the sight."

"But how? Venice is small. Were there a lot of them here?"

"Venice wasn't so small before the fall of the Republic in the late eighteenth century," Samael said. "

Cassiel nodded. "And before Napoleon came, Venice was a thriving home for orphans who were cared for by the church and trained in art and music. Children from all over were brought here, some even by their parents hoping for a better life for them."

"To this day, there's a plaque outside the church threatening parents with curses for trying to pass off their legitimate children as orphans," Samael said with a smile.

"During that time, a small group of nuns discovered Benedetta Giuliani had a divine connection with the supernatural. She had the ability to see angels. Then Maria Testa presented the same talents, and the church made the connection with the mismatched eyes. They brought children with the gift from all over Europe," Cassiel said.

Samael crossed his arms. "Thanks to genetics and the gift being hereditary, there's still a very high population of those with the gift here compared to other places in the world. Unfortunately, that has made them a target for demons."

"Azrael believed the demon Uko was trying to rid the city of those with the sight," Cassiel said.

"Uko?" My head snapped back. "We saw him last night outside Iliana's home."

Samael sighed. "I wish I could say that surprised me."

"He's carrying a sword these days," I told him.

He smiled. "Very medieval."

"Right? I need a sword," I said.

Samael chuckled.

Cassiel wasn't amused. "In 1795 or 1796, we believe Uko began influencing Vito Saez to kill those with the gift one by one."

"Was he possessed?" I asked.

"No. Only impressionable," Cassiel said.

Samael tapped his fingertips together. "Vito had killed before the serial murders began. And he continued long after Azrael banished Uko from Venice."

"Where'd he finally catch him?" I asked.

Cassiel tapped her index finger on the table. "Right here. Many of the murders happened on the Calle dei Morti at the end, so that narrows our search area a bit."

I looked carefully at the pages spread in front of me. "Heterochromia. That's the medical diagnosis for different-colored eyes?"

"Correct," Cassiel said.

"And then and now, all the victims were beheaded with the eyes removed and forced into the throat, right?"

Samael nodded sadly. "All their heads were mounted near the bodies as they are this time." He turned his head. "The mark is new though."

"He's letting us know he's back," Cassiel said.

The waiter returned with our pizza, announcing something I didn't understand in Italian.

Cassiel forced a smile as he put it down. "Grazie."

When he was gone, we all just stared at it.

"I'm not so hungry anymore," she said with slumped shoulders.

I pushed the pie toward her. "Come on. Have a slice. Carbs and cheese are the human cure for almost all emotional turmoil."

She picked up a slice and took a deep breath. "Here goes."

I smiled, waiting for her reaction.

She bit off the tip of the pizza, and a long string of mozzarella pulled away with the slice. With an embarrassed grin, she broke the cheese string with her finger and lowered it to her mouth.

"Well?" I asked, leaning on to the table.

Her eyes closed as she slowly chewed. Then she swallowed. "You're right."

I cupped my hand around my ear. "I'm *what*?"

"You're right. I do feel better. This is the way food on Earth is supposed to taste." She sucked the crumbs off her fingertips, and I had to tear my eyes away.

Needing a distraction even more than food, I picked up a slice for myself.

The pizza was pretty damn good. Easily, the best I'd ever had. Cassiel had ordered something with spinach, fresh tomatoes, and gobs of white cheese that tasted like it had been made in Eden.

"So we'll stay for a couple of days, and if we can't find him, we'll get help from Metatron. Is that our plan?" I asked.

Cassiel's mouth was full.

"Do you even know where Metatron is?" Samael asked as we ate.

I wiped my mouth with a napkin. "I've heard he's in Lunaris. Can you confirm?"

"I know he spends a lot of time there."

"Why do you want to ask Metatron? Any Angel of Life can help us," Cassiel said.

"Because Metatron can identify the Morning Star, and if I find him, maybe you'll leave Iliana alone."

She laughed. "Have you met Metatron?"

"Not yet."

Even Samael was grinning.

"We'll be lucky to get him to help us resolve the situation here. For that, he doesn't have to leave home." She picked up her slice of pizza again. "Getting him to traipse around the planet with you looking for the Morning Star won't happen. You should prepare yourself for that now."

"You've met Sandalphon, yes?" Samael asked.

"Once. He came to Earth to help Sloan."

"That was a long time ago in Eden years," Samael said.

I shrugged. "He's a bit of a recluse."

Cassiel grinned over her wineglass. "Metatron makes Sandalphon look like the life of the party."

My shoulders slumped. It had taken me months in Eden to find Sandalphon when we needed him the last time. While that didn't equal as much time on Earth, it was still more than I wanted to spend looking for Metatron.

I set my jaw. I was *not* about to get discouraged. "I'll find him. Even if I have to get the Archangel of Ministry to call him."

Cassiel refilled her wine. "But if he's reluctant—"

"He won't be," I said.

She took a slow drink of wine. "I must say, I admire your

resolve." She looked at Samael. "Do we have accommodations nearby?"

He reached into his man purse, then slid a key card across the table. "The villa is at our disposal."

Cassiel smiled and tucked the key into her pocket. She must have known where it was. "Lovely. If I have to be stuck on Earth, at least it's at the Casa Cafiero."

CHAPTER SIXTEEN

*T*hey say Venice is one of the most romantic cities in the world. And from my small taste of the city between the restaurant and the Casa Cafiero, I wholeheartedly agreed.

Streets dotted with painters and musicians. Restaurants with candlelit tables under the open sky. Arched bridges crowning the canals where gondoliers offered romantic sunset rides...

Too bad I was visiting with Cassiel.

And too bad we were hunting a monster.

The rain had cleared by the time we finished eating, and the tourists had reemerged onto the streets. Hopefully, it would be easier to spot our killer if the potential victims were out in the open.

We took our time on the Calle dei Morti, following the stone-paved street through buildings and open plazas. We dipped in and out of shops, picking up fresh clothes and toiletries. We scanned the patrons of the bars and taverns, and scoped out restaurants I planned to return to.

After the first hour of wandering without spotting anything

more sinister than two drunk men yelling in a bar, Cassiel seemed to settle into her role of blending in as a tourist. She took her time at the shop windows. She stopped and tipped all the street performers, and she checked out every single magnet on every single street-vendor cart for the last three blocks of our walk.

She also hummed a *lot* without realizing it. Mostly eighties rock ballads, which I found hilarious.

"This is it," Cassiel said before we passed over yet another bridge.

Casa Cafiero was a two-story stucco villa that overlooked a canal. The sand-colored structure had dark chocolate shutters and a double front door made of wrought iron and frosted glass. Fresh red flowers lined the second-floor balcony that faced the street.

Cassiel pulled out the keycard Samael had given her. I watched her curiously as I held our shopping bags.

She noticed me staring as she put the key in the card reader. "Our powers don't work on the locks."

"Really?"

She opened the door. "Not the outdoor ones anyway."

"Who owns this place?" I asked as I followed her inside.

"Theta, the Archangel of Prophecy, but a lot of us have a key to it. She's not here often, and it's for all of us to use. She confiscated it from Uko when the demons were sent out of Venice."

"Demons have good taste. This place is beautiful."

She closed the door behind me. "Yes."

A marble-floored living room, kitchen, and dining room were downstairs. It had expensive furnishings and central air conditioning, a rarity in Venice, I'd learned.

"The bedrooms are upstairs," she said, crossing the living room to a staircase near the back.

A second living area was at the top of the stairs. There were two comfy-looking beige couches, a leather recliner, and a big-screen TV. *When was the last time I watched television?*

She entered a door to our left. "There are two bedrooms. We can share this one. It doesn't look like Samael has made claims to it."

I nodded and followed her inside. A large king bed was centered on the wall. Beyond it were two large glass doors that faced the building on the other side of the canal. I walked over to them and found they led out to the balcony we'd seen from the street.

Then I sat down on the fluffy white comforter and bounced on the mattress. "This bed feels amazing." I flopped back onto the pillows.

"No sleeping on the floor this time?"

"I might make you sleep on the floor."

"Ha, ha." She walked to the bathroom and washed her hands. "I doubt any of us will be here much."

I draped my arm across my forehead and stared at the ceiling. It was covered with decorative aluminum tiles. "I'd hoped we would have seen him on our walk here, and the job would be done."

"So we could get back to Asheville?"

"So we could stop and eat again."

She laughed as she dried her hands. When she was finished, she spread all our purchases on the end of the bed and carried our toothbrushes and toothpaste back to the bathroom.

"When do you think Saez will strike again?" I asked.

"It seems he's picked up his old habits right where he left them all those centuries ago. So I assume it won't be long. New bodies turned up almost every day the last time."

"How many?"

"Thirteen, I think."

My eyes widened. "As disturbing as it is, it's an impressive kill record at such a quick pace. I can't believe he didn't get caught sooner, especially with the bodies being dumped in such a tight location. If we saw all of it today, the Calle dei Morti isn't that long."

"He operated mostly at night, and back then, there wasn't electricity."

I swung my leg back and forth off the side of the bed. "Which means he probably sleeps during the day."

"Probably."

"Maybe we'll have more luck tonight."

She tossed the map she'd made me buy onto my chest. "Circle the places where the girls disappeared, and we'll check them out first."

"I still can't believe you bought a map. We need to get you a smartphone."

"No thanks. That would be my own personal form of Nulterra."

I smiled and opened the map over my head.

She started folding her clothes. "What will you do when we find him?"

"I'm going to kill him." I wanted to add a "duh" at the end, but I thought better of it.

"You'll take him back to Reclusion and kill him?"

"Why bother?" My eyes strained looking for the first location on the map—an apartment near the corner of the Calle dei Morti and the Calle Regina.

"Because it's forbidden to—"

I looked up at her and smiled. "Not forbidden for me. I have free will, remember?"

Her eyes widened. "There's a reason it was forbidden. It's dangerous."

"It worked though, didn't it?"

"Just because something's possible, doesn't mean you should do it."

"My only interest here is to finish this job so I can find

Metatron. Going to Reclusion is much like this map." I crumpled it. "It's a waste of time. Do you know how much work I have waiting for me? I'll never get out of there." I pulled out my phone and opened Google Maps. I put the first address into it.

She stared at me so long I wondered if she was debating on a rant about my work ethic. She didn't. "What makes you believe Metatron might be able to identify the Morning Star?"

"I don't know for sure, but I don't know that he can't either. It's worth a try."

"It isn't possible, Warren."

"It's never been done, so you don't really know. Besides, Sandalphon recognized Iliana even when Sloan was still pregnant with her."

"I'm sure that was only because Iliana is the most powerful angel to ever exist. She stands out to all of us."

"Have you met her?"

"I've only seen her through the spirit line. We all have."

Crunching my abs, I propped up on my elbows to look at her. "Why did Sandalphon enter Cira? And why wasn't he present at the Council's verdict?"

"That's two questions."

"So give me two answers."

"I don't need to. I don't know why he went to Cira. He was making a lot of wild accusations lately that I know were untrue."

"Like what?"

"He thought the Council was having secret meetings, which we *weren't*. The final blow before he left for Cira was the ruling to bring Iliana to Eden. He didn't support it."

I flopped back down again. "I knew it. I knew he'd be on our side."

"But he was overruled. The rest of the Council agreed."

My jaw was tightening. "We need to change the subject. I'm tired of fighting with you."

She walked over to the side of the bed by me. "Think we can be friends then?"

"Friends?" I shook my head. "But I will agree on a temporary truce." I held my hand toward her.

She smiled and shook it.

By eight o'clock—dinnertime by Italian standards, so I was told — Cassiel and I had wandered the streets for an hour without any luck. The outdoor tables were filling up and the sights and smells from the kitchens were making my stomach rumble again.

"Why do you think hunger pangs are so intense on Earth and yet we eat so much more here than we do in Eden?" I asked, halfway to myself, as we crossed over a bridge.

"Filling a void?" she asked.

"Maybe."

"You hungry?"

"If you walk any closer to me, I might take a bite out of you."

Her head snapped back.

I squinted one eye. "That came out way more sexually charged than I intended."

She chuckled and shook her head. "Come on. I know a great place to eat where we can still do our job."

We stopped at a *trattoria* at the edge of the plaza.

It was quaint, with tables draped with white tablecloths facing St. Mark's Basilica. After some direction from Cassiel, the waiter showed us to a table on the outside row with a clear view of the piazza.

"Grazie," I said as he handed me a menu, overworking my pronunciation and staring at Cassiel.

She grinned and asked the waiter for red wine. That much, I could understand.

"I need to wash my hands." Then she looked at me seriously and lifted an eyebrow.

I put my hands up. "I'm not going anywhere."

"Good."

The entire menu was in Italian, so I put it down and scanned humans enjoying the piazza.

The local life was back out in full force after the rain and the crime-scene cleanup. Artists painted the skyline along the water while street musicians jived in the square. A few people danced in the crowd. It was hard to believe so much death could be found in a place so alive.

"Have you decided what to order?" Cassiel asked as she sat back down across from me.

I picked up the menu again. "I have no idea. I can't read it." A word snagged my eye. "Oh, I do like gnocchi."

"It's very good here," she said, not looking at me.

I lifted an eyebrow. "How many times have you eaten here?"

"Never, but this is Italy," she said. "Be sure to order a main course after the gnocchi or you'll sound like a tourist."

"Can't have that," I said with a smirk. "Am I allowed to have some of your wine when it comes, or should I have ordered my own?"

"I'll let you have some."

"Thanks."

She winked. "You're welcome."

After deciding on the *filetto di bue all griglia* and praying to the Father that meant some kind of steak, I put my menu down. The waiter walked over and poured both of our wine-glasses full.

He took Cassiel's order first, then turned to me. I pointed at the things on the menu I wanted, and he smiled...which hopefully meant he understood. I assumed as much because I was far from the only American on the piazza.

Cassiel picked up her glass. "Look at you. Ordering all by yourself."

"I hope it doesn't backfire me. I accidentally ordered fried tarantulas once in Cambodia." I gagged. "Still can't even think about it."

She laughed and shook her head.

I sipped my wine, then looked at it. "That's pretty good."

"Yeah. It's usually a good bet to order the house wine whenever you're in Italy."

"Good to know." I put the glass down and scanned the piazza. "It's a shame I never came here when I was alive. From what I've seen, Italy's worth all the hype."

"The food is even better in Rome and Florence."

"Judging from the pizza alone, I'm having a hard time believing that's possible."

"Maybe once all the madness settles, we can go," she said.

I smiled.

"What?"

"I think you're starting to like me."

"I've always liked you. That's never been a question," she said over the top of her glass.

Too bad we were on opposite sides of such a deal-breaking fence.

I turned my attention back toward the tourists surrounding the basilica.

My phone buzzed. I pulled it out and read the text message from Azrael. *The team from New Hope just left. Ahab is fine.*

I tapped out a reply. *Thanks for the update. Another dead girl here in Italy. Still no killer.*

"Everything all right?" she asked.

"Yeah. Just Azrael letting me know everything's fine with Ahab."

"What was it like when you found out Azrael was your father?" she asked, balancing her chin in her hand and leaning on an elbow.

"It was an eventful day all around." I crossed my arms on the tabletop. "I'd just surprised Sloan by coming home early from a military deployment. In almost the same sentence she told me she was pregnant and that I had a father."

"Wow."

"Yeah. For an orphan, it was a lot of new relatives in one conversation."

She laughed. "But you already knew he was an angel, right?"

"Yeah. Kasyade, Sloan's demon mom—"

She held up a hand. "Oh, I know Kasyade."

I chuckled. "Yeah, I guess you would. Anyway, she told me I was the son of an Angel of Death."

"How long was it before you found out he betrayed all of Eden?"

My brow scrunched. "That's not fair. He fell in love with my mother. And I'd say he more than redeemed himself there at the end."

She didn't look convinced.

I straightened in my chair. "Cassiel, Sloan would have died had he not destroyed himself with Iliana's power. And if Sloan had died, Kasyade would have taken Iliana across the spirit line and destroyed it. He saved us all."

She held up both hands in defense. "I'm not arguing that what he did wasn't noble. But he was cleaning up his own mess."

I sat back. "There you go again, wishing I'd never been born."

"It's not personal. Few things with angels are. But if you'd never been born, the demons would not have had Sloan. You two wouldn't have met and created the Vitamorte."

"I feel like if we keep talking about all this, we'll break our truce."

She bowed her head. "You're probably right. What shall we talk about instead?"

"Let's talk about your Bon Jovi obsession."

"My what?"

I started humming the melody to "Livin' On A Prayer."

She covered her mouth with her hand and laughed.

"You hum *all the time*, Cassiel." I chuckled.

"I do not."

I laughed harder. "Yes, you do. I think the eighties must have been very good to you. Was it only Bon Jovi or was it Guns N' Roses and Def Leppard too?"

She wadded up her napkin and threw it at me. It missed my face, but I caught it with my power, suspending it just off the ground.

Cassiel's mouth formed a perfect *O*. "You're not supposed to do that here," she whispered loudly.

I snatched the napkin out of the air. "We passed a guy on the way here pulling roses out of ladies' ears. I fit right in."

She giggled again as I handed it back to her. "Do you tease everyone as you tease me?"

I picked up my wineglass. "I actually don't tease anyone. Ever." I took a long swig.

Her laughter faded. "If it makes you feel any better, neither do I."

"*Nooo*," I said, drawing out of the word.

"Oh, shut up."

"What do you do for fun, Cassiel?"

"Fun? What's that?" she asked, shaking her head. "I'm an Angel of the Council."

"I'm aware."

She looked down at her wineglass, holding its stem with both hands and staring at it so hard, I feared the glass might crack. I reached over and put my hand on her forearm. She relaxed and smiled at me.

"Fun is not what we do. It's what *they* do." She looked out at the piazza.

"I felt that way when I was human. Like I was always on the outside looking in." I swirled my wine around in my glass. "At least until I met Sloan. She lightened me up a lot."

"You really loved her."

I nodded. "Yeah. I did. Still do, and probably always will."

It was her turn to squeeze *my* arm. "It's a funny thing, love. Truly the most powerful force on either side of the spirit line."

"That's for sure. I never thought I'd feel anything close to what I felt for Sloan." I shook my head. "I was wrong."

Her brow lifted.

"Iliana. I gave up my life with Sloan for this tiny person I hardly know."

Cassiel opened her mouth to speak. Then she closed it. Perhaps she felt the same worry that was stirring in my mind. That if we kept up the current conversation, it would lead to another fight.

And that was the last thing I wanted just then. I was enjoying laughs, the banter, the warmth of her hand still on my arm...

I was enjoying it too much.

We searched the city the rest of the night, traveling from street bench to street bench, posing as a couple while monitoring the city. Nothing turned up, and there were no more reports of dead bodies.

But it all hadn't been a waste of time. By the end of the long night, I knew a lot more about Cassiel than when we'd started. Like, on Earth, she couldn't get clean enough. She must have washed her hands fifty times between sundown and sunup. And in the purse she'd brought from Eden, she carried hand sanitizer, wet wipes, and travel disinfectant spray. Really ironic for an angel who couldn't get sick.

She talked about Eden and told stories about Azrael. About the days before he'd given up his place in Heaven for my mother. During the first great war, Azrael had been the angel who'd quite literally *thrown* the Morning Star out of Eden, sending him like a blazing meteor across the spirit line into the galaxy.

I'd always thought Azrael was a badass, but by the time Cassiel finished, one thing was clear: my father was a legend. I understood a little better why his betrayal (her word) carried such a lasting sting.

She'd genuinely seemed curious about me as well. She'd asked about my time in the military. About my travels with the Marine Corps and with Claymore. And about what it had been like to find out I was the son of the Angel of Death.

When the sun came up, we were scouting for signs of fresh death again. But the Calle dei Morti was dead—in a good way—so we journeyed beyond it.

Venice by day was very different from the Venice we'd stalked all night. Most dinner restaurants were still closed, but in a few, we could watch the chefs making fresh pasta and hanging it to dry. We also strolled through the Rialto Market as most of the fisherman were unpacking their fresh catches.

The whole experience was dizzying and almost made me forget the horrors of why we were there.

After a quick breakfast at a Venetian bakery, Cassiel and I started back toward the Casa Cafiero. Leaning on my arm, she yawned.

"Tired?" I asked.

She nodded. "My stomach's full, and now I need a nap." She held up a finger. "Only after I take a shower and change into some sanitary clothes. Earth is gross."

I thought of her incessant hand washing and chuckled. I couldn't argue though. Earth *was* gross.

We never *needed* showers in Eden. There, our bodies didn't shed skin cells, we didn't sweat, and germs couldn't survive in the atmosphere. Everything on Earth seemed to stick, and after being so purely clean for so long, it was hard to stomach the filth of everyday life.

The more I thought about it, the more I agreed. "A shower sounds glorious."

"I'll fight you to go first," she said.

We both laughed.

When we reached the villa, I followed Cassiel upstairs, and she walked straight to the bathroom. She did pause in the doorway as I sat down on the bed. "Do you *want* to go first?"

I smiled. "It's kind of you to offer." And uncharacteristic, but I didn't say the last part out loud.

She was already untucking her shirt, flashing bits of smooth, taut skin. A dangerous image danced through my rotten brain... beads of water and soap bubbles sliding down her wet skin.

With a gulp, I got up and walked toward the doors to outside. "Go ahead. I'm going to sit on the balcony." *Where it's safe.*

"I'll make it fast." She paused. "Hey, Warren?"

I turned back around.

"Aside from the part where we were hunting an undead serial killer, I had a nice night with you."

"Yeah. I did too."

With a smile, she closed the door. Then I heard the shower water running. I walked outside and leaned against the railing. "Get a grip, Warren."

"Get a grip on what?"

Samael's voice nearly made me jump off the balcony. He and Jaleal were sitting around the corner on lounge chairs. I grasped at my chest to make sure there wasn't a hole left by my exploding heart. "Oh my god! Don't do that!"

They were both laughing. "Jumpy?" Jaleal asked.

"I didn't know you guys were here."

"Clearly," Samael said, closing the book he was reading.

I walked over and pulled a chair around to face them. "What are you doing here?"

"I came by to see if any of you found anything interesting. I certainly didn't," Jaleal said.

"Nothing, and we were out all night," I said.

"I didn't either, so I'm reading." Samael held up his book. *A Secret History of Creation.* "I found this on Theta's bookshelf. Looked like it might be interesting."

"Is it?"

He grinned. "If you like fiction."

"Is it fiction?"

He glanced at the back cover, then put it down on the glass coffee table. "I don't think it's supposed to be."

"I've been told the beginnings of Eden and Earth, but I don't know much about the Morning Star creating Nulterra."

"There isn't a lot I can tell you. No one knows much about it because it's forbidden for us to enter."

"Why did he create it? Do you know?"

Samael thought for a moment. "I have theories. The first being he wanted a place to rule as his own. Or maybe, like anyone, he wanted a place to belong. Cassiel might have better ideas than I do."

"That's sort of her specialty, isn't it?"

"Ideas? Yes."

He cut his eyes at me. "Do I sense a spark there?"

"With me and Cassiel?" I looked away. "There's no spark."

"OK." Jaleal chuckled and crossed her ankles. "I think you're good for her. She's much more...what's the word in English?"

"Chill?" I asked with a laugh.

She pointed at me. "Yes! Chill."

"Maybe. Still, I kind of hate her."

"There's a very fine line between love and hate. Especially among angels," Samael said.

I put my feet up on the coffee table. "Well, it's a line that's staying definite between us for the foreseeable future."

Samael just nodded.

Jaleal smirked.

"Bad news, Warren." Cassiel came out the door in a white robe, dabbing her long wet hair with a towel. She froze when she saw the other angels. "Oh, I didn't know you were here."

"Why *didn't* we know you were here?" I asked them.

Samael's finger circled the air. "Theta put a shield around the building. It conceals the supernatural inside."

I looked around but saw nothing. "Like Echo-5?"

"Not quite as secure. More of an illusion than an actual defense," Samael said.

"Cassiel, you said you had bad news?" Jaleal asked.

"Yeah." She looked at me. "Unfortunately, there's no hot water, so you'll want to make your shower snappy."

My eyes fell to the split in the front of her robe, but I quickly pulled them up to her face. "Thanks. I'll do that."

I stood and walked past her.

A cold shower was exactly what I needed.

Cassiel was drying her hair in the bedroom when I finished my shower. She'd thankfully changed out of the tantalizing robe and was wearing the cotton pajamas she'd purchased when we arrived.

I was only wearing the sweatpants I'd bought.

This time, I got a reaction.

She turned off the hairdryer and spun all the way around as I walked to the bed. "What is that?"

Her tone was more panicked than impressed. *Not* what I expected. I looked down a little self-consciously.

Pecs, check.

Abs, check.

Respectable sweatpants bulge even after a cold shower, check.

"What are you talking about?" I asked.

She walked over and grabbed my shoulder. "What have you done to yourself?"

Her fingers traced the thick black lines of ink wrapped around my torso and upper arm. I breathed a man-sized sigh of relief. "Oh. The tattoo. Geez, you scared me. I thought I'd contracted angel leprosy or something."

She walked all the way around me. "What is it?"

"A dragon claw."

The design was massive, covering almost half my upper body. One talon came down the center of my chest, curving to a point toward my ribcage. Its top wound over my left collarbone and across my shoulder and down to my elbow. My back had three more claws stretching halfway down my spine.

"It looks like it's going to carry you away."

I smiled. "Maybe it did."

Rolling her eyes, she laughed and shook her head. Her eyes fell to my right hip. "Is that...?" She hooked her finger into the waistband of my pants and pulled.

My breath hitched, and I flinched, pushing her hand away. "Whoa, whoa, whoa. What are you doing?"

"Looking at that." She pointed.

I looked down. "Oh."

"Is that Azrael's name?"

I tugged down the waistband a couple of inches. "Yeah. That's where I used to wear my weapon holster when I was human. That was my first tattoo. Got it when I was in the military."

"Why?"

"When I was in Iraq, this old guy with the sight saw me and thought I was Azrael. I didn't know who Az was at the time, but our translator told me the name meant the Angel of Death. Since I knew I could kill people, it seemed appropriate."

Her fingertips sent hot tingles straight through my hips as they graced the script. My abs tensed and chill bumps rippled over them. I shuddered and she noticed.

I smiled. "That tickles."

Her hand lingered a second past naïve curiosity. My eyes fell to her mouth. I leaned in and...

Alarm bells sounded on my phone on the nightstand.

Ahab.

CHAPTER SEVENTEEN

"That's never happened before," I said, looking at the screen.

Cassiel looked over my shoulder. "What?"

"Ahab went offline right after I got the breach warning."

"Moloch."

The phone rang before I could answer. Azrael. I tapped the answer button. "What's going on?"

"We have a problem."

"I'm aware. What happened? Why is Ahab offline?"

"I'm not sure, but I'm here with the whole team."

I glanced at my watch. "At three in the morning?"

"We were already here running night ops."

"Is everyone safe?"

"I believe so. There doesn't seem to have been contact with the building. But right after the breach, everything went dark."

"Who was it?"

"I don't know." There was commotion on his end of the line. I walked to the bathroom and grabbed the shirt I'd discarded into the hamper. "What's happening?" I said, stuffing my arms into it.

Gunfire blasted over the phone. Voices were yelling in the distance. I ended the call and shoved my bare feet into my boots without socks.

I needed to go. Now.

I tried to breach.

Nothing.

Cassiel was watching from the bathroom doorway. "You must go outside. Theta's shield around the building won't allow us to breach in or out."

I walked past her. "If you're coming, hurry. I'm not waiting."

She caught up with me on the stairs. "Did Moloch attack the building again?"

"Looks like it." I threw open the front door and ran out into the street. About twenty tourists stopped to gawk at the crazy man in sweatpants and an unbuttoned shirt.

Cassiel skidded to a stop beside me. She was barefoot, carrying her shoes. "We can't do this here. Too many witnesses."

"Screw the witnesses."

She grabbed my arm. "Come on, just a few feet to the alley."

My phone rang again. Azrael. I tapped the screen.

"We're OK! We're OK!" he was yelling.

"I'm on my way."

"Just wait."

I was still jogging toward the alley with my untied boots flopping up and down on my feet. "What was that?"

"Moloch and his minions. Whatever he tried to do failed, and they left."

I slowed. "Is everyone safe?"

"Yes, I think so. The power has come back on, but Ahab is still offline, so I can't talk to whoever is inside—" I heard Enzo's voice in the background. "Nate's on the radio. Everybody's safe. Nothing got in."

My whole body relaxed. "Thank God."

"Let me talk to Nate. I'll call you back."

"I'll be there in two minutes."

"Is Cassiel still with you?"

She was standing right next to me. "Yes."

"Don't. Not yet. Let me figure out what's going on. I'll call you back."

"I want to be—"

"Warren! I said *wait*."

My hand clenched the phone. "All right. Call me back."

He ended the call.

"Well?" Cassiel asked.

"Azrael wants me to wait. He'll figure out what's going on and let me know."

"Oh." She looked down at her pajamas. "At least we might have a little time to get properly dressed." We started back toward the villa. "I assume the attack failed?"

"I think so. The power came back on, but the security system is still offline."

"Why does it need to be *on*line?"

I held up my phone. "When the system is online, a few of us have the ability to remotely secure the building or disable Ahab if there's an emergency. I can also see the cameras inside and outside the building if I need to."

"Inside? You can see Iliana and Sloan?"

"I can, but I don't."

"Too hard?"

I didn't answer.

She trailed her fingers down my arm. "Is there anything I can do to help?"

If she wasn't here now, I could go to my family. Instead, my presence had become a liability.

I shook my head and let Azrael's warning replay in my mind...

"Don't let your guard down."

If I didn't watch it, my guard would be down around my ankles soon.

An hour later, I was dressed and sitting on the balcony to avoid being alone near a bed with Cassiel.

A video call came through from Azrael. I hit answer, and his face filled the screen. He appeared to be inside the guardhouse at Wolf Gap. He was yawning when I said, "Hello."

The yawn faded and he shook his head. "Sorry. It's late."

"Or very early."

"Yeah."

Cassiel must have heard me talking because she walked out of our bedroom.

Azrael turned the camera around. "I've got Nathan, Enzo, and a few others here."

"Cassiel is here with me."

Azrael didn't comment.

"What did you find out?" I asked.

"It seems Moloch may have fried part of the system. None of us can bring Ahab back online."

"I figured as much. I've been refreshing my app for the last hour. What happened?"

"I'll let you talk to Nate."

The camera wobbled as he passed the phone. Cassiel sat down on the love seat beside me.

"Hey, man," Nathan said when he steadied the phone.

"Hey. What happened?"

"The breach alarm went off, then ten seconds later, it was a total blackout except the emergency lights. Nothing worked. The high-Z locks bolted the doors, so it was still secure, but the entire system completely crapped out.

"Justice finally got it rebooted, but when he did, the whole system went haywire."

"Haywire?" Cassiel asked.

"Yeah. It went crazy. The cameras started moving. Icons were being clicked. The temperature controls were going up and down." Nathan looked behind him, and the camera moved enough for me to see Justice in the corner. "But neither one of us were touching it."

"It's like the computer was possessed," Justice added.

Cassiel looked at me. "Possessed."

"Then there were a lot of sparks and smoke and the whole thing shut back down and went offline," Nathan said.

Enzo leaned into the screen's view. "One of the defense mechanisms is for the system to shut completely down when it's attacked. That's why it went down and stayed offline."

"Cassiel, do you think Moloch tried to disarm Ahab?" Azrael asked in the background.

Cassiel looked at me. "I think Moloch tried to control Ahab."

"Hack the system?" I asked.

"*Become* the system," she said.

Nathan pulled the camera close to his face. "You think a demon tried to upload himself into our security system?" He looked at someone to his right. "Didn't Johnny Depp do that in some movie?"

Cassiel was not amused. "Moloch has the most advanced consciousness in existence next to the Morning Star. Your computer system isn't smarter than he is."

"Apparently Ahab is close. It shut down to keep him out," Nathan said.

"But something was messing with that screen. I saw it myself," Justice said off-camera.

"And what if Moloch figures out a workaround and defeats the system next time?" Cassiel said.

"So what do we do?" Nathan asked.

"Leave the system offline?" she suggested.

Enzo shook his head. "That's not a good idea. That means none of us will have the ability to monitor the system or secure the building remotely if there's an emergency."

"And I won't know what's going on there at all," I said.

"Me either," Azrael added.

We were all quiet for a moment. Nathan sat back and handed the phone back to Azrael.

I took a deep breath. "I'm calling Fury's hacker, Chimera." I waited to see if my father would argue.

After a moment, he pinched the bridge of his nose. "That might be a good idea."

Had I not already been dead, I would've been a goner. Then again, if Azrael was worried enough to consider he might be wrong, we had a serious problem on our hands.

"Does Fury's guy know about threats from our world?" he asked.

"Yes."

"Get in touch with him as soon as possible. Let me know what he says."

"Will do."

"We'll get the Nerd—" Nathan stopped himself. "The *tech team* from Claymore back out here."

"I already called them and woke them up," Azrael said. "For now, Ahab will stay offline."

"Nathan, call me if there's the slightest issue," I said.

Azrael turned the phone's camera toward Nate again. "I will." His head pulled back with alarm. "Oh, my phone won't work inside without Ahab to boost the signal through the walls."

I swore.

"This is going to be a problem," I heard Azrael say.

"We'll find a solution. We're safe for now, and if anything happens, I'll send a pigeon to Italy."

I wished that was funny.

Azrael angled the phone back toward himself. "Don't worry. We've got this under control. You and Cassiel *stay in Italy,*" he said with a little more emphasis than I cared for.

I nodded.

"And let me know as soon as you talk to Chimera." Then he ended the call without saying goodbye.

I stared off into the distance for a while until Cassiel's nails scratched lightly across the back of my neck. "With the system offline, nothing can get in, right?"

"Not without the passphrase entered at the door," I answered almost to myself. God, I wanted to be there. I looked at Cassiel. "Mind if I make another call?"

"To the hacker?"

I nodded.

"Go ahead. I'm going back inside."

She got up and walked back to our bedroom door. I realized then I'd have to call Fury first for the number. My eyes widened. I might have a moment to talk to her privately. I stood and walked to the edge of the balcony to be certain the door had closed behind Cassiel. It was closed, and she was in the bathroom washing her hands.

I quickly tapped Fury's name in my recent-call list. She answered on the second ring. "If you're calling with more bad news for me, my vagina hurts too much to talk to you."

Any other time, I'd probably have laughed. "Hey. I only have a minute. Where are you?"

"In the damn car headed to an undisclosed safehouse. Azrael specifically told me not to tell you where."

I sighed. "That's probably for the best."

"Do you know how painful car rides are after giving birth?"

"No," I said with a grimace.

"Be glad."

"Fury, I need your help. I need to get in touch with Chimera."

"Why?"

"Remember I told you Moloch attacked Echo-5?"

"Yeah."

"He might have tried to take over Ahab."

"Damn."

"I'm hoping Chimera can help us plug the holes in the system's security. Azrael's team worked on it yesterday, but Moloch was still able to get into it."

She chuckled on the other end of the line. "You want Chimera to help out Claymore? Do you realize the irony of that?"

"Yes, but even Azrael is feeling desperate."

There was a pause. "That's never good. I'll text you the number. It will go to a secure voicemail, and Chimera will call you back. Sometimes it takes a while."

"Thank you, Fury."

"Where are you right now?"

"Venice."

"As in Italy?"

"Yep."

"Are you alone?"

I glanced back toward the bedroom. Cassiel was laying on the bed. "Sort of."

"Why is Eden coming after Jett?"

I looked up at the blue sky. "Because they're afraid."

"Warren, desperate angels are dangerous. Be careful."

"I will be. Please be safe, Fury."

"You know I always am."

I smiled. "I know. I'll be in touch when I can be. Don't forget to text me that number, OK?"

"Stand by," she said and disconnected our call.

"I hate it when she does that," I whispered, ending the call and holding the phone over the balcony.

"Did she hang up on you again?" Cassiel asked behind me.

Startled, I dropped my phone. I swore and threw my power toward the concrete below to catch it. I stopped it just before it smacked the ground.

"Jumpy?" Cassiel asked, walking up beside me.

The phone flew back up into my hand. Several tourists gasped down below. "Uh..." I held up both hands. "Ta-da!"

They all clapped.

Cassiel laughed and leaned on the rail beside me. "How's Fury?"

"Sore."

"I'll bet. Childbirth looks dreadful." She made a sour face.

I waited for her to press me for details about Fury and Jett. She didn't. My phone buzzed. It was a contact card for Chimera with a long overseas phone number. I looked at the number. "I wonder what country code starts with forty-one."

"Easy. Ukraine."

My mouth fell open. "You know all the country codes too? What about area codes? And zip codes?"

She rolled her eyes. "Don't be a donkey hole, Warren."

I laughed, and it surprised me.

"I used to live in Europe, remember?"

"Right. What time is it right now in Ukraine?" I looked at my watch. It was after four in the morning in Asheville.

"Look it up yourself." She leaned on my arm. "That's why man created Google."

I smiled as she walked back to the bedroom, leaving the door open behind her.

I did a quick search on my phone. It was only an hour later in Ukraine than in Venice. I dialed the number. At the end of five rings, there was a long beep. No message. No identification.

I left a brief message and my phone number before ending the call.

I walked into the bedroom. She was lying on the bed, reading what had to be an ancient copy of *People* magazine. Brad Pitt was on the cover as "The Sexiest Man Alive"—his *Interview with a Vampire* days.

Two other sexiest-men issues were laying beside her: David Beckham and Johnny Depp.

I lifted an eyebrow. "Is it your turn for some alone time?"

"I'm trying to understand American men. And Theta has all these magazines."

I laughed. "Well, you won't learn much from them. And David Beckham is British."

"But he is beautiful." We both laughed. She closed the magazine and laid it on her chest. "What do you want to do?"

I didn't want to lie down beside her. That's what I told myself, anyway. Truthfully, I could really use a nap. Or more food. I looked at the clock on my phone. "Want to get lunch? Scope out more tourist spots?"

"I could eat."

"Good. Let's get out of here."

We ate lunch near the Rialto Bridge, another prime spot for people watching. Our view was so great, we decided to stay for dessert. And another carafe of wine. Fortunately, our bodies metabolized everything so quickly, we could indulge in all the excess without much consequence.

Still, nothing. No purple haze. No disjointed human souls. And no more dead bodies.

We finally gave up, left the restaurant, and crossed the busy bridge. When we reached the other side, she veered toward another street vendor's cart and made a beeline for the magnets.

With a laugh, I shook my head and looked around at the other items for sale. Intricately painted Carnival masks, decorative plates, and..."Hey, Cassiel, they have hot priest calendars over here. It's like the sexiest priests alive. That sounds right up your alley."

"Ha. Ha. Ha."

"You want one?"

She rolled her eyes. "Where would I put it?"

"I think it would look great in the Onyx Tower. The whole Council could enjoy it," I said.

The vendor offered me a deal. "It's only ten euros, Cassiel. Are you sure?"

"I'm sure." She'd plucked a magnet off the metal display board. "Can you buy me this instead?"

It was a small rectangle with a colorful painting of a canal with a gondolier. "Sure, but I was really hoping you'd pick the *David* statue's penis," I said with a frown.

She leaned in and lowered her voice. "I already have one from Rome."

I laughed and paid the vendor.

Just beyond the cart was a walk-up gelato window. "Ooo, gelato," I said, mindlessly taking a few steps toward it. Then I stopped and shook my head.

Cassiel was right behind me. "What's the matter?"

"I think I've been hanging out with Reuel too much. We just ate tiramisu."

She laughed and tugged on my sleeve. "Come on. You can blame it on me if it makes you feel better."

A young woman behind the glass half-window was staring at us. My head tilted, and the woman flinched.

I knew that look. She *saw* me.

I grabbed the back of Cassiel's shirt to stop her. "Behind the counter," I whispered.

"What?" She spun toward me.

"Your six o'clock."

"What does that mean?"

"Turn around and look behind the gelato counter."

"Why didn't you just say that?"

She turned and then froze. I nudged her forward. "Come on, we don't want to freak her out, remember?"

I did a full three-sixty, my eyes peeled for purple smoke. The immediate area was clear. No one else seemed to be working the small counter with her. She was exactly the killer's type. Her eyes were blue and brown.

Cassiel reached back, fumbling for my hand. I locked my fingers with hers as she inched forward. The woman cowered back as far as she could toward the far wall. She was visibly shaking.

Cassiel said something to her in Italian, but instead of the woman being comforted, a small cry slipped out. I squeezed Cassiel's hand. "She knows you're not supposed to speak Italian."

"Oh no."

It was probably the wrong time to point out again that the language rule of the angels was stupid.

She pointed to the gelato case and spoke to the woman again. Cassiel put her hands up in defense and said something else. Finally, the woman crept forward and reached for the gelato scoop.

"What flavor do you want?" Cassiel asked me.

I peeked around her shoulder at the case. "Cookies and cream."

When I spoke, the woman jumped back again, holding the scoop like a weapon.

"Warren, maybe you should go outside," Cassiel said.

"Not a bad idea." I reached into my wallet and handed her a stack of euros. "I'll see you out there."

Outside, I found a bench still in view of the gelato shop. After thoroughly scoping out the square, I sat down. Several minutes later, Cassiel walked out carrying two white bowls of gelato. Mine, cookies and cream. And Cassiel's, mint chocolate chip.

"How'd it go?" I asked as she handed me mine.

She sat down beside me. "That girl is terrified."

"Clearly."

"Her name is Bettina."

"She told you that?" I asked, surprised.

"No. I read it on her name tag. She did, finally, talk to me a little, and I think I convinced her we weren't dangerous. She knows someone in the area is killing people with the sight. Two of the victims were friends of hers. There seems to be a small community of those with the sight."

"What do you think we should do?" I asked, picking up my spoon.

"I think we need to make sure she gets home safely. We can hang out here until she gets off work. As much as I hate to say it, this is probably the most likely place for Saez to show up."

My spoon stopped halfway to my mouth. I groaned. "Now it feels an awful lot like we're using her as bait."

Cassiel didn't respond. She didn't strike me as the type that would be sorrowful about using humans for anything she deemed a greater purpose.

A man with a dog on a leash approached us to sit down. But when he neared the bench, he spun on his heel and walked in the other direction.

"Force field," I muttered.

"What?"

"People run when I'm near."

She pulled on the tail of my shirt. "Scoot closer. It *will* help."

"When Sloan and I were together, she thought our powers balanced each other out somehow. Like her presence made me more approachable. Was that true?"

"Yes. Probably even more so with Sloan because she was an Angel of Life."

I slid next to her. Then I sighed as the stress left my body. I looked down at our thighs pressed together. "This helps me too," I admitted.

She smiled and lifted a spoonful of green gelato to her mouth. "I'm glad."

For once, I believed her. Had we not been hunting a brutal killer, our time together in Venice might have actually been pleasant.

My eyes scanned the area again. No purple smoke. Then I turned back to my dessert. "Why do you suppose our powers work like that here?"

"It's pretty simple. Missing Eden leaves your spirit with a void. And that's true of angels and humans alike. Humans try to fill it in all sorts of ways, much like how we spoke of the hunger pangs yesterday."

I smiled. "Right."

"But the power in us is straight from Eden's core. You and I lessen the sting of that void for each other, simply by our proximity."

"You feel it too then?"

She swallowed another bite. "Does that surprise you?"

"Honestly, yeah. I've always assumed you were superior to me."

"I am," she said with a laugh.

I rolled my eyes.

She nudged my arm with her elbow. "I feel the void too. Though it might be worse for you since your body is still part of this world."

The biggest way Cassiel and I were physically different was

that my body would continue to age as long as I was on Earth. In Eden, the process stopped, but here, I was subject to cell death and decay just like anyone else.

Cassiel, however, was frozen. Her skin, hair, and organs would always stay as flawless as they'd been for the few centuries since she'd been born.

Using my spoon, I dug around in my ice cream for a hunk of chocolate cookies. "What would happen to me if I stayed on Earth for the entire span of a human life?"

"You'd get old."

"I know that." I thought of Yaya and George. "But would my body be reset to my youth like other souls in Eden?"

"You're the only one of your kind, so I'm not sure. If your body wears out to the point that it dies, it's possible. Or you might cross over and remain old like Sandalphon and Metatron."

My eyes widened. "Metatron is old too?"

"Oh yes. Much older than Sandalphon, even. The Father brought him to Eden when he was over seven hundred years old."

My head tilted. "Seven hundred?"

"Humans lived much longer before the creation of Nulterra. It seems to have poisoned the Earth."

"Why didn't the Father shut that shit down a long time ago?" I asked.

She sighed. "We've all asked that question many times."

"Azrael has always said Iliana won't die on Earth. She'll be brought to Eden like Metatron and Sandalphon were. So whenever she's brought over, no matter how old she is, she'll be frozen at that age?"

"Yes. And I'm sure Metatron would tell you, the younger, the better."

We were tap dancing very close to the conversation about making Iliana a seraph. Thankfully, my cell phone rang. I angled to the side and pulled it out of my pocket. On the screen was a foreign number with a Ukranian country code. "It's Fury's guy. I need to take this."

Cassiel nodded and focused on her ice cream.

I tapped the answer button. "Hello?"

"Is this Warren?" The voice on the other end of the line wasn't a guy at all. It was a woman.

"It is."

"This is Chimera."

My mouth opened, but no sound came out.

"Hello?" she asked.

"Sorry. I expected a man," I admitted.

"Most men do."

"My apologies. I meant no offense."

"None taken. I vetted you through Fury. She says you're a friend. What can I do for you?"

Fury called me a friend twice in one week? Mind blown.

"Are you familiar with Claymore?"

She laughed on the other end of the line.

"That was a stupid question," I said.

"Yes, it was. What about Claymore?"

"We've had a security breach in one of our top-secret facilities. I need the best of the best to get it back online and make sure it's secure."

"What's so important that Damon is trying to protect? His real identity?" she asked.

Wow. This chick was ballsy. No wonder she and Fury got along so well.

"My daughter, actually."

Silence. "Oh."

"Can you help us?"

"Since you are a friend of Fury's, I will come. But I'm not cheap."

"I expected as much. Whatever your rate is, I'll pay it."

"That's good to hear. Is it the Claymore property in New Hope, North Carolina?"

"No. It's on the other side of the state, just outside Asheville."

"Wolf Gap?"

My head snapped back. "How did you know that? It's a secure facility."

She chuckled. "OK."

I wasn't sure if that made me feel better or worse. "We can put you on a plane, or whatever you need."

"I can be there in a few hours."

"I thought you were in Europe."

"Sometimes I am, but right now, no one is hunting me."

I liked this woman already. "Thank you, Chimera."

"That sounded promising," Cassiel said when I ended the call. Sitting so close, and with her elevated hearing, she would have been able to listen to our whole conversation.

"She'll help us."

I pulled up a blank text message and typed out a message to Azrael, Enzo, and Nathan. *Chimera will be at Wolf Gap in a few hours.*

"I'm sure that eases your worry some. Will she be able to bring the security system back online?"

"After that conversation, I'm confident that if anyone can, it's her."

"The system sounds very sophisticated."

"It is." I opened the app on my phone. "If it weren't offline, I could show you more."

She leaned closer for a better look. "Can you control the system with the phone?"

"Only some of the features."

"You need a key card then?" she asked with a teasing grin, pressing her elbow into my ribs.

"It's a little more complicated than that."

"If you're wanting to convince me that Azrael can secure the Morning Star, maybe you should enlighten me on how he handles security."

Whoa. She was entertaining the idea.

"If the system isn't on Security Level Alpha, I can get through the front door with a retina scan. If it is on Alpha Alert, the system can only be disarmed from the mainframe computer inside with a unique passphrase." I held up the phone again. "From the phone, I can check all the cameras in and outside, as well as monitor the atmospheric conditions in the area."

"May I?" she asked.

I gave it to her.

"I'm amazed by how technologically advanced humans have become," she said, taking my phone into her hands. "All this power in such a tiny box."

The phone's screen lit up with a text message. I saw it was from Nathan. She handed it back to me, and I swiped the screen open.

That's excellent news. Ahab is still dark. I'm out running errands and getting takeout.

I didn't respond.

"You two are still close friends. That's interesting given your twisted love triangle with Sloan."

"Nathan fell for Sloan before I ever met her. It was always clear that had I not shown up, the two of them would have been together from the beginning."

"I imagine there wasn't much he could do to compete once you were in Sloan's life."

"There wasn't. Sloan and I were like magnets. Our attraction was out of anyone's control."

"And yet, Nathan still allows you to come around."

I held up my phone. "Well, he does control a serious system to keep me out."

"He controls it?"

"Nathan runs everything at Echo-5."

"Sounds like a lot of responsibility. Is he up to it?"

I nodded. "More than any other human on Earth."

"But he *is* human. What does he think about all of us? Especially you, now that you're the Archangel?" she asked with a smile.

"As you can probably guess from the *Angelo Suave* on my passport, he doesn't take me very seriously." I glanced down at my phone. "Lately, he's been calling me his Area 51 Reject."

She laughed. "That's hilarious."

My phone buzzed again. This time, it was a text from Chimera. *Be there by 6pm. Tell Claymore I want to meet him.*

"I need to call Az."

Azrael answered quickly. "Hello."

"Hey. I talked to Chimera, who is a *woman*, by the way. She'll be at Wolf Gap by six tonight. And she wants to meet you."

"Me? Why?"

"Probably to rub your nose in the fact that you're asking for her help."

"Probably," he said with a grumble.

"Be nice to her, and pay her whatever she wants."

He sighed. "I will. I'll stay here at the guardhouse until we figure this shit out."

"What about Adrianne?"

"Adrianne's gone on a baby-furniture shopping trip to Hickory with her mother. They left today."

My brow raised. I doubted her timely departure was a coincidence.

"Iliana and Sloan are still safe?"

"Yes."

"Good."

"How's the search going in Venice?"

"We still haven't found the killer, but if he follows his MO, he's overdue for a victim."

"Every day almost."

"Correct. And no one died last night."

"Think you scared him off?"

I'd been wondering the same thing. "I hope not. We're exploring a lead now, but if he doesn't turn up soon, we'll go to Eden and have Metatron summon him to Samael."

"That sounds like a more reliable plan anyway. Too bad Sloan can't access her powers."

"Trust me. That was my first thought."

"Good luck, son."

"Thanks. I'll be in touch."

We stayed in the immediate vicinity until well after dark. The gelato shop closed at ten o'clock. Bettina locked the shop behind her and looked very carefully around. She saw us, and Cassiel waved.

After a moment's hesitation, Bettina power walked in the opposite direction. We got up and followed her at a distance. She must have sensed it because she zigzagged in and around different alleyways, like she was trying to lose us.

She didn't.

We watched from an alley corner as she entered a building just off the Calle dei Morti. It was tucked back away from the busy streets, far away from where passersby might notice anything sinister. Cassiel and I were not random passersby, and we both immediately sensed danger. Close.

We exchanged a worried glance just as my keen hearing heard it...a piercing scream.

CHAPTER EIGHTEEN

I didn't bother with a clean entry. Using my power, I ripped the door off its hinges. It flew out toward me and Cassiel, and I batted it out of our way. It landed on the stone street with a loud clatter.

Inside, we took the steps two at a time toward the sounds of shouting. I turned left when we reached the landing into a bedroom.

A naked body was strapped to the bed. And a man swirling with purple smoke had Bettina pinned against the wall. A knife was to her throat. "Let her go!" I bellowed, extending my hand toward him.

The man turned, a dripping snarl on his face, as I twisted the knife out of his ashen hand. I flung the knife so it embedded itself in the wall.

Cassiel grabbed my arm. "Don't kill him. We need him alive."

It was a good thing she stopped me because I was ready to obliterate his soul. He released Bettina, and she fell to her knees. Cassiel rushed toward her as the man squared off with me.

"Vito Saez?" I asked.

I had no idea what Vito Saez looked like. This guy was of Italian descent with short black haircut. His skin, however, had lost its classic golden undertones. He was almost gray.

"You're not Azrael." The man was speaking Katavukai, though I understood him in English.

I kept my killing power ready at my fingertips. "That won't help you any. Who are you?"

"You know who I am," he hissed.

Behind him, Cassiel was inching toward the bed. The girl bound to it wasn't yet missing her head. She was still alive, but only just.

"How did you get here?"

"I walked."

"Bettina!" Cassiel screamed something else about a *paramedico* and Bettina scrambled off the floor. "Warren, you need to get out of here. You're killing this girl faster!"

"Warren? You're the new Archangel everyone is talking about." His eyes narrowed. "How's the baby girl?"

I closed the space between us in one stride, extinguishing my power and slamming my fist into his face. With a satisfying *crunch*, Saez crumpled to the floor. My hand closed around his throat, and I lifted him off the ground.

There was a balcony off the bedroom. I looked over at Cassiel. "Meet you back at the villa?"

She was carefully peeling back the tape from the mouth of the woman on the bed. My symbol had already been carved into her chest; thankfully, her eyes were still in the sockets. "Yes, but I don't know how long this will take."

I curled my arm around Vito's throat. "Don't worry. He's not going anywhere. How bad is she?"

"Getting worse by the second with you here. Go!"

I blasted the balcony doors open and dragged Vito outside.

After checking the street for onlookers, I stretched my wings but kept them dark.

"Whoa, whoa, whoa, what are you doing?" Vito struggled to say in the crook of my elbow. He clawed at my arm, desperately trying to keep his feet underneath him.

"Taking you for a ride. You better stop struggling so I don't drop your ass."

With a powerful thrust, we lifted into the air.

Samael was waiting when we reached the villa. I had called him from the air. Thankful for the cover of darkness, I silently landed in the alleyway Cassiel and I had run to the day before.

I dragged Vito across the street and through the front door Samael was holding for us. "Where did you find him?" he asked.

"In the middle of a work in progress." Once we were inside, I released Vito and shoved him into the center of the downstairs living room.

Hopefully realizing he was cornered, Vito took in his surroundings. Samael walked slowly around behind him, and the two of us circled the killer like hungry sharks ready for a meal.

He looked worse here in the bright light of the villa than he had in the bedroom where we'd found him. Dark veins spiderwebbed his face, and his cheeks were drawn, and his eyes were sunken.

"How did you get here?" I asked again.

"Why should I tell you?"

"Because if you don't, I'll do this." I gripped his body with two invisible fists and twisted his torso in opposite directions like he was a human dishtowel.

Nothing happened.

Anybody else would be crying in pain, bent to my will so I wouldn't break them. Vito Saez—or rather, the body he occupied —didn't even grimace. I released Vito, and he stumbled forward.

I looked at Samael behind him. Samael just shrugged.

I conjured my power into my hands once more. "This is the last time I'll ask. How did you get here?"

Vito's head tilted, and he laughed until he began to wheeze. "Are you really going to kill me? Go ahead. I'm not afraid to die *again*."

He really wasn't. I let my power extinguish. "You're right. I won't kill you. How about I send you back to the pit?"

That got his attention. His spine straightened, and his eyes doubled.

"Oh, you don't want to go back to Nulterra?"

He didn't answer.

Time to close in for the kill. I took a step forward. "How did you get—"

A fly crawled out his nostril.

I gulped. "How did you leave Nulterra?

Vito swayed. "I told you. I walked. I walked right out."

"Walked right out to *where*? Where is the gate here on Earth?" Samael asked.

Vito staggered a few steps.

I looked at Samael and switched to communicating silently. "What's happening?"

He shook his head. "I'm not sure. He's controlling the body without occupying it. I didn't even know that was possible."

Vito bent at the waist and spewed blackish blood all over the hardwood. It smelled putrid, like rotting meat. I jumped back to keep it from splashing my boots. "Oh damn," I said, covering my nose to block the smell.

Samael sidestepped quickly toward me as Vito fell to the floor.

Vito vomited again.

I grabbed Samael by the shirt. "He's dead, and our presence is feeding it."

He nodded. "At this rate, he'll die before we get any answers out of him. What do we do?"

"We need to wait for Cassiel."

"And in the meantime?"

I looked around the living room then smiled. "Think we can find any rope?"

A few hours later, the nearby sirens had quelled and the emergency boats were gone. The only noise that remained in the Venice night was the gentle slosh of the canal water against the buildings. And the sloshing of Italian beer against our glass bottles.

"Think we should check on him?" I asked.

Samael tilted his bottle up to his lips again. "Nah."

Coming down a side street, I heard the subtle, rhythmic rustle of pants rubbing with a walker's stride.

Cassiel emerged from the darkness and paused over the bridge when she saw us. "What are you doing?"

I held up my beer. "Drinking. Isn't that what we do here in Italy?"

Shaking her head and staring at the ground, she trudged forward. I stood from the patio chair we'd dragged down to the front walk. "You OK?"

She didn't look up until she reached me, and when she did, she walked right into me, dropping her head against my shoulder. My arms froze, suspended for a moment before they closed around her. I looked at Samael for help. He just shrugged.

I leaned close to her ear. "What's the matter?"

Shaking her head, she took a step back. "Later. Where is he?"

"Inside."

Her head tilted.

"You told me to keep him alive."

I followed her into the villa. "My stars," she said when she saw him.

Vito Saez was duct-taped to an armchair.

She turned and looked at me and Samael in the doorway. "We couldn't find any rope," he said.

"What happened to the floor?"

"He started vomiting blood. That's when we decided it best to step outside," I said.

With a heavy sigh, she walked over to him, then turned and looked back at us when we didn't follow. "Am I doing this alone?"

"If you want him to keep breathing long enough to get an answer," Samael said.

"We tried, but that's when the blood spray began." I closed the front door and leaned against it. "We'd better watch from here."

I wasn't even sure she'd get an answer from Vito. He was alive, but I wasn't sure for how much longer. His disjointed soul seemed to be pulling away from its temporary host. His eyes were slowly darkening, and every few seconds, the swirling purple soul seemed to flicker to a position just outside the body.

Cassiel ripped the tape off the man's mouth. Part of his lip came off with it. She dropped it on the floor and gripped his head by his black hair, forcing him to look at her. She gripped both sides of his ashen face. "Who are you?"

"Il mostro de Venezia," he said with a bloody smile. "Signore Vito Saez."

"How did you come back from Nulterra?"

"Moloch brought us through the gate."

"Us? How many other humans?"

"Two others."

Cassiel looked at me.

"We're missing one," I said quietly to Samael.

"Who were the other two?" Cassiel asked him.

"I don't know."

"You don't know?"

"Nulterra is not a social club," he said.

Her hands were squeezing his skull so tight her fingers were turning purple. "Where is the gate?"

He didn't answer.

She leaned closer. "Where is the gate?"

"La Isla del Fuego," he hissed.

"What does that mean?" I asked.

"The Island of Fire," Samael translated.

"Where is it?"

He shook his head. "I'm not sure."

"Sounds appropriate."

"Yes, it does," he agreed.

"I only know of two islands with that name, or a variation of it, anyway." Cassiel forced Vito to look at her again. "Where is the island?"

"In the sea."

"Tell me the truth!" Cassiel shouted, her fragile patience finally cracking along with Vito's cheekbones and jaw.

He gasped and coughed and showered her face and shirt with blood. I crossed the room and grabbed her arms, pulling her backward. "That's enough for now. Come on, Cassiel."

Vito slumped forward as much as the tape would allow. Dark blood oozed out of his mouth and dribbled down the front of his shirt. Cassiel turned and crumpled against me again.

I held her head against the crook of my neck. "What is it?"

"I want him to die," she whispered into my shirt. "I want you to kill him right now."

I nodded against her hair. Then I caught Samael's eye and jerked my head to beckon him forward. I passed her off to him, then turned toward Vito once more.

He was close to death already.

I finished him.

Then the world swirled to black.

———

I woke up sometime later in the guest bed upstairs with no memory of anything following Vito's final execution. My head throbbed, and when I sat up, I nearly passed out again from the pain and dizziness. I took several deep breaths and rubbed my throbbing temples.

The shower was on in the bathroom, and I heard it cut off.

I waited for Cassiel to emerge.

She didn't.

I finally pushed myself up. Thankfully, the pain in my head had calmed. I walked to the bathroom door and knocked. "Cassiel?"

Nothing.

Then I heard the tiniest shaky gasp for air.

I waved my hand in front of the knob. The lock clicked, and I pushed the door open slightly. "I'm coming in." When I heard no objection, I walked inside.

Cassiel was wrapped in a towel, sitting against the side of the tub on the floor. Her hair was hanging wet over her bare shoulders, and her face was red from crying.

I sat down beside her and held her hand.

After a few beats of silence, she let out a quiet sigh. "The girl he attacked tonight...she's dead. Well, her body's on life support, but Jaleal took her to Eden."

My face fell.

"She's pregnant too. It's a boy."

Damn.

I leaned my head against hers. "I'm sorry."

She sniffed. "I'm not supposed to care about them."

"Yeah, you are." I looked down at our hands joined together. "Otherwise, why would the Father have put you in charge?"

"Maybe." She looked at me. "You fainted."

I frowned. "I passed out. Men don't faint."

A small smile spread on her face.

We were quiet for a while. I squeezed her fingers. She squeezed mine. Then I drew her hand to my mouth and kissed her knuckles. "Come on," I said. "Let's go to bed."

While Cassiel dried her hair, I lay on the bed and texted Azrael. *Vito Saez is dead, but not before claiming another victim. A pregnant woman.*

My phone rang. It was him. I tapped answer and put the phone to my ear. "Hi."

"I'm glad you caught him."

I sighed. "Yeah, me too. When I killed him, I passed out. Has that ever happened to you before?"

He laughed. "No."

"It's not funny. My head still hurts."

"Poor kid."

"Shut up, Azrael."

"Did you find out where Vito came from?"

"A place called La Isla del Fuego. Ever heard of it?" I'd tried googling the place. A big island off the southern tip of Argentina came up, but its name was slightly different.

"Seems like I remember an island by that name or something similar in the South China Sea."

"Thanks, I'll try searching for that."

"What's your plan?"

"Tomorrow, I'm coming back to Asheville to return your blood stone before we go to Eden."

"I appreciate the heads-up."

"You're welcome. What's going on with Adrianne?"

There was a beat of silence before he answered. "I've tried

to convince her to do fetal blood sampling, but she's afraid it could hurt the baby."

"Is that why you've sent her away?"

More silence.

"Az?"

"She's gone with her mother on a shopping trip."

Sure. But the less I knew, the better, so I let it drop. "Has there been any more trouble at Wolf Gap?"

"No. Your family is safe, and as much as I hate to admit it, Chimera is making them even safer."

"What did she find out today?"

"She was able to pinpoint how Moloch got into the mainframe. He tapped into the connection coming in from the main Claymore servers in New Hope. Tomorrow, she'll set up Wolf Gap to run independently, and add a few more fail-safes to Echo-5."

"That's excellent."

"It really is. You made a good call bringing her in."

I smiled. A father's pride never gets old.

The bathroom door opened and Cassiel walked out wearing a white cotton T-shirt and gray cotton shorts. Her hair hung loose over one shoulder, and she was barefoot.

"Az, I need to go. We'll see you sometime tomorrow, probably late morning."

"All right, have a good—"

I pulled a Fury and hung up before he could finish.

I sat up and put the phone on the nightstand charger. "Feel better?"

She walked around to the other side of the bed and pulled back the covers. "No. But I'm glad he's dead. At least he can't hurt anyone ever again."

I rolled onto my side to face her, propping my head up in my hand. "Yeah. *Never* again."

Lying on her back, she gripped the comforter that was

pulled up to her chest. "I hate being on Earth. Everything *feels* too much here."

The tension radiating off her was almost palpable. "I know. We'll go home tomorrow."

She nodded. "Would it be all right if we slept close tonight? My nerves are still so—"

"Shh." I scooted closer, pulling my pillow over beside hers. Then I tangled our feet and slipped my forearm under her neck. "Better?"

"Thank you."

I was still propped up on my elbow. My black hair falling around my face as I looked down at her. She reached up and pushed it back, then let her hand linger on the side of my neck.

Slowly lowering, I kissed her.

And she kissed me back.

Nothing happened.

At least not after that kiss, anyway. That mind-blowing, Eden-shattering kiss.

When the sun rose the next morning, she was still in my arms. I hadn't slept that well on Earth...maybe ever.

Samael had cleaned up the mess in the living room, vaporizing the body and all the blood. The smell was thankfully gone.

We said our goodbyes downstairs. "What's your plan?" he asked.

"I'd like to have one last meal before we leave Italy. Then I want to return to Asheville and make sure Iliana is safe and give the blood stone back to Azrael."

"Please send my regards," Samael said.

"I will." I offered him my hand, and he shook it. "Thanks for all your help."

"Of course. I'll see you back in Eden. Goodbye, Cassiel."

She smiled. "Goodbye."

When Cassiel and I left, we had a quick late breakfast on the Calle dei Morti, then we walked to St. Mark's Square and toward the water. She paused in the middle of the open piazza to admire the basilica one last time.

Bright rays of sunlight bounced off the church's domes and the colorful mosaics that filled its arches. "I must say, Venice is as beautiful as I'd always heard it was," I said, unable to keep my arm from slipping around her waist.

She nodded and smiled. "It really is."

"That's a big compliment coming from a snob like you." My fingers dug into her hip, and she flinched, laughing.

After a second, she rested against my side. "I ate pizza from a bar. You are no longer allowed to call me a snob."

"Whatever you say." Looking up at the church again, my head tilted to the side. "It looks a little like the Avronesh, doesn't it?"

"I can see that. If the Avronesh was about a hundred feet shorter and had tiny people standing on top."

I squinted, looking at the building. "I think those are angels."

She laughed. "That's funny. If they only knew, right?"

"If they only knew." My laughter faded, and I rested my head against hers. "You know, even with hunting a killer, this is my first time away from Eden that I've had even a little bit of peace." I sighed. "Thanks for that."

She turned around in my arms. "After last night, I should be thanking you."

I bent to kiss her again. This time, she dodged.

I pulled back with the surprise.

She flattened her palms against my chest. "Warren, with everything going on and my position on the Council..."

I stepped away. "Say no more."

"I just think it's better if we stay friends until everything's resolved, and then see if maybe—"

I laughed, but none of it was funny. "OK."

She was saying we should cool it until after the fate of my daughter had been carried out.

Awkward silence hung between us for a moment. "Come on. We'd better catch the water taxi back to the mainland," she finally said.

"You're right."

Then I turned and walked off without her.

CHAPTER NINETEEN

*R*euel was the first to see us when Cassiel and I arrived in the front yard of Echo-5 again. He waved from the entrance to the building. I waved back, and we started toward him. Even though I'd checked when we were inside the breach, I scanned the building to be sure its emergency shutters were closed.

The parking lot was now full. Two heavily armed members of SF-12, Pirez and Wings (I remembered their names without a problem) stood with Reuel near the armored door. The three of them were laughing. Hard.

"What's so funny?" I asked as we walked up.

Pirez had tears sparkling in his eyes. "Reuel's telling us stories about the boss. Did he tell you about Azrael's invention for a floating tank?"

Reuel shrugged. "It was just a boat...with guns."

Pirez and Wings cracked up again.

I pointed at Reuel. "Az is going to kill you."

He grinned.

"Is he here?" I asked.

"You just missed him," Wings said, still laughing.

That was strange. "I assumed he'd be micromanaging the cybersecurity issues."

Pirez dabbed the corners of his eyes dry. "He was, but Ionis stopped by with a message. Then they left together. Said he'd be back as soon as possible."

My head snapped back. "Ionis?" I hadn't seen him since we were at the Avronesh.

Wings nodded. "Skinny dude with white hair and weird clothes."

"I know who he is. Just wondering why he was here."

"He told the guardians about the mandate concerning the Morning Star. Then he spoke with Azrael in private, and they left," Reuel explained.

"Why did they leave?" Cassiel asked, speaking for the first time since our awkward departure from Venice.

Reuel just shrugged his large shoulders.

"Did you need something?" Wings asked me.

"I wanted to return Azrael's blood stone, but I guess I'll hang onto it for a while." I looked around the parking lot. "Is a woman named Chimera still here working on Ahab?"

Pirez and Wings exchanged a wide smile. "Oh yeah," Pirez said.

"What does that mean?" I asked.

"It means she's attractive," Cassiel said with an eyeroll.

"Can you call Nate and ask him to come out here, please?" I asked.

"Roger that, sir." Wings pressed the button on the side of the radio Velcroed to his shoulder. "Kane, tell the commander that Warren is here to see him."

I cocked an eyebrow. "He makes you call him the commander?"

"Yes, sir."

I laughed and shook my head.

"What happened in Venice?" Reuel asked.

"We got our guy. Let's just leave it at that." I glanced back at the building. "How are things here?"

"Better now, but the system is still offline."

The front door opened and Nathan walked out. "You're back a lot sooner than I expected," he said, slipping on his sunglasses.

"And we can't stay. This is a pit stop on our way back to Eden."

"I heard you caught your killer. Congratulations."

"Yeah, but unfortunately not before he killed someone else."

"Saw it on the Italian news. Did they find the girl's family?" he asked.

I had no idea.

"I don't think she has any," Cassiel said.

"They say she's still on life support. Any way you can get an Angel of Life in there to save her like Sloan saved me?"

Sloan.

It hadn't even occurred to me that she was inside the building. That was a first. I looked at Cassiel. We hadn't touched since we left Italy. But maybe she'd had a bigger effect on me than I'd realized.

I hadn't been hung up on wistful thoughts of my old life so far on this trip, and I didn't want to start now. "It's too late. Her soul already crossed the spirit line."

"We didn't want her suffering to continue," Cassiel added, her face falling.

"I'm sorry," Nathan said.

Cassiel took a deep breath. "So am I."

"Want some good news?" he asked.

I crossed my arms. "I'd love some good news."

He jerked his thumb toward the building. "Fury's girl Chimera knows her shit. She's been here less than a full day and has accomplished more than the New Hope team has in months."

"That's great," I said.

"She thinks the system will be back online in an hour or so."

"Will my passphrase change?"

He had a teasing grin. "You don't want it to, do you? It's so appropriate."

I rolled my eyes and ignored him. "Are Sloan and Iliana still inside?"

"Of course. Ahab may be offline, but inside, it's been full-on DEFCON Two around here since that shit went down with Moloch. I thought I was going to have to do a retina scan just to access the refrigerator this morning."

I chuckled. "Good. Keep them safe. I'll be in touch when I know more."

"You're leaving now?"

"Yes, but I'd like for Reuel to stay on here." I looked at Reuel, and he nodded. "I'll be gone for a few days, at most I would think."

I prayed so anyway.

"We can keep Iliana inside for a few more days. Not a problem." His face fell. "But it will be a problem before too long. It's not right to keep a kid locked up indoors. We've got to find and neutralize the Morning Star."

Glancing up at the two-story structure that looked more like a prison than a home, I couldn't argue. "I'm working on it, Nate."

He put a hand on my shoulder. "I know you are."

"I'll be in Eden, so call out to Samael if you need to get in touch with me quickly."

"Call out like..." Nathan folded his hands in prayer and cocked his head to the side.

I laughed. "Something like that. He'll hear you, just do it outside the building."

"So weird."

"I know." I gave him a firm handshake, then pulled him in and slapped him on the back.

"We'll be fine," he said in my ear.

Forcing a nod, I released him. "Please thank Chimera on my behalf for coming so quickly."

"Will do."

"I'll be back soon."

"Godspeed," Nathan said with a grin and a wink.

Laughing, I stepped back beside Cassiel and looked down at her. "Are you ready?"

She nodded. "Goodbye, Nathan. I'm sure we'll see each other again very soon."

I didn't like the sound of that at all.

Together, she and I walked toward the open field to lessen the blast of our departure for the humans. Midway through the grass, a crackling sound caught my attention. "Warren, it's Lachlan. Where are you?" one of my angels asked in my head.

"Asheville, why?" I responded.

"I need you in Chicago. There's a human spirit here glowing purple."

"This can't be good."

From the parking garage where we emerged from the spirit line, I could see a familiar triangular tan building.

"Where are we?" Cassiel asked.

"Downtown Chicago." I pointed. "That's a federal prison. The last time I was here was with Sloan."

I pressed the two spots beneath my earlobes and my supernatural communication system clicked back on. I couldn't believe I'd had it off for a few days.

At the garage's exit, a brawny figure was silhouetted against the sunlight. I didn't need to see his face to know who it was. His name was Lachlan, another Angel of Death.

"What have you got?" I asked as we approached.

He reached inside his jacket and handed me a sheet of paper. "Know this guy?"

I took the page. A color mugshot was printed in the center of it, a man with graying blond hair, a severely wrinkled face, and two empty eyes. "Please tell me this guy's dead," I said, studying the booking sheet.

"I don't know what he is, boss. I saw him last night when I slipped into the prison—"

"When you slipped into the prison?" Cassiel asked.

Lachlan's head bobbed side to side. "I might have some business with one of the female guards."

I scowled.

He grinned. "She didn't think I could get inside. I proved her wrong in more ways than one."

Cassiel rolled her eyes.

"Anyway, on my way out early this morning, I saw this guy in solitary glowing bright purple. I remembered something Jeshua said about a spirit glowing purple, so I thought I should let you know."

"What's he in prison for?" Cassiel asked, leaning sideways to read the paper.

"Says armed robbery. He was convicted four years ago."

"But apparently this dude had the shit beaten out of him with a broken bathroom pipe about six months ago. He was on life support until he randomly woke up a few weeks ago and was brought back here."

Cassiel covered her mouth to stifle a laugh.

"What?" Lachlan asked.

Smiling, I handed him the paper. "A spirit escaped from Nulterra and claimed this man's body. Little did the spirit know, he was bound for a maximum-security prison. That's hysterical."

"If it's not this guy"—he looked at the sheet—"Gary Hughes, who is it?"

I shrugged. "Somebody Azrael killed a long time ago, would be my guess. Where is he now?"

He pointed the paper at the three-hundred-foot building. "Nineteenth floor. Solitary."

"You're going in?" Cassiel asked.

"Yes, ma'am. You coming?"

"Absolutely."

"Lachlan?" I asked.

He hesitated. "I'd like to keep working this area."

"Of course. Do me a favor and let Samael know what's happening here."

"I'll let him know, and then I'm headed back to Eden," Lachlan said as Cassiel and I started toward the building.

"We'll hopefully see you there soon!" I called back to him.

Cassiel threw her arm across my chest to stop me. "Wait. Do you have a plan or are you just going to barrel your way in there?"

I turned my palms up. "Barreling sounds fun."

She frowned.

"If we can get into the Capitol building in Malab, this should be a breeze."

"You don't have anyone to escort you in, and you can't knock out the cameras here. It would put the guards in danger."

I hadn't thought about that. "What do you suggest?"

With her hands on her hips, she looked up at the three-hundred-foot building. "We need to cross the spirit line and enter inside."

I chuckled. "And me strong-arming my way into an elevator is too much?"

"It's quicker. We can get in without drawing as much attention to ourselves."

"You don't think it will affect the building?"

She looked up again. "It's steel and concrete. It's designed to take worse."

"If you say so."

"Getting out might be harder if we try to take him alive. Think we should?"

"You're the brains of this operation. Do you think he'll tell a different story from Vito?"

"No, but if we have trouble finding the island, an Angel of Life could summon him back to where he came from. Then we could follow."

My head tilted as I considered it. "All right. We'll strong-arm our way out."

"OK."

We vanished right there on the street, crossing into the breach but staying in the same area. Everything was distorted, like looking at the world through kaleidoscope glasses.

Together, we rose into the air, and Cassiel counted the floors of the building. At floor nineteen, we passed through the wall to find a long hallway lined with heavy metal doors.

"This is it. He's somewhere on this floor," she said.

One by one, we checked the small windows of each cell. Recognizing faces would be difficult with our fractaled view, but spotting the purple fog was much easier.

"Got him," I said passing through a cell door. Cassiel followed me.

The man was lying on his bed, and even though we were still invisible, he sat up straight when we entered. I studied his face and his disjointed soul. He'd never killed anyone, which was something else my power as an Angel of Death could tell me.

It was rare for Azrael to kill someone who hadn't committed murder. Then again, Haile-what's-his-name hadn't had a death tally on his soul either, even though he'd been responsible for the deadly starvation of many.

"Warren, don't look at the camera when we enter." Cassiel was pointing to the corner near the door behind us.

"I'll destroy it once we're in," I said. "Do you know this guy?"

"I don't know the body or the spirit. That might be different once you separate them."

"Ready?" I asked.

"Ready."

Crossing the spirit line indoors was like throwing a concussion grenade into an armored ammo box. The whole building shook around us. Sirens blared. Red lights flashed.

The prisoner had fallen to the floor screaming, his arms wrapped around his head. I threw my hand toward the camera, and it exploded. Cassiel marched toward him, grabbed him off the floor, and pinned him against the wall. "Who are you?" she demanded.

Impressed, I smiled and hung back.

The spirit cackled. "I don't want to talk to you, woman."

Cassiel threw the body with so much force into the ceiling that the concrete fractured. I chuckled.

An actual living human would *not* have been OK after such a collision. This one stood with blood trickling from his ears.

Out in the hallway, voices were shouting. I conjured darkness and threw it over the window before sealing the door.

"Who are you?" Cassiel demanded again.

The man arched his back to stretch it. I suspected she'd done some damage to his spine. Then he pointed at me. "He knows who I am."

I crossed my arms. "Oh really? I think you have me confused with my father."

"Oh, I know Azrael. You're not him."

I cocked an eyebrow.

"It's good to see you again, Warren."

Something about the way my name dripped off his tongue made me shudder.

In two inhumanly fast strides, he closed the gap between us and his hands grasped my skull. The purple energy swirled around both of us, and somewhere in the distance, a voice was screaming.

He leaned in and hissed. "How's *Alice*?"

A memory flashed across my mind.

Alice was tiny, and she was crying, pulling on my arm and begging me not to go in the house. Charlie Lockett's car was parked in the driveway. I wanted to run, but I didn't.

Charlie stood from his recliner when we walked inside and walked toward Alice, but I stepped in front of her, my tiny fists clenched in balls at my side. "No more."

His head jerked with surprise, and he cackled with the same laughter echoing around the cell. "No more?" His eyes narrowed to angry slits. "Maybe I'll make you come too."

Tears spilled down my cheeks. I was shaking. "I said no!"

Inside the swirling purple fog, I grabbed his throat with one hand and his face with the other. I pushed and pulled, ripping his trachea through his skin as I screamed. His body crumpled, but the familiar wicked spirit that still stalked my nightmares remained.

I unleashed my killing power on him for the second time in both our lifetimes, and Charlie Lockett's spirit detonated. The building shook again. The window in the door exploded. Prison toilet water sprayed everywhere.

Cassiel screamed and cowered against the wall.

The guards in the hall were clambering to get inside and yelling, "Get on the ground! Get on the ground! Get on the ground!"

I slowly turned as one of them fired stun-gun prongs through the window. Rage pulsed through me, throbbing against the veins in my neck as the electric *whirr* sizzled all my nerve endings.

Extending both my hands, I let my power dance at my fingertips, then I dropped my head back and let out an ungodly howl that rattled the floor beneath my feet.

Then with another loud *crack!* I disappeared across the spirit line.

My hands were covered with blood.

Cassiel caught up with me at the Chicago safe house. She was breathless when she ran down the stairs into the bunker. I was slumped over the dining table, my head still spinning with fury and endorphins.

"I thought I lost you," she said, panting.

I straightened, but only barely. I could hardly hear her over the static crackling in my ears from all my angels checking in. Charlie Lockett's destruction had been felt around the world and beyond.

Cassiel must have realized why I was squinting because she knelt in front of me, cradled my jaw in her hands, and switched off my ears. My whole body relaxed.

"What happened back there?"

I opened my mouth to speak, but no words came out.

She grimaced. "At least you didn't pass out. It was probably all the adrenaline." She put her hand under my quivering chin. "Come on. Let's get you cleaned up."

I followed her to my bathroom, where she turned on the hot water in the shower and sink. Looking at myself in the mirror, I was sickened by what I saw.

Human blood.

And weakness.

When steam began wafting from the sink, I splashed my

face and arms with the scalding water and scrubbed. And scrubbed. And scrubbed until my skin felt raw and burned.

"Enough," Cassiel said gently, handing me a towel and reaching around me to turn off the sink.

I dabbed my face with the soft towel as Cassiel's hands slid up my sides from behind. She was pushing my ruined shirt up over my ribs. "This thing is trashed."

It was. My white shirt was covered in blood spatter. When she reached my shoulders, I helped pull it the rest of the way off and dropped it in the trashcan.

"Shower. You'll feel better."

I turned toward her. "Thank you."

Reaching up, she touched my face, and the whole world calmed. My eyes closed, a single tear slipping from each of them. She stretched and kissed one away. And then the other.

Her fingers trailed down my cheek and traced my bottom lip. Then her mouth touched mine. Gently. Tenderly.

I forgot to breathe.

"Warren," she whispered.

Looking down, my gaze fixed on her icy-blue eyes as they searched me. That piercing, all-knowing stare, seeing me as I was in that moment.

Angel. But human.

Powerful. But weak.

Ripe with all my doubts and insecurities. My vulnerable heart ripped open by a past I feared I'd never be free of.

She stretched up on her toes again, kissing my lips this time without reservation. Her arms slid around my shoulders, and her tongue short-circuited something in my brain. Unleashing a long-suppressed need deep inside me.

My lips worked fast. Hard. And desperately as they consumed her. I fisted her hair with one hand and undressed her with the other. The pants first, letting my palm slide over the gentle swell of her backside.

Then I tore my lips from hers long enough to pull the shirt from her perfect body. My gaze fell to her breasts; then my mouth followed.

"Warren" was the last thing I heard before my body was lost to a tsunami of sensation.

"I think we're in for another cold shower."

With her head still on my bare chest, she laughed. The water in the bathroom was still running, and we'd been in my bed for a glorious hour.

Considering it had been about seventy years (Eden time) since I'd been with a woman, I held on shockingly long. Of course, I'd laser focused my mind on everything but the magic of being inside her. My sex-starved brain leapfrogged from one subject to another:

Possible locations of the Nulterra Gate.

Alien vs. Predator.

Our battle plan to protect Echo 5.

Did I lock the Challenger?

All the work I was behind on in Eden.

World peace. Hell, we'd already tackled world hunger. Maybe it was time to aim a little higher.

"We need to get up," she said, tracing her finger around the edges of the blood stone.

I tightened my arm around her. "Five more minutes."

She laughed softly.

"You've never done that before, have you?" I asked.

"Of course I have," she said, looking up at me.

I cocked an eyebrow.

"Well, I haven't done it on Earth, but—"

I smiled.

"What? Did I do something wrong?"

"Not at all."

"Then how could you tell?"

"You seemed very *shocked* by a lot of it."

She settled back down and turned her face away from me. "Well, maybe I was. It's different here."

"How so?"

She was drawing circles around my bellybutton. "You know..."

"I really don't. Please enlighten me."

Her head jerked up. "You've never"—pink flushed in her cheeks—"had sex in Eden?"

I shook my head. "Never."

"But you've been there so long."

"Trying to give me a complex?" I asked with a grin.

"I don't mean it like that."

"It's OK, Cassiel. I'm kidding." I raked my fingertips up and down her back. "What's it like?"

"Everything works the same, but...I don't know. I guess we're more uninhibited there. And here, getting past that inhibition is kinda fun. Like, the nervousness makes it even better."

I smiled.

"I mean, Eden *is* ecstasy. How do you make that better?"

"Makes sense." I rolled, taking her with me across the mattress. "Or maybe you're not doing it with the right person." My weight settled between her thighs.

She put her arms around my neck. "Or maybe it's because I've never done it with a *person* at all."

My eyes doubled, and I pushed back on my right arm. "Are you telling me I'm your first human?"

She bit down on the insides of her lips.

A low growl came from my chest, and I kissed her.

On my nightstand, my phone chimed. My head popped up. "Ahab." I reached for the phone, then bent my arm on the bed to look at it. "The system's back online." My phone rang. "It's Azrael."

"Go ahead."

I rolled off her and pressed the answer button. "Hello?"

"Ahab's back online."

"I know. I just got the message." With one hand, I was mindlessly stroking Cassiel's arm beside me.

"Chimera put Echo-5 on a private server that can't receive inbound information, so we'll still receive status updates, but we'll no longer be able to disable it remotely. That will have to be done by one of us at the panel or from the inside."

"Same passphrase?"

"No. She said the part of the system where the passwords are stored wasn't compromised, but that it would be a good idea to change them anyway."

"What's mine?"

"Nathan picked it."

I groaned.

"AREA 51 REJECT. All caps, with spaces."

"Of course it is," I said, rolling my eyes.

Cassiel sat up, drawing the bedsheet around her. "I'm turning off the water," she whispered.

I held onto the sheet as she got up. Then she smiled over her shoulder and let it drop.

God, she was gorgeous.

"Thanks for letting me know, Az."

"Where are you now?"

The water shut off in the bathroom.

"At the safehouse in Chicago. We found the last soul Moloch released from Nulterra."

"Who was it?"

I sighed. "I'll tell you about it later." Nothing in me wanted to relive the memory. "We're heading back to Eden soon. I'm still going to try to convince Metatron to help us."

"Good luck, son."

"Thanks. I'll call you as soon as I know something."

Cassiel walked back into the room carrying her clothes.

"Bye, Az." I ended the call and put it on the nightstand. "It's not time for clothes again already, is it?" I reached for her and she sat down beside me.

"We need to get back home, and unless you want to raise a lot of eyebrows at the gate, that requires clothes."

I sat up and kissed her shoulder. "Nobody at the gate will notice."

"Samael will notice."

I pulled her over onto my lap. "And I will threaten him with Cira if he tells."

She straddled my thighs and said...something. I couldn't hear because her breasts were near my face.

"Warren?"

I looked up and met her eyes.

"We can't tell anyone about this. If the Council finds out, they'll send me back to the Onyx Tower, and I won't be able to help you."

"Help me?"

She pushed my hair behind my ears. "I'll help you find Metatron."

I blinked. "You will?"

"Yes."

My brain was scrambling. "But why?"

She kissed me softly on the lips, then pulled away. "You know why."

I wanted to ask "I do?" but she kissed me again.

She pulled away and started to get up. I held her still. "Cassiel, how?"

"I know where he is."

CHAPTER TWENTY

*B*ack in Eden, we stopped at the safe room outside the gate to stash our stuff. Cassiel's locker was much bigger than mine. The inside of its door had a couple of magnets. With a glance over, I could make them out: London, Sydney. Now she would have Venice. I'd expected there would be more given her fascination with them.

She was unloading the bag she'd brought along. No phone. Nothing personal. Just hand sanitizer, a toothbrush, and a small collection of travel-sized supplies.

Cassiel had only ever been a traveler.

She caught me staring.

I smiled and turned back to my own stuff. I flipped through my Iliana book until she closed her locker door. "Ready?" she asked.

"Yeah." I stuffed the book back inside and shut the door.

We kept our distance as we neared the Eden steps. It was a little exciting carrying such a secret into the purest place in the universe. I smiled over at her. She smiled back.

My smile faded as I caught sight of my chamber up ahead.

Sooner or later I'd have to do some work—or the bodies (figuratively speaking) would start piling up again.

Just looking at my door, my shoulders sagged. Nothing in me wanted to go in there. I wasn't sure how Azrael had done the job for so many millennia. I was starting to understand why he spent so much time on Earth.

"You all right?" she asked as we neared the Eden Gate.

"Can I confess something?"

She looked surprised. "Sure."

"I hate my job."

"What?"

"The final death. Making people *cease* existing. I hate it almost as much as I hate sentencing souls to Nulterra."

She was smiling. "Tell me how you really feel."

"OK, I will. The Angels of Death got screwed."

"What?" she asked with a laugh.

"Think about it. The messengers have the Avronesh." I pointed back at her. "You guys have the Onyx Tower. The guardians have the Keep in the auranos. The prophets have Celestine. And the Angels of Life have the Throne Room.

"The Angels of Death are supposed to be the most powerful in all of Eden, and we got stuck with Reclusion. Undoubtedly, the most miserable place in all of Eden."

"The Angels of Death are the most powerful in Eden?" She scoffed. "You sound just like your father."

"Are we not? It says so in the Canon."

"You are the *first* choir in Eden. Nowhere in the Canon does it say you're the most powerful."

"Same thing."

She laughed. "It's really not."

"Still," I said, shaking my head.

"What's wrong with Reclusion? It's gorgeous. All polished obsidian and domed ceilings. You even have an oculus."

I made a circle with my fingers. "That looks *this big* from the floor."

"But you can go to the landing above the oculus. It has some of the best views of the auranos."

I stopped walking and crossed my arms. "Oh really? How do the stars look from the Onyx Tower?"

She pressed her lips together to fight a smile.

"See?" With a huff, I walked on and she followed. "Reclusion is depressing. It's always dark. And cold. And...do you hear that?" I pointed above our heads.

She looked up. "The music?"

"Yes. There is absolutely no music in that place. It is dead silent *all the time*."

She smiled. "Pun intended?"

"No, because this is not a laughing matter." I pointed toward the giant black door. "Would you like to step inside and see for yourself?"

Her nose scrunched.

"Exactly. Because it's awful. I wish I could take all the souls locked up in there and destroy them on Earth."

She grabbed my sleeve. "Hold on. You're perfectly fine."

"Why thank you," I said awkwardly.

"No. I mean, you delivered the final death three times on Earth without it affecting you."

I considered flexing to show how powerful I was, but Cassiel was serious. Per usual. "And this is such a big deal because...?"

"It's forbidden to perform the deed outside of Reclusion because it's supposed to be physically harmful."

"Maybe it was true for Azrael, but not for me. We might look similar, but we are *very* different."

She shook her head, her face still puzzled. "That can't be it."

"Maybe I'm tougher than what you give me credit for." That time, I flexed.

She laughed. "What's the matter with you?"

"I don't know." I dropped my arms. "Sex does weird things to the male brain."

"Shh." She looked around for anyone who might have heard.

"Relax. Nobody cares." We started up the steps. "Stop trying to change the subject. What are we going to do about my job?"

"We?"

"Yeah. You make the rules, right?"

She rolled her eyes.

"If that's not it, then what do you do?" I bent toward her. "Besides make decisions that ruin people's lives?"

Her face whipped toward me.

I put my hands up in defense. "It's a joke. Ha. Ha. Funny, funny."

"Not funny."

"No, I guess it's not. I'm sorry."

After a moment, she exhaled, the sound heavy with regret. "You're actually right. We do make a lot of decisions that ruin people's lives for the sake of the greater good. We allow things to happen on Earth without intervening. We set things into motion that can really damage certain individuals."

"That's why you don't like spending time on Earth. At least here, you don't have to see the ripple effect your decisions have."

She didn't answer.

I wanted to hold her hand, but I didn't.

She was looking down at the moonstone steps. "This trip has been eye-opening for me in ways I didn't expect."

"Is that why you're willing to help me now?"

"That's why I'm willing to *try*."

"Thank you, Cassiel."

"Don't thank me yet. We still don't know that he can actually help."

"Where are we going?" We were nearing the Eden Gate.

"You were right about Metatron being in Lunaris. He's in a place called the Fiery."

If I'd had any questions about whether or not it was the gloom of Earth that drove me to Cassiel, those questions vanished when we crossed into Eden. As we walked into the buzzing Idalia marketplace and my knuckles graced her hand, I felt thirteen again. Downright giddy.

Still, aside from a private smile, I kept my affections to myself. The marketplace was busy, and it was no place to unveil an angel affair.

"How far is Lunaris?" I asked.

"Several hours in the air. We can take a ship, but it's much slower."

"I don't mind flying. It just makes me feel weird to do it around other humans who can't."

"I wish I could say I understand that, but I don't."

"I don't expect you to."

She looked up ahead. "Let's walk through the village, and we'll fly from the beach. We should be able to make the Fiery before dark."

"What is the Fiery?"

"It's a light garden."

"A what?"

She smiled. "You'll see."

My nose caught a whiff of something delectable nearby. I looked around and saw the Heavenly Delights manna cart was open for business near the end of the lane. A sparkling black-and-white stardust sign out front said "Fresh and Hot: Death by Chocolate Manna!" I stopped walking. How could I not?

Holly and Heather—Reuel's favorite bakers in all of Eden—

were both working the stand. Holly was all smiles as we approached. "Hello, Warren. Death by Chocolate manna?" She offered us her basket and pulled back the checkered blue cloth that covered it.

My eyes nearly rolled back in my head. "That smells sinful."

She laughed. "Help yourself."

I pulled out a piece and offered it to Cassiel. "Ladies first?"

Holly and I both watched as she lifted it to her mouth and took a small bite. Closing her eyes, she licked her pink lips. "It's positively delectable, Holly. Bravo."

"Thank you." Holly held the basket toward me again. "Your turn."

I took a piece for myself and slowly bit into it, savoring its warmth, flakiness, and molten chocolate. My body quivered with sweet happiness. "Holly, Heather, I'm nominating you for sainthood."

The ladies giggled.

"Warren?" A woman's voice across the lane made us all turn. Audrey Jordan, Sloan's mother, was walking toward us with a basket full of food. Audrey had died when Sloan and I were still together.

"Audrey," I said, meeting her halfway. I greeted her with a tight one-armed hug, carefully holding the manna away from her white dress. Chocolate, no matter on what plane, was messy. "It's so good to see you."

She stretched onto her tiptoes as she hugged me back. "And you, my sweet Warren. How are you? Have you been to Earth lately?"

"I just got back."

"Did you see Sloan?" she asked, her eyes full of hope.

I shook my head. "Not this trip, but I saw Nathan, and he brought me new photos of Iliana. She still doesn't have hardly any hair."

"Sloan didn't either until she was almost two."

"Really?"

"Yep."

"She's really cute, though, and *so* smart. She's talking now and crawling a lot. Nathan says she and Sloan both are doing really well."

She put a hand on her chest and smiled. "I know. I feel her."

That was the thing about humans in Eden. Their souls were still connected to those they loved on Earth. Turns out, love is a bond so strong even death can't sever it.

Audrey looked past me at Cassiel. She offered her hand. "Hello. I'm Audrey Jordan. I don't believe we've met."

I stepped to the side. "Audrey, this is Cassiel. Cassiel, this is Sloan's mom."

They shook hands. "It's a pleasure to meet you, Audrey. I'm very familiar with your daughter."

"Most angels are. It's very nice to meet you too." Audrey touched my arm. "It's good to see a smile on this guy's face. It doesn't happen nearly enough. Even in a place as happy as this."

She was right, but was I really smiling that much? Maybe we weren't being inconspicuous enough.

Audrey pulled her basket around in front of her. "I'd better be off. I'm having dinner with my family tonight. It's so wonderful to see you, Warren. I hope you come visit soon."

I smiled. "I'd really like to."

She waved, and I watched her walk away. Cassiel was watching me. "You didn't mean that."

I sighed. "It's complicated."

"We have a long walk unless you want to fly," she said as we started down the street again. "And I know you'd rather walk."

I took another bite of manna and chewed slowly. "It's not that I don't want to see her. I'm just not a fan of visiting her at home. It's exactly like her place back on Earth."

"And that makes you sad? Even in Eden?"

"Maybe not *sad* exactly, but I don't like the way it makes me feel."

Her head tilted. "That's curious."

I thought of Audrey putting her hand over her heart. "I'm a little more connected to Earth than most angels."

"Understatement," she said with a chuckle.

When the street ended at the main road, we turned right and started down a stone staircase. At the bottom was the trail that would lead us to the Eternal Sea. "Is it such a bad thing I was born part human?"

"Do you want the truth?"

"Isn't that what we do now?"

"I used to think it was a bad thing. That you were an inferior angel."

I clutched my chest. "Ouch."

"But I'm starting to think you might have an advantage on all of us. You understand things about the world we never will, and you certainly have more incentive to fight for Earth than any other angel in Eden."

"That's true. And I don't hold it against you that you thought I was inferior. Sometimes I feel the same way."

"I was wrong, Warren."

"Really? How many other angels have you had to chaperone since the beginning of time?"

She smiled. "Your father. On a few occasions."

I laughed. "Touché."

"You're just different. I realize now that's not a bad thing."

One stone was very tall, so I stepped down ahead of her and offered a hand.

She laughed as she took it. "This. This right here is a perfect example of another good way you're different."

"Huh?"

"I have wings. No one in Eden helps me on the stairs." She held onto my hand after she was standing beside me.

"You're wearing a long dress. I don't want you to fall."

With a genuine smile, she nodded. "I know. It's sweet and refreshing. Thoughtfulness in Eden is rare because no one *needs* help."

"I guess you're right."

"You guess? I'm an Angel of Knowledge. Warren, you *know* I'm right."

Laughing, I squeezed her fingers before she released my hand. We reached the bottom of the steps and turned toward the sound of trickling water.

"You know, we could leave from the cliffs if you'd like to stop by and see your mother."

I smiled. "Yeah. I'd like that. Might drop by my house first and check on Alice and Skittles."

"Skittles?"

"My dog."

She laughed softly, shaking her head. "Pets are for humans. Angels don't have dogs."

"This one does."

Music and laughter echoed through my house when Cassiel and I walked through the front door. Skittles barked and ran through the open living room, slipping and sliding happily across the dark hardwood floor toward us.

I knelt down to greet her. "There's my girl. Who's a good dog?" I leaned down to let her lick my face.

"You're home!" Alice cheered, running in from the back patio through the open door in the living room. She wore a pink bikini with some kind of skirt wrapped around her waist.

I stood and caught her around the middle. "Not for long," I said, kissing the side of her head. "Who all is here?"

There were lots of people and angels in our infinity pool overlooking the bright-blue ocean.

"Just some friends." She draped her arms around my neck. "You know I get lonely when you're not here."

I laughed. "No, you don't."

Her blonde hair whipped around her face as she shook her head. "No, I don't." Her eyes landed on Cassiel behind me. "Oh. Hello, Cassiel."

Cassiel waved.

I pulled Alice close and inhaled. "Had a little bit to drink, have we?"

Alice held her index finger and her thumb millimeters apart. "Just a little."

"Is that my grandson?" Yaya called, waving from the pool through the sliding-glass wall of the house. She held a wineglass in her other hand.

I looked at Alice. "You're hanging out with my grandmother?"

"George and your mom are here too." Alice counted on her fingers. "And Sagen, Lachlan, and Forfax."

"Lachlan, really? Good for him."

Outside, Lachlan and Sagen, Forfax's male partner in the auranos, were playing a pool version of a game I liked to call hoverball. It was like volleyball, except often telekinetic.

"I hope you don't mind," Alice said, pulling me toward the kitchen.

"Of course I don't mind." I looked back at Cassiel. She was lingering near the front door. "Come on in. You can meet the rest of my family."

The kitchen was full of food. Thanks to my mother, I was sure. Alice stopped at the kitchen freezer and pulled out a pitcher made from an Eden blend of dry ice. It was filled with something pink and fruity. She poured two tall glasses full and handed one to me and one to Cassiel.

I tried to refuse it. "We can't stay."

"You can have one drink. It's delicious. Gazenberry and crystal water."

Uh oh. Crystal water was like the white lighting of the after-life. "Be careful with that stuff," I said to Cassiel as she took a sip.

She shuddered. "Whoa."

"It's good, right?" Alice turned up the volume on the house speakers.

"It's something," Cassiel said, still grimacing as she carefully set the glass on the countertop.

Alice took my hand and twirled under my arm. Then she danced out the patio door over to Forfax on the pool steps. We followed her outside, both of us leaving our drinks behind.

Sagen caught the ball in his large hands. A guardian, much like Reuel, Sagen towered over everyone else in the pool. "Great, you brought the Council to the party."

"Be nice," I said.

"I'm just curious. Is she here to hang out, or has she come to tell us we require approval to be here now?"

Lachlan and Forfax both laughed.

I shot them all a warning glare.

My mother got out of her lounge chair to greet us. She wore a black sundress, a wide-brim hat, and giant sunglasses. Mom looked like a Kennedy.

I greeted her with a kiss on the cheek. "Hi, Mom."

"Hi, son." She took off her glasses and smiled at Cassiel. "Hello again. Nice to see you, Cassiel. You look lovely as always."

"Thank you, Nadine. So do you." Cassiel glanced around the party. "Looks like everyone is having a wonderful time."

"Yes. This is what Eden is all about, isn't it?" Mom asked.

Cassiel nodded and smiled, sort of. She looked more confused than anything.

Yaya waved her hands over her head in the pool. "Warren, introduce Yaya to your friend!"

I looked at Mom. "Is Yaya drunk?"

Mom chuckled. "What do you think?"

"Where's George?" I asked.

Mom stretched on her toes, looking out toward the water. "Down by the dock. They sailed over on their boat. I think he's washing it."

"Was it dirty?" I asked, confused, knowing that wasn't really a thing in Eden.

"No," she said, smiling.

Yaya, refusing to be ignored anymore, clapped over her head.

I laughed. "Yaya, this is my friend Cassiel. Cassiel, this is my grandmother. You can call her Helen."

Yaya waved her hand. "Hogwash! She can call me Yaya."

"It's nice to meet you, Yaya," Cassiel said.

"Heads up!" Lachlan shouted from the pool as an inflatable ball sailed toward our heads.

I caught the ball in a shower of pool water, which had to be intentional given either one of the angels could have stopped the ball before it reached us. Using my power, I smacked the water in front of both of them, splashing their faces before I hurled the ball back at Lachlan's face. It bounced off his forehead.

We all laughed. Except Cassiel. She took a small step back.

Mom smiled warmly and touched her arm. "It really is wonderful to see you. Please help yourself to something to eat if you're hungry. There's plenty of food."

"Ah yes. Thank you." She sidestepped back toward the door. "I'll do that now actually."

Mom and I watched her go. "Think it was Sagen's greeting? Should I have a word with him?" I asked her.

Mom linked her arm with mine, watching Cassiel float

around the kitchen. "That probably didn't help, but I think she'd feel like a fish out of water in a situation like this anyway."

"What do you mean?"

"I mean, they're not like us. It's harder for them to relax and have fun when their whole lives have been about service and duty."

Perhaps Mom was right. As much as I bitched about my job in Reclusion, at least it wasn't all I'd ever known. Cassiel and the others had been created for their destinies. There had been no childhood. No decisions. No options.

Was it really any wonder that a backyard pool party had her mildly freaked out?

Mom leaned on my arm. "It took a long while to soften your dad up too. Give her time. She'll come around."

I slid my eyes over at her. "I don't know what you're talking about, Mom."

She laughed.

My mother didn't have to be an angel to know when I was lying.

"How long can you stay?"

"Not long. We're on our way to find Metatron."

"I hate it when you leave."

I smiled and kissed her forehead. "I know."

She squeezed my bicep. "We have all of eternity to celebrate your success."

My mind drifted to Iliana. "I really have to go. Wish me luck."

She looked at me seriously. "You don't need luck. You are your father's son. You can do anything."

"Thanks, Mom." I hugged her. "I love you."

"I love you too."

I waved to Yaya in the pool. "Bye, Yaya. Give my best to George. Tell him I'm sorry I missed him."

"Your grandad and that stupid boat," she said, shaking her

head. "Well, at least Yaya loves you." She blew me a drunken kiss.

I laughed and knelt down to pet Skittles. "To be fair, George doesn't know I'm here. Maybe you should eat some manna."

"You're not leaving, are you?" Alice called from the pool. "You just got here!"

I stood and walked toward her with Skittles trotting beside me. "I know, but the universe won't save itself."

"Warren, hold up!" Lachlan hoisted himself out of the pool and jogged over.

I patted his shoulder. "I'm glad you're here."

"Me too. What happened in Chicago?"

I sighed. "It was a mess, but I handled it. There will probably be lots of media attention for a while."

"That bad?"

"Yeah."

He lowered his voice. "What was that *thing*?"

"It was a soul that should have been destroyed a very long time ago." My eyes drifted behind him. Alice was laughing at something...at *everything*. I smiled. "It's done now. Forever."

Lachlan nodded. "Whatever else you need, just let me know."

"Thank you."

"Warren, wait!" Alice called, sloshing her way out of the pool. "Please stay!"

I put my arms around her. "I wish I could, but Cassiel and I are on our way to Lunaris."

"Lunaris?" Her eyes widened. "Can I come?"

"You'd better stay here and take care of Skittles and Forfax. I don't know how long I'll be gone, and I'll probably have to go straight to Earth when we're finished there."

Her shoulders drooped.

I put my finger under her chin and raised her eyes to meet mine. "I promise, I'll take you to Lunaris soon."

She smiled. "Hurry back."

"I do try."

Alice clung to my waist until we got inside. Cassiel had finished almost half the potent drink. Alice pointed at her. "It's good, isn't it?"

"It's an acquired taste," Cassiel said, lowering the glass from her lips.

Smiling, I cupped her jaw and used my thumb to swipe away a drizzle of pink gazenberry juice from the corner of her mouth. My thumb lingered a second too long.

Alice gasped and wagged her finger between me and Cassiel. "Ooo, what's going on here?"

I dropped my hand. "Nothing. Go play in the pool with Forfax." Laughing, I playfully pushed her away.

"I saw that. I know what you guys are up to."

"And you'll keep it to yourself, right?" There was no point in lying. Alice knew me even better than my mother.

As she walked backward toward the door, she pretended to zip her lips shut. Then she blew me a kiss.

When she was gone, I looked at Cassiel. "Sorry about that. She won't say anything."

She nodded, still staring past me. Outside, Alice squealed as Forfax pulled her into the pool.

"What's the matter?"

"You're changing Eden, Warren."

My brow crumpled with confusion. "What? Alice was here long before I came."

"I'm not talking about Alice. There are angels *playing* in your backyard." She shook her head. "That's not normal."

"Maybe it's time for normal to change."

She smirked. "I guess we should start giving everyone time off."

"Maybe you should. I think that's the only thing I've done

right since I got here. That's part of the reason you hear happiness right now."

"We have about a million years of experience on you—"

"Sure you do. But the Earth was created to evolve. Wasn't Eden?" I picked up an *arenapple* and bit into it.

She stopped and stared at me. Something in her eyes told me her mind was spinning for a rebuttal. "Eden's perfection is held together by an intricate tapestry of laws and tradition—"

I burst out laughing. "Bullshit."

Her eyes doubled.

"Laws and tradition? Would that be the Father's answer if I asked him about the tapestry of Eden?"

Her jaw went rigid. But she didn't argue.

"I'm pretty sure the rules were created out of necessity to keep *Earth* in order. Otherwise, what the hell did you all do before you had us as a welfare project? Was this place just a shitshow until the Father decided to test out humanity?"

She was scowling, but I knew she was trying to keep a straight face. "Eden has never been a shitshow."

It was funny to hear her swear. "So what was it like before us humans? Was it all choir meetings and Council hearings?"

She finally cracked a smile. "No."

"So maybe it's held together by something else. The Father told me in Africa, the Council was appointed to make the hard calls. He's not a god of laws and tradition. He's a god who'd rather fish with the locals than rule the world."

Her shoulders relaxed. "Maybe you're right about some things."

With a gasp, I grabbed my chest. "What did you say?"

"I won't repeat myself." She smiled again.

I took her hand. "Come with me. I want to show you something."

After putting Skittles back outside with the others, I led

Cassiel to my bedroom and closed the door behind us. "Have a seat," I said, gesturing to the bed.

She raised an eyebrow.

I laughed as I opened the nightstand drawer. "Trust me."

She sat down.

From the drawer, I pulled a small, smooth stone. I handed it to her.

"A memory stone?"

I nodded. "The Father gave it to me when I first came to Eden."

Similar to a blood stone, it could hold one memory from Earth at a time, preserving it in perfect clarity to be recalled by the holder whenever they desired.

Sitting down beside her, I clasped my hand around hers with the stone between our palms.

A memory surged to life in our minds. The day I took Azrael back to Earth. I had just dropped him in the front yard of Sloan's house, and against my better judgment, I'd stopped in Iliana's nursery. It was the first time I'd ever seen her face-to-face, except the moment she was born.

I was standing over her crib, and she was reaching her tiny arms up toward me. I didn't dare hold her, but I did let her grasp my finger.

"I love you so much, Iliana," I'd said, but not out loud.

Her spirit must have heard my voice because she started smiling and kicking her legs. She sputtered back a lot of baby babble. Nothing in existence could have meant more to me than the look on her face.

The memory faded.

When I looked at Cassiel, tears had streaked her cheeks.

"You really love her, don't you?"

Cassiel would've been able to do more than simply see Iliana in the memory. She'd feel exactly what I felt in that moment.

Because that's really what memories are—everlasting snapshots of the way we felt.

"Of course. She's my daughter." I closed her hand around the stone. "And she's the future for all of us. Imagine not fearing the Morning Star anymore because *she* is on our side."

Another tear slid down her face. I brushed it away. "Why are you crying?"

"Because I've never loved anyone or anything with such intense affection. And I'm sure no one has ever cared for me." She was still clutching the memory stone, letting all my most vulnerable—most pure—emotions mingle with her own.

My hand slipped beneath her hair and curled around the back of her neck. "You're wrong." I pulled her lips to meet mine and kissed her slow and deep.

The sound of singing outside broke our kiss. It was Yaya belting out "Dancing Queen" by ABBA. We both laughed.

I stood and offered Cassiel my hand. "Shall we do this?"

"Let's fly."

CHAPTER TWENTY-ONE

*B*y the time we reached the Lunaris shore, I could've almost been convinced that flying was the only way to travel. The wind in my hair. The sea spray on my face. The rush of adrenaline thumping through my veins.

I felt like Superman.

And the view. Holy shit, the view. The first sun had just begun its descent beneath the watery horizon, splashing pinks and purples across the crests of the waves. Dolphins jumped to greet us. And every once in a while, Cassiel would glance over and smile.

The second sun was setting by the time land came into view. Beach shops and restaurants alive with music, colorful lights, and laughter lined the shore.

We landed a few minutes later at the top of a waterfall in a lush green gully far away from the beach. We were the only beings in sight.

"Well?" Cassiel asked over the noise of the water. She was running her fingers through her hair to straighten it.

"That was..." Smiling wide, I let out a loud sigh, then grabbed her and kissed her. She was stunned at first, but then she relaxed in my arms and kissed me back. "Exhilarating," I said when I pulled away.

"Exhilarating." She was breathless. "That's a good word."

"I mean it." Still smiling, I rested my hands on my hips and looked back over the path we'd flown. "I've flown plenty before, but that was spectacular."

She laughed. "I think we might have a convert."

"Maybe."

I surveyed our surroundings. Vegetation unlike any I'd ever seen on Earth *or* in Eden colored the rocky landscape. Thick moss carpeted the ground, and a leafy vine snaked all across the tall rock formations that framed the narrow waterfall. I peeked over the rock face. It was a long way down.

Far in the distance, I could see an empty beach. The sand shimmered like glitter.

I sighed. "Eden never stops taking my breath. It's incredible."

"Especially Lunaris. I love it here."

"Where do you live?" I asked, feeling a little stupid for not knowing such a basic detail of a woman I had carnal knowledge of.

"I have a few places, but my main residence is in the Onyx Tower."

Her answer made me feel a spark of sadness. The Onyx Tower was beautiful, but she literally lived at work. The thought of me doing that was nauseating.

"What is it?" she asked.

"I was just thinking what it might be like to live in Reclusion. Ugh."

She laughed and the sound tingled my spine.

It was starting to get dark. "Do you think it's too late to visit?" I asked.

"No. The Fiery doesn't operate on regular days and nights.

We're just as likely to catch its residents sleeping as we are to catch them eating lunch."

"What?"

"Come on. You'll see."

"Where are we going?"

"Down."

I pointed off the rock. "Down there?"

"Yep. Let's go."

Cassiel started down a trail between two boulders. The path was steep. Almost too steep for even me. "If Metatron is older than Sandalphon, how would he manage this?" My foot slid on a patch of loose dirt.

"He wouldn't. There are a few ways in and out of the Fiery. This is just the most beautiful. I like to bring all first-timers in this way." She glanced back over her shoulder. "Why? Is it too much for you?"

"No." Though I wasn't so sure. On Earth, I would've needed a rope and a belay for such an incline. At least here, my wings could catch me. Whether or not I'd take out Cassiel before my wings caught was another question. I slowed my pace to put some cushion between us.

"Do you come here a lot?"

"Not in years."

"But you know Metatron?"

"Very well. I haven't seen him in a long time, but I get letters occasionally."

We passed a couple of full gazenberry bushes. Gazenberries looked like pink currents, but they tasted just like Nerds candy. I plucked a few ripe berries off and popped them into my mouth.

"When we were in Italy, you were so adamant he wouldn't help me. What's changed your mind?"

She shook her head, and her long loose curls swooshed

across her back. "I still don't think he will, but I may know of a piece of leverage we can use to convince him."

"What's that?"

"Let's just say, Iliana has the power to give him what he wants most. We'll see how the conversation goes just asking him."

At the bottom of the falls, Cassiel crept along the rocks toward the waterfall. I stopped and looked up. In the cool mist, rainbows arched in different directions thanks to Eden's double suns.

Around me, the water seemed to vanish under the mountain.

"Come on!" Cassiel called before disappearing behind the falls.

I followed her and found that the rocks formed a bridge over where the water poured *into* the large mouth of a cave. She was waiting for me on the other side.

It was dark inside the cave except for glowing blue stalactites that hung from the ceiling and small patches of bright, colorful plants that lined the banks of the river.

"Wow," I said, my mouth gaping as I took in the expansive cavern. "It's like *Fraggle Rock.*"

"What's a fraggle rock?" she asked.

"It was a cartoon when I was a kid. Is it this dark everywhere?"

"More or less."

A hollow thump made us both look behind her. It was a small wooden boat bumping against the rock. "That's our ride," she said.

We walked over to it. There was no driver. No ropes. No anchor I could see. Cassiel held up the hem of her skirt and stepped over the railing. Then she turned and motioned me forward. "Your turn."

I stepped onboard and the boat rocked. "Now what?"

She sat down on the bench and patted the seat beside her. "Sit here, then reach back and push off the rock."

I raised an eyebrow.

She smiled. "The boat won't move with the stream until you make it."

"OK," I said, my voice full of melodic doubt.

I sat beside her, then reached back and pushed against the rock wall.

The boat lurched forward into the current, and my upper body toppled backward. Cassiel's arm came around my back to catch me. Our laughter echoed off the walls of the cavern.

"Remember how I said no one needs help in Eden? Perhaps I was wrong," she said.

I kissed her to shut her up.

Blushing, she checked our surrounds. We were alone. "No one will see us down here, right?" I asked.

"No, I don't think so."

"Good. Come here." I kissed her again, then put my arm around her.

The boat moved slowly down the river, gently bouncing off the rocks as the stream curved through the cave. Cassiel pointed toward a small cove in one of the bends. It was covered with fluorescent mushrooms and flowers. "See the lights? That's what all of the Fiery looks like."

I leaned against her. "No. This is what all of the Grateful Dead's music videos looked like."

She nodded. "They said the same thing."

My head snapped back, and I turned all the way toward her. She just laughed.

We floated for about ten minutes (or it could have been an hour in Eden time, who knows?). Cassiel softly hummed "Time after Time" with her head against my shoulder, and I almost forgot we were on an urgent mission. Easy to do in the land of *ever after*.

The farther we went, the thicker and brighter the gardens were. We went over two small waterfalls before it seemed we reached the end of the cave.

On the other side, the auranos was dark except for the stars and planets, but the land was alive with a brilliant light show. "Holy smokes," I said, my eyes full of wonder.

Purple and blue cascading flowers covered the riverbanks. To our right was a field of glowing orange, pink, and gold spindles that twisted up toward the stars. On Cassiel's side of the boat were tall trees, the brightest green I'd ever seen.

She was watching me.

I was smiling so wide my face felt like it might cramp. "This is the most beautiful place I've ever seen."

"I knew you'd like it."

"It's like all the plants are made of neon."

"They are. Well, at least some of them are. Other gases produce different colors. Mercury creates blue. Helium, yellow."

"You're serious?"

"Yeah. It's a lot like Earth's neon signs. The energy of auranos"—she pointed to the sky—"causes the gas to glow."

Tiny blue gnats floated around us. I relaxed against her. "This is beautiful." I looked at her admiring the lights like it was the first time she'd seen them. All the colors of the rainbow reflected off her face. I pushed her hair behind her ear. "You're beautiful."

My hand lingered on her cheek, and she turned her face into it, closing her eyes. She pressed a kiss to my palm.

There were faint voices up ahead, and music—there was always music in Eden.

We rounded another bend toward what looked like an outdoor restaurant. A pergola draped with glowing white vines crowned the tables. There were only a handful of patrons.

I immediately recognized Metatron sitting with a woman

and watching the river. His hair was white, and his tan face was creased with deep wrinkles. He sat his chair with the weight of a few hundred years. His spine was bent. His head was down. Even from our distance, I could see the tremor in his hand as he slowly lifted his fork to his mouth.

My mind flashed forward to my face in the mirror as an old man. Gray hair. Deep lines. Tired eyes. Even though I was quasi-immortal, my body was far from perfect. In Eden, it was better, but I could still feel a slight ache in my spine from where Azrael had ripped out the bullet a few days before.

What would eternity feel like after I'd spent a few more decades on Earth? Which I fully intended to do once Iliana was older and my presence was no longer dangerous.

Metatron didn't only look his age—it was obvious, he felt it.

The boat slowed at a small wooden dock near the eatery. I got out first, then offered my hand to Cassiel. She took it, then lifted the front of her skirt as she stepped out.

"Cassiel, is that you?" a woman asked behind me.

Cassiel pulled away from me and straightened her dress. "Hello, Miriam."

I followed her up the bank. The woman who had been seated with Metatron was walking out onto the glowing landscape. The two women embraced.

They turned toward me when I neared them. "Warren, this is Metatron's wife, Miriam. Miriam, this is Warren."

"The American angel." She reached for my hand.

I laughed and shook it. "That's me. I can't believe you've heard of me all the way out here."

"You're a legend. Just like your father."

"You know Azrael?"

She just smiled, waiting for me to answer my own question. I felt stupid. "Of course you do. I forget you've been here for what? Hundreds of years?"

"Hundreds, ha. Try again."

"Well, you've aged very well." She actually looked younger than me.

"Sweet boy." She motioned me forward. "Come. I'll introduce you to Enoch."

I leaned toward Cassiel. "Enoch?"

"Earth name. Someday you'll get the hang of living here," she said with a grin.

I sighed and shook my head. "One sec." Kneeling down, I plucked a blue flower from the ground. It still glowed as I stood.

"Beautiful isn't it?" Miriam asked. "It will burn for about a day. Then it will go out."

I twirled it in my fingers. "What happens if I take it home?"

"It dies outside the Fiery."

"That's so cool."

I carried the flower toward the table. Metatron started to stand as we approached, but Cassiel held her hands up. "No, no. Don't get up on our account."

With a grateful *humph*, the old angel settled back in his chair.

Cassiel walked over and knelt by his chair, putting her hand affectionately on his arm. "Metatron, it's so good to see you."

He covered her hand with his own withered one. "Shalom, Cassiel. It's a pleasure as always, my old friend."

Friend? Interesting.

Their plates on the round table looked like giant red flowers with the food in the center of the petals.

"We didn't mean to interrupt your meal," Cassiel said.

"Nonsense. I insist that you join us," Miriam said, sitting back down beside her husband.

I couldn't help but think of Sloan and be grateful that she wouldn't be chained to an ancient angel someday.

Cassiel stood and touched my arm. "Metatron, this is Warren. Though, I'm sure you already know that."

Metatron smiled and reached up. "Of course. Warren, it's nice to finally make your acquaintance. We've heard a lot about you for many years."

I gently shook his hand. "Good things, I hope?"

He smiled. "*Things*, anyway."

I laughed. I could appreciate an angel with a sense of humor. They were rare. Then again, he'd been born on Earth, so he was different like me. "It's a pleasure to meet you, sir. I understand this is quite the privilege."

"I don't know about all that." He gestured toward the table. "Please join us for a meal. The Fiery has the best *gonganut* manna in all of Eden."

"Gonganut? I haven't even heard of that." I turned to pull out a chair for Cassiel, but she'd already sat down.

Metatron slowly lifted his shaky hand and pointed over our heads at the vines growing on the pergola. "Gonganut. The white flowers wither and fall to the ground and form a pod under the soil."

"Like peanuts," I said.

Cassiel's brow lifted. "I'm surprised you know that."

I tapped my temple. "Not all spiderwebs and dust up there, my dear."

Metatron laughed—and wheezed.

In front of Cassiel and myself, two eight-inch circles in the tabletop began to glow red. Then they swelled. I pulled my hands back and watched. The centers cracked in a star shape, then peeled back like petals.

My eyes widened, and I looked at Cassiel.

She was watching me again with a smile. Then she grabbed one of her own petals and peeled it back. Then another and another until the food in the center was unveiled.

Manna, fresh fruit, and some kind of chocolate were all inside...even for Eden, it was impressive magic.

The berry-sweet smell was intoxicating. I picked up a piece

of manna and bit off the edge. It melted like butter in my mouth, and my eyes closed with pleasure.

Metatron had an expectant smile when I opened my eyes. "Well?"

"Delicious."

Cassiel cut her manna with her fork and knife. "We had some chocolate manna in Idalia today that was to die for."

He chuckled. "Perhaps I should try it."

Cassiel's face fell.

"Stop making jokes like that. You know I don't like it," Miriam said.

"I apologize, my love." Metatron laid his napkin across his flower plate. "Not that I don't love the visit, but why have you come? I doubt it's only to appreciate the *luxem* blooms."

Cassiel swallowed the bite in her mouth. "No doubt you know of the Vitamorte's birth."

"Yes, we've heard," he said.

"Congratulations," Miriam said to me.

I smiled. "Thank you."

"There's a plot for the demons to take the child into the spirit world," Cassiel said. "They plan to use her unbridled power to destroy the spirit line, forever separating the mortal world from Eden."

Metatron nodded. "You told me about that in your letter."

"Did she tell you what the Council wants me to do with Iliana?" I asked.

"She didn't tell me, but we heard it from a shopkeeper in the village. They want to make the child a seraph," Metatron said.

My stomach twisted. I dropped the manna on my plate, my appetite suddenly gone.

"Yes," she said.

Metatron folded his hand on the tabletop. "I don't understand what this has to do with me."

"I need to find the Morning Star. I believe he might be my

only bargaining chip to convince the Council to allow Iliana to stay on Earth." I took a deep breath to steel my nerves. "I'm hoping you will return with me to Earth to identify him."

Metatron turned his ear toward me. "Am I going mad, or did I hear you say you want me to return to Earth?"

"You heard me correctly, sir."

His wife tried unsuccessfully to stifle a smile. "I'm sorry, Warren, but if you only knew how hard of a time I have getting him to go to the market once a century."

Cassiel took my hand across the table. "Metatron, please consider this. You know I wouldn't ask if it were not important."

"Yes, I know. Which is why I'm sorry I must be a disappointment. Does the Council know you are moving against them? Undermining their decision?"

I squeezed Cassiel's fingers.

Her eyes fell. "No, they don't. But I'm sure it won't be long before they find out, which is why it's imperative that you help us now."

The angel shook his head. "I'm sorry, I can't—"

"The Vitamorte can give you what you want most in this world," she blurted out.

Her words landed on the table with a nearly audible *thud*. Metatron sat back in his seat. Miriam covered her face with her hands.

Cassiel leaned forward. "But only if she's allowed to come into her power. To do that, she must grow up on Earth."

Metatron and his wife locked eyes. Finally, he turned back to Cassiel and bit back an angry smile. "You toy with my emotions, my friend."

"Please help us," I said.

The angel closed his eyes. "Where do you believe the Morning Star is now?"

I could have fist-bumped everyone in the restaurant. "We

believe he's either been recently born to a friend of mine or that he's still in utero."

Metatron laughed. "Well, why didn't you start with that?"

His tone made the hope go out of my chest like air from a sliced balloon. Cassiel's hand tightened around mine.

"I can't identify an angel child before they come of age." He looked at Cassiel. "You should know that."

Her eyes closed.

"How do you know?" I asked, desperation in me welling like a tidal wave.

"When the Morning Star was born the last time as Leviathan, I visited Earth to see the child. Then, of course, we knew it was him." He shook his head sadly. "But had I not been told, I wouldn't have known."

I released Cassiel's hand. Balancing my elbows on the table, I cradled my skull.

"I'm sorry. I know this is not the news you were hoping for," Miriam said.

My eyes were fixed on the center of the table.

Metatron's wrinkled hand closed around my forearm, and a wave of peace washed over me. He was an Angel of Ministry. I took a deep breath and pulled my arm away.

He looked surprised.

I pinched the bridge of my nose. "I know you're trying to help, but I can't let my senses be dulled. There must be another way."

We were all quiet for a while. No one had any ideas, least of all me. Cassiel put her hand on my back. "We'll figure something out."

I didn't look at her. I was afraid I'd see deceit in her eyes.

"If there was any way for me to help, please know I would." Metatron sighed heavily. "Your daughter could be of great value to me personally."

I folded my arms. "Why?"

Miriam looked like she might cry. "Because she will have the power to destroy angels."

Cassiel put her hands in her lap and looked away.

"Well, yeah, but why does that matter to you?" I asked.

"Because he wants to die," Cassiel said.

I sat back in my seat. "So my success is a suicide mission for you?"

Metatron pushed his plate back. "That's a very harsh way of viewing it, but yes. I've lived for thousands of years. I'm tired and I'm old. This body has been worn out for far too long."

My human nature wanted to judge, but the sadness on his face wouldn't allow it.

"Do you know why I stay in the Fiery?" he asked.

I didn't try to guess.

He waved his hand through the air. "It's dark. It's easy on my exhausted eyes."

"How old are you?"

"When the Father brought me to Eden, I was aged three hundred and sixty-five years. No one should live that long."

"But they were good years," Miriam argued.

He reached for her hand. "Yes, they were. I have many children, and I would do it all again, just for them." He offered me a weak smile. "You will find a way, Warren. Never underestimate the power of the connection with a child."

"Thank you, Metatron. I'm sorry we've wasted your time," I said.

"My boy, *time* is all I have."

CHAPTER TWENTY-TWO

We left the Fiery a different way than we'd come in. Our exit was on foot through a maze of ramps and stairs. Neither of us spoke. How could we have come all this way to fail?

Metatron's words were on a loop in my mind. *"Never underestimate the power of the connection with a child."*

Maybe he overestimated me. Hell, maybe I overestimated myself.

We ascended another staircase and turned a corner, then daylight pierced the darkness. My face turned up to see blue sky and the Eden suns shining down on us.

How long had we been down there?

The sound of crashing waves and the smell of the sea drifted down the shaft. And when we emerged, we were on a rocky beach. Looking out over the ocean, I breathed in deep the salty air.

Standing beside me, Cassiel's golden hair blew across her face. "Are you ready to return home?"

"Mind if we walk the beach for a while?"

Nothing waited for us back on the mainland that couldn't be worried about beside the sound of soothing waves.

Her gaze was fixed on the water. "I don't think it's a good idea."

"Why?"

She looked at me. "We're not far from the Haven."

My spine went rigid. Cassiel didn't have to explain. I knew in my bones it was the home of the seraphs.

"I think I'd like to see it."

"OK."

We carefully crossed the rocks until we reached the sandy beach. The pearlescent white sand looked even finer than that of my backyard, and it shimmered against the suns. I knelt and scooped up a soft handful.

"It's crushed moonstone and diamonds," she said as I let it run through my fingers.

Shaking my head, I dusted off my palms as we walked on. "Diamonds. Who would have guessed sand would be so valuable to humans?"

She smiled. "We regularly get a lot of amusement out of the things valued on Earth."

I looked up at the sky. "The Father told me in Malab that he had faith in me. That if I could find the Morning Star, he'd help convince the Council." My eyes fell to the sand again. "I'm starting to think he might have been wrong."

She laced her fingers with mine. "The Father is a lot of things. *Wrong* is never one of them."

"Well, you're far smarter than me. What am I going to do?"

She had no answer.

We continued on down the beach in silence, rounded a peninsula, and started into an inlet. She stopped walking. I looked up. In the distance was what looked like an old Victorian beach house in the cove.

We were close enough to hear a child laughing somewhere outside.

My throat burned.

"Warren, are you all right?"

It was a beautiful three-story structure with tall windows and a wraparound porch. It had a rounded tower that overlooked the sea and decorative trim that made the whole thing look like a gingerbread house. Or a doll house. Appropriate for a place where children can never grow up.

"Would she *have* to live here?" I finally asked, the question hitching in my throat.

"No, not at all. Iliana can stay with you and your family like the other children in Eden. The seraphs here have no human families. So other angels from their choirs take care of them."

I couldn't tear my eyes away from the light-yellow house.

"Warren?" She stepped in front of me to block my view. My eyes connected with hers. They were worried. "We don't have to do this."

"I need to." I was sure my shaky voice didn't sound too convinced.

"It's better than you imagine. I promise." She smiled at me, but her eyes betrayed her doubt.

I took a brave step forward. "Come on. Before I change my mind."

With each step, my heart filled with dread, something very few could say in Eden. We reached the house far faster than I wanted to.

The front door bells jingled when Cassiel opened it, announcing our arrival to anyone inside. My feet seemed glued to the front stoop. I had just opened my mouth to tell Cassiel I had to leave when a tiny boy ran down the hallway toward us. He had black hair and dark-tan skin.

"Karma! Karma! We have visitors!" he squealed, sliding to a stop in front of Cassiel. "Hello, what's your name?"

Cassiel knelt in front of him. "My name is Cassiel. We've met before."

"We have?"

"A long time ago. Your name is Ofaniel."

His chest popped out. "Guardian of the light squire."

My eyes widened. Ofaniel was so small, but his speech was developed like an adult.

"Have we met too?" he asked, looking up at me.

I knelt down. "No. My name is Warren."

"Warren, Warren..." He drummed his fingers over his lips. "I've heard that name before."

Suddenly, the boy spun around as if his name had been called. Then another Angel of Protection walked around the corner. She *had* called his name, only I hadn't heard it.

"I'm not overwhelming our visitors," he argued. Then he looked back at me. "Am I?"

I forced a smile. "No."

But *oh*, he was. It just wasn't his fault.

"Cassiel?" The woman smiled as she approached. "We weren't expecting to see you today."

Cassiel and I stood. "Hi, Karma. I hope we're not intruding."

"Of course not. Visitors are always welcome." She looked at me. "Hello, I'm Karma."

I shook her hand. "Warren Parish."

Her hand froze in mine. "The Archangel."

"Yes."

She looked around and behind us. I knew why.

"My daughter isn't here."

"Oh." Karma nodded and put her hand on Ofaniel's head. "Go find Amaiah, please."

"Wait." Ofaniel held up a finger and slowly looked up at me again. "You're the new girl's dad? The new girl who's coming to live with us?"

My insides twisted.

Karma ran her fingers through Ofaniel's black hair. "You've been eavesdropping again."

The boy scrunched his nose.

Cassiel cast a worried glance at me. Then she knelt back down in front of Ofaniel. "She might not be coming to live here in Lunaris. She has a family."

"Like Gaelish?" he asked.

I worried I might vomit. "Excuse me," I choked out.

Without another word, I bolted from the house and didn't stop walking until I collapsed to my knees in the sand a hundred yards up the beach. Deep and painful sobs bubbled up inside me, and perhaps for the first time in Eden's history—tears of anguish flowed.

The flight back to the mainland helped ease my aching heart. Cassiel and I touched down in the front yard of my house. I turned toward her, a little embarrassed of my meltdown earlier.

"I'm sorry I fell apart back there," I said, looking down at her sandals.

She lifted my chin so our eyes met. "Never apologize for caring so much."

My mouth smiled, but the rest of me still slumped.

"I'm afraid I must go. I was summoned by the Council when we were in the air."

"What will you do?"

"I'll try to convince them to explore other options."

"You will? Why?"

She thought for a moment. "Because you were right about a few things. The Council is afraid of Iliana coming to power. Afraid of someone raised as a human sitting on the throne. We fear change, but maybe that's exactly what Eden needs."

"What else?" I asked, sensing she was holding something back.

She twisted a button on the front of my shirt. "And if Iliana has even a fraction of the heart of her father, I think the benefit of having her on our side outweighs the risk."

Smiling, I meshed my fingers with hers. "Do you think they'll listen?"

Her head bobbed side to side. "I don't know, but we are inherently bent toward reason. I'll do my best."

"Thank you, Cassiel. For everything."

"Don't thank me yet. So far, I feel I've just helped make this another shitshow."

I chuckled and pulled her to me.

She rested her head in the crook of my neck. "Will I find you here when I'm finished?"

"Yeah. I don't have plans to go anywhere without you."

When she pulled back, she was smiling, but her eyes were red and glassy. "I like the sound of that."

With both my hands, I cupped her jaw. Then I kissed her, savoring every sweet detail of the moment. The velvet stroke of her tongue. The pressure of her fingertips into my sides. The needy whimper that escaped her throat.

I pulled away. "You'd better go before I never let you leave."

"Do you promise?" she whispered, her eyes still closed.

I touched my lips to hers again. "I promise."

She stepped back. "I'll be back as soon as I can."

Then, standing on the beach, I stuffed my fists into my pockets and watched her fly away.

"Looks serious." Alice's voice behind me made me jump.

"Geez, don't do that." I turned around and saw her standing in the front doorway. "How did you even know we were here?"

Skittles wiggled through her legs and ran across the yard. I knelt and scooped her up into my arms.

"Skittles heard you. She knows her daddy's voice."

I froze, and my eyes doubled.

"What the matter with you?" Alice asked.

My hand was suspended over Skittles' back. She squirmed as if to remind me I was supposed to be petting her.

"Alice, you're a genius." I walked to the house and right past her inside.

She followed me. "I know, but why do you say so?"

I didn't stop until I reached my bedroom. I deposited Skittles on the bed and opened the nightstand drawer. In it, I found my memory stone. I held it in my hand and let the memory spring to life.

My daughter was holding my finger. "I love you so much, Iliana."

I hadn't said those words out loud. Yet she heard me, and even though she couldn't talk, she *tried* to answer.

I opened my eyes. "My god. That's it."

"What's it?"

Tucking the stone in my pocket, I grabbed Alice and kissed her hard on the forehead. "I must go to the Onyx Tower. You might have just saved us all."

CHAPTER TWENTY-THREE

I flew to the Onyx Tower, landing just outside the main square. Then I raced up the steps and through the market. As I marched toward the large marble doors, someone shouted my name.

My hand was halfway to the door handle. I swore. "Not now." I slowly turned as Gabriel landed in front of me.

"Thank the Father you're here," he said.

Gabriel showing up to deliver a message personally was never a good sign. "Why? What's the matter?"

Before he could answer, there was a static crackle in my ears. "Warren, where are you?" Samael asked.

"Getting ready to save the world. Can't talk."

"You're in Asheville?"

I paused. "No, I'm at the Onyx Tower. Why? What the heck is going on?" I was asking both him and Gabriel at the same time.

"Ionis just called me from your daughter's home—" Gabriel started as Samael was talking in my ears.

I held up a finger to pause the messenger, then pressed it to my ear. "Samael, I'm gonna call you back." I clicked off my ears. "Sorry. What?"

"Ionis is reporting multiple angels crossing on or near the grounds of your daughter's home."

My feet were already moving before he finished talking. He hurried to catch up with me. "Is Ionis here now?" I asked.

"No. He's still there. Said it was an all-hands situation."

That may have been the most worrisome thing he could have said. Ionis staying for a battle? Unheard of.

"What?" I broke into a run.

Gabriel and I launched into the air toward the gate. I called out to Samael. "I'm on my way."

Samael was waiting for us when we touched down on the other side of the crowded market a second later. "I'll come with you," he said, falling into step beside us.

I didn't slow as we pushed through the gate. "What happened?"

"I'm not sure, but help is already on the way. Reuel sent for more guardians. Cassiel and another Council member went with them."

Cassiel. Thank the Father.

Samael and Gabriel were right behind me as we raced down the Eden steps. We entered the breach, and I searched for Iliana. Nothing.

Good.

The closer we got to our target, the more the air hummed, almost buzzing with activity. Whenever angels gathered in mass numbers on Earth, we could feel it in the breach.

War was close.

The three of us landed so hard in the front yard of Echo-5 that it shook the building. It was late evening. The sun was setting in a cloudless sky.

All heads whipped in our direction: the humans and

guardians who stood ready to defend the building, and the angels who looked ready to attack.

None of them were demons.

"What's happening here?" Samael asked, sounding as confused as I felt.

Half the SF-12 team, along with Nathan and Azrael, were armed in front of the building. Reuel and the four guardians that had been with him the last time stood with them. So did Ionis, but I barely saw him hiding behind Reuel.

"Warren, what the hell's going on?" Nathan called, holding an assault rifle toward the other angels.

I wish I knew.

Facing off with them across the yard were two other guardians: Sagen, who was just at my house, and Barachiel, a good friend of Reuel's. They were standing in front of Zaphkael and Cassiel.

Her eyes were fixed on me, filled with terror.

"Warren! I didn't know!" she screamed. Then I saw of a flash of something else in her eyes.

Deceit.

In front of her, Zaphkael had a wicked grin. "So glad you could join us, Warren. How are you feeling?" He started toward us.

"What are you doing near my family?" I shouted.

Gabriel had relaxed. But Samael, like me, had his hand up, ready for a fight.

Zaphkael's eyes were searching me. Inside and out. Scorching my spirit so that I could physically feel it. He paused midstep, then turned back toward his group. "I thought you said he destroyed the last of the extricated."

I spoke out of the side of my mouth to Samael. "Extricated?"

"I think he's talking about the souls released from Nulterra."

"I knew that."

Samael was biting back a smile.

"Doesn't he mean escapees?"

Samael shook his head. "It doesn't sound like it."

"I wasn't lying Zaphkael! He destroyed all three souls from Nulterra. I was with him," Cassiel cried.

"I know you weren't lying, witch. But you haven't told me the whole truth." Zaphkael extended a hand, and an unseen force gripped her, bending her backward nearly in half. From where we stood, I heard Cassiel's bones crack and pop. Her painful shrieks sliced through the still mountains.

I blasted Zaphkael's feet from under him, and he landed hard on his back. Cassiel fell to the ground. I started toward her, but Samael held me back.

"Don't. Something's wrong," he said, his golden eyes searching the angels around Cassiel.

Zaphkael shot me a hateful glare and pulled himself off the ground. Then he stormed toward me, ranting about something being impossible.

Energy sizzled at my fingertips. "Samael, call the Angels of Death. All of them."

"Yes, sir."

Zaphkael reached up like he was about to grab my face. Instead, I gripped him around the throat with my power and forced him to his knees. "You should be a vegetable," he choked out.

I squeezed tighter. "It would really help if I knew what you were talking about."

Cassiel staggered toward us. She fell down on one knee, then forced herself up again. "He has a blood stone!"

Surprised, my grip loosened enough for Zaphkael to throw his hands forward and knock me back. Then he charged before I could recover and grabbed the thick chain around my neck.

With both hands, I grasped the front of his robe. I yanked him forward and slammed my skull into his. Stars danced in my peripheral vision, but Zaphkael released the chain and crumpled to the ground.

That time, I gripped his throat with my actual hands. "Why are you here?"

He laughed, saliva dripping from his teeth.

Cassiel stumbled again, this time collapsing onto her hip a few feet away. "They're here for Iliana."

"No shit. Why now?"

"They needed the passphrase." She slumped sideways and tried to claw her way across the grass toward me. Tears streamed down her red face.

Realization hit me like an atomic bomb. An image flashed through my mind.

My bed in Chicago.

She was on top.

I was inside her...

She'd been inside my head.

Zaphkael started laughing, his face red from oxygen deprivation. The color deepened to a dark crimson, and spit spewed from his mouth when he tried to yell. "Moloch, now!"

I snapped his neck, and he went limp in my grasp. It wouldn't kill him, but it would hopefully buy me some time to figure out what the hell was going on.

Thunder erupted all around us as countless demons breached the spirit line. They hit the parking lot lights first, shattering the glass bulbs across the asphalt and sending electric sparks into the darkening sky. Then the spirits swooped toward the building in a uniformed assault. The guardians flew up to fight them off.

The sky lit up like a war zone in Baghdad.

A collision with the building triggered the big siren. It

wailed and waned, and the spotlights flashed on. Gunfire rattled through the air as SF-12 shot wildly into the sky. Demons flew into the lights on the roof blowing them apart in showers of sparks.

Something caught my eye at the top of the fake tree—the communication tower. It was the silhouette of what looked like a tiny demon perched on the peak.

Samael and Gabriel soared into the air to join the fight.

Cassiel pushed herself up again and fell toward me, grabbing my arm. "I didn't know."

"Sure you did." I pushed her off me. "Don't act like you weren't tagging along with me on their orders. Is that why you slept with me too?"

I didn't give her a chance to answer. Anger pulsing through my veins, I stormed over Zaphkael toward the middle of the action. "Reuel!"

He looked at me.

"Instruct your guardians to seize the Council members!"

Reuel nodded and bellowed, "Barachiel! Sagen!" Then he barked orders they immediately followed. They'd probably unwittingly been brought along to storm Echo-5 on behalf of the Council. Good thing their boss was on *my* side.

Saleos, the sorceress with a flair for theatrics, turned toward me. Her long black hair defied gravity, swirling around her head. She raised her hands. In them, flames danced. Her eyes glowed green, daring me to attack.

Without breaking my stride, I hurled a ball of energy at her and knocked her a hundred feet back into the tree line.

Two demons dive-bombed toward me, but Reuel sailed like an airborne bowling ball headfirst at them. The three angels collided with the force of an atomic blast. The air rippled around us, and Ionis and several SF-12 operators were knocked to the ground.

Nathan was one of them. I grabbed the front of his shirt and hauled him to his feet. "You all right?"

He gave a quick nod before jerking the barrel of his gun up over my shoulder and firing. The sound nearly ruptured my eardrum. I flinched to the side in time to see the demon Uko fall to his knees.

Nathan had put a bullet right between his eyes.

"Yes!" Ionis screamed, raising both fists in the air.

Uko face-planted at my boots, dropping the sword he'd probably been aiming at my head. I bent and picked it up, then gave Nathan's shoulder a grateful squeeze.

I grabbed the sword with both hands, squared my feet in front of Uko's twitching head, and drove the tip straight through the back of his neck. The blade severed the spine with a piercing screech. Light fractured through Uko's body, splintering his spirit. It detonated with a violent quake that shook the earth beneath our feet.

Startled, I stumbled back a step.

Most of the warring angels were startled as well. The fighting in the sky and on the ground came to a stop. Ionis's mouth was gaping.

Reuel gasped. "What the coitus?"

We all looked at him and burst out laughing.

Azrael grabbed my arm. "What did you do?"

"Beats the shit outta me." I laughed and looked at the sword.

The fighting around us resumed.

"You'd better keep that close," Azrael said.

I swung the heavy blade up into striking position. "Oh, I plan on it."

Azrael grabbed Nathan's sleeve and pulled him back. A spirit-form demon plunged toward me, and I swung the sword like a baseball bat. It sliced through the spirit with a shrill metal-on-metal screech. Then light splintered through the demon and *boom!*

I laughed. And swore with delight.

Behind me was another explosion. Saleos had set the woods on fire. Shit. The last thing we needed was the fire department showing up.

My wings spread and launched me into the air. I landed in the tree line where Saleos was hurling fireballs into the pines.

"Saleos!" I raised my new sword.

She froze and turned toward me with an evil smile. "Fighting dirty, are we?"

"All is fair in war, right?" I charged toward her, then spiraled through the air like a torpedo. A sword-swinging torpedo.

Fire shot from her hand like a blowtorch, but I intercepted it with my blade, deflecting it right back at her. Her dress caught fire and blazed around her.

I swung.

She ducked.

Then I somersaulted, landing hard on my feet. My boots tore up the forest foliage as I slid to a stop, and a wall of dirt sprayed over the flames in front of me. With a quick turn, I raced back to Saleos, swinging my sword like a feral gladiator.

Her hands aimed. Fire burst from her palms. I swung the sword again, slicing off her arms.

With a deafening shriek, Saleos fell to her knees. Her glowing green eyes turned black. Then I buried the sword up to the hilt in the center of her chest. Light discharged through her and exploded into sparks and dust around the blade.

I held the sword up in front of my face. "I could get used to this." Then I flew back to the building and landed near my friends on the ground.

As soon as my feet touched down, a bright light seared through the sky with the pitchy squeal of a falling missile. It collided with the fake-tree tower in an explosion of sizzling electricity.

"What the hell was that?" Nathan shouted over the fighting.

"That would be Moloch," Ionis answered. He was using his $700 jacket as a shield over his head.

I looked back at the building. "If Moloch gets into the mainframe, he has my passphrase!"

Azrael shook his head. His face was covered with mud and sweat. "No, he doesn't."

I'd started to launch into the sky again, but I jerked to a stop. "What?"

"We knew, with you being so close to Cassiel, you couldn't be trusted."

I wanted to argue, but he had a solid point. "Who's *we*?"

"Chimera and myself."

"Chimera's making calls for security clearance now?"

"You'll understand someday." Azrael was watching the sky as he sidestepped toward us. "There's too many of them. Too few of us."

"Not for long." I pressed a finger to my ear. The static rustle in my head was almost drowning out the war. "Now," I said to whoever was listening.

Above us, the sky peeled back. Inside the breach were the Angels of Death. Thousands of them. They rolled through the purple-and-pink Asheville sky like an airborne militia.

Azrael squeezed my shoulder. "Well done."

I smiled.

Then something slammed into him from behind, throwing him forward into me as a bullet pierced the left side of my chest. My left arm closed around Azrael's torso before we both went down. Behind his back, I pulled my fingers up and found them covered in blood.

Kane, one of the members of SF-12, still had his rifle

pointed in our direction. His eyes were horrified. He lowered the gun. "I don't know why I did that!"

He'd shot Azrael in the back.

I looked around. Nybria, the Goddess of Confusion was laughing nearby. She aimed her hands toward Enzo and Cruz. They immediately turned toward each other, weapons aimed and ready to kill.

"No!" a woman screamed.

Cassiel.

She broke free from Sagen's grasp and blasted Nybria off her feet in my direction. Nybria's spell on Enzo and Cruz broke, and they both dropped their weapons.

My eyes locked with Ionis's. "Please, help me!"

He hesitated, making a gagging face.

"Ionis, please!"

He dropped his jacket and grabbed Azrael from behind. The small angel went down under Azrael's weight, but Nathan stepped in to help him. As soon as I was free, I sprinted toward Nybria, my sword ready to swing.

Before she recovered her footing, the sword cut sideways, slicing right through her throat. Her head toppled off her neck, but before it hit the ground, cracks of light spiderwebbed through her, blowing her spirit apart. The body—head and all— turned to dust.

Cassiel caught my eye across the yard.

But I broke our gaze to return to my father.

Azrael was laying across Ionis's lap on the ground in front of Echo-5. Nathan was holding pressure on Azrael's chest—with Ionis's jacket—but blood was sputtering out of Azrael's mouth, all over his face.

"The bullet tore through his lung," Nathan said.

I looked down at my bloody shirt. "I know. It went into my chest. It's working its way back out now."

Ionis gagged again.

A buzzing sound above caught my ear. It was the tiny demon on top of the tower. It vibrated with energy, and it seemed to be rattling. "What is that thing?"

Azrael could barely breathe, but that didn't stop him from chuckling and spraying more blood from his mouth. "It's Moloch."

"What?"

Enzo pointed to it. "Chimera figured out that Moloch accessed the mainframe last time by coming through the datalink between Claymore headquarters and the tower. She set up a loop to trap him if he tried it again."

"Is that a gargoyle?" I asked.

Azrael tried to laugh again. "Yeah."

"And a demon's trapped inside it?"

Nodding, he laughed harder. So did the others around us. Then Azrael began gasping for air. His face turned a deeper shade of red, and the veins bulged in his neck.

I searched the sky for an Angel of Life. There wasn't one. I swore. "Ionis, go to Eden and get help. Enzo, call Doc and 911!"

"Already done, sir. Doc's on his way."

"And Gabriel went to the Throne Room," Ionis added.

There wasn't any more I could do for Azrael, except get away from him. I backed away and inventoried our surroundings.

The angels fighting in the sky were vanishing—the evil ones fleeing, and the Angels of Death hopefully in their pursuit. Still, the hum in the atmosphere seemed to be growing, not dwindling as the depleting numbers would suggest.

"This isn't over," I said, searching the area for an explanation.

Samael landed beside me. "What happened to Azrael?"

"Nybria cursed one of the operators. Azrael was shot."

Samael shook his head, his eyes still fixed on Az. "He doesn't have much time."

"I know."

Headlights flashed down the road. It was a Claymore SUV. Hopefully Doc.

I looked over at Samael. "Do you feel that?"

"I do. What do you think it is?"

"I don't know. There were four demons in human form last time. The only one I haven't seen yet is Elek, the weather demon."

Samael looked up. "Whatever I'm sensing, it's far more powerful than Elek."

The Claymore vehicle veered off the paved road and onto the grass toward us. Doc was out of the passenger's side, running with his first-aid bag, before the SUV stopped rolling.

"It's weird that Azrael is mortal now," Samael said, almost to himself.

"Lay him down!" Doc shouted as he ran.

Nathan helped Ionis ease Azrael onto the ground, then they both moved out of Doc's way. Doc immediately started to work. Nathan walked toward us, but Ionis stayed close to Azrael. His fancy clothes were now covered in blood.

I searched the sky again, certain something else—something powerful—was headed our way.

Nathan bent to pick up the leather scabbard where Uko's body had dissipated. He walked over and handed it to me. "If you're gonna carry a sword, you need one of these."

"Thanks." I loosened the strap and put it over my shoulder, tightening it across my chest. Reaching back, I put the sword into it...or tried, twice.

Nathan grinned. "Need help?"

"Please." I handed him the sword.

Turning it sideways, he balanced it between his hands. "Too heavy for steel. What do you think it is?"

"I have no idea, but it can destroy angels." I looked at Samael. "Have you ever seen anything that can do that?"

"Only your daughter."

I turned so Nathan could put the sword in the scabbard and saw Cassiel on her knees across the yard. Barachiel still had hold of Zaphkael behind her.

Cassiel's eyes were pleading.

The full weight of the sword pulled on the scabbard's strap, and Nathan slapped my back.

"Thank you," I said.

There was commotion around Azrael. Enzo got up and ran with Kane to the SUV. "What's going on?" I asked.

The SUV spun around and left the way it had come.

"Cooper and I passed some old guy walking up the road," Doc said over his shoulder as he cut open Azrael's shirt. "They're going to check it out."

"Old guy." My head turned toward the road. "Metatron?"

"Warren, please." Cassiel's voice twisted all my nerves.

Nathan glanced back at her. "You'd better go deal with that."

I groaned and turned on my heel.

Zaphkael struggled hopelessly against Barachiel's grip as I approached. "Let him go."

Barachiel flung the Angel of Knowledge onto the ground, and he landed on his hands and knees beside Cassiel.

I walked slowly toward them. "You know, Zaphkael, I find it humorous that you recently tried to accuse me of blasphemy. And all the while, you were plotting with the fallen to what end? To destroy the spirit line?"

Breathless, he sat back and looked up at me. "No. To *protect* the spirit line. From you."

"Come again?"

"Had we forced the Father's hand and dealt with you the first time, none of this would have happened. And such desperation would not have been required."

"The first time?" I turned to Samael who was a few feet

behind him. "There was a plot to kill me once upon a time, wasn't there?"

Samael looked at the ground.

"They sent me to do it." Reuel's voice turned my head. "To kill you."

My mouth fell open. "What?"

Samael stepped forward. "You were a few months old and still with your first foster family when the Council ordered your death. Reuel was their chosen henchman because none of the Angels of Death would move against Azrael. I tipped him off, and he intercepted Reuel in the house while the family slept."

"You were going to do it?" I looked at Reuel, afraid of the answer.

Reuel's face fell. "I was. Azrael stopped me. Threw himself across your crib to protect you."

I looked past them to where Doc was still working on Azrael.

"In the end, I couldn't do it."

Samael put a hand on Reuel's shoulder. "He risked everything for not doing it."

"Which is why Azrael has always trusted you," I said.

Reuel nodded.

I shook my head in disbelief as I turned back to Cassiel. "That's what Azrael meant about them doing this *again*. You really meant it. You think I should never have been born."

"No, Warren. I don't think that," she cried.

"Is it true? Did the Council vote to kill me when I was born?"

Her mouth opened, but no words came out. Just a quiet, whiny, tearful squeak.

I nodded, crossing my arms. "And now you've gone so far as to conspire with the fallen to steal my daughter?"

She pulled herself up on her knees. "I swear I didn't know Zaphkael was plotting with Moloch and the other demons."

I ignored her. Whether she knew or not didn't matter. I walked over and stood kicking-distance away from Zaphkael's face. "Why release the souls from Nulterra?"

"A real angel wouldn't need to ask such a question." The bastard spat at my boots.

I gritted my teeth. Then I reached back behind my shoulder blades and grabbed the hilt of my sword. Slowly, I drew it from its scabbard. (I'd always wanted to do that.)

Lowering the sword, I knelt in front of him. Then I pointed the tip of the blade straight at his Adam's apple. "Feel free to use small words."

He visibly swallowed but shook his head. "Go ahead and destroy me. I don't have to tell you anything."

"Maybe not, but you'd have to tell her." I pointed the sword at Cassiel. "Cassiel, you're good at getting inside people's heads. How about doing something useful with that gift?"

Her lower lip trembled, but she fought back her tears and grabbed Zaphkael's head. "Tell us why you released the souls from Nulterra."

Zaphkael tried not to speak but failed. "The power of the final death is not without consequence. It's forbidden to be performed outside Reclusion as a matter of safety, not because we enjoy making rules for the sake of having them."

"Safety?" I asked.

"The final death consumes its intended target, but the excess energy must attach itself to something. Reclusion was created to be that *something*."

A death sponge. No wonder Reclusion was so depressing.

"Doing the deed here should have been detrimental to you," he said.

"You were trying to kill me?" I asked, pushing the blade farther.

"Unfortunately, that's not possible. It should have, however, destroyed the bit of humanity you so desperately cling to. The only problem was you were wearing a blood stone."

The hand not holding the sword went to Azrael's heavy stone around my neck.

Cassiel said. "It safeguarded your mind. It acted like a backup."

"You knew about this?"

"I didn't. I only realized what was happening when Zaphkael brought me here. Sandalphon was right. There were secret meetings. I just didn't know about them."

"So what was the deal?" I asked Zaphkael. "What did Moloch want out of all this?"

Zaphkael tried to resist.

"Tell him," Cassiel demanded.

"Moloch wants the throne of Nulterra. If the Morning Star were to be reborn, he'd be powerful enough to reclaim it. I promised we'd keep the Morning Star in spirit form if he'd help us take the Vitamorte."

"But you already told me to take Iliana," I reminded him.

His eyes narrowed. "And were you ever going to do it?"

Well...

"What was in it for you?" I asked.

"Nothing, I am but a servant to Eden—"

"Bullshit."

"Tell him," Cassiel said, digging her fingers deeper into Zaphkael's temples.

"Moloch agreed to transfer the power of the Archangel to me," Zaphkael admitted through clenched teeth.

"The Father would never allow that," I said.

"Wouldn't he? It would take Moloch out of this realm, peace would return to Malab, and the spirit line would be safe from the threat of Iliana." Zaphkael narrowed his eyes. "Do you even understand why he appointed the Council? To keep his perfect hands clean and still accomplish what needs to be done."

I swallowed. Could Zaphkael be right?

"No," Cassiel said calmly, as if answering my silent question. "The Father appointed the Council to protect the Earth from *us*. To make the hard decisions of ruling against angels to protect humanity."

"And that's what I was doing—"

"No." She shook her head. "You only considered options that would elevate you and ensure an angel raised as a human would never be more powerful than the Council, correct?" Her hands were still clasped around his head.

"Yes," he hissed.

I twisted the blade at Zaphkael's throat. "Give me one good reason why I shouldn't end you right now."

He smiled and laughed through the fear in his eyes. "Because deep down, you know I'm right. And you know you'll never be what we need you to be. What *Earth* needs you to be."

My knuckles were going white around the sword's handle.

The headlights reappeared on the road.

I removed the sword and stood.

"We're not finished," Cassiel said.

My head jerked with surprise.

She looked at Zaphkael again. "How did you open the Nulterra Gate?"

"I didn't. Moloch did. Someone on the inside has a key."

"Who?" she asked.

He looked at me, his eyes boiling with hatred. "Anya."

Fury's sister.

Cassiel and I locked eyes. I nodded, and she released his head.

"Zaphkael, I'll deal with you back in Eden. You'll have to answer to the Father for what you've done here."

Reuel came over and stood beside me. He spoke Katavukai. "Barachiel, take Zaphkael back and lock him up in Cira."

Barachiel nodded and with a thunderous crack, the two angels disappeared across the spirit line.

"What about me?" Cassiel asked, her voice small and shaky.

I shook my head. "What about you? You betrayed me after I trusted you. How am I supposed to ever forget that?"

"I didn't know," she pleaded.

"Were you or were you not trying to get the ability to access Echo-5 out of my head when we were together in Italy?"

Her eyes fell.

"See? Whether or not you knew Zaphkael was working with Moloch is irrelevant. I'll never trust you again."

Tears streamed down her face. Tears I didn't want to see. "Sagen, keep an eye on her."

"Yes, sir."

Then I turned, and Reuel and I walked back to Nathan and Samael.

Samael was grimacing. "That's a shame. I liked her much better with you."

Sadly, I did too.

Lifting the sword over my back, I tried again to slide it back into its scabbard. "Stop. Stop," Nathan said, holding up his hands. "Keep that up and you might kill yourself. Give it to me." I gave him the sword, and he put it back in its place again. "You're really gonna need some lessons, brother."

I looked at the building. "Is Iliana safe?"

He pulled out his phone and showed me the screen. It was a video feed of Sloan pacing the panic room, bouncing Iliana in her arms.

It was the first time I'd dared to see either of them in months. I put my hand on his shoulder and squeezed.

"What's the status of the ambulance?" Doc shouted, probably realizing the SUV wasn't it.

"Enzo said it's on the way," Cruz answered.

"How's he doing?" I asked.

"He's got a collapsed lung, and he's losing a lot of blood."

The SUV stopped in the grass. God, I hoped it was Metatron. We all turned toward it as the doors opened up. My eyes strained. But my spirit felt exactly who it was.

The angels around me went down on one knee as the Father stepped out of the passenger's seat.

CHAPTER TWENTY-FOUR

"Father?"

I crossed the yard toward the SUV. He was taking in the landscape, the building, and the tower tree crowned with a living gargoyle. He put his hands on his hips. "What on Earth is that?"

"The ridiculous tree or the demon?"

"Both."

"The tree is a communications tower. The demon is Moloch. He's trapped inside the gargoyle."

The Father laughed, loudly. "That's hilarious."

"Father, what are you doing here?"

"I told you I'd deal with the Council if you determined the identity of the Morning Star, and after the bang-up job you did in Malab, I figured I'd fulfill my end of the bargain sooner rather than later."

My brain was spinning. "But I haven't found the Morning Star."

His head fell to the side. "Haven't you?" He smiled and walked past me toward the building without giving me a chance to explain. "What's happening here?" he asked as we neared Azrael and Doc.

"Az was shot in the back," I said. "Can you help him?"

"No." The Father looked up at me. "But you can."

"What?"

"Your daughter is here, is she not?"

Fear rippled through me.

Perhaps, he sensed it because he put his hand on my arm. "It will be all right, Warren."

I nodded, then turned and walked over to Nate while the Father talked to Azrael. I looked up at the top story of the building. "I need you to get Iliana and bring her out."

"Have you lost your mind?" Nathan was almost shouting.

I jerked my head toward the Father. "Do you know who that is?"

"I'm guessing from the way the supes went all knights-of-the-round-table, he must be important."

"That's *him*. That's the Father."

Nathan crossed his arms, looking behind me. "God looks like Mikhail Gorbachev in overalls?"

Laughing, I glanced back over my shoulder. "Never thought about that before."

Nathan, for once, wasn't amused. "I don't like this."

"If he says it's OK, it's OK. Go get her."

With a heavy sigh, he started toward the door.

I walked back to the Father. He was talking with Samael and Reuel. "How did you get here?"

"Delta," he answered with a smile.

The rest of us laughed.

"You'll be pleased to know Umar Tadese is doing good work for the people of Malab. Aid began arriving almost immediately. You made the right choice trusting him," the Father said.

"That's good to hear. At least my douchebag radar still works on humans," I said, shaking my head.

"Douchebag," the Father said with a chuckle.

Realizing what I'd said, I was glad he thought it was funny.

"I heard about the souls Zaphkael and Moloch released from Nulterra. They're destroyed now?" the Father asked.

"Yes."

"Good."

I pulled the blood stone out from under my shirt. "I guess this thing saved the day once again. Wonder what happens if I take it off?"

Azrael's memory had been wiped completely when he gave it to me the first time in Eden and then crossed the spirit line without it.

"Maybe I should do it?" the Father asked.

I lowered my head, and he reached behind my neck and unclasped the chain. Nothing happened.

I exhaled. "Thank you."

The Father smiled. "My pleasure."

I wrapped the stone's chain around my hand.

He looked across the yard to where Cassiel was sitting in front of Sagen. "What happened there?"

"It's a long story."

The Father grinned. "They usually are." Then he leaned to the side to look around me. "Ah, there's your little one."

My heart clambered into my throat, nearly doubling me over. Reuel put a hand on my shoulder as I turned around slowly.

There they were.

Sloan.

My baby girl.

Iliana's eyes connected with mine, and she smiled and clapped her hands. "Appa!"

Everything in me turned to mush. My knees wobbled, but Reuel grabbed the back of my collar to hold me upright.

Sloan was holding her, and Nathan was standing behind

both of them. "Come on over!" he called. "We're all going to pay for this visit either way."

My feet wouldn't move, frozen with fear to the ground. How the hell would my heart ever recover from this?

Reuel shoved me forward. I stumbled a few steps, then thanked him over my shoulder.

When I reached them, what felt like a million years later, Iliana reached for me. "Appa."

I swallowed.

Sloan smiled up at me. "Go ahead, Appa. Take her."

When I lifted her tiny body, I feared my heart might explode. I pulled her to my chest, letting her sit on my forearm. She put both her hands on the sides of my face, then rested her forehead against mine.

Tears flowed and dripped off my chin. "I love you so much, Iliana."

She giggled and patted my cheeks.

I pulled back to study her face, to memorize every detail. She had my eyes, dark as night with a faint halo of gold around the pupils. Puffy pink cheeks and a heart-shaped mouth. The little bit of black hair on her head was standing on end. She wore footed pink donut-print pajamas.

"I hate to break up the family reunion, but if we don't act fast, we'll be short a grandfather here," Doc said on the ground with Azrael.

The Father stepped up beside me. "Hello again, Sloan. May I?" he asked both of us.

Sloan nodded, and I handed him the baby. He took her and bounced her in his arms. "Hello, sweet Iliana."

She giggled and grabbed his nose.

Sloan followed the Father and Iliana over to Azrael. I dried my face on my sleeve, and Nathan walked over beside me.

We couldn't see what was happening on the ground, but there was a bright light and then we heard Azrael gasp.

Iliana squealed with delight.

"You're going to introduce me to God, right?" Nathan asked.

I smiled. "I'd never dream of leaving you out."

He jerked his chin toward them on the ground. "What consequences is this going to have for her?"

"I don't know." I looked up at the sky. Once again, it was empty. "Hopefully, we'll all be safer for it in the long run."

Sloan and the Father moved to the side, and Doc helped Azrael sit up. His face was ghostly pale and still covered with blood, but he was alive.

"You all right, old man?" I asked.

He rubbed the spot where the hole had been on his chest. "I don't like being shot anymore."

Nathan laughed. "Did you ever?"

"Well..." Azrael gave a noncommittal shrug.

"Weirdo," Nathan said.

The Father groaned as he stood, still carefully balancing my surprisingly heavy toddler on his arm. He carried her back over to us. "You know, I think she looks like you, Warren."

"Nah." I smiled over at Sloan. "She's beautiful, just like her mom."

Nathan shook his head. "I should've let that angel chop your head off when I had the chance."

I put my hand on his shoulder. "Father, you know Nathan."

Nathan reached to shake the Father's hand. "It's a pleasure to meet you, Your Honor."

"Your Honor?" Sloan asked with a smirk. "This isn't *Night Court*."

"Your Highness?" Nathan was clearly panicking.

"Just call me Father John." He shook Nathan's outstretched hand. "Oh, I have something for you." He reached into his pocket and pulled out a pack of Skittles.

Nathan laughed as he took it. "Look, Warren."

"Thank you, Father John." Nathan pointed the red candy packet at him. "You know, I have a lot of questions for you."

The Father chuckled. "Most people do."

"Appa," Iliana said, clapping her hands toward me.

I smiled at her. "Yes?"

"Dynos, Appa." My baby looked me square in the eyes.

Nathan shook his head. "I swear that kid speaks your language."

A chill rippled my spine. "She does."

Excited, Sloan touched my arm. "Really? What did she say?"

"She said *danger.*" I immediately began scanning the grounds.

A crackle somewhere above us caught my ear. The Father heard it too. He curled a protective arm around Iliana.

Kaboom!

A lightning bolt shot straight through me, lighting every nerve ending I had on fire. It blew everyone else backward. Except Sloan, who was still touching my arm. Her hand clamped down as her muscles tensed with the electric current.

There was a scream somewhere in the distance, but inside the bolt, nothing except for electricity crackling all around us. I pulled Sloan's rigid body against my chest. I couldn't see anything beyond the wall of white light.

The bolt vanished as quickly as it had come. Sloan and I collapsed to the scorched ground in its wake. Only the Father and Iliana were anywhere near us; everyone else had been knocked back at least twenty feet. Nathan had collided with the building and was lying dazed at the bottom of it.

I grabbed Sloan's jaw and rolled her head over to see her face. "Sloan? Can you hear me?"

Her eyes opened, and she blinked a few times. "I'm…I'm OK. The baby?"

"She's fine." I looked again to be sure. That time, Iliana opened and closed her fist at me. "I think she just waved."

Sloan tried to laugh, but she was too stunned. "My...my shoe."

Looking down at her feet, I saw her right shoe was missing and her sock had melted to her foot. I touched it. "That hurt?"

She shook her head.

It didn't appear to be burned.

Nathan had pulled himself off the ground and was running toward us. As soon as he reached Sloan, I moved out of his way and stood.

"What the hell happened?" I asked, searching the clear sky again.

"I saw it! I saw the whole thing!" Ionis announced, waving his arm in the air as he hurried toward me. He pointed toward the top of the building. "There was another demon up there."

"On the roof?"

"Yeah. That's where the lightning came from."

"Elek." With the excitement of the Father's arrival, I'd forgotten he was still MIA.

"Samael and Reuel went after him."

"Was anyone else hit?" I asked.

"No. Just you and Sloan."

I looked around. Cassiel and Sagen were brushing themselves off. The members of SF-12 looked stunned but otherwise OK. Azrael was walking toward us. He looked like he'd been bowled through the dirt—maybe he had been—but the color was returning to his cheeks.

The Father was standing closer, still bouncing Iliana on his arm. I walked over, and Iliana lunged for me. I smiled, my heart flooding with joy. Even after almost being blown to smithereens by an electrical surge, that was easily the most powerful feeling in the world.

I took her, hooking my arm behind her thighs. I jerked my head toward Sloan and looked to the Father for an explanation. "Those volts should have killed her. What did you do?"

"Not I." The Father smiled and tickled Iliana's cheek. "I believe we're right to assume we can expect great things from this little one. She is remarkable." His voice was full of wonder.

"What did she do?"

"She defended her family, of course."

It was clear the Father wasn't going into details, so I looked at Ionis, who was standing behind him. He raked both hands through his white hair. "I don't know, man. She did one of those mad crazy-baby screams and something happened." He wiggled his fingers.

The Father grinned. "Maybe it was magic."

Azrael rolled his eyes.

There was a loud clap of thunder that made us all flinch. It was PTSD at its best, even rattling the Author of Creations. We all looked up to see Samael and Reuel returning from the spirit line with Elek restrained between them.

I carried Iliana over to Sloan and Nathan. "Take her for a minute?"

Nathan got up and took the baby. Then I walked back to the Father, drawing my sword as I crossed the grass. "Mind if I kill him?" I asked, pointing the blade at Elek.

"Where did you get that?" The Father's old eyes were wide.

"Uko had it. Any idea what it is?" I carefully turned it sideways.

He ran his finger along the blade. The metal seemed to shriek. He withdrew his hand. "It's nothing I've ever seen."

"I think it was forged in Nulterra," Azrael said.

"Then I think you should have a very informative journey there." He lowered his voice. "Do it, but not in front of the baby."

"Yes, sir." I waved toward Reuel. "Hold him? We'll take him with us when we go."

Reuel nodded.

"Samael, can you go find Gabriel and cancel the call for an

Angel of Life?" I put my hand on Azrael's shoulder. "I think Az will be just fine."

The Father smiled at us. "If you'll excuse me, I'd like to speak to Cassiel."

My eyes flashed across the lawn. She was still waiting and watching for some sign that I might forgive her.

Not today.

"Father?" I asked.

He stopped and turned back toward us.

"I owe you the truth."

"The truth about what?" he asked.

"I haven't found the Morning Star. I don't know where he is, how he's coming back, or how to stop him."

The Father looked straight at Azrael and lifted his white brow. "Oh really?"

I could have sliced through their loaded stare with my sword.

My face whipped toward Az. He didn't meet my eyes.

"In the meantime"—the Father looked at the sky—"I think I know what we can do to make little Iliana a bit safer."

"You'll close the spirit line around Asheville?" Azrael asked.

"Maybe around the whole state, just to be safe."

"That means I won't be able to warp in and out of here," I said.

Azrael looked over at me. "Neither will anyone else."

"And Warren?" the Father asked.

"Sir?"

He leveled his all-knowing gaze at me. "Unforgiveness grows like a cancer in *your* heart...not theirs." He glanced toward Cassiel. "Or *hers*, in this case."

I nodded. Then he walked away. My eyes drifted beyond him and connected with Cassiel's. I held her stare for a moment, felt my heart tug, and then I turned away.

Other problems were at hand. I looked at my *other* father

and crossed my arms. "Is there something you're not telling me?"

His lips pressed together.

Realization poured over me like hot lava. "Oh god. It's Adrianne."

He didn't answer, which was answer enough.

Azrael grabbed my arm and pulled me in the other direction, toward the large crater he was building in the ground, away from everyone we knew. "You don't tell anyone. Not human or otherwise."

I ran my hands down my face. "How did you find out?"

"Sandalphon. That was the message he sent via Ionis the day Fury's son was born. It was a warning."

"A warning?"

"He worried the Council was dirty. And he knew if the Morning Star was reset to spirit form, we'd never have control of him. When they ruled to destroy the newborns, he knew we must hide Adrianne's child."

"But Ionis said—"

"I saw Sandalphon's vision myself. He sent it in a memory stone."

"The trinket box."

Azrael nodded.

"That was why he locked himself in Cira. So no one could get the truth out of him." We stopped in front of the massive crater behind Echo-5. Support beams had gone in since the last time I'd been there. Somehow the giant hole made me feel even more empty, more hopeless. I swore and put my hands on my hips. "Azrael, what are you going to do?"

"Son, the less you know, the better." He stared out across what would someday be a safe house we would hopefully never need.

I rubbed my hands slowly down my face. "I can't worry about this right now. I want to spend the little time I can with my daughter, but after that, you and I are going to have a serious chat."

I started to walk away, but he put his hand on my chest to stop me. "Go back to Eden and heal after this. You'll need it."

I wasn't exactly sure what he meant, but the look in his eye told me not to argue.

"We've got time, Warren." He was looking off into the distance. "Twenty weeks, give or take."

Nausea churned in my stomach. I gave a slight nod. "Before I forget." I reached into my pocket and pulled out the blood stone.

He didn't accept it. "My mind is clearer now than it has been since I came back to Earth. I think your daughter fixed that too."

"Well, take it anyway. Just in case."

He took the necklace and stuck it in his pocket. I shook his hand, and he pulled me in for a hug.

Nathan and Sloan were standing when I returned. Sloan was holding Iliana, but once again, she reached her tiny arms toward me. I knew she was probably drawn to the power she sensed inside me, but it didn't matter. Nothing even in Eden felt *that* good. She laid her head against my collarbone.

Closing my eyes, I let the memory soak in. The smell of her hair. Her hand gripping my sleeve. The way her head fit perfectly under my chin.

"Appa, tan," she said softly.

I kissed her forehead, not even trying to stop the tears that leaked from my eyes. "I wish I could, sweetheart. I wish I could stay forever."

When I opened my eyes, Sloan was crying too. Nathan had his arms around her. I pulled back and looked at Iliana, then I spoke to her silently in Katavukai, the language I was pretty sure she could best understand.

"Iliana, look at me."

She lifted her head and met my eyes.

"There's nothing else I love more in this world or the next than you. And though I have to go away, it's only for a little while on this earth." I tugged on the front of her pajamas. *"And I will always come back for you."*

She put both hands on my face. *"Akai anlo alis, Appa."*

I lost it then, and I kissed her cheek through my sobs. "I love you too, Iliana."

CHAPTER TWENTY-FIVE

I spent the next few days alone in Eden, understanding fully what Azrael meant about needing time to heal. The beach in Lunaris was good for that. I spent a lot of time flying. Even more time thinking. And ate my weight (and then some) in all sorts of manna.

Physically, I'd never felt better. Or looked better, if I do say so myself. The faint crinkles around my eyes were gone. So were the stray gray hairs that had welcomed me to my thirties. It took a few days for me to realize why.

Iliana had somehow used her life-giving power on me and her mother when we were inside that lightning bolt. It had kept Sloan alive, and it had dialed the years back for me.

That gave me an idea. I was already in Lunaris, so I paid another trip to the Fiery. There I told Metatron to hang onto hope just a little while longer. Help was on her way.

Then I was finally ready to go home.

Home to Alice and Skittles.

When I left the Fiery, I hiked out through the shaft that led to the beach. The bright light from the suns was blinding, momentarily obscuring the face of the woman on the shore.

Cassiel.

I drifted over the rocks and landed beside her on the sand.

The wind whipped behind her. "I thought I might find you here."

"Why?"

"It's where I would come to mend what you went through on Earth. How are you?"

I nodded. "I'm OK." And I meant it. "What are you doing here?"

"I have something for you." She reached into her bag, the one she'd taken on our trip to Earth, and pulled out a scroll.

"What is this?" I asked, breaking the seal.

"A treasure map."

I unrolled it. It was definitely a map. One that looked like the map she'd forced me to buy at the souvenir shop in Venice. Only this one was global.

There were colorful dots on Thailand and Turkey.

"I backtracked Vito Saez's travels, following the other murders he committed to an island known before the twentieth century as La Isla del Fuego. I found the Nulterra Gate."

Just like Azrael had said, there was an island marked with an X in the South China Sea. A tiny speck of land near the Philippines.

"You'll feel the gate once you get on the island, so you won't have any trouble finding it. The lock, on the other hand, will be trickier. I didn't have any luck, but I took pictures." She reached into the bag again and produced a few photographs.

I took the pictures. "Photos? A map? How did you get them across the spirit line?"

She held up the bag.

I pointed at it. "I wondered why your locker wasn't jam-packed with magnets."

"What?"

"Never mind."

She tapped the first photo of a pond or a lake, I couldn't tell. "I believe this is the entrance. When I stood on it—"

"When you *stood* on it? Who are you now? Jesus?"

"It's not water. It's salt."

"It looks like water."

"It actually looks like a mirror." She pulled out a photo behind it. "Look at this shot from the air."

"Dang, it's like a perfect circle." Inside the circle, I could see Cassiel's tiny reflection.

"It's a perfect circle, actually. Too perfect to be made by nature or humans."

"That's crazy."

"When I was in the air, I tried to use my power to open it, the way we do locked doors. Nothing happened, except it glowed purple." She thumbed through the stack and found another photo. This one had a faint purple ring with a line through the center. She turned it diagonally. "Is it a 'no' sign?"

Something snagged in my memory. Fury's hospital room. The burn on her hand. A charred circle with a line through it.

"It's not a sign." I looked at Cassiel. "It's the key."

"What?"

"I thought we were looking for a key, like a car key or house key." I looked at the photo again. "The key isn't a *thing*. It's a person. Fury and Anya *are* the keys to Nulterra."

Her head pulled back. "Wow. Really?"

"Yeah, Fury had this burn when I saw her in the hospital." I held out my palm. "It was a circle with a line through it. Just like this picture."

Cassiel looked excited, but the light in her eyes quickly dimmed. "I guess you and Fury are all set then."

I forced a smile. "Yeah. I guess so."

"No, take this too." She took the bag off her shoulder. "You'll need something to transport these things back across the spirit line."

I took the bag. "Are you sure?"

"Positive. You can return it when you come back." There was a small sparkle of hope in her eyes.

"I will." I lifted the bag and laughed. "You know Samael is going to give me a rash of shit about this."

She laughed too. "Yes, he is."

I put the map and photos inside it, then I held the bag in my hand because I wasn't yet ready to drape it over my shoulder. "Thank you, Cassiel."

"You're welcome. I hope it's a start on making things up to you. I really am sorry. I'm sorry I didn't figure out how very wrong I was until it was too late."

"On the bright side of all this, I finally figured out how to identify angels in infancy."

"Really?"

"I think Fury's son is an Angel of Protection. A guardian."

"How do you know?"

"When we visited them in the hospital, I'm pretty sure the baby recognized Reuel's voice. He woke up when I touched him, but when Reuel spoke, that baby paid attention."

"I think you might be right." Her head tilted. "Even as babies, they should still be able to recognize angels from their own choirs."

"Reuel will go with me when I tell Fury about her sister. We'll test the theory more thoroughly then."

"Good luck with that. Everyone is still eager for you to find the Morning Star."

I looked out toward the ocean and didn't respond. Cassiel and I might be speaking civilly, but we were a long way off from me trusting her again.

"The Father banished Zaphkael from Eden."

"Good. I would have killed him." I thought about the sword that was now locked up in Reclusion. "I still might."

She didn't respond.

"One thing I can't figure out. Why do you think Zaphkael picked the souls he did to be released from Nulterra?" I asked.

"I've thought about that a lot too. I think he knew Menelek would likely keep the Father preoccupied in Africa. He knew Vito Saez would make huge waves in this world, forcing us to act. And as for the last one...he knew Charlie Lockett would affect you the most."

Understatement. My eyes fell to the ground again.

Then my mind drifted to how Cassiel had walked with me through that.

Cassiel's voice interrupted the memory. "What I've been puzzled over since I got back from the Nulterra Gate is how all three souls picked right up where they left off all those years ago."

"Even Charlie. The hospital where he found the body he was using was the same hospital where his old girlfriend, my former foster mom, was a registered nurse."

"It's like they were never gone at all." Silence settled between us. Then she touched my arm. "At least now, thanks to you, they'll never hurt anyone else again."

I looked down at her hand. "I need to ask you a question, Cassiel." I pulled my eyes back to hers. "Did you tell Zaphkael willingly how to get Moloch into Echo-5? Or did they force you to tell them?"

"Zaphkael got his hands on me and saw it in my mind." She took a step closer. "As you know, we can extract information with a touch."

I nodded.

She took another step closer. "We can share it the same way." Her hands trembled as she placed them on the sides of my face. My eyes closed at her touch, and a moment later a rush of elation pulsed through me.

Scenes flashed through my mind.

Holding hands on the boat.

Us sitting on the bathroom floor.

The first time we kissed.

The night we made love.

Me dismissing her in Asheville.

Me telling my daughter goodbye.

And then she kissed me on the beach. Timid but needy, like the waves lapping the sand. The sensation sent my heart through a gauntlet of emotion. *Her* emotions.

Joy.

Love.

Sorrow.

Brokenness.

Regret.

Hope.

Breaking the kiss and the spell, I leaned my forehead against hers and breathed slow and deep to slow my heart. "I want to love you too, you know?"

I felt her nod.

I kissed her again. Gently. Carefully. A kiss full of absolution and possibility.

Then I eased my lips toward her ear and whispered, "For the first time in a lifetime of brokenness, you've made me fly."

Her eyes were still closed as I backed slowly away. Then I spread my wings and lifted off the beach.

CHAPTER TWENTY-SIX

*A*nother week of being at home was just what I needed. Mom brought food. Yaya brought wine. George took me out on his boat.

Neither Alice nor Skittles left my side.

Samael brought word about Iliana. Serious migraines would have been expected for her from the exposure to and sudden withdrawal from so many angels. Thankfully, the Father had spent his last few days on Earth in Asheville to gradually wean her off her connection with us. So Iliana's symptoms had been mild. I'd experienced those headaches myself, and wouldn't wish them on anyone—much less, my daughter.

I didn't see Cassiel again, but I would.

Someday.

Alice and I had just finished a quiet dinner at home alone when Skittles ran to the door and started barking.

"What is it, girl?" I asked, crossing the room.

I pulled open the door.

"Hark!" Ionis said.

I shook my head. "You're so weird."

"I've come with a message."

"Shocker." I stepped out of his way. "Come on in."

He walked into the house, and Alice came in from the kitchen. "Hi, Ionis."

"Hello, Alice. How's star-making these days?"

She smiled. "It's great."

"Tell Forfax I said hello?"

"You bet. You hungry? We have plenty of leftovers."

"No thanks. I can't stay long. Just stopping by on my way back from Italy to make a delivery."

"What were you doing in Italy?"

"Handling some business with your father."

My brow scrunched. "You two have been very chummy lately. What gives?"

"Let's just say Azrael has finally figured out who he can trust. He even hired Chimera to take Fury's open spot on SF-12."

"Really?"

"She's good."

"So I've heard. What did they do with that gargoyle she trapped Moloch inside of?"

"They moved it to the vault at Claymore headquarters in New Hope. As far as I know, they're keeping him locked inside it."

"That's brilliant."

"I must say, Chimera is brilliant. Azrael's paying her to keep working with Fury. The search for Anya is now a top Claymore priority."

"That's good news."

"There's more news. He sent you a message."

"What is it?"

Ionis reached into his pocket and pulled out the blood stone.

My shoulders fell. "I've barely put myself back together from the last time I dipped into that world."

Ionis pushed the stone into my hand. "Trust me. You want to see this."

With a heavy sigh, I walked to the sofa in the living room. When I sat down, Skittles waddled in place at my foot until I picked her up and put her on my lap. Alice sat down beside us, and I put on the necklace. "How far back do I need to go?"

Ionis sat down on the coffee table in front of me. "He hasn't been wearing the stone much, so the most recent memories should be fine. You'll know it when you see."

I closed my eyes, and the world around me faded to black. Memories skipped in reverse until I saw Sloan's face and the viewpoint jostled. I started watching.

It was just like I was there.

I was looking at the screen of a smartphone. Sloan was in the picture. "OK, I'm ready. Do it again," I heard Azrael say.

Sloan was rocking nervously side to side on her feet. She wore a slouchy sweatshirt that hung off one shoulder. God, I had always loved her collarbones.

"You sure you're ready?" She held up her hands facing each other.

"Do it! Do it!" people were chanting. Someone in the background made a drumroll.

She smiled at the camera.

And sparks of white energy sizzled to life between her palms.

THE NEXT BOOK

Book 8 - Coming Soon!
Want to be the first to know about its release?

Join Elicia Hyder's newsletter at
www.eliciahyder.com

JOIN HYDERNATION

AUTHOR ELICIA HYDER

OFFICIAL FAN CLUB

★ Want leaked chapters of new books?
★ Want the first look at a new series I'm rolling out?
★ Want to win some awesome swag and prizes?

Join HYDERNATION, the official fan club of Elicia Hyder, for all that and more!

Join on Facebook

Join on EliciaHyder.com

OFFICIAL MERCHANDISE

Want Nathan's SWAT hoodie?
Want to start your own patch collection?
We've got you covered!

www.eliciahyder.com/shop

ALSO BY ELICIA HYDER

Britches Get Stitches

IN STORES NOW

Turn the page to start reading.

BRITCHES GET STITCHES

CHAPTER 1

The whole house smelled like eggs.

Not the best way to start off girls' night. I pushed open the window letting the cold Nashville night air rush into the house. Sure, the gas heat was going right out into the neighborhood, but did I care? Nope. No longer my bill. No longer my problem. I threw open the sliding-glass door too.

Heavy paws thudded down the hallway as the sliding wheels of the patio door announced canine freedom throughout the house. Bodhi bounded past me, water dripping from his golden snout. He'd probably been drinking from the half-bath toilet again, his preferred water bowl over the expensive filtered fountain I'd had installed in the laundry room.

As I drank the last drop of the 2013 Chateau St. Jean Cinq Cépages we'd been saving for a special occasion, I watched Bodhi romp unbridled through our backyard. Well, Clay's backyard. Err... Make that Clay and *Ginny's* backyard.

Dr. Virginia "Ginny" Allen, MD—or as my friends and I had taken to calling her, "Dr. Vagina"—was the cardiologist, quite obviously, now occupying my bed. Lab coats and mall-bought dresses hung in my closet, and a PhD*iva* mug sat by the coffeemaker.

Bitch. I hoped she *was* a diva.

In hindsight, I should've seen the affair coming. But to my embarrassment, I'd sexistly assumed "Dr. Allen" was a man for the first few months my husband rattled on about her.

"Grace, you would love Dr. Allen in the new TennStar office."

"Dr. Allen told me the funniest story about a patient today."

And, oh let's not forget: *"Grace, you and Dr. Allen would really hit it off. You've got so much in common."*

Yes. The same shitty taste in men, apparently.

I tried to drink from the glass again, but alas, empty. I leaned on the doorway for support. Emotional and vertical.

Bodhi lifted his leg on the corner of Clay's toolshed. I appreciated the canine solidarity.

The backyard had always been my favorite part of the house. With the vintage lights strung between the ancient oak trees and the vine-draped pergola built by my father's own hands, it could have been a fairy's paradise. Ripped straight from the pages of *A Midsummer Night's Dream.*

Our first year in the house, Clay and I had spent the warm summer evenings snuggling on the wicker chaise lounge under the pergola. Me sprawled against his side, my head on his chest as he read to me.

The Martyr's Wife by C. E. Frost had been our favorite. That wine-soaked memory now so acute I could almost feel the warmth of his breath against my blonde hair as he'd read aloud. *"This moment in time is ours, completely ours. Even if for but a moment, I will hold you as though the light of the sun may not burn tomorrow."*

We'd made love right there without bothering to go inside.

Only happy meant-for-each-other couples do that sort of thing, right?

I wonder if I can strap the pergola to the roof of my car?

Except for the victorious holes it would leave in the sod,

Clay wouldn't mind, even if the pergola hadn't been listed among my assets in the divorce. The happy couple would probably need the room for a swing set or a sandbox anyway. For the baby.

Their baby.

I could steal bungee cords out of the garage.

I needed more wine.

Pushing back from the door casing, I stumbled a half step. Maybe more wine wasn't the best idea. I had practice the next day, and the team had a strict policy about sobriety on the track. Which, in all honesty, was probably the only thing that saved me from going full-blown Amy Winehouse during my divorce.

Thank God for roller derby.

I also couldn't afford to be sloppy. Not this night. My very last night in the house I'd worked so hard to make a home. The house where I was now a guest, only allowed in to gather the last of my things.

Seven years, gone.

"Bodhi!" I whistled, and the dog froze on the grass, letting the tennis ball he'd found drop from his mouth. His big head flopped to the side as he stared at me. "Come on. Let's go inside!"

He picked up the ball again, slung it sideways across the yard, then fetched it.

"Come on, boy!" I slapped the side of my leg, and he ignored me.

The doorbell rang.

Bodhi jerked to attention, then charged, nearly knocking me out of the doorway like a bowling pin. He barked all the way to the door. I followed, depositing my empty glass on the marble countertop with a scraping *clink* as I passed. The bell rang again.

"I'm coming!" I grabbed Bodhi's collar with one hand and

pulled open the heavy wood-and-iron door with the other. It was a vintage piece we'd found in Franklin during the house's remodel.

A party horn sounded in my face, followed by the flash of a Polaroid camera. Then my friends began to sing off-key. "*Ding! Dong! The jerk is gone! Ding! Dong! The jerk is gone!*"

"Oh my god!" I was laughing as they carried in fuchsia and black balloons, champagne, and a cake. I released Bodhi, letting him sniff and tail-whip my friends who were all in matching black T-shirts with different sayings scrawled in pink.

Monica's shirt: I NEVER LIKED HIM ANYWAY.

Zoey's shirt: SHE'S FREE AT LAST.

Lucy's shirt: GOODBYE, MR. WRONG!

Olivia's shirt: SHE GOT THE RING. HE GOT THE FINGER.

Tears spilled down my cheeks. "You guys!"

"Wait, we have one for you too!" Monica thrust a bright fuchsia shirt toward me.

I held it out as everyone read it aloud. "We now pronounce you single and fun!" I pulled it to my chest. "I love you guys."

They all gathered around me for a group hug, Bodhi tangling himself in the middle of our legs. "We love you too," they echoed back.

After a second, Olivia sniffed over my shoulder. "Grace, why does it smell like eggs in this house?"

I wiped my eyes as we all stepped back. "It's a long story."

"And I'm sure it's a great one." Monica held up a bottle. "But first, champagne!"

Lucy grabbed my arm. "No, first, Grace has to put on her shirt."

"Yeah, we all changed in the driveway," Olivia agreed.

"OK, OK." I unzipped the Music City Rollers hoodie I was wearing and slipped the T-shirt over my camisole.

Monica twisted off the cork's metal cage and handed me the champagne. "Grace, you do the honors."

"Smile for the camera!" Lucy said, holding up the Polaroid again.

I smiled, and she snapped the picture, then grabbed it when the camera spat it out. Gripping the bottle by its neck, I put both thumbs on the cork and pushed.

Pow!

The cork zoomed across the living room, catching a lampshade and knocking the three-hundred-dollar mouth-blown glass lamp off the end table. It shattered on the floor.

The girls gasped. Bodhi barked and ran a lap around the kitchen island.

Laughing, I handed the bottle back to Monica and grabbed Bodhi's collar as he passed so he wouldn't run through the shards. "Clay got that in the divorce. Oops." They all cackled behind me. "Who's thirsty?"

I let Bodhi back outside, and Olivia helped me sweep up the glass while Monica poured the champagne. When we were finished, Monica held her flute high into the air. "A toast, shall we?"

I smiled and raised my glass with the others.

Monica, my best friend, smiled gently. "To Grace, may this be the beginning of the very best years of your life. I love you."

I mouthed the words "I love you" back to her as everyone shouted, "Cheers!"

Without pause, I drained the champagne, then punctuated the moment with a tiny burp. The girls laughed.

The best years of my life...who knew I'd be in my thirties before those would roll around?

ORDER BRITCHES GET STITCHES NOW

Lightning Source UK Ltd.
Milton Keynes UK
UKHW022038011119
352741UK00014B/192/P